MY FATHER'S SECRET

SEAN PATRICK DOLAN

FriesenPress

One Printers Way
Altona, MB R0G 0B0
Canada

www.friesenpress.com

Copyright © 2021 by Sean Patrick Dolan
First Edition — 2021

All rights reserved.

No part of this publication may be reproduced in any form, or by any means, electronic or mechanical, including photocopying, recording, or any information browsing, storage, or retrieval system, without permission in writing from FriesenPress.

ISBN
978-1-03-911635-1 (Hardcover)
978-1-03-911634-4 (Paperback)
978-1-03-911636-8 (eBook)

Fiction, Thrillers, Terrorism

Distributed to the trade by The Ingram Book Company

TABLE OF CONTENTS

CHAPTER 1: TERROR   **1**
   A son's duty   1
   On board an ill-fated flight   7
   Out of the mist came the unimaginable   8
   Conscience and a quest   13
   Bloody Sunday   17

CHAPTER 2: A NEW THREAT   **25**
   The Irish Desk   25
   The legend of Darcy Byrne: Origins   31
   Connecting with Warren Belwood   35
   From a manpower perspective, we're it   42
   A spy at the pub   44

CHAPTER 3: FATHERS AND SONS   **51**
   A trip to the cottage   51
   The legend of Darcy Byrne: Evolution   54
   A meeting near Shelburne   64
   A Canadian and a Provo   67
   The legend of Darcy Byrne: Resurrection   68
   The elusive Irish   71
   We better get started   76

CHAPTER 4: THE EMERGENCE OF EVIL — 83
- Charisma casts its spell — 83
- Shock, anxiety, and commitment — 88
- Potentially next level stuff — 90
- Back to school — 94
- A problem with Sully and a potential informant — 99
- A shocking lack of academic research — 105
- Leveraging Eamon Kerrigan — 108
- Digging deeper — 111
- The summer of 1972 — 113

CHAPTER 5: AS THE PLAN EMERGES — 117
- Redmund's take and the first tape — 117
- An out-of-town guest — 123
- Arranging the tutorial — 125
- A trip to Montreal — 127
- In the woods behind the farm — 138
- The second tape — 145
- Committed to the rifle theory — 148

CHAPTER 6: IRISH GAMESMANSHIP — 153
- Target: Prince Charles (?) — 153
- I'm not Redmund — 155
- They can enjoy their hockey moment — 158
- Choosing family — 163
- A trip to Rosedale and an unsettling dream — 166
- The bigger target — 172
- Misdirection — 175
- The plot to kill the prince — 177

Time for the fireworks	180
Trimming the fat	185

CHAPTER 7: RIGHT UNDER OUR NOSES — 189

A new year of promise and revenge	189
They're up to something	193
The tickets	196
The best laid plans	199
Crisis averted	203
Plan B	205
Redeployed	207
Planting the devastating cargo	213
The story of a Samsonite suitcase	219
It's time to commit	220

CHAPTER 8: IT GETS WORSE — 225

What's our exposure?	225
The legend of Darcy Byrne: Rejection	231
Maybe you should do it	235
They're burying it	238
He did it	243
A perfectionist and a narcissist	245
A discovery in Moose Jaw	247
The legend of Darcy Byrne: Reckoning	250
Charges and a trial	255

CHAPTER 9: DECLAN'S LAST STAND — 259

Belwood breaks and a graveside visit	259
What do we know?	267
A candid conversation with Heather Jansen	271

Close enough to publish	277
Nugent's had enough	281
Do it. Tonight.	283
A mysterious fire	285
Farewell to a king	288
Requiem for all that was lost	296

AUTHOR'S NOTE   **303**

ACKNOWLEDGEMENTS   **307**

CAST OF CHARACTERS

1972-1986

Terrorists – The Irish
Darcy Byrne – IRA sympathizer, plot leader
Owen Ryan – Byrne's main ally
Collin Boyle – entrepreneur, IRA fundraiser
Paddy Kerrigan – Boyle's main ally
Eamon Kerrigan – Paddy's son, Security Service informant
Quinn Foley – proprietor, Foley's Irish Pub
Cathal O'Dwyer – IRA sympathizer, bombmaker
Dylan Costello – IRA Commander of the South Armagh Brigade
Jimmy O'Connor (alias *Thomas Driscoll*) – IRA explosives expert

RCMP Security Service – The Irish Desk
Patrick Keenan – agent, surveillance
Warren Belwood – agent, surveillance
Terry Maloney – undercover agent, aka *Terry 'Sully' O'Sullivan*
Mike Nugent – agent, field operative
Dave Stratford – agent, field operative
Heather Jansen – Watcher Service
Bill Short – Watcher Service
Paul Dawson – Sergeant
Gord Millington – Staff Sergeant
Oliver Hunter – Crown Attorney

2003

Declan Keenan – son of Patrick and Kathleen Keenan
Karuna Patel – Declan's spouse
Jack Redmund – journalist
John Bakersmith – retired Director of Intelligence for Foreign Affairs
Terry Maloney – retired RCMP Security Service agent (undercover in 1973)
Heather Jansen – retired RCMP Watcher Service agent (active in 1973)
Mike Nugent – CSIS Deputy Director, Ontario (Security Service field operative, 1973)

Groups

RCMP – Royal Canadian Mounted Police; two branches: Security Service and Criminal Branch
IRA – Irish Republican Army; the Provisionals (Provos) were active during the Troubles (1969–1998)
RUC – Royal Ulster Constabulary
The Irish diaspora – persons of Irish nationality who live outside the island of Ireland
CSIS – Canadian Security Intelligence Service (Canada's spy agency)
CSE – Communications Security Establishment (Canada's cyber security agency)
OPP – Ontario Provincial Police

CHAPTER 1: TERROR

A son's duty - *November 21, 2003*

The death of a parent is a watershed moment for any person. It forces one to reconcile their life with the life that has been lost. Inevitably, whether conscious love or hate is the mode of expression, a grief process—governed by the unconscious—is initiated. This is the situation I found myself in shortly after the death of my father in the autumn of 2003.

I approached the rust-coloured brick house in suburban Toronto with more of a numb feeling than anything. It was a two-story home, built shortly after the Second World War. My parents were the second owners of the property, picking up the three-bedroom house for $16,000 in the fifties. Our family had lived there for most of my life, until death had taken both my parents within three years of each other. Looking down the street, you could think only of the mediocrity of it all, with its long line of small, identical houses interrupted only by the odd mega-home. Wealthy Torontonians had started to gentrify the neighbourhood with ostentatious structures that towered above the originals.

I parked my car in the driveway and waited a moment. I noticed that the red maple tree that my father had planted so many years ago had grown to an ominous height, the width of the trunk more than sturdy enough to hold the weight above it. 'What a tree,' I thought. Its leaves had been swept away by the autumn breeze as Toronto braced itself for the coming of another winter.

I stepped out of my car and walked along the stone path—a path I had traversed so many times over the epochs of my life. I remembered walking out of the house with my mother on my way to my first day of school. I remembered walking along the path toward the house when I was ten years old to receive the news from my mother that her father—my grandfather—had died. And I remembered striding confidently along it after graduating from university, my parents brimming with pride at my accomplishment in becoming an honours major in history, a scholar of notable distinction out of York University, *en route* to a teaching job at the high school I had attended as a young man. My father snapped two or three photos of my mother and me standing on the path that day with the red maple hovering over us in the background. It seemed strange to consider the personal evolution that the tree had been witness to—both mine and my parents—as though the maple had consciousness.

While my father had been present for these milestones, I have to admit that I never really knew the man. For all intents and purposes, he was emotionally (and many times physically) absent from my life. Nonetheless, as a man who'd recently turned fifty myself, I felt a bond of love for my father that went beyond rational explanation. Dad had worked as a spy for the Canadian government. A former agent for the Royal Canadian Mounted Police's Security Service, Patrick Keenan had learned some of the secrets of the enemies of Canada. In turn, he'd embraced more than a few secrets of his own, resulting in an almost permanent state of disconnection between himself and the people he loved.

Yet here I was, Declan Keenan, the only son of Patrick and Kathleen Keenan, full of resentment toward my father, knowing that (in many ways) my dad did not deserve my love but loving him anyway. Admiring him anyway. Seeking his approval anyway. Perhaps the unconditional love that seems so incomprehensible to the average person is really just something as a simple as the unexplainable bond that a child feels for a parent.

Now I stood on that same path; it was guiding me to another milestone in my life, this time into the unpredictable and burdensome dimension of grief. I passed the skeleton of the maple tree, devoid of leaves and preparing for its winter rest, ascended the three steps up to the house, unlocked the door, and made my way inside. The process of packing my parents' life away was about to begin. While my wife had offered to help, I wanted to make this first foray into my family home on my own.

As I entered the tiny foyer, a fresh wave of resentment hit, as if my father's stony resolve had swept down through the house in a unified icy wave. I was still bitter about Dad's response to the death of my mother less than three years earlier. She had fought a brief battle with an aggressive cancer. The disease had been found in her stomach and moved quickly to her other vital organs. The process had ended her life while those around her watched her endure unyielding pain before her passing. It had been emotionally exhausting for my wife and me, but my father had hidden behind a frozen detachment as the disease took the person who, I assumed, was the love of his life.

My mother had been stoic through the whole process. A kindhearted woman with a positive view of life, when death had come for her, she'd gone as gracefully as the cancer would allow. Where I'd always felt disconnected from my father, I'd felt connected to my mother. I still did. Our bond was strong, loving, and compassionate. If there was a divine plan for how a mother's love could be bestowed upon a son, I felt Kathleen Keenan was in sync with the plan.

After Mom died, I knew I needed a break from work, and one was coming. Throughout my career with the school board, I had opted into the four-over-five plan (working four semesters and getting the fifth semester off). The school board simply spread my pay out over the time frame to make sure I drew a salary when I was off work. My hope was that, during my semester off, I'd be able to travel a bit with my wife and get some rest at my uncle's cottage, north of the city. Instead, Dad's health had taken a turn, and it looked like I would be spending the downtime settling his estate.

In terms of taking care of the house, I am not going to bore you with the details. It was a cumbersome job involving many trips back and forth to the car, retrieving boxes and tape, filling those boxes, and stacking them in the middle of each room that I conquered. Finally, I was left with the room I dreaded going into most: my father's study.

I stood in the hallway and stared at the door going into the room. It was slightly ajar, inviting me (*daring me?*) to come in. I hesitated and turned, catching a glimpse of myself in the hall mirror. My short brown hair looked dishevelled, my face a bit drawn and in need of a shave, and I had gained a small belly on my once-slim frame. 'A typical fifty-year-old man,' I thought. 'Letting yourself go a little bit at a time.' Maybe I thought I could hide the weight behind my nearly six feet of height. What struck me most as I looked at my reflection was how tired I looked—the bags under my eyes and the way the blue around my pupils appeared somehow dull.

I turned my attention back to the task at hand and made my way into the study. I hesitated once I was in the room. It was immaculate: everything in order, stacked in the right spot, and put in its proper place. The desk was the focal point of the room, and there were a lot of books, along with a small filing cabinet. Dad had a little media area: an antiquated reel-to-reel tape recorder and player, a stereo receiver attached to a cassette player and a turntable, and a pair of ancient Koss headphones with their spiral cord resting on one of the two tall cabinet speakers. 'Dad was a bit of a tech nerd,' I thought. There was also an oxygen tank in the corner by the desk chair, with a plastic nose inhaler draped across the start valve, a remnant of his final days alive.

I went over to the desk and sat down. After mindlessly sorting through an assortment of items on top of the desk, I noticed that a drawer to my left was slightly open. My father was obsessive about everything, so I couldn't help but notice this small evidence of disorder. 'Perhaps the old man was starting to slip near the end.' Then another thought came: 'The open door and the open drawer. Not very typical of Patrick Keenan at all.'

Up to that point in my life, I had never gone into his desk. The family taboo was clear: Don't you dare go near Dad's desk. The only emotion my father knew how to express with clarity was anger, and the few times I'd gone near the desk, I'd felt his wrath. I looked inside the drawer and found nothing of consequence at first, just some office supplies that I removed from the drawer and placed on the desk. But underneath the supplies was a letter-sized manilla envelope with a jagged inscription that read *"Declan."* Inside the envelope was a VHS videotape with a note attached to it: *"I'M SORRY."*

Almost stunned by the bizarre apology note and the mystery tape, I made my way into the living room across the hall. On my way out of the study, I noticed a VHS camcorder on a tripod in the corner of the office. I wondered.

My father had an old VCR/DVD combo player attached to his television in the living room; he just had too many old VHS tapes to fathom abandoning the outdated technology. I knew this because I had just packed up four boxes of old movies. I turned on the television, inserted the video cassette, and pressed Play. After five seconds of snow and static, an image of my father appeared. The video must have been recorded close to his death, because Dad looked pretty ashen, and the oxygen breathing tube I had noticed in his office was under his nose to keep him going. His salt-and-pepper hair was a mess, and his clothes hung loosely on his body, a not-so-subtle indication of how much weight he had lost. He was in a sad state. I sat down and listened.

"Son, I am going to make this brief. I know I haven't been much of a father," he began, the stereo system in his study resting behind him, his voice weak and rough as if he hadn't spoken in days. "I know you will not make the same mistakes I have made. I am going to take a lot of secrets to my grave because of the work I have done over the years, but there's one secret I can't allow myself to take with me, so I need to share it with you now. This will be a burden for you, Declan. I know it is a lot to ask, seeing that I was a cold and distant person for most of my life, but I need you to know this secret, and if you've got the courage, to do something about it. I didn't have the moral strength when I was alive to fully deal with this, and too many people suffered because I was a coward. Put it this way: I have confidence in you because you are your mother's son." A memory of my mother flashed through my mind: Kathleen Keenan in her prime, a tall woman of grace and pride, pretty in a wholesome way, with a face that invited conversation and a demeanour that welcomed and never threatened.

My father paused after his last statement and stared into the camera. He looked so tired and so sad. There was a hint of torment in his eyes. I felt sick to my stomach. I worried that the confession, and the secret he was about to share, would change the course of my life.

"In 1973," he swallowed hard before continuing, "I was a witness to the planning and execution of a terrorist attack—a terrorist attack that the RCMP Security Service could have prevented. Declan, I know who bombed BOAC Flight 281. May God forgive me for my part in the death of those three hundred and twenty-nine people. If you can find it in your heart to deal with this information, I think I can steer you toward righting at least part of the injustice that followed the bombing of that plane. Listen carefully, son, or turn off the VCR and destroy this tape. Once I deliver the next part of this message, there's no turning back. You will feel compelled to do something with the information I am about to give you."

On board an ill-fated flight
- February 14, 1973, 9:00 a.m. (GMT)

Young Elizabeth Jacks was restless and started squirming in her seat. Her mother tried to settle her down.

"Lizzy, we are going to be there in just a little while," Mary Jacks pleaded. "Do a bit more colouring in your book."

But the six-year-old girl would have none of it. She needed some kind of change. After sitting in the same seat for hour after hour, the novelty of flying in an airplane was long gone, and she was desperate for something different. So, the normally delightful little girl did what little girls are apt to do when they are unhappy: She got fidgety and asked if she could go for a walk. Her mother had to say no, as the plane was preparing for its descent. They were just off the coast of Ireland, and the pilot had told the passengers they would be at the terminal at London's Heathrow Airport in less than an hour.

The flight attendant was making her way down the aisle, checking that everyone was settled and directing many to put out their cigarettes, when she noticed the upset little girl. She leaned toward her, smiling a calm, nurturing, comforting smile—

In that moment, everything changed. Calm turned to chaos. The smile was gone and so was the little girl. The fuselage that protected them had shattered, everything flew in different directions, and gravity began to do its work.

Out of the mist came the unimaginable
- February 14, 1973, 9:30 a.m. (GMT)

Seamus O'Hearn's fishing rig *The Dagda* began navigating its way back to Cork. The fog that they had seen in the distance a few hours earlier had now enveloped the ship that carried O'Hearn and his crew of twelve men. They had set out to sea at four that morning, and now, at a little after nine, they were sailing blind back to port with a scant collection of cod and haddock comprising their daily haul. O'Hearn was a rugged seaman who looked the part, with a heavy beard and muscular stature, along with a commanding presence that inspired confidence among those on board his ship. A forty-two-year-old fisherman and a product of three generations of O'Hearns in the fishing industry, Seamus was content to work the seas but always preferred to get back to shore to his wife and children.

He was a bit angry with himself for not turning back to port sooner on this particular morning. A captain of his experience should have known that the fog would roll in quickly and force him to navigate back to Cork on instruments and instinct alone.

Combine this with the cold maritime air of the Celtic Sea, and one could appreciate that Seamus might have been better off staying in bed that Valentine's Day morning. However, he had navigated these frigid waters before, and he would have to do it again today.

The Dagda bobbed northward through the rocky sea. The seasoned crew was used to the sea's perpetual movements, and while this winter morning was not calm, it was a far cry from some of the more violent storms they'd had to contend with in the past. However, it was cold, hovering just above freezing, which certainly affected the spirits of the men on board. A few of the seaman were disappointed that Seamus hadn't turned back to port sooner. Some were angry with their captain, but they knew better than to voice their displeasure.

Seamus attentively monitored his speed and instruments to guarantee that he didn't get *The Dagda* turned around and delay the return of the ship and her crew. 'The boys will be pissed if we're not home by mid-afternoon,' he thought.

For Eoin Fitzgerald, the youngest of the twelve-man crew at nineteen years old, navigating through foggy waters was a combination of two sentiments: eerie and boring. The fishing was finished, and now it would be a long, monotonous trip back to port. He would probably have a shower and a rest before hitting the pub on Garrett Street that night.

But he had to get back to port first. He was sitting at the bow of the ship, staring blindly into the sea, when he saw something floating in the water, which gently bumped the side of the boat. No sooner had it hit the ship than it was gone again, swallowed by the fog. A short time later, another object grazed the side of the ship and deflected off into oblivion again. Eoin turned toward the captain's perch and shouted, "Captain, there's some kind of debris floating around out here." Seamus gave a dismissive nod and turned his attention back to navigating the ship. Eoin returned his gaze to the sea and saw another object hit the boat, and this time he was able to discern a suitcase. Before he could finish processing what he had seen, Eoin looked in horror as a man's body careened off the side of the ship and drifted off into the fog. He sprung to his feet, stepped backward, and shouted, "I just saw a body, for Christ's sake! Captain, stop the ship! There's something going on out here!"

Several crew members rushed to Eoin's position. 'He must be seeing things,' they thought. The sea can be a cruel mistress, playing games with the minds of men, who become hypnotized by her vast unpredictability. But Eoin knew what he had seen, and no sooner had they arrived to console him than a large piece of steel hit the side of the boat. Now all their eyes were fixed on the water; the crew looked overboard in shocked amazement.

And then they saw the unimaginable. The fog lifted in a small pocket. Strewn in front of them were bodies, some intact and some not, scattered luggage, and a jigsaw puzzle of steel debris. The air reeked of petrol. It was as if the sky had quietly deposited its refuse into the Celtic Sea for the crew of *The Dagda* to reckon with.

Seamus watched in horror from behind the ship's controls as the image unfolded in front of him. He reached for his radio, but before he could call for help, a dispatch came over the airwaves, "Attention all vessels sailing the Celtic Sea. Shannon air-traffic control has lost contact with an aircraft headed for London. Please make your way to the following coordinates and report any sign of an aircraft." The dispatcher delivered the coordinates, but Seamus did not hear them. He was consumed with a foreboding sense of despair. He had just inadvertently navigated his ship into a scene of indescribable carnage.

The despair gave way to a resolve that would be described as heroic in the days to come. O'Hearn mustered the mental focus to compel his men into action. "All right, word from Cork is that this is the site of a plane crash, and it looks like we are the first on the scene." Then he started to bark out orders. "Fitz, you and O'Reilly take the life raft and pull as many survivors out of the water as you can. Bring them back, and we'll tend to them onboard. Collins and O'Malley, you take the other raft and do the same. The rest of you are my spotters. Get to the bow, and be on the lookout for anyone who's moving. Keep your eyes open, and let me know what's going on. Move! Move!"

Adrenalin was surging through the bodies of the crew of *The Dagda*. There were no thoughts of heroism, only feelings of hope—hope that they would find someone alive.

It didn't take long for them to realize that all they were going to encounter was death. Fitzgerald and O'Reilly, along with Collins and O'Malley, did take on as many bodies as they could, but they were all dead and many of them were missing arms and legs. Each boat went out numerous times, and each trip they returned with their macabre cargo. Men, women, and children, some clothed and some naked. Mothers and daughters, fathers and sons, grandparents—generations of people dumped into the Celtic Sea from somewhere high above.

For four hours, the men of *The Dagda* searched in vain for survivors. They were joined by other vessels about an hour into what became a recovery operation, and shortly after that, military helicopters began to hover over the site. O'Hearn had led them to the area, and he was the man who communicated each grisly discovery to whomever would listen on the other end of the radio. In the midst of the recovery effort, O'Hearn noticed for the first time that, at some point, the fog had completely lifted.

By mid-afternoon, Seamus had stepped away from the controls of his ship to check on his crew. The twelve men were sitting despondently facing each other on deck with no one speaking a word. Then he looked beyond his men; strewn across the belly of the ship were too many dead bodies to count. And lying prominently among the collection of corpses was the frail frame of a little girl. She was no older than six. Her clothes ripped from her tiny body; her dignity stripped away by some unimaginable evil, delivered mysteriously from the sky into the arms of O'Hearn and his crew. Seamus took off his coat, moved through the mass of death that had been brought on board his ship, and laid it over the little girl's body. He turned to his crew and told them that they were heading back to port.

By this time, the sea was alive with hopeful rescuers. But Seamus knew that hope had died that day. It had disappeared with the lives of those who'd fallen from the sky that February morning.

The Dagda was back in port by early evening. It took some time for the authorities to remove the bodies and take them to the makeshift morgue at a nearby school gymnasium. Exhausted and heartbroken, O'Hearn went home. His wife greeted him at the door. He stood anchored in the doorway, as if he didn't know what to do next, his children staring at him from inside the house. His wife motioned to the children, a gesture indicating that things would be all right, before she guided him inside and up to their bedroom. She closed the door as he sat on the bed. Then Seamus O'Hearn wept like he had never wept before. Tears burst from his eyes, agony and grief beyond description emanating from his tormented soul, and an anguish that only those who have witnessed the unimaginable can feel engulfed him.

His wife held him closely, saying nothing, knowing that her husband had helped to recover the bodies of some of the victims of British Overseas Airway Corporation's Flight 281. The news outlets were reporting that a London-bound Boeing 747, which had departed from the city of Toronto in Canada, had suddenly dropped from the sky. Since there had been no sign of trouble from the plane, the authorities assumed the worst and were looking for terrorist connections to the crash. All of the three hundred and twenty-nine people on the plane were dead. Seamus O'Hearn and his crew managed to bring on board thirty-six of the ninety-three bodies that were recovered that morning. The remainder would find their final resting place at the bottom of the Celtic Sea.

Conscience and a quest - *November 21, 2003*

I pointed the remote at the screen and stopped the VCR. I was caught between a rock and a hard place. I could destroy the tape and be forever haunted by what I might have done to unravel a mystery related to one of the greatest crimes ever perpetrated on Canadian soil, or I could watch the rest of the tape and see my life turn into a crusade to right the wrong that my father, the "great spy" Patrick Keenan, had been too afraid to take care of himself.

Dad knew which choice I would make. He even played the "you are your mother's son" card to guarantee my compliance. Sure, my dad was a distant man emotionally, but behind the stern facade was a man in the grips of profound fear. And now his fears were about to start haunting me.

And he knew me: I was a brooding introvert with an overly active conscience. I was also a social science teacher who prided himself in all things Canadian. The downing of BOAC Flight 281 had been a tragedy that had shocked the nation, not only for the horror of it all but also for the inability of investigators to expose the full nature of the conspiracy that had brought down the plane. No one was ever able to answer the question of how this evil had emerged from Canada, and why all the perpetrators weren't brought to justice.

Before I started the tape again, I went to the kitchen, pulled a beer from the fridge, hoping it hadn't gone skunky from sitting there for who knows how long, and twisted off the cap. I sat down at the kitchen table and thought about my mother and my father and this often-joyless brick house. There had been times in my life when I wondered if I had been born to be an adult. I couldn't really wait for my childhood to end, maybe because I wanted desperately to escape the shadow of the introverted and guarded patriarch who ruled this particular roost. Maybe it was simply because I was raised in a home devoid of play. While my mother was the civilizing influence in my life and earned a loyalty from me that transcended rational thought, she was always plagued by a sadness that kept her from expressing any prolonged sense of joy. She was subject to her own demons, no doubt exacerbated by the shadow of Patrick Keenan.

At this particular point in time, as I sat motionless at my family's kitchen table where my mother and I had shared so many meals without Dad and so many tense meals under his silent and bitter moods, I confirmed a conclusion that I had long felt: My father had earned nothing in my eyes. I recalled a few of Dad's RCMP buddies telling me what a great man he was at the funeral. I had smiled politely, but deep down, I felt empty and dejected—not because my father was gone, but because my father had achieved nothing of consequence from my point of view. Sure, Patrick Keenan was good at his job, but he wasn't good at being a father to his only son or a husband to his wife. He was cold and distant almost all the time. Now this cold and distant man was trying to warm up to me by handing me his unfinished business. "Fuck," I said out loud, before getting up and dumping my half-finished, semi-skunky beer into the kitchen sink. I walked back into the living room and pressed Play on the remote.

My Father's Secret

After a few seconds, the late Patrick Keenan resumed his monologue. "I really never talked to you about my job with the RCMP Security Service, partly because I wasn't supposed to and partly because of the events of 1972 and 1973. I was part of the surveillance unit working out of the Toronto Airport Detachment. We were directed by the top brass to keep an eye on a group of ex-patriot Irish living in the west end. After thirteen people were killed in Londonderry in 1972, the infamous Bloody Sunday incident, this ex-pat group wanted to inflict IRA-style damage on the British from over here in Canada.

"We had an operative on the inside, and we put wiretaps on the pertinent phones and bugs where we could put them undetected. Our operative was there, playing his part as an angry, disenfranchised, Irish sympathizer who wanted to go after the Brits. Not long after joining the group, he got wind of the repatriation of an IRA militant who was coming back to Toronto. This fellow, a dual citizen of Canada and Ireland, was universally regarded as 'bad news.' He was essentially a member of the Provisional IRA, a heavy-handed paramilitary group that had a propensity for violence throughout the conflict called the 'Troubles.' They were routinely shooting people and planting bombs in a variety of spots across Northern Ireland and Great Britain. After this man's return to Toronto, some members of the Irish community started exploring the idea of bombing British assets, eventually settling on going after airplanes leaving North America to head for the United Kingdom. They set their sights on the British Overseas Airways Corporation, BOAC, the airline that eventually became British Airways. They had a number of Toronto to London flights scheduled every week. That's how it all began. Within a year of this man's return, the plan was hatched, Flight 281 was blown up, and three hundred and twenty-nine people were incinerated off the coast of Ireland.

"Son, this is where the tape ends. A sick, old man talking about what looks like a government cover-up is not going to make this case believable to anyone other than the people who think that *everything* is a cover-up. You are about to start gathering evidence. Eventually, you'll deliver the evidence to a person I trust who will hopefully expose the conspirators for what they have done. In the meantime, I want you to go to Warren Belwood's house and ask him for my files. He was my most trusted colleague at the Security Service, so I asked him to keep these files for me. He thinks they are copies of some financial documents that were pertinent to my estate. You'll need to look over the files very closely.

"Warren knows you and I haven't been getting along too well since your mom passed, and that's why I asked him to hang on to them until you came around to get them. He thinks you are being directed by my estate lawyer to retrieve them." A barely detectable expression of bitterness flashed across his face while he paused.

"That's everything. You are on your way to potentially righting a wrong and exposing the bastards who committed this terrible act. I hope you have more courage than I did in my life. You certainly have more of a conscience than I ever had. You are your mother's son." He paused again after saying this, staring at the camera as if to convey a deeper message. He stoically added, "I just wish I could have been more of a father to you, which sounds like a cliché, but you'll find out part of the reason why I was such a sullen man once you start digging into this story."

I looked hard at my father's face. What was I seeing? Sadness? 'Is that a tear welling up in his left eye?' I asked myself. But before the tear could come to life, he sucked the moisture back, and his face reinstated its morose and stony frame.

"I am sorry I have to leave this burden with you."

Then he got up, approached the camera, and stopped the recording. While the old man had tried to dole out a compliment about me being "courageous" and "conscientious," I wondered if I wasn't just being manipulated into doing my father's bidding. Whether I had been manipulated or not, I knew the unsolicited invitation had been extended, and I was morally bound to accept it. I was about to call Warren Belwood and see what the hell was in those files.

Bloody Sunday - *January 30, 1972*

It is difficult to put into words the level of hate, anger, and resentment, or the thickness of the emotional air that hung like a fog over Northern Ireland in 1972. On the one hand, the Irish Catholics, who made up a majority of the population in most areas, despised the Ulster Protestants and the freshly dispatched British forces. On the other hand, the Ulster Protestants and British saw the Irish Catholics as wild and reckless savages. This seething caldron of mutual hate is what bubbled and boiled in all of Northern Ireland in 1972, with Derry (or Londonderry, depending on who you were talking to) representing a major hotspot in the feud between the two sides. This is the atmosphere that Jim Reilly and his friends Adrian and Colleen Murphy willingly walked into that January day.

They left mass at St. Eugene's Cathedral, grabbed a late breakfast, and headed to Bishop's Field to take part in the anti-internment rally that was being staged by the Northern Ireland Civil Rights Association. Internment had become the policy of the British authorities that ruled the six-county cluster in the North of Ireland. Thousands of Catholics, many from Derry, had been arbitrarily arrested and detained without a trial in the early days of what came to be known as the "Troubles." The authorities had banned public protests, but people defied the ban and held protests anyway. The tension seemed to grow with each *illegal* protest leading up to the Derry march in late January. Internment. This was the cause that Reilly and the Murphys came to fight against that Sunday after mass and breakfast.

The British responded to news of the march by sending in the paras—an elite and ruthless paratrooper force who were well trained, well disciplined, and fiercely efficient at achieving their objectives. Today's task was to stop the civil rights demonstration from breaching the barricades at the corner of Chamberlain and Little William streets, foiling the protestors efforts to assemble at Guildhall Square. This would prevent a clash with Protestant loyalists who had planned a counter-demonstration, which was slated to end at Guildhall Square at the same time. The paras would also be confining the Catholic protestors to Catholic neighbourhoods.

Jim, Adrian, and Colleen made their way through the Creggan estates and arrived at Bishop's Field early in the afternoon. As they walked from their favourite breakfast haunt, they found themselves merging with a great deal of foot traffic. Everyone was going to the same place, and by the time they got to Bishop's Field, over seven thousand people had already gathered.

Jim Reilly was a pretty realistic civil rights man. The Irish Republican Army hadn't popped up out of nowhere, he reckoned. They obviously fed on the historic and communal grievances of the Irish people, which dated back centuries. While people weren't rushing to join them in the early days of the Troubles, the IRA had a solid base of public sympathy that allowed their operatives to wage a guerilla war on the British and Ulster authorities and then scurry into hiding in Catholic neighbourhoods. The most recent incarnation of the IRA—the Provisionals or "Provos"—believed that violence was the only way to go. From Jim's perspective, while he was a civil rights man, he could see the need for the Provos, especially with internment escalating across the north.

My Father's Secret

Jim had convinced his best friend, Adrian, and Adrian's wife, Colleen, to join him on the civil rights march. They were less zealous than Jim, but they still felt mortified by the British decision to opt for internment. Adrian was a lawyer, and the idea of detainment without trial was something he was dead set against. Colleen, a schoolteacher in Derry, was equally aghast at the policy.

And so, they gathered at Bishop's Field to (in a sense) vote with their feet. As republican nationalists in a land where British loyalists had the power, they sought to grab a little power back by taking part in what they hoped would be a massive public protest.

The protest exceeded the expectations of the organizers. The numbers swelled as they left Bishop's Field and made their way south on Creggan and then down William Street. The three friends were near the rear of the cohort, which by the time it was halfway down William Street into the Bogside had grown to over fifteen thousand people. In the midst of what could only be described as a boisterous atmosphere, Jim heard someone shout out to him.

"Reilly! Over here!" Out of a mass of people, Mike Walsh and Tim O'Brien made their way toward Jim, Adrian, and Colleen.

"I didn't expect to see you guys here," Jim shouted at them with an uncomfortable smile on his face.

"What the fuck are you talking about?" Walsh replied. "We are civil rights activists," he said sarcastically.

Jim knew full well that Walsh and O'Brien were Provos. He'd had a long conversation with the two men over many pints to see if the IRA option was one that he could consider. Walsh and O'Brien were adamant that violent resistance was the only way to free the North, and if Reilly wanted to join, they would make the necessary arrangements. Reilly had declined, but he maintained a casual friendship with the two men, sharing beer and conversation with them when they met at some of the local republican pubs.

In conversation with a few of the protest organizers, Jim had learned that the civil rights people did not want the IRA in attendance, because they might provoke the British troops. They had met with the local Provos and were assured that this was a civil rights association protest and not an IRA event.

'What the hell are these guys doing here?' Jim thought. He had a bad feeling about their presence at the rally. While a part of him appreciated the IRA's ability to intimidate and antagonize the British, he was concerned that this edition of the IRA—the Provisionals, the ones who had broken away from the Official IRA—could ramp up the cycle of violence to unprecedented levels.

"Don't worry, Jimmy. We come in peace," O'Brien said, waving an exaggerated peace sign and flashing a charming smile. Then leaning into Jim, he added, "Our bosses told us there should be no trouble today, or they'll chop off our balls and throw them in the River Foyle. We are just here to show our support," he said with a wry smile. Then he leaned in closer and whispered (albeit loud enough for the others to hear), "And if the paras try something, we just might be ready to respond to that too."

Jim let out a heavy sigh. The last thing this protest needed was for the Provos to antagonize the British and a massive riot to break out. Nonetheless, Jim was not deluded. Provo antagonism or not, he knew that—once the front end of the protest reached the barriers at the foot of Lower William Street—the British would try to break up the march and a small riot was likely to occur. This was pretty typical of a Derry protest. People march; the authorities respond with water cannons and tear gas. Rocks are thrown, rubber bullets are shot, people get hurt, and then the masses divert their course to Free Derry Corner for a round of speeches and a public rally.

Jim, Adrian, and Colleen moved south, with Mike Walsh and Tim O'Brien not far behind them. Jim had been to a number of protests around Northern Ireland (in defiance of the British ban) and had noted the high security presence. Usually, the Royal Ulster Constabulary teamed up with the British army to police the event. They'd station themselves along the parade route, many of them in riot gear, and jump into action if they thought things were about to get out of hand. Today, the RUC was nowhere to be seen, but there were plenty of British paratroopers around, the same unit believed to be responsible for the Ballymurphy massacre the previous summer in Belfast. These guys were not your garden-variety British military outfit; they were essentially a special-forces unit, and as Jim passed different clusters of paratroopers, he could not avoid their menacing gaze. This did not disturb him; soldiers' death stares were pretty common for protestors. What did disturb him was a group of paratroopers, in full combat gear, who were lying in the tall grasses by the derelict buildings on William Street. Most protestors ignored the soldiers and continued marching and chanting their way forward. But Jim took note; this scenario was different, because the soldiers were in battle position, seemingly ready and willing to pounce. Jim pushed the image to the back of his mind once he passed the buildings and allowed himself to become reabsorbed into the protest atmosphere.

Then the expected happened. The protestors at the front of the cohort of fifteen thousand strong reached the barricade at the foot of Lower William Street. The authorities must have told them to turn back. A standoff ensued, and all that the people at the rear of the crowd could see were the plumes of coloured water being sprayed at the crowd from the British water cannons. They also saw CS tear-gas canisters vaporizing into the crowd and rifles firing what they assumed to be rubber bullets at any protestors the soldiers could pick off. The crowd began to force their way back, and as if part of some fantastic multi-thousand-person dance, everyone retreated to provide relief for those being peppered with tear gas and rubber bullets at the front of the pack. The typical Derry protest skirmish was on.

'This will run for about an hour, and then it's off to Free Derry Corner,' Jim thought.

Jim led Adrian and Colleen up William and across Rossville Street to Glenfada Park, where they waited with a throng of people. Jim wanted to stay far enough away from the riot to avoid getting hurt, but close enough to hear that it had been dispersed. Many others, coughing wildly with tears streaming down their faces from the CS gas, were heading up Rossville Street toward Free Derry Corner. A group of hardcore protestors, mostly young men, could be seen in the distance with kerchiefs over their faces, hurling rocks at the British and their armoured vehicles.

"We'll let the people from the front head down Rossville first, and then we'll follow," Jim told Adrian and Colleen. "Let's just hang here in the wings until the crowd thins out."

A short time later, four loud gunshots came from the direction of the rubble barricade near Kells Walk. The shots were explosive, a far cry from the sound of a rifles firing rubber bullets. The people in the crowd ran wildly, hiding between buildings, seeking shelter wherever they could find it. Jim, Adrian, and Colleen managed to find cover, but when they looked back to Glenfada Park, there was Mike Walsh and Tim O'Brien lying on the ground with blood streaming from their bodies.

"They shot your friends!" Adrian said to Jim.

"It's like they picked them off," Colleen added.

By this point, most of the crowd was either in hiding or running frantically away from the scene. Walsh and O'Brien were in a great deal of pain. They were no more than ten metres away from Jim, so he decided to make his way over to help them.

"I'll be right back," Jim said, scurrying in a crouched position over to O'Brien. He waved a small white handkerchief to demonstrate to the soldiers that he was unarmed and meant no harm. Jim had just about reached his friend when two shots were fired. He was sent flying away from O'Brien, landing face first on the ground, wailing in agony. He knew he was badly hurt and summoned all his faculties to determine what he needed to do next. He was quick to conclude that, even if he wanted to, he couldn't move.

"Jim! Jim!" Colleen shouted. "Are you okay?"

"I'm all right!" Jim shouted back.

"We're going to come and get you," Adrian said.

"No!" Jim shouted. "You'll just get shot like me. Stay there. Wait until it's safe."

Then a silence fell over the area in the immediate vicinity of Walsh, O'Brien, and Reilly. And out of the silence, Adrian, Colleen, and about six others who were hiding with them heard someone walking toward the men. They held their breath, careful not to make a sound, and looked out to see a lone soldier: a para who had been brought in specially for today's protest. Walsh and O'Brien played dead, but Jim's breathing was laboured, and this must have drawn the attention of the soldier. He regarded the helpless man and fired two shots into him before casually walking away. The soldier had randomly selected Jim for execution. It could have just as easily been Walsh or O'Brien, but instead the soldier chose Jim.

Adrian and Colleen sat in shocked disbelief. They had just witnessed the summary execution of their friend, but they dared not make a sound for fear of suffering the same fate. They turned to each other and shielded their faces from the sight of Jim's dead body.

The rest of the day was a daze. Adrian and Colleen stayed where they were for what felt like an eternity. Eventually, they made their way over to Jim and wept by the side of their murdered friend. By this time, the area was flooded with ambulances and soldiers. The wounded were tended to and the dead carted away. The sun began to descend in the western sky, and the presence of the soldiers began to fade.

The chaos of Bloody Sunday led to the deaths of thirteen people at the hands of the British paratroopers. A whole new chapter in the Troubles had begun.

CHAPTER 2:
A NEW THREAT

The Irish Desk - *January 31, 1972*

In 1972, the Royal Canadian Mounted Police consisted of two branches: the Criminal Investigations Branch, which enforced Canadian law like a regular police force, and the Security Service, which handled both foreign and domestic national security issues. While the criminal side worked to lay charges that would lead to convictions, the national security side didn't have to pay much attention to things like the criminal code. They pursued leads and gathered intelligence that served and protected the nation's interests.

Patrick Keenan and Warren Belwood were scheduled to arrive for their first day on the job at the RCMP Security Service's Toronto Airport Detachment at nine in the morning. They agreed to meet in the parking lot and walk into the building together.

Keenan was the first to arrive. "*Early is on time*" was the motto he had lived by since starting his career. He looked at his new work home from the confines of his car, the heater working overtime, drowning out the sound of the old Buick's radio and keeping the January cold at bay. The detachment was housed in a nondescript grey building in an industrial park—a typical one-floor concrete box in the middle of nowhere on a street with a similar cluster of concrete boxes—not far from the Toronto airport. The architects had tried to jazz up the place a bit with a few modern accent columns, but the station couldn't help but give off a sterile vibe.

He thought about his new role and the information shared with him by his superiors. Both he and Belwood, standout electronic surveillance and countersubversion agents from the downtown detachment, had been transferred to the airport unit amid rising fears that RCMP intelligence resources were too concentrated on the Cold War-Soviet threat and not enough on others. The government responded by reallocating assets in the aftermath of the attacks of the *Front de Liberation du Quebec* on the Canadian confederation. Certainly, the FLQ, the most violent of the separatist factions in Quebec, had made their point since 1969 with close to a hundred bombings in the Montreal area, along with the high-profile kidnapping of James Cross and Pierre Laporte. Cross, the British Trade Commissioner, was freed two months after his abduction, while Laporte, a Quebec cabinet minister, was found dead in the trunk of his car. The hysteria surrounding the kidnappings prompted Prime Minister Pierre Trudeau to declare martial law, enacting the War Measures Act in October 1970, which suspended the civil liberties of all Canadians.

While the so-called October Crisis was pretty much put to rest by the end of 1970, politicians across Canada were paranoid that further cracks in the Canadian federation were about to emerge. FLQ efforts to achieve the separation of Quebec from Canada via violence were greeted mostly with alarm. However, the seeds of separation had been planted across the nation, and fringe groups from coast-to-coast hatched plans to rip the country apart—or at least, that is what the politicians were thinking. As a result, funding was funnelled into the RCMP, with a handsome chunk of the money heading to the Security Service and the establishment of a counterterrorism unit aimed at the Quebec separatist movement. Canadian politicians wanted enemies of the state rooted out, and the Security Service was the group mandated to do the job.

With most of the Cold War concentration of assets centred in Ottawa and the newly formed Quebec separatism unit based in Montreal, the Toronto unit was left to deal with other threats. Most of those threats had to do with immigrant populations who were aligned with rebel factions in their former homelands. For this reason, the Toronto Airport Detachment housed a variety of ethnic units that focused on potential problems emanating from these groups.

The challenge for the detachment was finding a way to see what threats were being imported from other countries. Toronto was an immigration hub. People from all over the world were leaving their homelands to settle in the relative affluence of Canada. While most immigrants quickly embraced the Canadian social and economic framework, they were less likely to assimilate into a unified Canadian motif and abandon their own cultural backgrounds.

The immigration statistics were clear. Immigrants came in multitudes and very few ever went back, other than to visit. Most got their Canadian citizenship as soon as they could. In fact, from the late sixties into the early seventies, the standard number of immigrants ranged from one hundred to two hundred thousand a year. Their arrival drove the economy upward in a way that most Canadians could not (or would not) appreciate.

The downside of the immigration wave was that a very small minority of immigrants continued to pursue the political grievances they harboured toward their homeland from their mostly suburban homes in Canada. Money was sent back to some pretty shady groups that were seeking to undermine the authority of the national governments of some of Canada's main allies.

Belwood's brand-new Chevy Impala pulled into the parking lot, bringing Patrick Keenan out of these thoughts and back to the present. 'Warren always drives a nice car,' he thought, before concluding that his ten-year-old Buick Skylark sedan was looking and feeling a little tired.

They got out of their vehicles at the same time and shared a hurried hello as the sub-zero temperatures penetrated their many layers and got right into their bones. They were bundled up in their winter gear: parkas, toques, and gloves. Neither man was terribly concerned with winter fashion; warmth was the priority on this particular winter morning.

No sooner had they moved through the front door than a short, burly man in a brown, tight-fitting suit with a bright yellow shirt and wide striped tie approached them. "You must be the two new agents. Meeting in the conference room, stat."

The men stared at the stranger who had just addressed them.

"I'm Sergeant Paul Dawson. Leave your coats with the reception girl and follow me," he said. "Come on, let's move, gentlemen."

Keenan and Belwood did as directed, abandoning their coats and following Dawson to the conference room. The chairs around the main table were occupied, and a few men were standing at the back. Keenan figured most of the agents were in their thirties, making him and Belwood among the older agents, with both of them in their mid-forties. The two newcomers found a place to stand while Sergeant Dawson advanced to the front and took his place beside Staff Sergeant Gord Millington. Keenan and Belwood had been warned about the staff sergeant's no-nonsense leadership approach. Millington was tall, with short, dark hair and a thick moustache. He looked like an army man and appeared quite fit for someone in his early sixties.

"Yesterday, in Northern Ireland, the British sent paratroopers into Londonderry to keep the peace," Millington told the service agents gathered in the briefing room. He stood erect and spoke with authority, perhaps a holdover from his military service. The combination of confident demeanour and imposing physique let everyone in the detachment know that he was in charge. "Londonderry is a pretty unstable city, and the Brits have had their hands full with so-called 'civil rights groups' for the past couple of years. According to the British MI6, these groups are essentially pawns of the Provisional IRA, a violent outgrowth of the Official IRA that the locals call 'Provos.' To make a long story short, what started as a mass demonstration turned into a riot. Thirteen people were killed in clashes with British troops. Many others were wounded.

"I don't care about the details surrounding what happened over there. What I do care about is how the Irish in Toronto are going to react. Ireland's greatest export is its people, and more than a few of them live not far from here. We know for a fact that many in the Irish diaspora have been sending money back to nefarious elements who live in Belfast, Antrim, and yes, Londonderry. Since the Battle of the Bogside in '69, they've started to refer to the conflict as the 'Troubles.' A few service members have been pulled off other desks to work on the file sporadically. They have identified a radical group of IRA sympathizers who congregate at a place called Foley's Irish Pub in the Junction here in Toronto. The proprietor, Quinn Foley, likes to play host to Irish nationalists. One patron, a rich Irish immigrant named Collin Boyle, is in our crosshairs for channelling money to Ireland for the IRA."

Millington's mention of the Junction caught Keenan's attention. The new service agent had grown up on Hook Avenue in the Toronto west-end neighbourhood, just a few blocks from the pub in question.

"The money is being used to buy guns and build bombs, weapons that the Provos are using to kill innocent people. We're not quite sure how they are moving the cash. They are also using these funds to orchestrate the assassination of cops and soldiers." Millington paused to make sure the agents were listening, quickly scanning the room to get a gauge on their state of attention.

"Dawson and the two new agents are going to put together a reconnaissance and surveillance plan for Foley's Pub. We need someone else to volunteer to go undercover and infiltrate the group," Millington said. "Maybe one of you Irish-looking guys can step up and do us proud." Another pause by Millington and then, "That's it. Dawson, introduce yourself to the new agents and get a draft surveillance plan on my desk by the end of the day. The rest of you, work your sources to see what the buzz is out there in light of the events I just spoke to you about."

The day was intense for the two new members of the Toronto Airport Detachment. Paul Dawson, a fifteen-year service veteran, showed the men around the station. The detachment was comprised of a large, open space that was separated into clusters; each cluster represented an investigative focus called a "Desk." This particular unit housed a counterespionage team made up of a Soviet Desk (working in conjunction with a larger downtown team), a Satellite Desk (focusing on the Eastern Bloc of Soviet satellite nations), a Chinese Desk, and a separate Countersubversion Desk (focusing on threats emanating from within Canada). The team that was investigating the Irish threat would work under the "countersubversion" umbrella.

By noon, Keenan and Belwood were in a service car, heading to what could be the lifeline between IRA extremists in Toronto and the Provisional IRA in Northern Ireland. They drove along Dundas Street through the Junction and stopped outside of Foley's, just shy of Pacific Avenue. It was a standard old Toronto west-end establishment, located in a block-long row of retail

My Father's Secret

units, with apartments upstairs, that were built in the late nineteenth and early twentieth centuries. Fortunately for the service, there was a vacant apartment down the street from the pub, one which could be commandeered for physical surveillance. Better still, the service, with its team of clandestine agents, would have no problem gaining access to the pub's main building undetected, if necessary. The agents made some notes before heading back to the detachment.

Once they were back at the office, they met with Dawson and gave him the pertinent information: the location on the street, the neighbouring units, the entrances and exits to the building, the positions of the ventilation system, gas line, water metre, telephone poles, and phone-connection access points. They also let him know what equipment they needed to conduct electronic surveillance on the pub.

While Keenan and Belwood were on their surveillance mission, Agent Terry Maloney volunteered to go undercover at the pub. Recently divorced with no kids, Maloney was an ideal candidate for the job. His Irish ancestry was written all over his face, and the fact that he had just moved to Toronto from Montreal meant he had no significant ties to the local community. His parents were also Irish immigrants, so his grasp of the accent was almost expert. He could play the part. His undercover name would be "Terry O'Sullivan."

This marked the birth of the Toronto Airport Detachment's Irish Desk.

The legend of Darcy Byrne: *Origins - 1939–1957*

If you heard Darcy Byrne tell the story, you'd think he was as Provo as Brendan Hughes or Gerry Adams (though you'd never hear

Adams admit to it). He'd have you believe that he emerged from a fiercely republican household in the city of Armagh, in the heart of "bandit country," watching his relatives fight operation after operation for the IRA and leading the charge in the battle to oust the British from the island. In terms of Darcy's personal actions, he'd have you believe that, after leading many missions himself, a deadly skirmish with the Royal Ulster Constabulary forced him to flee to Canada to save himself from internment and to lead the fight for the IRA in the diaspora. This was the legend he had built for himself, a legend that he propagated every chance he got. A legend that was given legs when he returned to Canada in 1972.

While reality reflected some of the aspects of the legend, there were many important points of distinction that Darcy left out of his story. These omissions necessitate a more faithful retelling of the tale.

Darcy was born in 1942 to Kevin and Rosemary Byrne in the town of Brampton, in the province of Ontario, in the country of Canada. Kevin had come to Canada from Armagh in the North of Ireland shortly after the Second World War began.

Kevin's uncle, Mick Fagan, had emigrated from Ireland to Canada when he was a young man and eventually founded the Brampton-based Fagan's Trucking, an all-purpose delivery company moving wood, coal, and crops to Toronto and the surrounding area.

Fagan had a keen mind and could see that things were going awry in Europe, so prior to war being declared in September 1939, he'd contacted his brothers and sisters back in Ireland (of whom he had eight!) to see if they had any children who could help him keep his fleet of trucks moving. Fagan expected every able-bodied Canadian male between eighteen and twenty-five to sign up to go to war. This would decimate his workforce and leave him in the lurch.

Fagan's sister, Anne Byrne, had contacted her brother and said that her son Kevin was eighteen, out of school, out of work, and needed to do something, so he'd be on the next boat bound for Canada. There was absolutely no danger that Kevin or any other Irish Catholic from Armagh would be fighting in the war for the British. He arrived in Brampton in the late fall of 1939 as the Germans got ready for the Blitzkrieg, the British mobilized, the French manned the Maginot Line, and the Russians negotiated the Non-Aggression Pact to stave off the Nazi threat.

Kevin was a quick study and became Mick Fagan's main man in no time. They managed to find a few other drivers, and the business dodged the wartime bullet. While in Brampton, Kevin met and fell in love with Rosemary Cullen, a local farmer's daughter. They were married in the summer of 1941 and had a son, Darcy, in 1942.

While Kevin was the most valuable employee at Fagan's Trucking, he longed for Armagh. Before they'd gotten married, he'd made it clear to Rosemary that, when the time came, he would like the family to move to Ireland. He knew he could easily make a livelihood driving a lorry there. And so, when the war ended in 1945, Armagh welcomed home Kevin, his bride, Rosemary, and their son, Darcy.

Darcy was just a toddler when they made the move, and he grew accustomed to Armagh quickly. But there was something distinctly different about Ireland when compared to Canada, a subcurrent that a boy would absorb into his consciousness without fully appreciating its presence. There was a constant flow of anger and tension from day to day. It was written on the faces of the people who lived there. It was an anger that felt as if it could explode at any moment. Darcy didn't really come to terms with this; he just soaked it in and lived the average life of an Irish Catholic growing up in Armagh.

Darcy had a revelatory experience shortly after he turned eight. His father had taken him on a trip to Crossmaglen by the border, going into the Republic of Ireland. They'd met Kevin's brother, Aidan, for lunch at a local pub. It was an emotional reunion since the brothers hadn't seen each other in years. The pub was bright and noisy and packed full of patrons. The summer sun shone outside with the warmth of the day, raising the temperature and the collective thirst for adult beverages of those gathered in the establishment that July day.

Over lunch and after more than a few pints, Aidan, the eldest of the Byrne brothers, had leaned in and said to Kevin, "You know, brother, I'm IRA."

"Really?" Kevin asked, surprised at the declaration. The men shared the glazed expression of two slightly drunken Irishmen.

"I fought in the Northern Campaign. I had to head up to Belfast for most of my service—it was a mess down here; the Irish Republic made sure of that," Kevin said. "Now that I got a taste for it, I'm IRA for life."

Then the brothers got into a long discussion about the state of the dis-union in Ireland: efforts by the South of the island to establish itself as a legitimate free and independent state; efforts by the North to oust those loyal to the British and to send the Brits packing. They talked about Irish history, the Easter Rising of 1916, partition, and the reasons for the failure of the Northern Campaign. Darcy was mesmerized, watching the two men wax not-so-eloquently as the drink got deeper into their systems while the conversation progressed.

Kevin Byrne was a republican at heart, but he was unwilling to turn to the gun to free the North of Ireland. Maybe it was because he was born and raised in Armagh and had migrated to Canada for a short time—two sanctuaries in a way, both far enough away from the violence of Belfast and Derry and Newry and Crossmaglen.

Clearly, Aidan was willing to pursue a path of combat, and as a boy, Darcy was captivated by his uncle's militant leanings.

While Aidan's membership in the IRA surprised Kevin, he knew better than to tell Rosemary about it. After losing two uncles in The Great War, she'd hardly be able to come to terms with the battle to unite the Irish republic. In fact, the deaths of her uncles had hardened her, made her feel more isolated, withdrawn, and untrusting. This is why Kevin kept that bit of news from her and told Darcy to do the same.

In the meantime, Darcy had become a full-fledged member of the community in Armagh. He attended St. Patrick's Primary School. He was a tall boy for his age with jet-black hair and a broad-shouldered, athletic physique. He was a small-time bully in the schoolyard, picking his targets carefully and using his charisma and persuasive techniques to keep the more seasoned bully's away from himself. By the time he reached high school—another school named St. Pat's, down the road—he was as republican as all the other kids at the all-boys school. He imagined the next IRA campaign—one where he could fight alongside his uncle to oust the Brits from Ireland and bring the Ulster loyalists to their knees.

Connecting with Warren Belwood - *November 22, 2003*

I arranged to meet Warren Belwood the day after viewing my father's video message. I had never really given my dad's work much thought. I actually hadn't found out that he was working for the spy branch of the Mounties until after he retired. Belwood was really just a work friend of Dad's who would occasionally come over to our house with his wife to socialize with my parents.

Warren Belwood lived in a small house in Mimico, a modest Toronto neighbourhood off the shores of Lake Ontario. He and his wife had lived in the same bungalow for forty years. The exterior of the house proclaimed humility—perhaps the message the Canadian government had had in mind when they'd built the homes for returning veterans after the Second World War.

The Belwoods were an affable couple. Sally was a doting hostess with an energetic step despite the fact that she was over seventy and a little on the chubby side. Her husband was a match—chubby and eager to please the son of his former friend.

Warren Belwood knew exactly what I had come for. He went into his den and pulled out the brown file box and laid it in front of me. Sally offered me a coffee, and I decided to oblige (the two seemed a little desperate for company).

"Your dad was a hell of a Mountie, Declan," he said, after his wife handed me my cup of coffee and retreated back to the kitchen. "He and I worked in electronic surveillance. We orchestrated the bugging of more places than I can tell you, and ninety-eight percent of the time, people didn't have a clue that we had the place wired. Of course, we never really enjoyed the two percent of the time when they found out what we were up to."

Belwood let out a small laugh. I smiled back.

"I know the two of you didn't always get a long after your mom passed. The service life was tough on its agents and their families. The fact that Sally and I, and your mom and dad, made it work is the exception rather than the rule." Belwood shot a look toward the kitchen. Sally was busy cleaning something and didn't hear his comment.

Belwood then went into a few minutes of war stories about the operations he and my dad had been involved in. He bitched about how unappreciated the surveillance guys were in the Security Service. "Christ, we gathered most of the intelligence, and the other Service Mounties took all the credit. Surveillance was a dead end if you were looking for a promotion. Good thing your dad and I weren't too ambitious," he said with another warm-hearted chuckle.

I wanted to get right to the point, so I decided to put out some feelers to see if Belwood knew anything about my father's plans to send me on a mission to unearth the mysteries surrounding the downing of that aircraft back in 1973.

"I've got a question for you, Mr. Belwood. My dad and I weren't completely on the outs. In fact, we did talk sometimes. Granted, the relationship was strained." I cleared my throat before continuing, "He did say to me once that the toughest case he ever worked on was related to the bombing of BOAC Flight 281."

The affable Belwood, a moment earlier smiling and showing genuine hospitality, went completely vacant. He wasn't shocked by the statement. He wasn't irritated either. Instead, he just went blank—emotionless, devoid of any discernable expression.

Then vacancy gave way to an intense expression as he looked me directly in the eyes. "I doubt he said that." His delivery was cool and concise. His look seemed to say, *"That secret is supposed to be buried."* With that one sentence, he was telling me that the conversation was over. An old man—over seventy years old and clearly not a physical threat to me—had just delivered a message, through a few words and a startling expression, that completely unnerved me. I picked up the file box and said an awkward goodbye to him and his wife.

I was pretty rattled when I got back into my car. 'What the hell was that?' I asked myself. 'Sure, I just tried to play a mind game with a former Canadian spy, but his reaction was *so severe*.' I knew I had struck a nerve with the man, and his message to me—through the few words he'd said and the expression on his face—was clear: *"You better watch your step."*

Belwood's reaction also told me that there was more to the story than what was conventionally known. The history of the event was pretty clear. A group of Toronto IRA sympathizers, likely working with the Provisional IRA in Northern Ireland, had brought down BOAC Flight 281. The Provos vehemently denied any involvement in the bombing, something that was uncharacteristic of the group. The conspiracy was so effective that only one person, the man who built the bomb, was ever convicted of the crime—this despite the fact that a man named Darcy Byrne was widely believed to be the mastermind behind the bombing. While Canadians were saddened by the events of 1973 and the subsequent inability of the authorities to arrest or convict anyone else, they put the event behind them pretty quickly—far too quickly for the families of the victims. While the Crown did make an effort to lay charges years later, the government side could not make anything stick, and the conspirators were acquitted.

I considered all these issues as I drove back to my house. My wife greeted me at the door, saw the expression on my face, and asked me what had happened. I made my way to a chair in the living room in a daze. I explained the situation, and she reiterated the fact that my direct approach had opened a can of worms with Belwood. Instead of reprimanding me for the way I'd handled the situation—something she didn't need to do because I'd been second guessing myself for most of the evening—she shifted her attention to the contents of the box.

You need to understand a thing or two about my wife, Karuna Patel. Primarily, she's a petite, five-foot-five, one-hundred-and-fifteen-pound, dark-haired, dark-skinned, no-nonsense dynamo. Her family had immigrated from India, part of an initial wave of South Asians who'd come to Canada in the mid-sixties. It must have been extremely difficult for them when they first arrived. They'd been the target of plenty of racial hatred. Her father recalls being called a *Paki* on a daily basis as he rode the TTC to and from his job as a junior accountant at Revenue Canada. Her mother stayed at home and raised Karuna and her brother, Raj. They were lovers of Indian culture, but they embraced the things that Canada had to offer, giving them a foot in each world. This is what saved Karuna from familial ostracism when she'd met and fallen in love with me. It was also what allowed her family to accept me despite the judgment of many members of their community, particularly the ones who believed the Patels should have arranged Karuna's marriage to a fellow Indian of a particular caste.

To be clear, they'd lost friends when Karuna and I got together. They'd also gained friends, namely my parents and a few others. But overall, the losses outweighed the gains.

To this day, I still can't believe how lucky I am. Here's this beautiful, intelligent woman—an immigration lawyer who works for a small Toronto firm—who fell for me, an introverted, cautious, fretful, high school teacher.

Karuna popped the cardboard lid off the brown file box and looked inside. Files were stacked neatly in folders from one end to the other. My father hadn't made it easy for us. The files were, in fact, financial documents that covered the last two years of his life. As we sifted through the pages, we encountered old bills, bank statements, and income tax returns. If Belwood had ever been tempted to look inside, he wouldn't have suspected a thing. The only file that didn't fit the scheme was called "Old Pictures." Inside, we found random pictures that gave a snapshot of my family's history. Some showed family gathering and birthday parties. Some showed scenic landscapes from holidays we'd gone on. Some were candid shots that involved my mother, and occasionally, my father. Many were of me as a child.

After two hours of reviewing the files and all the photos, I threw my hands in the air. "I'm stumped. I have no clue where my father is trying to lead me. Are you seeing anything out of the ordinary?"

Karuna looked at me with an equally confused expression. "I'm as baffled as you are."

By this time, we were both exhausted and decided we needed to step away from the files. We moved to the adjacent kitchen and cooked a late supper together without saying a word. Every once in a while, one of us would cast a glance across the open space between the kitchen and the living room, back toward the files that were scattered on the floor. Even after we'd sat down at the table, we both kept looking over toward the files, so frustrated by the puzzle that we refused to let it beat us.

We went back to the files after dinner. We reviewed every financial detail and looked over every photo too many times to count. Still nothing.

"That's it. I'm done," Karuna finally said. "You coming to bed?"

I considered the invitation, because I was exhausted. "No, I am going to keep at it for a bit. I'll be up soon."

She kissed me gently on the top of the head, placing a warm hand on my shoulder and wished me luck.

I kept at it for another hour before I decided to rest my eyes for few minutes, rolling onto the nearby couch. When I closed my eyes, all I could see were files, numbers, disjointed financial statements, and a slideshow of family photos. I started to drift off to sleep with this bizarre visual circus unfolding in my mind. Soon, the circus faded, and a dull silence set in.

And out of the silence came my father's voice—the same voice from the video that had started this whole ordeal. *"You are your mother's son."* And then an image from one of the photos floated into my dreamy mind: my mother and I, sitting on a rock in front of the cottage where we used to stay when I was a boy. The cottage belonged to my uncle Liam, my mother's brother. I could honestly say that the best days of my youth were spent at that cottage.

My Father's Secret

I was jarred awake by the image and forced myself up off the couch. I found the photograph. *"You are your mother's son."* I didn't know who took the picture, but the photo featured my mom, wearing a pretty summer dress, embracing me. I was around seven, and she was giving me a warm, playful hug while I tried to squirm away. In the background, sitting on the cottage porch, was my father, a book resting on his lap, looking at us with a half smile on his face. This was usually all we got out of him—a half smile. I flipped the picture over, and printed in the jagged scroll of a sick, old man, I saw the letters, "Y.A.Y.M.S."

You Are Your Mother's Son.

A memory popped into my mind. When we'd stayed at Uncle Liam's cottage, my dad would lead me in a kind of hide-and-seek game. He would take a dollar bill and hide it somewhere in the living room. The living room was rustic with the main window looking out over Georgian Bay—a positively spellbinding view. If I found the dollar, I got to keep it. Most of the time, I won the game because I was too stubborn to give up. Sometimes he really challenged me, hiding the dollar in a pretty obscure place.

On one occasion, I was deep into a search; I was probably seven-years-old at the time (around the time that that picture had been taken as a matter of fact). My father was staring out the living-room window when I finally gave up. He slowly brought his attention back to me and encouraged me to give it one more shot. "It's closer than you think," he said. I checked under the seat cushions on the couch and underneath a nearby lamp. I checked under the carpet and flipped through a couple of magazines on the coffee table. Nothing. Finally, I opened my mother's *Jerusalem Bible* that was lying right in front of me on the living-room coffee table. She had bought the Bible a few months earlier with some friends of hers from the church. I flipped through the Bible, and there it was—nestled somewhere in the middle of the Old Testament. Feeling tremendous pride in my great victory, I held the dollar bill over my head like a true champion. My father looked at me, smiling (a full smile this time), and said, "You are your mother's son."

At the time, I wasn't really sure what my father meant by this, and to be honest, I didn't really care. I was more preoccupied with my new dollar bill. However, over the years, whenever I did something that my father approved of, he would say to me, "You are your mother's son," and it would always trigger my memory of that episode.

Now I knew I was on to something, but what was I on to? Was the next clue in my mother's old Bible? Where the hell was that Bible anyway? Or was I supposed to go up to my uncle's cottage and play hide-and-seek in the living room with the ghost of my dead father? That seemed more than a little odd. Meanwhile, part of me wondered if I was just chasing a phony lead.

From a manpower perspective, we're it - *February 1972*

Patrick Keenan was at his desk, reviewing a list of surveillance gear needed for the Foley's Irish Pub job, while Warren Belwood was on the phone with the service tech department, checking on inventory, when Sergeant Paul Dawson made his way over to the cubicle where the two agents worked. He motioned to Belwood to tell whoever it was that he would call them back.

"Well, it's kind of a good news, bad news scenario," Dawson started. "The good news is that we've obtained a warrant to wiretap the phone lines of the pub, and Collin Boyle's home and office. The bad news is that the courts won't let us bug the bar itself."

Keenan and Belwood looked at Dawson in disbelief. "We're not going to get much from those phones. We need electronic surveillance *inside* the pub," Belwood said.

"And isn't the standard for getting a warrant a little more generous when it comes to Security Service applications? I mean the warrant is obtained in secret and in a closed courtroom. If our surveillance needs are going to prevent an attack on our nation, you'd think they'd be more willing to give us what we need," Keenan added.

Dawson was quick to respond. "Gentlemen, I understand your frustration, but until Maloney can get us something substantial—something we can use to expand the warrant—the surveillance will remain restricted to whatever he can discover from the inside, and the wiretaps on the phones."

The room went silent again.

"There's another thing," Dawson said with a note of apprehension. "The higher-ups have officially confirmed that we will be called the 'Irish Desk.' We're focused primarily on assessing threats coming out of the Irish community in Toronto. In terms of resources, we have the wiretaps and access to the apartment across the street from the pub. From a manpower perspective, we're it."

"You gotta be kidding," Keenan protested.

"Two surveillance guys and an insider? How are we supposed to get a handle on these guys, Sergeant?" asked Belwood.

"I know, I know," Dawson said, "and believe me, I pled our case, but the Security Service is allocating its resources back into Quebec. They think that a resurgent FLQ is likely to team up with the Parti Quebecois and stir up Quebec nationalism to the point of politically motivated separation from the federation. This is the greater threat to the nation at the present time, and this Irish thing looks like it's small time compared to the FLQ and the PQ. I'm sorry, gentlemen."

Keenan shuffled the papers in front of him. "So, what does this mean? Are Belwood and I supposed to spend all our time monitoring the ins and outs at the pub and listening to the wiretaps? With just two guys in the field..." He ended his query mid-sentence.

"That does seem a bit unreasonable," Dawson said. "We'll do evening surveillance. Both of you can work out of the apartment we acquired five evenings a week. There's no money for overtime. We'll decide on which evenings based on the information that Maloney provides. You can also take the tapes of the calls and review them on shift at the apartment." He sighed. "Let's see where this goes. This might be a dead end anyway."

He left them, and the two RCMP investigators just sat back in the chairs and stared blankly at the desks in front of them. Keenan burned with a quiet anger. Belwood eventually shook his head and picked up the phone. It seemed that the RCMP Security Service's concern about the Irish threat was not as serious as they had initially let on.

A spy at the pub - *February 1972*

Terry Maloney assumed the cover persona of "Terry 'Sully' O'Sullivan" and prepared for his assignment at Foley's Irish Pub, gathering intelligence and familiarizing himself with the impact of the Troubles on the ex-pat Irish community in Toronto. Foley's had all the telltale signs of a typical Irish drinking establishment: a fully stocked bar that was adorned with too many bottles to count; a handful of Irish stouts and ales on tap; handcrafted, detailed wood décor; and the odd splash of stained glass to accent its appearance. The lighting was also dim, lending a little more mystery to the pub's atmosphere. The proprietor, Quinn Foley, had done his best to recreate the experience his customers would expect if they walked into a pub in Dublin, Derry, or Donegal.

However, the one fundamental difference was that Foley's, despite possessing all the welcoming features of an Irish pub, was distinctly unwelcoming unless you were a patron who had been accepted into the fold. Maloney (*Sully*) figured this out the minute he walked through the door.

It was a little after seven when Maloney arrived at the pub. He'd dressed the part—tight jeans, a flannel shirt, and scuffed-up boots that suggested an off-the-clock construction worker who was looking to unwind. The eyes of most of the patrons turned, quickly noting the presence of the stranger, before refocusing on the beverage in front of them. Mental notes were made: average height, fairly muscular, short, sandy-brown hair, and a thin beard. If they were going to toss the guy out, they needed to know if they could handle him. Maloney concluded that he would either be driven out of the place inside of ten minutes or he'd be accepted as a probationary patron until he could justify the fact that he belonged as a regular.

He made his way to the safest place for a newcomer to go—the bar seat closest to the door—in case he had to make a hasty escape. The bartender, Foley himself, shot him a few glances before he made his way over to serve him. Maloney could feel the tension in the room. Everyone was waiting on Foley to deliver his initial verdict.

"What can I do for you?" the publican asked, not offering service but inquiring for an explanation of his presence.

"A pint of Harp, please," Maloney responded, not taking the bait and hoping his faint Irish accent was up to par.

Foley stared at him for a moment before he made his way to the taps, flipping a towel over his shoulder and starting to pull the interloper a beer. 'No Irish hospitality yet,' thought Maloney.

Quinn Foley was like a lighthouse beacon at this point. He was tall enough that he stood above the taps, so most of those gathered in the pub could see his face. His receding hairline and short, brown hair helped those interested in seeing his eyes get a grip on what he was thinking. Of course, they didn't need to see much. Foley's signal would be clear to them, and they would respond accordingly.

He headed back to Maloney and delivered the pint. "Here you go," Foley said. "Now, I need to know why you're here."

Maloney looked up and smiled. "I'm just here to unwind. I just got to town for work and moved into an apartment a short drive from here. I saw your place and thought an Irish pub could give me a taste of my roots." He held up his beer as he finished his sentence.

Foley let out an impatient sigh. "Take a look around, friend. The clientele doesn't exactly seem pleased with your presence."

Maloney cast a quick look around the pub. They were almost all men, and most of them looked ready to toss him out. One man—seated at a large booth by the corridor heading to what he assumed was the kitchen and the restrooms—looked completely disengaged. Maloney knew the man must be Collin Boyle.

"Where's the accent from?" Foley asked. "It sounds like the west coast. Not very strong, but it's there."

"Donegal," Maloney answered. "By way of my parents who immigrated to Canada when I was a teen. They're still in Montreal. I left because of all the shit going on with the Quebec government. An Irishman's better off working in Toronto than Montreal these days, let me tell you."

"The Quebecois do seem to hate anyone who doesn't speak French exclusively." Foley was finished sizing him up, preparing to deliver his verdict. "What do you do?"

"Construction," Maloney answered. "Just got a job working on one of the new skyscrapers downtown."

Another pause followed before Foley held out his hand. "My name is Quinn Foley. I run this place."

"Terry O'Sullivan," Maloney replied, shaking the man's hand. "But my friends call me Sully."

"Well then, Sully it is," Foley said, looking out at the patrons. The handshake signalled the fact that "Sully" was fit for probation.

Over the ensuing weeks, Sully proved his fitness to be a regular at the pub. He didn't waver from his cover story and focused on his main target: Collin Boyle, the quiet, distinguished-looking man with short, salt-and-pepper hair who was a fixture at Foley's. His stern expression and stocky frame suggested that he was both guarded and prone to anger, which would make it tough for Maloney to enter into his inner circle.

The service file on Boyle told the story: Collin Boyle was a pharmaceutical importer who spent most evenings at the pub. He always sat at the same booth—a semi-secluded, open-concept, six-seater that was not far from the bar. He could see every person who came into the pub. A wealthy businessman, Boyle had made his relative fortune as an early investor in the burgeoning generic pharmaceutical sector. Irish entrepreneurs had started manufacturing drugs and exporting them to North America in the sixties. Boyle had worked a few of his contacts, made the appropriate investments, and positioned himself as the Canadian lead for Irish generic drugs.

He immigrated to Canada from the town of Monaghan—technically in the Republic of Ireland, but situated near the border between Ireland and the British controlled North. When the island was divided in 1921, many Protestants were left on the wrong side of the border. A tense period ensued, and while some uprooted and moved into the Protestant-dominated North, others stayed and did battle with hostile Catholic groups, most notably the IRA. Many claimed that border towns like Monaghan, Donegal, and Cavan were the birthplace of Protestant agitator groups like the B-Specials, the Ulster Specialist Constabulary, and the Ulster Volunteer Force—this despite the presence of a sizable and militant Catholic population.

Maloney knew that Boyle, born in the late twenties, would have spent his entire Irish life watching the IRA do battle with Protestant forces. Monaghan was the place where IRA operatives would murder British loyalists, and the loyalists would murder members of the IRA or their families. It was a vicious and continuing cycle of brutal violence, the horror of which could never be put into words. One could only surmise that, by the time Boyle had left Ireland as a thirty-year-old man, he hated the Northern Protestants with every fibre of his being.

Maloney would make his way to the pub shortly after Boyle arrived most evenings. He would take his place at the bar and make small talk with Foley. Small talk often garnered important logistical information for a Service Mountie. In no time, Maloney was not only able to figure out the comings and goings of the main players in the pub but was able to cozy up to a few of the players themselves. He was fortunate to have made inroads with Quinn Foley, as he was one of Boyle's closest allies.

Maloney (now accepted as Sully to the pub faithful) had grown to admire Foley. He was a striking man, a gracious host once you received his approval, and a skilled entrepreneur. The maintenance of his Irish accent (Foley had lived in Canada for most of his adult life) was as much about business as it was about being a proud Irishman, something that lent credibility to his role as host to ex-pat republicans. He made it very clear that Foley's was a pub for men and the women they chose to bring with them to the establishment. In other words, it was a pub for drinking and scheming, not necessarily for families and wholesome fun.

This wasn't a problem for Maloney. The Service Mountie had been on a variety of assignments at home and abroad. He had dealt with far more sophisticated characters than Foley and Boyle. He also knew how to work his way into a group's inner circle. If Maloney had one fault, it was his love of Jack Daniel's Tennessee Whiskey. His work early in the evening was solid and professional, but by closing time, Maloney was a bit of an intoxicated mess. Since his divorce, he had taken his drinking to a new level. The service knew this, but they needed to turn a blind eye because Maloney was their only asset working the case at Foley's Irish Pub.

However, Maloney made major inroads one Friday night, deep into a bout of drinking, when Foley spent about a half hour at the bar, speaking with the man he called Sully near closing time. They went through the typical topics: weather, sports, work, and family. Maloney played his part as best he could. He opined that the weather's better in Dublin than in Shannon, suggested that hockey's a fine game once you get the hang of it, and mentioned that he was a newly single man who was trying to find his way in Toronto. Despite his heavy drinking, he maintained his faint Irish accent, albeit with a bit of slurring brought on by his alcohol consumption.

Foley listened and shared some of his own background. He told Maloney about his wife and four kids. He attended St. Veronica's down the road for the sake of his family and "his rotten Irish soul." He said the pub was his real church. He liked to cater to the tougher crowd—a crowd that looked rugged and wasn't afraid to see the world the way it really was: as a hostile battleground playing host to an ongoing struggle that saw the fittest survive. Foley finished off the pint in front of him and said, "A lot of folks in these parts would like to exact a little revenge on the fuckin'

Brits for the shit that went down in Derry on Bloody Sunday." This was the comment that Maloney had been waiting weeks to hear.

Fully cognizant of his duties as a Service Mountie and not drunk enough to screw up, Maloney responded, "As if internment wasn't enough. The fuckers had to send in the paras and start killing us. If I was back in Donegal, I would be talking to a few of my Provo friends about hopping the border and doing some damage to those British bastards." This led into a spirited exchange between the two men. As luck would have it, a few minutes before closing time, Foley brought Maloney over to the table of Collin Boyle. An introduction was made, and one had to wonder if the agent was about to infiltrate the group and bear witness to the seeds of conspiracy.

CHAPTER 3:
FATHERS AND SONS

A trip to the cottage - *November 23, 2003*

Ridiculously early the morning after I reached the revelation about the photo, I bid Karuna goodbye with a gentle kiss on the forehead while she lay sleeping (I think it was around five) and made my way back to my mother and father's house. I left her a note on the bedside table to tell her where I was going.

I searched for the Bible through the boxes I had packed from the bookshelves during my previous visit. It wasn't there. I checked the boxes in my parents' room. Still nothing. I even went down to the basement to see if they had packed the Bible away—something I know my mother wouldn't have done, but I wouldn't have put it past my father. After a futile search, I gave up and went back upstairs to the kitchen. I pulled out my cellphone and called my uncle Liam. By this time, it was around seven.

Uncle Liam, a gentle and generous soul like my mother, had been very good to my family. In a sense, he was the polar opposite of my father; instead of carrying a despondent demeanour, Liam was outgoing and (for lack of a better word) joyful.

I asked him about the Bible, and he told me that my father had given it to him for safekeeping. He said that Dad had told him, shortly before he died, that someday I would come looking for it, and he wanted to make sure he was leaving it with someone he could rely on. My uncle said that my father wanted him to store it up at his cottage. While he'd thought this request was strange, who was Uncle Liam to argue with a dying man? So, the next time he'd gone north, he'd put the Bible on the bookcase in the living room of the cottage.

I asked my uncle if I could head up north to fetch the Bible. He reminded me about the secret hiding place of the key, and I was on my way to Georgian Bay. It was a crisp, clear autumn day, and the drive was smooth sailing. I avoided the congestion of Highway 400 and headed up the backroads, weaving through Orangeville and Shelburne, eventually venturing toward Craigleith. The drive north on County Road 2 is stunning; you crest over the Niagara Escarpment, and the next thing you see is about ten kilometres of farmland and forest with the vast expanse of Georgian Bay and the Nottawasaga shoreline in the distance.

I went north until I could go no further, then took a right on the local highway, followed shortly by a left onto the road that led to my uncle's beachfront property, where a solid A-frame cottage (*circa* 1960) stood. The rustic exterior and natural perennial garden welcomed everyone who ventured up the driveway. I parked the car, grabbed the key, and made my way to the front door before stopping in my tracks. What was I doing? What was the rush?

I decided to forgo a quick search of the cottage bookshelves for the Jerusalem Bible and opted for a visit to the back porch for a bit of airtime with Georgian Bay. This body of water is the source of retreat for so many people from Toronto. It was certainly a source of rejuvenation for my family in particular. My mother seemed to sink into a deep state of calm whenever she was in the presence of the great bay, and while sitting on Uncle Liam's dock, my father was not nearly as intense as he normally was. I looked at the water; today, it varied from a serene teal to a deep blue. It was disarmingly beautiful.

I looked out over the bay and wondered what this little adventure—an adventure created by my father (who was far from adventurous)—had in store for me. I took a deep breath, made my way back around front.

The cottage itself was large, but from a design standpoint, pretty dated. While my uncle's neighbours had sunk a ton of money into their properties, he preferred to keep things modest (it was a cottage after all). I opened the door and kicked off my shoes, even though the floor was a bit of a mess with sand and dirt, remnants from summer beach time and early autumn hikes. The living room was straight ahead with a huge window that stretched up to a vaulted ceiling, providing a stunning view of the bay. There was nothing fancy about the furnishings, mostly cast-offs from Uncle Liam's house in Toronto.

I crossed the living room and started to search through the bookcase. In no time, I had the Bible in my hands. I flipped through it and found an old Canadian one-dollar bill on the first page of the Book of Job. Written on the side edge of the dollar bill was a note from my father: *"You are your mother's son."* There was that message again. Behind the dollar bill was a newspaper clipping from the 1990s. The clipping was about a government-spending scandal in Ottawa and made no reference to the downing of Flight 281. However, the article was written by a well-known Toronto reporter. His name was Jack Redmund, an excellent journalist and a social-justice crusader who'd worked for *The Toronto Star*. Redmund had been shot while he was working on a story in the late seventies. If memory served me, and (in this case) I knew it did, Redmund was pursuing a theory that highlighted the botched investigation into Flight 281 and those he believed to be responsible for the downing of the plane. Redmund had been gunned down in a drive-by shooting on Front Street, just steps from the *Toronto Star's* main office building. They'd never caught the shooter, but the cops assumed it was a local Irishman Redmund had implicated in his story. A rush to the hospital and two surgeries later found Redmund alive but paralyzed.

At the bottom of the article was a phone number. I pulled my cellphone out, flipped it open, and punched in the digits. A man answered. "Jack Redmund. Who's this?"

The legend of Darcy Byrne: *Evolution - 1957–1972*

One way to understand the emotional state of Armagh in the late fifties and early sixties is to envision the impact of generation after generation of poverty and oppression—and the corresponding anger and resentment—on a group of people who felt like they were captives in an occupied territory, with their overlords preventing them from living meaningful lives. While Kevin Byrne was making a livelihood as a truck driver serving the city of Armagh and the surrounding area, he had not come even remotely close to the financial freedom he'd enjoyed in Canada. A few years after arriving in Northern Ireland, he'd realized that he had been drawn back to his homeland by a sentimental attachment to things familiar and had failed to recognize or remember the harsh reality that encapsulated life on the island.

And while the town of Armagh was no IRA bastion when compared to Newry, it was republican enough that, when tensions grew in the late-fifties, the anger that was perpetually on the verge of explosion felt as though the fuse and the match were about to make contact. This is when it happened.

One day in the early winter of 1957, Kevin was driving his truck to a farm in Killean to pick up some produce. He was on a remote road when five men, rifles in hand and balaclavas over their faces, came out of the bushes and onto the road. Two of the men pointed their rifles at the front of the truck while one of the others gestured for him to stop. A little over a month earlier, things had flared up in the county in what came to be known as the "IRA Border Campaign."

The man who'd ordered him to stop came to the driver's side with one of the gunmen behind him, pointing his rifle up at Kevin.

"Where do you think you're going?" he said.

"Down to Killean for a pickup," Kevin responded nervously. "I don't want any trouble."

"Well, trouble's what you've got, friend. We'll be taking your truck, and you'll be walking back to where you came from."

Kevin hesitated before grabbing his lunch pail and a newspaper and stepping down from the truck.

That's when one of the gunmen further back lowered his rifle to his side and removed his balaclava.

"Oh, for fuck's sake! This is my brother," Aidan said as he walked toward the truck. "Kevin, what in Christ's name are you doing out here? Have you not been following the news of the campaign? Anything south of Armagh is a war zone. They're calling it 'bandit country.'"

Kevin was in shock, but not too shocked to say, "Aren't you a little old for this, Aidan?"

Aidan smiled slightly, looking at his brother. "Can we just turn this one around boys? Kevin is republican. He'll just head home, no harm done."

"I'm afraid not, Aidan. This truck is ours now. You can swing him home in your car, but we're taking this truck back to the outpost," the leader of the group responded. "Go now."

Aidan walked a ways to where his car was parked. He eventually pulled around, and Kevin climbed in.

As they drove away, he said, "You could have got yourself killed, Kevin!"

"Killed picking up crops from a farmer in Killean. I'm sorry, Aidan, but I didn't think that was a dangerous thing to do."

"Well, it is in 1957 in South Armagh!"

The two men were both angry.

"What am I supposed to tell my boss about the truck?"

"Tell him the IRA appreciates the fucking donation; that's what you'll tell him. He should have given us a truck when we asked him for one at the beginning of the month."

Kevin was dumbfounded. "You mean you approached old man Findlay about a truck?"

"Of course, we did. We need trucks and cars and guns and explosives. It's a war for God's sake!"

"But you knew I worked for him."

"Indeed, I did, brother."

That's when an uneasy silence emerged between the two of them—a silence that lasted for the rest of the ride back to the city of Armagh. Aidan dropped Kevin off at the trucking depot and sped away, back to join his compatriots in another ambush no doubt. When Kevin told Findlay what had happened, his boss claimed he was in cahoots with the IRA and accused him of willingly giving away the truck. He fired Kevin on the spot.

At this point, all sentiment for Armagh and Ireland was lost. Kevin and Rosemary had a brief discussion that evening and decided to move back to Canada and away from the madness. Kevin could not reconcile the fact that he could be driving on a country road and face being shot or robbed by his own brother. War or no war, he wouldn't have to deal with this in Canada.

It took a few months, but eventually the necessary arrangements were made. By early April, the Byrnes were heading across the Atlantic. As the ship pulled away from the pier in Belfast, Kevin and Rosemary breathed a sigh of relief. Meanwhile, their son, Darcy, seethed in a mental cauldron of anger and resentment.

In a sense, the person who had arrived as a Canadian boy had become an Irish man—albeit a man of fourteen. That was the nature of adulthood in Ireland. Boys became men far too soon. Things they should have been shielded from invaded their minds years before they should have, and as a result, teenagers spoke like adults—at least when it came to expressions of profanity-laden anger about the state of affairs in the North of the island. So, when Darcy Byrne made his move to Canada, he made it abundantly clear to his parents that it was against his wishes, vowing to return to Ireland someday.

For his parents, the return to Canada gave them the opportunity to breathe again. Kevin and Rosemary had not realized how much they actually missed the freedom and serenity of life in Ontario. For his part, Kevin got a job with a transport company by tapping into some of the connections he had made prior to his return to Ireland. He was a good driver and a dependable worker, and despite the fact that Brampton had changed so much, he still had enough of a grasp of the area to be able to make his way to and from the places he needed to go.

Meanwhile, Rosemary felt the relief of knowing that Kevin was safe to go to work without the threat of a republican or loyalist ambush, and Darcy could finish his education at a Canadian school that wasn't even aware of the conflicts in Ireland.

But Darcy had become too Irish. He had the Irish accent and the suspicious gaze—that gaze of assessment, always sizing people up to gauge whether you can trust them or not. It was in his blood now, and memories of the struggle for independence, born in the stories told by his father and enlivened by the example of his uncle, caused him to feel dissociated from his contemporaries at school in Brampton.

Nonetheless, Darcy had developed a certain skill set. He was still taller than most and his jet-black hair and steely blue eyes drew people to him. So did his Irish accent. He was a gifted student and a skilled communicator, verbally and in writing. When he graduated high school, he opted to attend the University of Toronto where he got a degree in history with a focus on Irish Studies. He developed an affiliation with a few of his classmates, and they would spend hours discussing the historic problems faced by the Irish.

Despite these contacts, he really didn't have a lot of friends. Only one stood out: a young man named Owen Ryan. Byrne and Ryan shared the same curriculum choice—Irish Studies—and led many impassioned debates on the events that had led to Irish oppression. Byrne always positioned himself as the one who knew the most, because he had lived in Ireland for a lot of his life. For his part, Ryan deferred to Byrne, conceding that his Irish heritage, dating back to the mass migration during the time of the potato famine, meant his view of Irish nationalism was tainted by his Canadian upbringing. The two bonded in a way that worked for them, with Darcy always the alpha, and Owen happy to be the beta in the friendship. While they did have a crew of Irish they would party with, Darcy and Owen kept to themselves most of the time.

That said, Darcy Byrne had no trouble attracting women. They remained interested in him until they lost hope, realizing that his emotional detachment, at least when it came to relationships, was irreversible. He could lure them into his realm with intellect and flattery and into his bed with his good looks and alluring features.

My Father's Secret

But he'd never let them see anything that hinted at any form of devotion or commitment.

Byrne and Ryan graduated from university in 1965. Darcy persuaded his parents to book him a ticket to see Uncle Aidan in Crossmaglen as a graduation gift. They reluctantly acquiesced, and he bid farewell to his family, Owen Ryan, and whoever his lover was at the time. When Darcy got to Ireland, he knew he would be staying.

His uncle had taken him in willingly. He had plenty more tales of republican adventures to share, a few of them from the Border Campaign. Darcy soaked them in. He also soaked in his uncle's love of the drink.

The next few years were highlighted by drunkenness, odd jobs that were of little consequence, a stream of women whose names he'd never remember, and a gradual descent into a pit of empty-headed debauchery. He was a young man adrift in troubled waters.

This all came to an end in 1969. The Irish anger, always ready to express itself, burst to the surface once more as civil rights activists staged demonstrations across the North of Ireland. The police attempted to suppress these protests with a heavy hand, eventually choosing to detain Catholics without charges in a policy called "internment." This peaked Darcy's interest. Suddenly, the drinking diminished, his promiscuity lessened, and he found his way into the IRA.

While civil rights associations were the order of the day for most of the Irish crowd who were younger than him, he was convinced that violence was the only option that would bring an end to the Ulster loyalist and British occupation problem in Ireland. Violence, employed in the right way, would make the Protestants of Ulster bend and make the British leave. Period.

Aidan Byrne was of the old guard, Official IRA. While violence had served a purpose when he was younger, Aidan, now in his fifties, was starting to have his doubts, which apparently reflected what was going on with the Official IRA leadership of the time. Moderation, tact, and synchronization with the civil rights movement were not out of the question for the Officials any more. Meanwhile, young men—many of whom were in their teens and early twenties, and had heard all of the old republican war stories—felt it was time to strike again at those who possessed the power.

And who could blame them? The Ulster loyalists and their pawns, the Royal Ulster Constabulary (along with the Ulster Volunteer Force, the B-Specials, and the Black and Tans), had engaged in a campaign against Catholics that was tantamount to kicking people while they were down. Already enduring poverty and political powerlessness, Catholics in the North of Ireland saw loved ones killed, houses destroyed or taken away, and family members thrown in jail without trial. "They're killing us!" the young Catholics cried, and while civil rights associations flourished, Darcy Byrne knew that it was just a matter of time before the ticking time bomb of Irish Catholic despair would explode.

That came when the British sent in the troops. Initially, Catholic neighbourhoods had welcomed the soldiers because they kept the loyalists from brutalizing them. But that welcome was short-lived as the British soldiers, propped up the RUC, turned on the Catholics.

Stories of the new war, famously known as the "Troubles," spread throughout the land. A split between the Official IRA and the violent youth wing called the Provisional IRA meant that violence was back on the table in the fight for independence. Byrne allied himself with the Provos under the mentorship of South Armagh Brigade Commander Dylan Costello.

He started his militant career by smuggling arms from the Irish republic into safe houses in and around Crossmaglen. He received arms training and helped sort the proceeds of raids on warehouses and shops into useful stockpiles for the Provos. He was not a leader by any stretch, but he proved to be a reliable operative when it came to supporting tasks. However, Costello noted that there was something missing when it came to Byrne: true, natural, pure Irish rage—the kind of rage that coursed through the blood and informed every thought and deed a man possessed. Ultimately, Byrne came off as too soft, too cerebral, and too detached for Costello's liking. This is why Costello held back in giving him a meaningful role in any operation.

That changed in December 1971. Costello believed it was time for Darcy to take part in an actual operation, mainly because they were planning to engage in multiple attacks on the same night and needed the bodies. The battle for a united Ireland was gaining momentum, and the IRA of South Armagh had started to earn a brutal reputation that, in many ways, was the envy of those in Belfast and Derry. The RUC and the British feared the IRA in Crossmaglen and Newry more than anywhere else in the country. These were the men who would take down a policeman or a soldier anytime, anywhere, consequences be damned. The moniker of "bandit country" was well earned. Costello told his men that December 13th would be a night no one would forget—policemen would be assassinated, British army barracks would be bombed, and Ulster businesses would be left in ruins.

Darcy Byrne was part of a three-man team that night. Costello wanted to give him a chance to prove himself. The Provos garnered intelligence that allowed them to target the home of an RUC officer in Newry. Byrne and two other men would go to the officer's house, assassinate him, and head back to report the success of their mission. As simple as that.

Only, when they got to the officer's house, they discovered that he was entertaining guests. The lead Provo operative saw lights in the front room and shadows moving beyond the curtains inside. After a few minutes of ruminating, he said, "Fuck it!" before exiting the vehicle on the passenger's side and heading toward the house. The other man in the vehicle followed suit as they both donned balaclavas and pulled out their handguns.

Darcy Byrne remained frozen in the back seat of the car. They waved for him to join them, and when he didn't budge, they left him, proceeded to the RUC man's front door, kicked it in, and shot every adult male there. The man's wife ran from the house, screaming, and headed straight to the car where Darcy was sitting. She banged her hands on the car window and yelled, "Help! Please! You have to help!" Their eyes were locked on each other for a long moment before she was pistol-whipped by one of her husband's killers.

The next day, the South Armagh Provos learned that they had killed four off-duty RUC officers—a coup of sorts and an early Christmas present for the IRA. The rest of the attacks took second billing. The barracks were hardly damaged by the car bomb (though they gave the sleeping British soldiers quite a fright). Several Protestant-run businesses were set ablaze as planned. But it was the cop killings that got the attention of the people on both sides of the Irish border and in London.

Public support was, in a sense, lukewarm to what the Provos had done that December night. Most people in the North of Ireland clung to the civil rights movement—modelled on the protests of Martin Luther King Jr. in the US—as the way to get the attention of Britain and the world. They felt that the British occupation could be brought to an end through non-violence, making the cop killings provocative and counterproductive in the eyes of most people.

After his night of inaction in Newry, Darcy Byrne had a private meeting with Dylan Costello. Coming off his greatest accomplishment in the IRA to date, Costello was pleased with everything and everyone, except Darcy Byrne. He had run out of patience. Byrne had never made the transformation into a full-on fighting soldier. While Byrne pleaded to be part of a complex and deadly operation, he was clearly not cut out for the role. To say the least, the meeting between the two did not go well for Darcy.

"Well, Darcy, you're in a spot of bother now," Costello opened the meeting, lighting a cigarette as he sat behind a large table covered with maps and documents. The room was pretty rundown. It smelled of must and spilled beer. The wallpaper was falling off the walls. Costello let his stern expression set the tone of the meeting.

It would shock most people to see how small Dylan Costello was, considering his reputation as a brutal IRA man. He was really nothing to look at: short, a bit chubby, a thick mop of light-brown hair on his head—hardly the look of a ruthless tactician and warrior. But if you were in a room alone with this man when he was angry, he was as massive as a grizzly bear.

Darcy just looked down at his hands.

"I'm not going to ask you what happened, because it is pretty plain to see that you failed to even participate in the objectives of the mission—a mission that has put the South Armagh Brigade on the map, I might say."

Costello leaned forward and put his elbows on the table. "Not only did you fail. You let that woman see your pathetic face."

The anger and tension hung in the air for a moment.

"You shouldn't have let her see your face," Costello said with malice in his eyes. "They'll be looking for you, and you can understand that we're not inclined to protect you."

Now Byrne looked up. "What happens next?" he asked from a position of abject fear and defeat.

"I should put a bullet in your fuckin' head," Costello said, raising his voice as a hint of red flashed across his face. "But I have another idea. I am sending you across the border. You'll lay low there for a while. You'll run some errands for us. When the time's right, you'll go back to Canada, because you sure as fuck aren't coming back here."

Costello leaned back and looked at Byrne. "Maybe that was the problem all along. Maybe you're too Canadian. Not enough Irish in you to do an honest IRA man's work."

He took a drag of cigarette and squinted as he looked at Byrne. "I'd like to think that you could find a way to make yourself useful to us across the pond, but I'm not banking on it. Now get the fuck out of my sight."

And that's what happened. Byrne went to the Republic of Ireland, worked at an IRA armoury (that had the unspoken approval of the host government), and after about a month, he was told to *get the fuck out of Ireland* by one of his IRA handlers. He'd had to ask his parents to lend him the money for a plane ticket back to Canada, then he boarded a plane in Dublin and headed for Toronto.

This is how the mastermind of the greatest terrorist act in Canadian history made his way back to the land where he was born. Coincidentally, Darcy Byrne's flight home occurred the same day as the Bloody Sunday massacre, which (had he not stumbled in Newry) would have opened new militant doors for him in the North of Ireland. Instead, he was flying home an IRA outcast.

A meeting near Shelburne - *November 23, 2003*

I was hanging onto my cellphone, a cheap knock-off of the Motorola flip, and didn't know what to say. I had impulsively called the number on the bottom of the newspaper clipping that I had pulled out of the Bible. I didn't think I'd get the author of the article.

"Who's there?" Jack Redmund asked again in an irritated tone.

At this point, I had to say something. "Hello, Mr. Redmund. My name is Declan Keenan. My father—"

"I know who your father is," Redmund interrupted. You could almost feel him moving forward in anticipation of what might be coming next.

"I don't quite know how to put this, but my father died about a month ago, and he left me a bit of a mystery to solve."

"We should meet," Redmund said a bit anxiously. "Where are you right now?"

"Well, I'm up at a cottage on Georgian Bay. I'm in Craigleith between Thornbury and Collingwood. I found your number on a newspaper clipping that my father tucked into an old Bible. I could meet with you once I'm back in the city," I answered.

"Not good enough. Get to Gary's Deli at the corner of Highways 10 and 89 just east of Shelburne. It's about halfway between where you're currently located and where I am right now. You know it?"

"Yes," I answered.

"Good. Let's meet there in about two hours." Redmund hung up the phone.

"Jesus," I said out loud. Redmund seemed to be a little overly anxious to arrange a get-together.

What had I gotten myself into? This reporter was willing to drop everything to meet me in the middle of nowhere to discuss … *what exactly?* Of course, I knew it had something to do with Flight 281, but what the hell did I have to offer that would be of any use to Jack Redmund?

I got in the car and drove away from the bay, weaving my way down through the back roads and heading south toward Shelburne.

My mind was racing, kicked into high gear by Redmund's urgent call for a meeting.

I got to the deli before the reporter. The place was a bit of a dump, and there were only a few other customers inside, sipping on coffee and reading the newspaper. I kept an eye on every car that pulled into the parking lot. I assumed that Redmund would be easy to spot; he would likely be in a van equipped to carry his wheelchair.

Sure enough, about ten minutes after I showed up, Jack Redmund pulled into the parking lot of Gary's Deli. I watched him swivel the driver's seat around, manoeuvre himself into the back, and climb onto his wheelchair. Then he opened the door, activated a platform, positioned himself, and a lift slowly brought him to the ground. He looked quite put together: clean shaven, his black hair parted neatly to one side, and a jacket and pant combination that worked well together. I figured he was in his early sixties. When he started wheeling toward the restaurant, I jumped up and got the door for him.

"We're over here," I said, gesturing to the table I had picked.

"What's your name, son?" he asked.

"It's Declan," I responded, even though I had already told him my name when we had spoken earlier on the phone.

"Well, Declan, I figure we don't have a lot of time before we get rudely interrupted."

"By whom?" I asked in confusion.

"You'll see. In the meantime, we need to get some things out in the open."

And with that, I accompanied award-winning *Toronto Star* journalist Jack Redmund to our table in Gary's Deli for a potentially life-changing conversation.

A Canadian and a Provo - *March 1972*

About a month after he'd infiltrated the group, agent Maloney (aka Sully) felt he was starting to make some progress. His friendship with Quinn Foley was growing, and he was getting invited to sit with Collin Boyle once or twice a week. However, most of the conversation steered clear of the Provos, the Troubles, and Bloody Sunday, at least when Maloney was at the table.

The wiretaps picked up the odd bit of scheming, but there was nothing of consequence. While Keenan and Belwood catalogued the conversations, most of the chatter had to do with pub business on the Foley line, pharmaceuticals on the Boyle business line, and the latest illness that Aunt Mary in Monaghan was suffering from on Boyle's home line. Boring work, but the calls still had to be mined for potential plotting.

While Collin Boyle avoided Irish-centred topics with Sully, Maloney took part in many discussions dealing with the Irish anger surrounding the Troubles and Bloody Sunday with other pub patrons. People reacted as if this was the last straw. According to Foley, Boyle felt that some kind of action needed to be taken against the British, but he felt helpless, sitting in a pub thousands of kilometres away.

As far as the discussions that Maloney was able to share with the Irish Desk, talk at the pub was gradually shifting from *"action needs to be taken"* to *"here's what we should do."* He noted the shift and reported it to his superiors. That got him a pat on the back and a kick in the ass. He was told to crack the inner circle as quickly as possible. The service needed to know if these guys were all talk or if they were getting ready to spring into action.

Maloney got his first significant break in late April. He showed up at the detachment and made his way to Sergeant Dawson's office. "I think they are getting serious. A regular at the pub named

Owen Ryan is getting everyone stirred up. He's spreading a rumour that Darcy Byrne has snuck out of Armagh and is making his way back to Canada."

Dawson, slightly irritated, turned to Maloney. "Who the hell is Darcy Byrne, Maloney?"

"According to Ryan, Byrne's a Canadian citizen and a Provo," he replied. "He's the topic of conversation at Foley's."

Dawson sat upright at his desk and took off his glasses. "And he's coming to Toronto? Well, that's interesting."

The legend of Darcy Byrne: *Resurrection – 1972*

Darcy Byrne was too proud a man to admit that he was depressed. But when his parents picked him up at Toronto airport, he looked completely deflated. They shuttled him back to Brampton where he'd lain in bed for weeks, emerging only for the odd meal and to go to the bathroom.

Meanwhile, Byrne's mind went on a melancholic journey down memory lane, from his arrival in Ireland to his conversations with his uncle to his affiliation with the Provos. *What had happened that night in Newry? Why had he frozen?*

Instead of recognizing that he was lucky to be alive, Byrne fixated on his ousting from the South Armagh Brigade and his ostracism to Canada. He had let his comrades down. Since his failure in Newry, the cause had taken on another dimension, with Bloody Sunday inflaming the violence of the Troubles. The civil rights associations were withering, and the Provisional IRA was signing on recruits at a steady pace—at least that was what he was gathering from the scattered newspaper articles that were making it to the Canadian press. He had blown it. He had missed his chance. Instead of becoming a republican hero, he was no better than a coward.

He festered in self-pity for the better part of a month. Then he got an idea. He was still young enough to make a difference. Maybe there was a way to prove himself to his comrades from the far reaches of Canada. This process of thinking is what lifted him out of the fog of depression that had enveloped him (though, again, he'd never call it a depression).

Step one was to reach out to his university friend, Owen Ryan. He did, and told him that he'd soon be *"coming back from Ireland on a special mission for the IRA."* It sounded and felt much more dramatic this way. Ryan didn't need to know that he had been back in Canada for some time.

Owen Ryan took this bit of news straight to Foley's. The Canadian Irish contingent were stirred to rage by Bloody Sunday, so when Darcy Byrne painted himself as IRA, bringing firsthand accounts from the frontlines in the North of Ireland, many people were anxious to hear what he had to say. Ryan and a few of the leaders at Foley's Pub, including Quinn Foley and Collin Boyle, took the bait. They arranged for a fundraiser, featuring a speech by Darcy Byrne, at the Irish Heritage Centre.

This marked Byrne's introduction to the most passionate and extremist Irishmen in Toronto. When the time came, he decided to have Ryan pick him up at the airport, making it seem like he had just flown in. Ryan had done so and quickly ushered him to Foley's for a meeting with Collin Boyle. It was March 17th—St. Patrick's Day.

After sharing their mutual understanding of the situation in Ireland, they slipped into what could only be described as a negotiation. It was Ryan and Byrne sitting with Boyle and his second-in-command, Paddy Kerrigan, at a neutral booth away from Boyle's corner of the pub. The two young men in their late twenties made quite a sight, with Byrne looking polished and slick, ready for a serious meeting, and Ryan looking ragged, his beard needing a trim and his curly red hair going in just about every direction and his ripped jeans and tight T-shirt making him look like a hippy. On the other side of the table sat two men who were a generation older: Collin Boyle, all business in his tailored suit and stony demeanour, alongside Paddy Kerrigan (and his well-fed belly), ready to do his boss's bidding.

"Bloody Sunday has garnered a lot of attention for the IRA and the plight of the Irish people," Boyle said. "We are feeling compelled to do what we can to help our brothers bring the British occupation to a close."

"I can assure you, Mr. Boyle, the Provos are best positioned to make this happen. I have been dispatched from the island to stir up support in the diaspora and take action," Byrne said in a confident, self-assured tone.

"Stir up the diaspora, eh?" Boyle said.

"And take action." Byrne nodded, adding, "Can I call you 'Collin'?"

"Of course. What kind of *action* are we talking about, Darcy?" Now the two men were on a first-name basis.

"Fundraising for the cause, obviously. Beyond that, I am afraid I am going to have to get to know you a little better before we get into any details."

Boyle looked at Byrne intently before shifting his gaze to Ryan. He took a final drag of the cigarette he'd been smoking, exhaled, and butted it out. "We'd like to do a little more than *fundraising*. In fact, we've been sending money home for a while now."

Byrne was quick to respond, "Trust, first. Then more."

Boyle turned to Kerrigan, "Paddy, everything's in order for Darcy's little speech?"

"Indeed, it is," Paddy Kerrigan replied, staring sharply at Byrne.

"Well, Darcy, I imagine the funds raised at the Irish Heritage Centre will make you feel like you *know me* a little better. In the meantime, as a demonstration of trust, I am willing to offer you a place to stay and a vehicle to drive. All you have to do is deliver an inspiring speech. Does that suit you, sir?" Boyle asked, lighting another cigarette.

"It most certainly does," Byrne replied with a grin.

The elusive Irish - *March 1972*

Collin Boyle wasn't an easy man to get close to. He had a pretty tight inner circle, so Agent Terry Maloney was going to have to be at his "Sully" best if he hoped to gain the trust of the leader of the Irish community working out of Foley's Irish Pub. While Maloney was able to learn that Darcy Byrne, an alleged South Armagh Provo, was coming to Toronto, he wasn't able to secure an invitation to the speech.

Meanwhile, across the street in their surveillance hub—a modest one-bedroom apartment above an antique shop—Keenan and Belwood reviewed tapes of phone conversation after phone conversation, all emanating from the pub and Boyle's private and business lines. The service had tapped into the target phone lines via the junction box located on or near the telephone poles in the vicinity of each line. While tech agents routinely picked up the tapes from the remote locations, the tapes from Foley's were funnelled right into the surveillance hub.

Each shift, Keenan and Belwood would take their spots in the apartment about an hour before the pub opened and wouldn't leave until the pub shut down early the next morning. They'd alternate. One agent reviewed the wiretap phone conversations on his headphones while the other watched and photographed the comings and goings at the front of the pub. Live calls, placed while the men were on shift, were transcribed on the spot, so that a review at a later time wouldn't be necessary. If things were slow for the man looking out the window and snapping pictures, he would help transcribe the tapes. The listening, summarizing, analyzing, and cataloguing of the conversations was a tedious and often dreadfully boring enterprise.

Nothing fruitful had surfaced in over a month. It was as if Boyle and his Irish compatriots were on to something—as if they had learned they were on somebody's radar. Either that or there just weren't any legitimately nefarious plans in the works.

One evening, prior to his stint at the pub, Maloney visited Keenan and Belwood at the surveillance apartment. He accessed the place by the fire exit in the rear of the building, so he wouldn't be seen by any of the Foley's faithful.

Maloney knocked, identified himself, and Belwood let him in.

"Well, this is a surprise. What brings you here, *Sully*?"

The men shared a smile. Maloney looked around the place. It was surprisingly neat. Keenan had the headphones on and was transcribing some tapes but threw him a wave. Belwood must have been over at the window, snapping photos, when he had knocked on the door. The tapes were organized and placed in a rack that was situated by Keenan.

"You need anything, Terry, or is this just a social call?" Belwood asked.

Maloney had to think about the question. "I'm not exactly sure, Warren. I probably just need a quick break from the Irish before I walk back into that pub."

By this time, Keenan had removed his headphones and started listening in on the conversation.

"How's it going over there?" Belwood asked, gesturing toward the pub.

"Well, a fellow named Owen Ryan is promoting the arrival of a guy named Darcy Byrne. Apparently, he's IRA."

"That's a development," Keenan said. "When's he coming?"

"Oh, he's here. He arrived on St. Patrick's Day," Maloney responded with a chuckle. "You probably snapped a photo of him the day he got here."

"Probably," Keenan replied. "Nice of him to show up on my special day."

"Yes, *Patrick*, your special day," Maloney said, as the agents shared a laugh.

Maloney took a seat in a nearby chair while Belwood went back to the window to keep an eye on the entrance to the pub.

"To be honest, these guys are doing a pretty good job of shutting me out. Sure, I have gotten close to the owner; Quinn Foley has been my main advocate. But this Ryan guy and the lead man, Collin Boyle … it's as if they are instinctively keeping me at arm's length." Keenan pulled his chair over by Maloney's.

"But it sounds like you're getting some information," Keenan said, almost framing it as a question but not quite.

"Yeah, but it's all from the periphery. There's lots being said. This Byrne fellow has been described as some kind of IRA hero who killed a few cops back in Northern Ireland. Some people are talking about a new war being waged from the diaspora. IRA cells in London and Manchester are already active. Apparently fundraising in Boston and New York is leading to substantial weapons purchases for the Provos. But it's all talk. I haven't heard anything directly from Boyle, and I've only talked to Ryan a few times."

"What's your next move?" Belwood asked, still looking out the window.

"Apparently Byrne is making a big speech as part of an event at the Irish Heritage Centre. I've *got* to get an invitation to that speech. The guest list is quite limited. I need to see this guy in action, so I can give our team more information to work with," Maloney answered.

There was a pause before Keenan smiled. "It sounds like it's time for you to go and get friendly at that pub across the street."

"Getting friendly with terrorists," Maloney said. "That's the Sully way."

He got up, bid his fellow agents goodbye, and headed to work at Foley's.

A few days later, Sergeant Paul Dawson, prompted by Maloney's intel that an IRA operative had arrived from Northern Ireland, called an Irish Desk meeting at the Toronto Airport Detachment. Prior to the meeting, Dawson and Staff Sergeant Millington decided on the next course of action—an action that was not exactly legal but *might* be permissible from an intelligence-gathering perspective. While the RCMP Criminal Branch had to worry about dealing with the burden of proof in a criminal trial, the Security Service could take some liberties and go outside the law to gather information if it was in the best interests of the nation. It was this understanding of the role of the service that prompted Staff Sergeant Gord Millington to direct Sergeant Paul Dawson to meet with and give instructions to the team running point on the Irish Desk.

The meeting took place in Dawson's office. Two additional agents joined Keenan, Belwood, and Maloney. One looked greasy, with his dark hair slicked back, a neatly trimmed moustache, and a suit that tried its best to flatter his roughly twenty pounds of extra weight. The other agent looked rather innocuous, the kind of guy who would be easy to forget. He was slim, dressed in a drab grey suit, and made very little eye contact with the people in the room. He seemed like someone who was perpetually nervous.

"Thanks for coming in to meet with me, gentlemen," Dawson began, looking around the table at those assembled in his office. "I'd like to introduce you to Agents Mike Nugent and Dave Stratford. They'll be joining the team. You can become acquainted after the meeting." Nugent was the heavy one while Stratford was the one who was easy to forget.

Dawson took a sip of his coffee and then a drag on his cigarette as he reviewed the contents of a file folder in front of him. "The assigning of two new men is our way of letting you know that this case is getting more attention, based on the arrival of the IRA man Darcy Byrne. Our British intelligence contacts don't have a clue who he is, so he is either a clandestine operative or a bit player who is exaggerating his importance. Nonetheless, more resources, besides manpower, are being assigned to the Irish Desk.

"Here's the deal: You've got your wiretaps. I want you to up the surveillance with recording devices inside Foley's. This is something that the service can authorize in extenuating circumstances. Nugent and Stratford are going to try to recruit an informant from within the Irish ex-pat community." He turned to Maloney. "Recommendations would be appreciated, Terry, preferably from within Foley's and with something we can use against them to leverage their cooperation. Gentlemen, we need intel so we know what we're dealing with. Keenan and Belwood, take the lead on bugging Foley's. Obviously, we'll need something at Boyle's booth and at the bar where Quinn Foley does most of his work."

Keenan asked for clarification. "Sergeant, didn't the original warrant prohibit us from bugging the pub?"

Dawson wouldn't make eye contact when answering Keenan's question. "Staff Sergeant Millington wants the bugging to be initiated. With Darcy Byrne coming to town, he feels this course of action can act as an extension of the original warrant." He quickly turned to Maloney in an effort to change the topic, "Terry, how are things progressing in terms of acquiring an invitation to the Byrne speech?"

Maloney looked down before answering. "I am getting close, Sergeant."

Dawson paused, removed his glasses, and looked at him, wondering whether to believe him or not. Then he addressed all the agents in the room. "Just to reiterate, we are working through the Security Service mandate. *Do not* discuss the upgraded surveillance with anyone outside this room. Dismissed."

We better get started - *November 23, 2003*

I got Redmund a place by the window and bought a couple of cups of coffee. Before I settled into my seat, Redmund dove into his story.

"We better get started. A few years after Flight 281 blew up off the coast of Ireland, I received an anonymous tip regarding the downing of the airplane. It was clear from the outset that a bomb had brought the plane down. That's not disputed. What wasn't clear were the identities of all those involved in the plot. Certainly, there was a lot of speculation, with most people thinking the IRA decided to attack British assets via the North American ex-patriot community. Everyone just figured it would happen in Boston or New York. Not Toronto." Redmund paused to take a quick sip of coffee.

"The RCMP investigated and pinned the bombing on one guy. The 'lone bomber' theory is what dominated the narrative for a few years after the plane went down. But many people assumed there had to be a wider conspiracy. How was it that over three hundred people could be murdered, and Canada's top police force, the agency that *'always gets their man,'* couldn't garner enough

My Father's Secret

evidence to find anyone other than the guy who built the bomb? It just didn't make sense.

"About five years after Flight 281 was bombed, a source inside the RCMP Security Service leaked a document to me. It was just enough for me to chase the story. It was a classified threat assessment dated a few days before the bombing. It was heavily redacted, but not shy about identifying Darcy Byrne, Collin Boyle, and Owen Ryan as being part of a larger plot to bring down an aircraft. It became clear that the service knew much more about the bombing than they had originally claimed."

"Was that source my father?" I asked.

"It could have been," Redmund responded. "The source was anonymous. I think the intention was to simply implicate the conspirators, but the threat assessment included a few details that, with a little digging, allowed me to identify some of the Security Service agents who worked on the case. One of them was your father."

"Did you reach out to him?"

"Of course. I reached out to him and a few others. Let's just say that Patrick Keenan wasn't much of a talker. However, I always knew that he had information that could bust the case wide open. He was very close to the situation." He took another sip of coffee and cast a purposeful glance toward the rural highway before he continued. "I used the threat assessment and dug into the story, eventually publishing a series of four articles in 1978. Those stories implicated members of the Irish community in Toronto who were inspired by the ongoing efforts of the Provisional IRA in Northern Ireland. It was pretty much a hearsay piece—enough information that I wouldn't get sued for libel but not enough for the Crown to lay charges. A week after the last article of the series was published, I was shot while walking out the front door of *The Star* on Front Street. The doctors did what they could, but I was left pretty much paralyzed. I have limited mobility below the waist."

"I remember hearing about that when I was in university. A reporter getting shot was big news in a peaceful city like Toronto. And they never caught the shooter?"

"No, they most certainly did not," Redmund replied, clearly frustrated with the situation that had plagued him since the late seventies.

"Why do you think they saw you as such a threat?"

"Well, the stories got a lot of play. I put together a compelling explanation of the attack that went beyond the sparse lone-bomber narrative that had made the rounds in the aftermath of the bombing. The TV and radio talk shows gave Flight 281 a bit of airtime once I started publishing the stories. And the media in Ireland and Britain also started re-examining the idea of a trans-Atlantic conspiracy, but their appetite for the story waned quickly. Thanks to the series of articles, I became the go-to guy for the Flight 281 story. I even wrote a book about the situation. It didn't sell very well, but I still put together the most comprehensive theory surrounding the bombing out there."

"Jack, I'm a little confused," I interjected. "You said you wrote your articles in the 1970s. I was in my twenties at that time, and I don't remember anyone really talking about the bombing until the conspirators went to trial in the mid-eighties."

Redmund let out a heavy sigh. "Sadly, insufficient evidence—and a lack of will to investigate—pushed the story off people's radar. There was also the complete absence of coordination between the Criminal Branch of the RCMP and the Security Service. The Criminal Branch hated the fact that so many people died in the bombing, but they also did not have enough evidence to pin the attack on anyone other than the guy who built the bomb."

He paused before concluding, "And Canadians—from your regular person to the prime minister—did not want to believe a terrorist attack could originate in Canada. They couldn't fathom the idea that the 'land of the peacekeeper' could bring to fruition a diabolical mass murder the likes of which the world had never seen. You know, prior to 9/11, it was the worst terrorist attack on the books in the world."

Now I was really curious. "So, why the emergency meeting? Everything you've told me so far I could just read in one of your articles."

"Fair enough. Here's the reason why I told you to meet me here," Redmund said, shooting another look out the window at the cars and trucks moving along the adjacent highway. "About six weeks ago, your dad contacted me. He was pretty sick, but he said that he was ready to talk. I told him that I could go over to his house right away, but he put off the meeting. I followed up with a few calls, and he wouldn't pick up. The next thing I knew, he had passed away.

"Then about a week after your dad's funeral, I got a package delivered to my desk at *The Star*. It was from your father, and it had a small note and a cassette tape labelled *'FEBRUARY 14A.'* The note read, *'Talk to Terry Maloney and expect a call from my son. It's time.'* I got someone at the paper to track down a cassette player, and we listened to the tape and transcribed it. You could hear two men arguing about BOAC Flight 281 and how the bomb was supposed to go off when the plane was on the ground at Heathrow. The people speaking were Collin Boyle and his closest ally, Paddy Kerrigan. At least, that's what the Irish accents suggested."

"Sounds like a pretty incriminating tape," I said.

"You've got that right. For two reasons: First, Boyle was long suspected of being the banker behind the bombing, and second, Paddy Kerrigan probably arranged for the purchase of the plane tickets they used to put the bomb on the doomed plan. You bet your ass that's incriminating."

"Where's the tape now?"

"I have it stowed away in a secure place; don't you worry about that," Redmund said. "In the meantime, we need to figure out how to find Terry Maloney. When I started researching the bombing back in the mid-seventies, the name 'Terry O'Sullivan' started surfacing on the fringes of the conspiracy, but I could never find the guy. I eventually determined that O'Sullivan, who spent a lot of time at Foley's Pub in the pre-bombing period, was actually Terry Maloney, a former Security Service Mountie. I outed him in my book, and this caused quite a bit of controversy."

"So, he was a Service Mountie like my dad."

"Yes, but he was working undercover at Foley's while the conspiracy was being hatched."

"Jack, this still doesn't explain why we are meeting in Shelburne to discuss this stuff. Why couldn't this wait until I got back to Toronto?"

No sooner had I finished asking this question than a dark grey Ford Taurus pulled up outside of Gary's. Two white men—one with brown hair and one with blond hair, both wearing sunglasses and both dressed in dark suits—sat in the car and stared directly at Redmund and me. One fellow looked a little more intense than the other; he really stared us down. They kept their distance, but there was no question that we were who they had come to see.

"They are probably CSIS," Redmund said. "The shades and suits make me think CSIS, anyway."

"Spies? Why would Canada's spy agency be following you, Jack?"

"If I could answer that question..." He paused, looking at the car and its occupants before continuing. "Anyway, the day after I got the package from your father, I started to suspect that, sporadically throughout the day, people were following me. My initial round of inquiries regarding the authenticity of the tape probably tipped them off. Besides thinking I was being followed, I also became a little concerned that my phone calls (cell, work, and home) were being monitored. Since getting shot, I've become a little paranoid about these kinds of thing. When you called, I guessed that, if my cell is under surveillance or if they have a tracker on my van (which is more likely), whoever was doing the monitoring would find their way to us, because a trip out of the city is so out of the ordinary for me. And look what happened."

I looked out at the two men. They held their gaze on Redmund and me. They certainly weren't trying to hide the fact that they were watching us.

"And now, you are on their radar, Declan," Redmund said. "They'll probably run your plate to identify you. Stop taking the same route home every day, be careful what you say on the phone, and act as if *Big Brother* is watching your every move. You married? Kids?"

"Yes," I answered, the gravity of the situation gradually beginning to weigh on me. "Wife. No kids."

"Let your wife know what's going on. Tell her to be careful too." Redmund went on. "She needs to be as cautious as you are."

"And we don't know who these guys are," I said, looking directly at the men in the Taurus.

"Nope," Redmund said calmly. "But we will know who they are soon enough. Come with me to my van and make it look like you are helping me get on the lift. Just inside the sliding door, beside the lift, you'll see a cellphone. Slip it into your pocket. My number is the only one in the cell's phonebook. I'll be in touch. Call me only if it's urgent. Hopefully, we'll dig up some answers sooner rather than later. Christ, it's been thirty years already. It's *time* to get some answers."

At that, we got up and made our way back to Redmund's van. I opened the van's sliding door, slipped the black Nokia cellphone into my pocket, and watched him work the lift before manoeuvring into the driver's seat. Neither of us said a word. Our encounter ended with corresponding yet different waves, Redmund's one of reassurance and mine of overarching anxiety.

As Redmund pulled away, the men in the Taurus drove past slowly, starring suspiciously at me. It was the most intimidating moment of my life. Then they sped down Highway 10 in pursuit of Redmund.

CHAPTER 4:
THE EMERGENCE OF EVIL

Charisma casts its spell - *March 1972*

Around fifty guests gathered to hear the words of Darcy Byrne in a large meeting room at the Irish Heritage Centre. Normally reserved for community gatherings, small dances, and pub nights, the centre was converted into a makeshift lecture hall for this evening's event. Smoked filled the room, and the largely male gathering, with their beverages of choice in hand, prepared for the speech they came to hear. Among the guests was Service Agent Terry Maloney, who had secured an invitation at the last minute after Quinn Foley pleaded Sully's case to Collin Boyle. A suspicious Boyle reluctantly agreed. He still didn't quite have a handle on Sully.

Byrne arrived early in a blue Chevy Nova sedan, provided to him by Boyle. The men had an arrangement. Byrne was being given his shot to assume a leadership role in the more extremist Irish community in Canada. Boyle thought that, if the scheme worked, he could, at the very least, use Byrne as an asset in his IRA fundraising efforts.

Byrne waited in his car as people made their way inside. He adjusted his rearview mirror and had a look at himself. His black hair was starting to give way to a sprinkle of white around the temples, and the emergence of a few lines on his face put a shade of doubt in his less than thirty years of life. Byrne would still be considered an attractive man by most people—attractive in the sense that, while he was thin without being skinny and handsome without being pretty, he had a presence or aura that caused people to gaze at him for a fraction of a second longer than was usual. His eyes were the thing that those who encountered him spoke about the most. A fierce, deep blue that sucked you in.

It was no secret to those in attendance that Darcy Byrne was IRA; Owen Ryan had been playing this up in a big way at Foley's, something Maloney had relayed back to his Security Service colleagues. It was also no secret that he had experienced the Troubles firsthand, and rumour had it that he had personally shed the blood of the republican movement's enemies in an effort to rid the North of the Brits and their Ulster allies. From the perspective of those heading in to hear what he had to say, this gave his words added credence.

One had to wonder why a man of Byrne's allegedly violent pedigree had chosen to make his way to Canada. Why hadn't he stayed in Ireland to become an operational leader himself? Wasn't the real battleground in the North of Ireland? Wasn't a trip to Canada to stir up IRA sympathy a demotion of sorts?

Well, here's the thing about Darcy Byrne. Sure, he was a Provo ally from Ireland, but he was also a Canadian citizen, which meant he held dual citizenship. According to Byrne, he willingly accepted the demotion, returning to Canada as a messenger, orator, and leader for the IRA in the diaspora. It was for the greater good, he claimed.

According to Owen Ryan, his chief promoter, Byrne was a Provo to the very ground of his being. He was driven to follow orders and do the bidding of the IRA, proving that he was as capable as any other militant. Ryan said Byrne could do more than raise a couple of bucks for the cause. Darcy Byrne was capable and clever enough to orchestrate something big.

Byrne headed backstage shortly before his speech. He was all business—no idle chatter with his hosts prior to his introduction. Once onstage, he dove straight into his oration.

He was preaching to the converted. He went on at length about the need to both get the British out of Northern Ireland and put the squeeze on the Ulster loyalists. As preaching goes, this was a well-constructed, direct, and inspiring sermon. He painted a compelling picture of Goliath—the British overlords and their Ulster pawns—crushing the Israelite challengers—the disenfranchised Catholics—with the IRA posing as David coming to save the day. He did this by telling a steady stream of stories about Ulster authorities murdering men, raping women, and routinely destroying Catholic homes and businesses. He combined truth with fiction seamlessly to bring the emotions of the crowd to a climax.

And there was something about the rhythm and cadence of his Irish accent that had the audience mesmerized.

"Let me paint a little picture for you," Byrne said to the crowd as his presentation was winding down. "Shortly after the Brits and their Ulster puppets thrust internment down the throats of our brothers and sisters, the true Irish of the North said *'enough is enough'* and began to band together to try to put an end to arrest and detainment without cause. What was different about this particular form of protest was that the people of the North of Ireland were trying to communicate their message through human rights and civil liberties associations. While I personally don't think these methods are very effective in the fight against British colonialism and Ulster unionism, the majority of our Irish brethren back home supported ... let's call it *a more intellectual approach* to fighting oppression. All that changed a short time ago."

Byrne paused and looked out at those assembled, his eyes holding the gaze of the captivated crowd, a quiet rage welling up within him, and by extension, them.

"On January 30th—what we now call Bloody Sunday—British troops attacked and killed thirteen of our brothers while wounding and maiming scores of others." Byrne continued in a tone of controlled anger. "This, my friends, is the latest instalment of centuries of oppression, proving once again that the British occupation of even a tiny portion of Ireland is unacceptable. Put simply, the Brits have to go." A smattering of applause emerged from the crowd. "The Irish civil rights movement is dead. We are at war—AGAIN—and I am not just talking about the Irish living in the North. I am talking about the Irish living in the republic. I am talking about the Irish living in America. I am talking about the Irish living right here in Canada. I am talking about all Irish. All Irish are at war with the British, and our sworn enemies continue to be their Ulster thugs who do the devil's works on the streets of Belfast and Derry and Antrim and Omagh ... and Armagh, the city where I was raised." More applause.

Byrne paused again, his eyes alight with passion. "So, it is on you to do your part. Sure, you can give money, and our comrades in the field can buy some weapons to go after British troops and Ulster loyalists. If that is all you would like to do, I'll make sure your money gets to where it needs to go. But we also need to do our part in the very nations that the Irish diaspora has landed. Bombs in Belfast are all well and good in furthering our cause, but we can also go after the assets of the British Empire abroad. There is a British Consulate right here in Toronto. There's the High Commission in Ottawa. There are also a number of British companies with branch offices in Canada—companies like British Petroleum or the British Overseas Airways Corporation. The only way we are going to win this war is to hit our enemies hard on multiple fronts." The crowd stirred. No applause this time.

Byrne took a long sip of the Guinness that had been sitting on a stool next to him for most of the speech. He took on a cavalier tone before continuing. "Maybe what I'm saying offends your Canadian sensibilities," he said, his Irish accent making it sound like he was daring the crowd to consider what he was proposing. "Maybe this path is too much for you to handle. Well, passivity won't allow us to achieve our objectives … and hundreds of years of *disorganized* violence hasn't worked to this point. What I am proposing is a multi-front assault on the British by the Irish diaspora while our comrades on the frontline wage a deadly attack on '*Her Majesty's*' soldiers and the Ulster authorities within Ireland. A multi-front campaign is the strategy that will work, and I hope you will do your part."

At that, Byrne stood, drank the rest of his beer, and walked out of the room. A stunned crowd of Irish Canadians, who had essentially just been given their marching orders, started applauding slowly. They were on their feet cheering wildly by the time Byrne exited the building and climbed into his Chevy. He lit a cigarette and drove away, knowing that he had accomplished what he had set out to do. His message had been delivered with a cold bluntness that no one had expected, and it had been embraced with a passion that bordered on fanaticism.

And while Darcy Byrne sped away in his car, Cathal O'Dwyer and his father, Ken, sitting just three rows back during the speech, regarded the response of the crowd and shared a glance that suggested their dreams had come true. Here was a man that could allow them to pursue their militant dreams. The time for idle chatter about the state of the Irish nation was over. The time for action was at hand. Ken O'Dwyer turned to his son as the applause died down. "Cathal, I think the Provos have just created a new regiment right here in Canada."

Shock, anxiety, and commitment - *November 23, 2003*

I arrived back at my Toronto home late that afternoon. I'd gotten stuck in one of the city's seemingly perpetual traffic jams before navigating through my suburban neighbourhood and pulling into our driveway. Karuna wasn't back from work yet, which was a good thing, since I was trying to figure out a way to tell her that the situation was starting to take on some disturbing dimensions. Redmund's assessment of the state of affairs up at Gary's Deli was not reassuring in the least. The fact that a meeting with a reporter could draw the attention of CSIS did not sit well with me.

I put on a pot of coffee and took a seat at the kitchen table. 'I don't need this. I'm not capable of handling this kind of a situation,' I thought as the pot brewed in the background. 'What have I gotten myself into? How can I get out of this?' Waves of self-doubt swept over me. Then came the fear—paralyzing and terrifying bouts of fear, with blood rushing to my head and a panicked sweat enveloping me. I am not sure how long I sat at the table. The coffee had long finished brewing, and I hadn't bothered to pour a cup for myself. The sun had set, and it was only the sound of Karuna's keys in the front door that brought me out my fear and back to the present.

She came into the kitchen, and when she saw me seated at the kitchen table, she asked, "Now what?"

In a state of numb shock, I recounted the day, from the trip to Craigleith to the meeting at Gary's Deli and the arrival of the

My Father's Secret

strange men in Shelburne. My voice was dulled by fear. I sat hunched over as if I were already defeated.

"Karuna, I am so sorry this has happened," I said after telling the story. "I thought going to see Belwood would be the end of the mission that Dad passed on to me from his deathbed. Now, it's created a situation that feels incredibly dangerous."

Karuna didn't say anything at first. She was calmly evaluating the impact these developments would have on our lives. Arms folded—her beige suit, black shirt, and neck scarf reminding me that she had just walked in the door from work—she was processing the matter at hand like she would a legal case at the office. Finally, she said, "Well, we are in this situation now. We have to pursue it, because we have already gotten somebody's attention, which must mean that the crisis your father wasn't able to resolve needs to be resolved. To whose benefit, I am not sure, but we will need to see this through to the end."

"I wish I had your confidence," I said. My voice was low and despondent. Inside, I was feeling astonished that she could be so understanding. "I just put us in harm's way. I just put *you* in harm's way."

I got up from my seat. "I am such an idiot. Why did I choose to take Dad's bait? He just gave me the old, '*Hey son, I need you to fix something for me,*' and I dropped everything and ran to the rescue."

Karuna didn't say anything. She just moved to the cupboard, pulled down two mugs, and poured two cups of coffee, preparing them the way we like them. She handed me a mug and then leaned against the counter and took a sip from her own mug.

"Jesus, Declan. When did you make this coffee?" she asked before breaking the tension with a little laugh.

"I don't know," I said with a smile. "I got home around four, and I made the coffee as soon as I got in. What time is it now?"

"Well, this burnt taste in my mouth isn't a surprise then, because it's almost seven," Karuna said as she playfully poured the contents of both mugs into the sink. "We better get some dinner and decide what we need to do next."

Potentially next level stuff - *March 1972*

The day after Terry Maloney attended Darcy Byrne's speech, he calmly led the briefing for the Irish Desk team in the detachment conference room. Seven Service Mounties were in the room: Millington and Dawson, representing the detachment leadership; Keenan and Belwood from surveillance; and Nugent, Stratford, and Maloney, representing the on-the-ground agents who were working the case. They were meeting to get an idea of what had happened at the Irish Heritage Centre the previous night. Maloney started by describing his efforts to infiltrate the IRA sympathizer group in Toronto:

"As you know, I have been on assignment at Foley's Irish Pub since February. Staff Sergeant Millington and Sergeant Dawson sent me to pose as an IRA sympathizer at the establishment after Bloody Sunday. I have befriended the pub's proprietor, Quinn Foley, and a few nights ago, he secured me an invitation to an event at the Irish Heritage Centre. About fifty people were in attendance for a speech by a Canadian man purported to be closely linked to the Provisional IRA in Northern Ireland. While his speech lacked certain specifics, he was, in a not-so-thinly veiled way, telling the Irish diaspora to do more than funnel money through their families back to Ireland. He was suggesting they take action, things like, *'Hey, there's a British consulate here in Toronto. Why not throw a couple of Molotov cocktails through its windows?'* For the most part, the crowd stared at him when he called for more extreme action. However, when he was done, and they realized that this was a call to arms, they were on their feet, applauding."

Maloney shot a brief and subtle look toward Millington and Dawson, wondering how his message was being received by his bosses, before continuing. "The present concern is that the IRA is bringing the Irish diaspora into the battle with the British. This is unprecedented in that it goes way beyond the anonymous monetary donations that have characterized diaspora conduct up until now. This change in behaviour has likely been inspired by the events of Bloody Sunday. You can review the details of that incident in your briefing notes."

Dawson took over. "Keenan and Belwood, anything from the wiretaps?"

"Nothing of consequence, Sergeant," replied Keenan. "A lot of hot air about the plight of the Irish, but no scheming. That said, the bugs were installed at Foley's a few days ago, and those conversations could provide us with the information we are looking for. We just need to review the tapes."

Dawson followed up with another question. "Who are the main targets of our investigation? Maybe a description would help too."

"Sure," Keenan replied. "Here's the brief that outlines the targets."

Keenan handed a file folder to the men in charge. The file contained five profiles that included a surveillance photo of each target, walking into or standing outside the pub, along with a few descriptive details.

- Quinn Foley, the pub's proprietor, six feet, brown hair, thin build. Dual citizen: Canada and Ireland.
- Collin Boyle, pub patron and owner of Nova Star Pharma, five feet eight, salt-and-pepper hair, stocky build. Dual citizen: Canada and Ireland.

- Patrick 'Paddy' Kerrigan, pub patron and Boyle's financial director at Nova Star, five feet seven, brown hair with a receding hairline, about thirty pounds overweight. Irish citizen.
- Owen Ryan, pub patron, five feet ten, long, wavy red hair, beard, thin build. Canadian citizen.
- Darcy Byrne, pub patron, just returned from Northern Ireland, thick black hair with some white coming in, five feet eleven, thin build. Dual citizen: Canada and Ireland.

While Dawson reviewed the file, Belwood had a couple of questions for Maloney. "Terry, two things. First, why didn't we wire you, so we would have a recording of the speech?"

Maloney looked over at Dawson. He knew that the decision not to wire him was more a budget issue than an operational one. "We determined that my attendance and report would be enough. We also didn't know if the group would have countersurveillance measures in place. If they caught me with a wire, my cover would be blown." Maloney hoped he had done an adequate job of covering for his boss.

"Makes sense," Belwood responded, continuing. "Here's my second question: You're on the inside; do you really think the ex-pat Irish are interested in taking the IRA battle to the streets of Toronto? It seems like a bit of a stretch to me."

"To date, these guys have just been echoing the bitter complaints of their Irish predecessors," Maloney replied. "Are they all talk? At this point, that's all I've seen. However, Boyle continues to distance himself from me, so I am genuinely not sure what he is capable of."

Dawson chimed in. "Nugent and Stratford, we need an informant connected to the men covered in this brief." He held up the file Keenan had shared with him. "Review it, and find someone.

My Father's Secret

Name, background, leverage—informant; that's the equation. We've got to start moving on this, gentlemen. Byrne's message is potentially next-level stuff, and we need to see if the Irish in Toronto are more zealous than we think."

Dawson adjourned the meeting. Maloney, Keenan, and Belwood hung back, shuffling their papers into some semblance of order. Maloney spoke first. "I can see where they're coming from."

Belwood looked at him. "Excuse me?" he said, more in a spirit of curiosity than surprise.

"People like Byrne and Boyle and Foley. They come from generations of indoctrination in a world of 'us' and 'them.' They believe all the wrongs that have been done to them will be corrected the minute the British are out of Northern Ireland and the Ulster loyalists are reigned in. They believe, rightfully, that they have been gravely mistreated, and they want to put a stop to it."

"But to what extent will throwing a Molotov cocktail at the British consulate in Toronto help their cause?" asked Belwood.

"It likely won't. But it will draw attention to their anger. And that might draw attention to their cause," Maloney responded.

Keenan spoke up. "That's not likely to work in Canada. As soon as the local Irish start resorting to violence, Canadians will encourage them to take that stuff back to Belfast and Londonderry. This is the land of the great escape, where immigrants come to kiss the violence goodbye, not to stir it up on a new frontier."

"I know you're right," Maloney countered. "But it's the belief that it 'can't happen here' that will be our biggest roadblock if something does, in fact, come to fruition."

No one knew what to say after that. While Maloney and Belwood left the room, Keenan looked out the conference-room window, watching a plane take off at the nearby Toronto International Airport.

Back to school - *November 24, 2003*

I got up around seven that morning with a general idea for where to take things next. Essentially, the scavenger hunt for the Bible had netted me a spontaneous date with Jack Redmund and the mystery men in the Ford Taurus. I was already dressed and staring blankly at my first cup of coffee when Karuna joined me in the kitchen.

"What's your plan?" she asked as she poured a cup for herself.

I looked up at her. "I think I'll head into the school and speak with Andrea Kenmount, the librarian. I know I shouldn't go in when I'm supposed to be off, but I need her to point me in the right direction when it comes to background information on the Flight 281 tragedy."

"That sounds like a good idea," Karuna said. "Listen, I've got some lieu time coming, and God knows, I never take advantage of that. Maybe now's the time. You do some research today, and then tomorrow, I'll join you on … *whatever* this mission is. I can probably put in for about five days, and since it really isn't too busy at work, the two of us can see what we can come up with together."

I hesitated before responding. "Aren't you worried that this might be dangerous?"

"Well, Declan, it may well be dangerous, but here's what I know. Despite your struggles with your father, he has entrusted you with an opportunity to uncover a truth. I also know that this happened thirty years ago. Maybe the passage of time will make this particular quest a little less dangerous. I really don't know for sure, but it seems that we can't let our fears get in the way of justice," she finished, crossing her arms, and putting on a proud smile. "Now, didn't that sound very *lawyerly* of me?"

I let out a small laugh, "You're incredible. Okay, Operation 'Whatever This Is' has officially begun. Let's see where it takes us."

"I better talk to the managing partner about those lieu days this morning. I don't imagine there will be a problem, but it's best that I deal with it first thing rather than wait for some crisis to emerge that will keep him from being cooperative."

"Sounds fair," I said. "I'm going to finish this coffee and head to the school. I'll call Andrea from the car and see what she suggests. She's pretty well-read in terms of historic and current events, so a face-to-face might be good."

"All right, love. I'll head up and get ready to go into the office, and you finish that coffee." Karuna gave me a kiss before heading back upstairs.

I got in the car and phoned Andrea Kenmount on her cell. She was almost at the school, and after exchanging the usual pleasantries, I got to the point. I also started driving.

"Listen, Andrea, I am about to begin some research on the 1973 bombing of BOAC Flight 281. I could use your guidance to point my research in the right direction."

Andrea must have been navigating her car into the school parking lot. "Well, I just got here, so come on in when you arrive. Check in at the office though, because they are going to want to see how you're doing. Most of the staff haven't seen you since your dad's funeral, so say your hellos and come see me in the library, but I have to warn you about two things. First, I have a period-two class coming in, so you've got me until around ten, unless they need me to cover a class," she sighed. "Let's hope that's not in the cards. The second thing is that there's really not a lot out there on Flight 281. You'd think we'd have a pile of books on the IRA-inspired attack, but shockingly, I can only think of one book of substance on the topic. It's by a Toronto journalist—"

"Jack Redmund, right?"

"That's right," Andrea responded quickly. "It looks like you already know who the authority is. I know we have a copy of the book, and I can share a bunch of online passwords for the scholarly websites we subscribe to. That should at least get you started."

"Thanks, Andrea. I should be there shortly." I was about a half hour away from the school by the time I hung up.

For the balance of the drive, I thought about going back into the building where I worked. I had been off since the start of the school year, having arranged to take the semester off. I was heading into a building that would, no doubt, be wrought with mid-term stress and grade-related anxiety among both staff and students. This didn't really bother me. What bothered me more was the feeling that I didn't belong. When you're off for an extended period of time, you are no longer part of the team when it comes to a school community. Sure, they'll pay you plenty of lip service about how they *"can't wait until you're back"* and *"it isn't the same without you,"* but when it comes right down to it, staff members come and go, and the community quickly replaces anyone who leaves. That would be the case with my absence. No doubt the administration had hired some young kid just out of teachers' college who was putting their youthful spin on my courses.

I am pretty good at my job. My department head tends to let me teach a few specialty courses (namely ancient history and philosophy). I also do my share of teaching the tougher kids—college level law is no picnic, and applied history can be a bit of a challenge. But, overall, I get along with staff and students. I am neither the most dynamic teacher on the block nor the dullest. I can be relied on to deliver curriculum in a professional fashion with little need for the school administration to deal with a misbehaving kid from my class or an irate parent who doesn't like something I said or did.

However, if I am being completely honest, I'd have to admit that, despite the fact that Dad died on my semester off, I really wasn't planning on doing anything exceptional during my time off. Karuna had been ready to take some vacation time prior to Dad taking a turn for the worse, but I put no pressure on her to make sure she was available for a couple's trip somewhere exotic. Here's the reality: I was tired—twenty-five years into my teaching career, the same courses year after year, the same cycle from one school year to the next, the same institutional issues, the same bullshit. The fatigue had started to affect my work. I wasn't reading student work as closely as I once had; I was recycling a lot of old instructional material, and I wasn't enhancing my curriculum with more research. In all, I considered myself to be an average teacher with an average (albeit slipping) work ethic. While I genuinely cared about the wellbeing of my students, I was running out of gas, and retirement was still quite a few years away.

My many ruminations eventually got put on hold as I pulled into the school parking lot—perhaps at the worst time. Classes would be starting in around ten minutes, and the traffic around the school was a mess. I inched my way closer to the school before I could make the turn into the staff parking area. I probably should have timed this trip a little better.

I am not going to share the tedious details of the chit-chat that I engaged in for my first half hour at the school. The head custodian, the secretaries, the vice principals, and the principal all asked me what lay ahead—that is, after they told me how sorry they were about my father. I don't doubt their sincerity. I just struggled with the attention. Once I did my duty and talked to a few folks, I made my way to see Andrea Kenmount.

Andrea is an extremely passionate teacher. She took a library that had been a dead zone and converted it into a vibrant learning area—a place where staff and students wanted to be. In my current state of professional exhaustion, I wondered where she got her energy. I always felt a genuine sense of calm, and … how do I put it? Warmth, I guess, when I saw Andrea.

She greeted me right away with her welcoming smile. Andrea was thin and pretty, her hair cut short and died auburn. She had a grace in the way she conducted herself and a distinguished style in the way she dressed. Andrea asked a lot of the same questions I had dealt with when I walked into the main office. I didn't mind the interrogation as much coming from her. Then we got down to business.

"Okay," she started. "I've already pulled the Redmund book. It's called *A Nation's Shame: The Downing of BOAC Flight 281*. I read it years ago, and as I recall, Redmund puts together a gripping story and a compelling argument against IRA sympathizers in Toronto. I also logged into my office computer and pulled up a few scholarly articles on the terrorist attack. You probably won't have to go to another library. A lot of the material is on the web now, and you just need a decent computer to access what the other libraries have."

"Wow, gone are the days of the microfiche and periodical books that you had to access in some corner of a university library," I said.

"Yeah, we're pretty fortunate to be on the front end of a lot of the online academic material." Andrea started to move away from me and toward her office. I followed while she walked and talked. "Leave the Redmund book for now. Start reviewing the articles. I won't interrupt you, and because you're in my office, any of your former students or current staff won't be able to bother you unless they happen to walk by and notice you."

"Okay, thanks a lot, Andrea. This is exactly what I need."

As I made my way into her office, she gently held my arm and asked, "Can I ask what has inspired the sudden interest in seventies terrorism?"

I looked her in the eyes, and with a wry smile, said, "Apparently, I'm the very man who can bring those who did this to justice."

Andrea shot me a confused look before assuming this was a joke, smiling, and saying, "Okay, Mr. Justice-man, get in there and start reading."

A problem with Sully and a potential informant
- April 1972

Over the previous week, Keenan and Belwood had spent every spare minute reviewing the surveillance tapes from Foley's Pub. Their efforts, combined with the inside work of Agent Maloney, were starting to pay some dividends. First, the listening devices at Collin Boyle's booth made it clear that Maloney (aka O'Sullivan, aka Sully) was going to have trouble getting much closer to Boyle. One tape involving Boyle and Foley was the main topic at an important Irish Desk meeting.

> **Boyle:** The Byrne speech has got people talking, but we have to be careful.
> **Foley:** I think this is a pretty tight group, Collin. People picked their sides generations ago. We are clearly pro-Ireland and anti-Ulster, which also makes us anti-British. We can talk openly about our disgust for the shit the Ulster fucks and the British pricks have been raining down on us for hundreds of years.
> **Boyle:** That's not what I'm talking about, Quinn. What I'm talking about is Byrne. He asked for us to do something to show our support—beyond money. We have to be careful about any talk of action unless it is around people we trust completely.

Foley: Look around, Collin. Do you see anyone in this pub that wouldn't back us up if we decided to do something to support our Irish families back home?
Boyle: I have looked around, and I can tell you that the number of people that could be trusted with a serious call to action is around three. And I'm especially worried about the way you're cozying up to that guy at the bar.
Foley: Sully? What's your problem with Sully?
Boyle: I don't know him; that's my problem.
Foley: Jesus, Collin. I have gotten to know the guy since he started coming here. He is as Irish as you're going to get.
Boyle: So you say.
(A five-second pause ensues.)
Foley: Well, I gotta close up. You want anything else?
Boyle: No, Quinn. I best be getting home.

After the tape was played, Sergeant Dawson wondered what form this 'action' might take. Staff Sergeant Millington felt it was just a couple of Irishmen, well into their pints, posturing about doing something dramatic and gossiping about the clientele. Maloney, Keenan, and Belwood, who were closer to the situation than anyone else, were a little more worried. First, it looked like Boyle had a problem with Sully. Second, they felt that something was beginning to brew—something potentially dramatic and deadly. Dawson and Millington had the final say, and as they had not yet acquired enough information to warrant additional resources, their call was to stay the course and "see what happens."

Meanwhile, the distrust of Maloney by Boyle meant that the investigators urgently needed an asset on the inside who Boyle would trust. Nugent and Stratford were given another push to find the asset, and by the middle of April, it looked like they had a prospect.

My Father's Secret

Eamon Kerrigan was a second-generation Irishman whose father, Paddy Kerrigan, ran the finance department at Collin Boyle's pharmaceutical import company, Nova Star Pharma. In fact, Boyle was the younger Kerrigan's godfather and Paddy's second cousin, earning him the status of *Uncle Collin* for Eamon.

Eamon Kerrigan was a troubled young man. Since his early teens, he had been a heavy drinker and drug user who some might describe as a functioning addict. Certainly, his father and (on a few occasions) his godfather had had to bail him out of some compromising situations. Despite this, Kerrigan, who was in his late twenties, had proven his worth in the family business. A Queen's University graduate with a Commerce degree, he was able to translate his academic success into relatively clear-headed thinking when he was on the job at Nova Star Pharma.

Nugent and Stratford dug into Kerrigan's history: a drunk-driving charge that got tossed, a minor assault at a bar on the Danforth, and three fines for public intoxication. Discussions with the Metro Toronto police officers involved in the incidents didn't amount to much. They either minimized the encounter with the young man, or they had forgotten about him entirely. In their assessment, Eamon Kerrigan was deemed a part-time drunk and druggie who should really get clean and sober.

A look at his finances indicated something significant for the agents. According to Revenue Canada, Kerrigan made a modest salary at the pharmaceutical company. However, he filed two tax returns: a personal return, where he accounted for his pay from Nova Star, and a corporate return (no company name, just a corporate number with him as director) that appeared to be the destination of a mystery income. The investigators' working theory was that he was stealing the money from Nova Star Pharma and funnelling it into his corporate bank account. Everything looked legitimate because the corporation was paying taxes, which would keep the Revenue Canada auditors away. He'd been running the scam for over two years.

Eamon Kerrigan was in a perfect position to defraud his godfather and deceive his father. While his father was the chief financial officer for Nova Star Pharma, Eamon had become his protege. His father had done well by the company, and as Eamon had begun to learn the ins and outs of the finance department and prove his worth as a *trusted* employee, the elder Kerrigan had begun to loosen his grip and slacken his oversight of the money coming into the company. Instead, he'd shifted that oversight to Eamon, and if Nugent and Stratford had it right, the younger Kerrigan was redirecting money from the company into his corporate account.

Now, they believed they had a potential asset, but they needed to find a way to confirm their suspicions and leverage them against Eamon Kerrigan. That leverage actually came from the wiretaps. Nugent and Stratford got permission from Sergeant Dawson to extend the wiretap warrant to include Kerrigan's direct line. For about a week, the office discussions were as innocuous as all of the other conversations coming out of Nova Star. But then a call came in from Lancaster LLP, Nova Star's tax-accounting firm. With the company's corporate tax return set for filing, a junior clerk had a question about the company's bookkeeping line that was labelled "admin fee," which had accompanied all of the invoices from the previous tax year. The clerk needed to know the nature of the administration fee so that he could put the fee in the right category on the corporate return. The call went straight to Eamon Kerrigan, and at one point, the exchange got a bit heated.

Kerrigan: The admin fee. Why is this a concern?
Clerk: Well, I was just reviewing your company's return and noticed the fee. We must have missed it last year.

My Father's Secret

Kerrigan: Oh, well, the admin fee helps to keep our office costs down. It's a small sum attached to our gross sales, so it doesn't cost the client much, and it helps us keep a few of our office staff working. Does that help?

Clerk: It doesn't really help from an accounting standpoint. It looks like an additional fee that should be treated as income for the company. If it is covering costs, I have no way of seeing a link between the costs and the benefits— equipment, salaries, and the like—that are associated with the fee. I also don't see where your bookkeeper is depositing the payment. That's a discussion that I strongly recommend you have with him when you get the chance.

Kerrigan: What are you implying?

Clerk: I'm not implying anything other than the fact that your bookkeeper is not accounting for some of the money you are invoicing your clients.

Kerrigan: All right, I'll have the discussion with him. It's probably an easy fix. What are we talking about? Like $25,000? Can't we just shift that into our expenses and be done with it?

Clerk: If you want to get audited, we can do that. This is income, Mr. Kerrigan. Revenue Canada doesn't take kindly to disguising income as expense. This is why I am bringing it to your attention. I recommend claiming the ... (the clerk pauses) actually it's $38,568.49 ... claiming that amount, as part of the invoiced income, and fixing the bookkeeping error next year. Mr. Kerrigan, I don't mean to be a pain here, but if you want to declare something as an expense, your bookkeeper really needs to categorize the expense properly.

Kerrigan: Fine. We'll fix it next year. Is that it?

Clerk: Yes, it is. Thank y—

(Kerrigan hangs up midway through the clerk's response)

Nugent and Stratford knew they had Kerrigan at this point. They just needed a way to talk to him so they could use his theft of company funds (and willingness to deceive his own family) against him. Nugent had an idea. He had connections in the Metro Toronto Police Department. With Kerrigan's noteworthy drinking and drug habits, maybe they could get a squad car to bring Kerrigan in on an impaired-driving charge. The key would be to make sure he was legally impaired when they pulled him over.

So, Nugent and Stratford set up a bit of a sting. Nugent got Millington's approval to have the RCMP Watcher Service—professionals at physical surveillance and following suspects—keep an eye on Kerrigan for a number of evenings. This is when they got a little lucky. Not only was Kerrigan a heavy drinker but he was also frequenting some of Toronto's gay bars, most notably The Parkside Tavern and The Manatee. Besides the drunk-driving charge that the service was banking on, they could also leverage his sexuality against him—and the RCMP were experts at this kind of mudslinging. A holdover from the early Cold War days, the service were still red-flagging homosexual civil servants as part of their security-screening responsibilities for the RCMP. At the time, the service and the government believed homosexuals were vulnerable to recruitment by nefarious groups willing to use the target's sexuality to blackmail them. For the most part, if the service found out that you were gay, you got fired. While the practice had diminished quite a bit in recent years, the Security Service was still a deeply homophobic institution. It was the late sixties before the RCMP had put an end to the use of the "fruit machine"—a device that *tested* for homosexuality by showing subjects pornography.

While Nugent and Stratford were not about to bring the fruit machine out of its inevitable retirement, they were going to use the RCMP homosexual-interrogation playbook to shame Kerrigan and threaten to reveal his sexuality to his family and friends.

They didn't feel badly about this because their target wasn't really Kerrigan himself; it was the men who frequented Foley's Irish Pub.

Opportunity presented itself one night when Kerrigan had knocked back quite a few rye-and-gingers and settled behind the wheel of his 1970 Dodge Charger with a man he had met at the bar. It was a little after one in the morning when the Watcher Service had informed Metro police, and a yellow cruiser got to Kerrigan shortly after he pulled away from The Parkside Tavern. They'd conducted a sobriety test and administered a breathalyzer, but there was really almost no need. Kerrigan had wreaked of booze and was obviously drunk. They'd sent his new friend away and told Kerrigan they were charging him.

The Watcher Service contacted Nugent and Stratford, and arrangements were made to interview Kerrigan once he sobered up. They strongly reinforced that the young man was not to be extended his right to a phone call until after the RCMP had finished with him.

A shocking lack of academic research
- *November 24, 2003*

I spent the entire day in the library without really knowing where the time went. I reviewed news clipping after news clipping, opinion piece after opinion piece, and more timelines than I could count until I had a reasonable grasp of what had happened to Flight 281 in 1973. I also learned quite a bit about the investigative struggles that had marred the case. It was really mind-boggling that such a high-profile, deadly attack remained virtually unpunished thirty years after it happened.

By the time I finished up at the computer, the final bell of the school day had sounded, and the students had all gone home.

Andrea popped her head into her office. "You know, you've been at it all day, eh? I am heading home in about ten minutes, so I am going to have to kick you out."

I cast a blurry-eyed look at Andrea. "Geez, that explains why I am suddenly starving. It's not like me to skip lunch."

Andrea smiled. "Did you learn anything?"

I stood up from the office chair and stretched. My joints ached from six hours of not moving. "You know what? I learned quite a bit. A lot of the databases confirmed my cursory understanding of the event. The bomb was planted on an Ottawa CP flight and transferred onto the BOAC plane in Toronto. It blew up off the coast of Ireland, killing everybody onboard. Canadians reacted with both shock and disbelief—shock that such a devastating tragedy could have occurred and disbelief that such a crime could be perpetrated on Canadian soil by Canadians. This came through loud and clear in the press reports you steered me toward."

I went on for a few minutes while Andrea listened politely. She handled my little lecture with dignity and understanding. Here's my summary:

Right out of the gate, the inability of Canadians to feel any kind of outrage toward those responsible for this reprehensible crime led to embarrassing mistakes both politically and in the investigation. One thing that stuck out for me was the fact that Canadian Prime Minister Bryan Stanfield had contacted his contemporary in Britain and offered his condolences the day after the bombing. 'For what?' I wondered. Ninety percent of the passengers on the plane had been Canadian. Did he feel bad that a British company lost an airplane? Stanfield tried to walk back the infamous "condolence call," but the damage had been done. The newspapers tore him to shreds. Unfortunately, his actions revealed a more widespread inability by the Canadian government to recognize that Canada was not as squeaky clean as they believed and that the world's deadliest terrorist attack (prior to 9/11) had emerged from the true north strong and free.

The newspapers were also clear about the prime suspects in the bombing. Most of the articles emerged after Redmund wrote his series of articles five years after the bombing. Journalist had a lot to say about:
- Darcy Byrne, a dual Irish-Canadian citizen and IRA sympathizer who fled Ireland in early 1972.
- Cathal O'Dwyer, the Barrie demolition man who built the bomb (they did manage to convict this fellow of manslaughter).
- Owen Ryan, the man who many thought had taken the bomb to the airport.
- Collin Boyle, the suspected financier behind the bombing.
- Paddy Kerrigan, the man who authorities believe bought the plane tickets.

While reporters did their utmost to move the story to the forefront, Canadians were in a state of denial and read the reports with passing interest. It was as if a collective decision was made to bury the event deep in the nation's unconscious. Maybe this is why it took over a decade to bring charges against Byrne, Ryan, Boyle, and Kerrigan.

This ambivalence, in part, explains why very little academic work had been done on the attack. Certainly, there was a large hill (I wouldn't call it a mountain) of newspaper reports on the bombing of BOAC Flight 281, but where were the books? The 9/11 attacks on the US had already garnered a library of comprehensive missives, and this was just two years after those devastating attacks. That kind of academic commitment did not exist for what could be deemed Canada's 9/11. Redmund's book was the most widely cited work on the tragedy, with two other books making the rounds—one a wide-eyed, conspiratorial account that blamed the British MI6 for instigating the bombing to tarnish the image of the IRA, and the other a powerful tribute to the families of the victims of the attack. Other than that, nothing.

God bless Andrea Kenmount, because she listened to this entire rambling lecture without batting an eye. I hadn't noticed that she was in her coat, holding a briefcase and her lunch bag the whole time. She said she had wanted to leave in ten minutes, and I held her up for about a half hour. After apologizing to her, she said, "No need to apologize. It is good to see you so passionate about something so historically important. I was glad you were able to spend the day here. Let me know how it goes with the Redmund book."

At that, I said goodbye to Andrea, headed for the car, and made my way home. I actually couldn't wait to read *A Nation's Shame*.

Leveraging Eamon Kerrigan - *May 1972*

Nugent got to 51 Division a few hours after receiving the call. The ringing phone in the middle of the night did not impress his wife, and they'd had words before he left because she was struggling to get back to sleep.

Nugent was overweight, living an openly loving relationship with a bad diet, beer, rye, and scotch. He was opinionated and irritable. He was also deeply homophobic, so the prospect of dealing with Eamon Kerrigan both thrilled him, because he could go to town on the young man for being gay, and disgusted him, because he had to share the same space with a queer. This is why he waved off Stratford and told him he would handle Kerrigan on his own that morning.

Nugent planned on making the interrogation quick and devastating. Kerrigan had sobered up by the time the RCMP agent sat across from him. Kerrigan was dressed in a T-shirt and jeans, his long, sandy-brown hair looking a bit out of sorts. Nugent lit a cigarette and ran his hand through his slicked-back hair before identifying himself and beginning to explain what was going to happen to Kerrigan if he didn't cooperate. But before he could get very far, Eamon Kerrigan delivered his *mea culpa*.

"Officer, we've been down this road before, and I'm sorry. I know I got behind the wheel after I had a few, and that I should have been more careful but—"

"Mr. Kerrigan," Nugent interjected calmly, "I am with the RCMP. Do you think I give a rat's ass about your drinking habits? I am here for a very specific reason."

Nugent paused, and Kerrigan took a deep breath, his eyes darting from side to side. He was thoroughly confused.

"The RCMP is looking for your assistance in a matter of national security. Your cooperation will help make your impaired-driving charges disappear—"

"No fucking way," Kerrigan said with a note of panic in his voice. "So, I drank too much and got in the car. Suspend my fucking licence if you want. Impound my car. But I'm not working with the Mounties to do any kind of dirty work."

Nugent stared at his target, letting the unease set in. 'This skinny little cocksucker should mind his manners,' Nugent thought. He took a slow drag on his cigarette before resting the smoke in the nearby ashtray, putting his elbows on the table, and leaning in. "Mr. Kerrigan, you really need to hear everything I have to say before you get all ... indignant. I can guarantee you will cooperate, and here's why. First, you drove drunk, but you've already figured out that's no big deal and that you can probably get your family to help make the charges go away. Second, you've been stealing money from your *godfather's* company. Either way, it sounds like something that could reflect badly on you if your family found out. Third, and this one's my favourite, you're a faggot, and the Mounties are experts at using this particularly *behaviour* against people from whom they need cooperation."

Kerrigan slouched back in his chair and let out a heavy sigh. His eyes were cast downward, his mind racing.

"How are you feeling now, Mr. Kerrigan? Your self-righteousness still at its peak? So, now we deal with your current dilemma. We have two pieces of information that you don't want your family to know about: the fact that you are a thief ... and that you are a queer." Nugent sat back, spreading his legs wide, his belly drooping over his belt. He assumed a posture of what appeared to be trained dispassion.

Kerrigan was desperate. "I'm not stealing from anyone ... and who I spend time with is my business."

Nugent butted out his cigarette and exhaled. "Not anymore, asshole. You think we don't know what we're doing here? We've been on you for weeks. We thought we had you when we saw your *admin-fee* scam, but when we followed you to your downtown homo haunts, we knew we had you. What do you think Daddy and Uncle Collin will be more interested in? The fact that you've been embezzling from the family company or that you're a cocksucker?"

Kerrigan slumped over, putting his head in his hands.

"But," Nugent offered, "today's your lucky day, Mr. Kerrigan. Both secrets can stay locked in the vault, and all you have to do is share some information with us—albeit, on an ongoing basis. We'll even pay you a small stipend for your efforts."

'Judas money,' Eamon thought. 'I am so fucked.'

"Let's just say you are now officially an employee of the RCMP," Nugent concluded.

That's when Nugent laid it out for Eamon Kerrigan. He was now an informant for the RCMP (he didn't say the Security Service because he thought that would only confuse matters and require some kind of deeper explanation). Kerrigan would let his handlers know about the inner working of Nova Star Pharma. He'd also start to frequent Foley's Irish Pub, endeavouring to get closer to Collin Boyle and his closest associates. While his primary focus would be on acts of disruption and sabotage planned by Toronto's Irish community, he'd also try to provide information on shady business practices and objectional behaviour that could be used against people at Nova Star and Foley's. By the end of the conversation, Kerrigan knew that there was no way out.

When he left the police station, at a little after seven in the morning, he was officially a rat—or a *"tout"* as the Irish liked to call them—whose task was to betray his family in what seemed a much more shameful way than he already had been.

While Kerrigan ventured home to shower and get ready for work (and act as if nothing had happened), Nugent made his way to the Toronto Airport Detachment. He was at his desk, typing up his report on Kerrigan, when his partner arrived for work.

"Well?" Stratford asked.

Nugent leaned back in his chair. "We've got the faggot."

Digging deeper - *November 24, 2003*

When Karuna got home shortly after six o'clock, I was already fifty pages into Redmund's book. We shared our days with each other, and while she prepared dinner (it was her turn to cook), I knocked off another twenty pages, taking notes as I went along. By the time I got to the dinner table, I was well into *A Nation's Shame*.

"So, now that I have the time off, what's next?" Karuna asked.

I wasn't really sure. "Well, I'll be finished the Redmund book tonight. I'll hand it off for you to read next." Karuna is a much faster reader than I am. The fact that I was going to be able to finish reading a book so quickly was a bit of a miracle for me. "Maybe I'll contact Redmund again tomorrow morning and see what he thinks we should do." I went on. "Thirty years along and this is pretty much a footnote in Canadian history. The more I read about what happened, the more confused I am that no one was really brought to justice."

"The weakness of the justice system." Karuna sighed. "Conspiracies are the hardest things to prove in court. Plus, the conspirators in this case probably knew how to reign each other in and tighten up their stories."

"What kind of access do you have to the legal documents that surround the trials of the conspirators?" I asked. "Transcripts and briefings? The public-record stuff?"

"If it's public record, I can access it at the Osgoode Hall library. Just keep in mind that the conspirators who are still alive were tried in 1986 and can't be tried again. They're protected by the principle of double jeopardy."

"So, when my dad asked me to right a wrong, he was really just asking me to expose the truth."

"Hence the connection with a well-known reporter who can tell the story," Karuna said. "I can still check out the transcripts to see what the Crown had on the conspirators. Maybe that's what I'll focus on tomorrow," Karuna suggested.

"Okay, it sounds like we have a plan. You'll do some legal research, and I'll connect with Redmond and maybe arrange a meeting."

At this point, everything felt like an academic-research project. That's when the memory of the Ford Taurus in the parking lot of Gary's Deli in Shelburne found its way back into my mind. We were on someone's radar. I imagined that the more deeply we dug, the more attention we'd get.

So, after dinner, it was back to Redmund's book for me. I found the whole story riveting. Redmund was a skilled storyteller who wrote in a methodical and purposeful way. He had details and names that pointed the finger directly at a number of key conspirators who'd met at an Irish Pub in Toronto and hatched a plan to bring down a plane bound for the United Kingdom. It was IRA-style terrorism, born, nurtured, and executed in Canada—the land of positivity and perpetual apologizing.

One question stuck out for me: If a reporter could dig up this information and implicate the conspirators, why hadn't the authorities prosecuted the lot of them for the bombing? It was mass murder after all.

I finished reading the book around midnight. Karuna had spent most of the evening online, seeing what she could dig up on the downing of Flight 281. It was tough going, as the dial-up Internet service was painfully slow, but she found a way to make it productive. She got pulled down a rabbit hole that dealt with motive. Lots of IRA stuff was happening in 1972 and 1973 as the Provisionals were gaining momentum and the British were pushing back aggressively. We settled into bed together, holding each other closely, minds racing, a shared silence between us until we finally fell asleep.

The summer of 1972 - *June–July 1972*

Now that they had an informant on the inside to complement Maloney's attempts at infiltration, the intel was starting to take on more of a shape—at least when it came to understanding who the key players were in the Irish extremist community in Toronto. The team began to see a common thread of emotion that ran through the Irish leadership and the people who followed them.

In fairness, the more rabid IRA sympathizers of Toronto were really a fringe group. Certainly, while a lot of Irish folks spoke approvingly of the actions of the Provos, few would go so far as to help the IRA initiate paramilitary attacks on British targets in Ireland or Canada.

That said, the investigative team understood the importance of not underestimating the subtle (and sometimes not so subtle) rage that inhabited the minds of most of the Irish diaspora. Generation after generation had lived through the conflict between the native Irish and their British overlords—or their surrogates in Ulster. This meant that generation after generation had heard stories of atrocities—stories that settled into the consciousness of the diaspora with the predominant emotion being a proclivity to express anger and rage. Most of this was verbal, as in the outrage voiced at social gatherings about the behaviour of the Ulster crowd in the lead up to the Troubles—an almost *"they started it"* outrage that could be justified by any number of horrific stories. This sense of anger was sometimes misplaced on wives and children. In some cases, it was aimed squarely at the Ulster loyalists who were the clear enemy of Irish republicans. This was the same rage that caused the ranks of the Provisional IRA to steadily grow, particularly after Bloody Sunday. It was also the rage that the Security Service needed to pay attention to.

For his part, Kerrigan started to frequent Foley's to fulfill his reluctant obligation as a confidential informant for the Security Service. He brought back information that mostly reflected what the RCMP team already knew. So far, no concrete plans were in the works. However, one important development emerged. Darcy Byrne, his apparent star on the rise, had started a cross-Canada road trip, raising a substantial amount of money for the Provos. The money was likely getting filtered back to Northern Ireland through a complex web of back channels, personally orchestrated by Collin Boyle. Kerrigan claimed that most of the money came from cash donations, and once the money was converted to US funds, republican "mules" took the cash to IRA leaders in Northern Ireland. As far as Kerrigan could tell, Nova Star was not being used to launder the money.

Clearly the Provos were putting their cash to work. On Bloody Friday, July 21st, they set off twenty-two bombs in Belfast, killing nine and injuring over a hundred people. The explosives—mostly car bombs—targeted transport infrastructure and Ulster/British interests in the Northern Irish capital. Most of the bombs were detonated within an eight-minute time frame, with a few others going off within half an hour. The incident demonstrated a level of coordination that told the world that the Provos were able to act like a formidable guerilla army.

The British responded with Operation Motorman, during which they forcefully and brutally moved into Catholic "no-go" areas in Belfast, Derry, and other urban centres. They executed this plan with the tact of the professional army they were, and only two people were killed (a civilian and a Provo); two others were wounded. The British message to the IRA was clear: *"If you want to play this game, we're ready, willing, and much more able."*

All this news was received with the typical outrage in the Irish community in Canada. Byrne was able to use these developments to extract more money from his infuriated audiences in Halifax, Moncton, Montreal, Calgary, and Vancouver. According to Kerrigan, who was getting closer to having a seat at the table with his godfather at Foley's, about eighty percent of the funds raised by Byrne was heading back to Ireland. The rest was being stowed away for action on the Canadian front, and a generous amount was lining the pockets of Darcy Byrne.

Meanwhile, back at the Irish Desk at the Security Service's Toronto Airport Detachment, the team wondered if the Irish extremist threat was really amounting to anything substantial. Keenan and Belwood continued to monitor and review tapes from Foley's, along with the wiretaps, but almost no fresh intelligence was surfacing (besides the fundraising). The top brass noted that similar fundraising was happening in the US, particularly in the New England states. Sergeant Dawson wondered if the passion for action inspired in the post Bloody Sunday era may have been reserved for the realm of rhetoric. While Bloody Friday and Operation Motorman had inspired an uptick in the rhetoric, formal plans on the Canadian front still seemed to be lacking.

It was summer after all. A time for reprieve and enjoyment of the sunshine that eluded Canadians over a long winter. Who wanted to think about the Troubles when barbecue and beach season had officially begun?

CHAPTER 5:
AS THE PLAN EMERGES

Redmund's take and the first tape - *November 25, 2003*

It was a little after eight in the morning when the cellphone Redmund had given me started to ring. I had it plugged into a kitchen outlet, so it was fully charged and easily accessible for me to answer as I ate my breakfast.

"Hello, Mr. Redmund. I'm glad you called. My wife and I have been researching the bombing—"

"I'm sure you have," Redmund interrupted. "Can you get over to my house sometime today to go over a few things? I can use the text function to send you my address."

"Text? Okay, I'm sure I can figure it out," I answered, remembering that, while my students were experts at this technology, I was a novice. "Yeah, we can both come over and meet with you. What time?"

"How about later this afternoon?"

"See you around five?" I suggested.

He disconnected without saying goodbye.

'Five it is,' I assumed.

Minutes after hanging up, the Nokia cellphone buzzed and the screen illuminated with a *MESSAGE* indication. I navigated to the message, and there was Redmund's west Toronto address, just a short drive from our place.

Karuna and I got organized later that afternoon. She had just gotten home from Osgoode, a little more enlightened after reviewing some of the court transcripts and evidentiary documents that were available at the library. We were like a couple of nerdy academics, shuffling papers, writing out Post-it Notes, bookmarking important items, and acting as though we were headed to a university seminar to discuss a topic we were studying.

Of course, that was precisely what we were doing. So far, our examination of the bombing of BOAC Flight 281 was simply an intellectual exercise. Other than my meeting with Redmund, our time had been spent reviewing literature on the bombing.

We got to Redmund's right on time, shuffling out of the car and toward the front door of his modest suburban bungalow just off Kipling Avenue. It wasn't much to look at, just wood siding with two large windows framing the front door. They had those fake decorative shutters to keep the house from looking too plain. The most prominent feature was a wheelchair ramp that led from the carport, across the front of the house, and up to the front door.

It didn't take Redmund long to answer the doorbell. "Come in," he said abruptly as we walked in, kicked off our shoes, and followed him through the front hallway to an office space near the rear of the house. I cast a quick glance toward the living room on the way; the old furniture looked dusty and tired, suggesting the space wasn't used very often. On the way, I introduced him to Karuna, and he simply grunted a hello.

"Shut the door," he said once we were in the office.

Karuna and I watched him as he positioned himself behind his desk and started fiddling with some electronic contraption.

"That should do it," he said, after turning on four or five switches.

"Do what?" Karuna asked.

"I installed jamming equipment just in case the office has been bugged. I try to sweep it every once in a while, to see if there are any listening devices, but I'm not sure I can keep up with the technology that these people have."

"Which people?" Karuna asked.

"Probably CSIS. Maybe the CSE when it comes to my computer and cellphone."

Silence took over. Redmund was coming off as paranoid.

I broke the silence. "Jack, I know that mystery car showed up when I met with you in Shelburne, so something strange is happening. But do you really think that CSIS and the CSE are monitoring your every move?"

Redmund stared at me for a few seconds before responding. "You're new to this game, so I'm going to cut you some slack. I got shot leaving work after publishing a few articles on the conspiracy to bring down Flight 281. Since then, I have written about all manner of corruption, and I've received death threats for something as minor as implicating a developer in a land-acquisition scheme. It's also my house, so my decision to implement counter-surveillance measures, I think, resides with me."

"I didn't mean to—"

"No," Redmund said, holding up his hand to indicate that he hadn't finished speaking. "And as for the matter at hand, CSIS took on the case files of the RCMP Security Service in 1984. Some of those files, the ones they could find, at least, included crucial documents that are related to the downing of Flight 281. It is my position that this incident involves both massive investigative incompetence and a cover-up of vital evidence by service members who transferred to CSIS. All this in the interests of *'national security'*. As for the CSE, they have come a long way since signal decoding in the Second World War. They are not above monitoring everything from a phone conversation to what we do on our computers today. So, Declan, I do think I am in a position to exercise some extreme caution when it comes to further examination of the Flight 281 fiasco. You good with that?"

I took a breath. "Yes, sir."

"Great, let's get to work," he said. "Tell me what you've discovered."

Karuna and I took turns telling Jack Redmund what we had learned about the downing of Flight 281. None of it was new to him. He complimented us on being quick studies and then discussed his current perspective.

"So, like me, if you believe there was a conspiracy to bring down Flight 281 in February 1973, you should feel compelled to prove it. Everything I have uncovered so far is the equivalent of hearsay." Redmund began digging through the mountain of papers on his desk. "I am going to share my version of events—all based on speculation and best-guessing."

At that, Redmund told his story. He claimed that a conspiracy had been hatched at Foley's Irish Pub in late 1972, the plan being to bomb a BOAC airplane destined for the UK from a Canadian airport—preferably Toronto, but Montreal was another option. The ringleader was a man named Darcy Byrne, a Provisional IRA member who had returned to Canada as the Troubles began to get heated. He'd come to Canada and raised a large amount of money for the Provos. As a thank you, the IRA had shared their knowledge of blowing things up with Byrne and his associates. Maybe the original plan had been to car bomb the British Consulate in Toronto or Montreal, or the High Commission in Ottawa. Eventually, Byrne had gathered a group of like-minded men and fleshed out an attack on BOAC. Byrne or one of his people had recruited an employee of a demolition company in Barrie, and together, they'd built a device. A few months later, a simple bomb had been concealed in a stereo receiver, placed in a suitcase, checked in on Flight 281, and when the timer went off, detonated, killing everyone onboard the aircraft.

"Now, two things to prove that you've earned my trust," Redmund said, shifting gears. "Here's the Security Service threat assessment that was sent to me anonymously back in 1978. It led to the articles that debunked the lone-bomber theory and sent me on my journey to write *A Nation's Shame* about the conspiracy to bring down the plane."

Karuna and I looked at the report. Parts were blacked out that, at a glance, probably dealt with the names of agents and other sensitive Security Service information. The rest of the report was very easy to read. Dated February 9, 1973, it identified Darcy Byrne and Owen Ryan as renewing strange, coded conversations that had been dormant for a few weeks. It also spoke of the activities of Paddy Kerrigan and Collin Boyle that, while not overtly problematic, indicated a change in behaviour that, in turn, suggested scheming of some kind. The author of the report wondered if this meant that the Irish had redoubled their efforts and were about to strike. They ended the report by claiming that the threat level was high and that the Irish Desk team needed to increase its vigilance.

Redmund let us finish reading before speaking. "And then, there's this: Collin Boyle and Paddy Kerrigan the morning of the bombing."

He shifted in his wheelchair and pressed Play on a small cassette player near the side of his desk.

Kerrigan: What the fuck, Collin! It blew up early.
Boyle: We shouldn't be talking about this on the phone.

Kerrigan: We thought it would go off in the baggage area, not while the plane was in the air!
Boyle: Paddy! Shut your mouth.
Kerrigan: They're all dead!
Boyle: For fuck's sake, Paddy! Shut up!
(Boyle hangs up)

"This is the tape your dad sent to me just before he died," Redmund said, sliding over the cassette, labelled *FEB 14A*.

Karuna and I were speechless. Together, the two pieces of information clearly implicated four conspirators: Darcy Byrne, Owen Ryan, Collin Boyle, and Paddy Kerrigan.

Redmund gave us the space to digest the information. "Okay, now that you are fully invested, I have something new to report. I have located Terry Maloney—aka Terry "Sully" O'Sullivan. He's living in Montreal and has long since retired from the service. I have reached out to him, and he is willing to talk. When I got ahold of him, he said (with a bit of an intoxicated drawl), 'You probably want to talk about the tapes.' I played along and told him I definitely wanted to talk about the tapes… If you take a look out the window, you'll probably notice that the Taurus is back."

Karuna and I peered out the window and took note of two men sitting motionless in the car.

"It's not there most of the time, but whenever someone walks through my front door, they seem to show up. There's no way I could get to Montreal with any degree of ease." Redmund pointed at his legs and the wheelchair beneath him. "And talking to him on the phone won't work, because he's insisted on a face-to-face meeting. However, the two of you could make the trip on my behalf. I could feed you the questions, and maybe we could make progress a little more quickly."

I looked over at Karuna who was looking at Redmund and nodding. "Yes, Jack," she said. "We'll do it. Let's work out the details—"

"Wait." I pointed toward the window. "What about the guys in the Taurus? Won't they just divert their attention to us? Or do you think there might be another set of eyes watching us? I don't want to get tailed to Montreal."

"A few excellent points, Declan," Redmund replied. "I have some ideas to share with you on that front. And it's good to see you're becoming as paranoid as me."

So, we set to work on a plan that would take Karuna and me to Montreal to see the Security Service man who had been on the inside back in 1972 and 1973. The man who had disappeared for almost thirty years. The elusive Terry *Sully* Maloney.

An out-of-town guest - *August 1972*

Eamon Kerrigan arrived in an agitated mood for his meeting with his RCMP handlers. It was their standard meeting place, the Howard Johnson's Hotel restaurant near the Toronto airport.

"I hope you've got something for us, because the intel's been a little light lately, Mr. Kerrigan," Stratford said. The two service agents were already sitting at a table near the window.

"Well, I am sure you've been following the news. The British bulldozed their way into the Catholic sections of Derry and Belfast, but we struck back in Claudy. Three car bombs, nine dead," Kerrigan said as he sat down and opened his menu.

"I don't know or care about what you're talking about, Eamon. Give us something we can use, or we unload all your secrets onto your dad and your godfather," Nugent replied.

Kerrigan looked at Nugent incredulously. "It would be nice if you were at least sympathetic to the plight of an oppressed people. So, fuck it. I'll keep my perspective to myself. You guys just need to know that there's a lot of pissed-off people at Foley's."

Nugent and Stratford looked back at him with a blank expression. Finally, Nugent gestured for Kerrigan to speak.

"Fine," he said. "There's one development. I overheard my godfather tell my father that there is an IRA man coming from either Armagh or Omagh; I'm not sure which. He is going to meet with Byrne to discuss the IRA situation in Canada. That's how Uncle Collin put it."

"We need an arrival date and where he's staying," Stratford said, stepping in. "We'll be able to handle the situation once he arrives, but those two pieces of information are essential for us to get started."

Kerrigan reluctantly responded. "He'll be staying with my godfather. You know where he lives. They weren't very clear on the 'when' part, but I am thinking it should be in the next week or so."

"Thinking doesn't cut it, Kerrigan." Nugent said. "You have until the end of the day to get us the arrival information. We need to be on this guy from the moment he gets here."

Later that day, a man who Owen Ryan had met after Darcy Byrne's speech was invited to a meeting at Foley's in Toronto. The three met and shared a smoke in front of the pub before heading inside. At this point, Byrne and Ryan were exploring options that would help open up a second front for the IRA in the diaspora. Cathal O'Dwyer, a tall, lanky man who worked for a demolition company in Barrie and had family ties to Crossmaglen in the North of Ireland, was eager to take part in any plans emerging from Canada. Ryan was glad to see some potential in the young family man and had taken down his contact information that night at the Irish Heritage Centre. Byrne and Ryan were getting ready to recruit him for a very specific objective. It would involve some minor wining and dining and coaxing and prodding, but if O'Dwyer was as committed as he claimed to be, they just might be moving from the planning to the operational stage of helping their kin back in Ireland.

Arranging the tutorial - *August 1972*

Darcy Byrne pulled up to Collin Boyle's house in his Chevy Nova at around two in the afternoon. The RCMP Watcher Service looked on as he butted out his cigarette, rolled up the driver's side window, and exited the vehicle. He was greeted at the front door by Collin Boyle. They shook hands on the landing and went straight into the house. He had no idea that he was being watched. He also had no idea he was being photographed. Either the Watcher Service were that good or Byrne had other things on his mind.

The RCMP got the details surrounding the arrival of Thomas Driscoll on a London flight from Agent Mike Nugent and had been keeping a close eye on him since his arrival at Boyle's the previous day. Driscoll was a short, portly man with thick brown hair and a beard. To be on the safe side, they'd also put a tail on Byrne, because since his return from his IRA fundraising tour, there had been plenty of chatter about him at Foley's. The service had also concluded, thanks to the wiretaps and bugs at the pub, that Driscoll and Byrne would be meeting to discuss IRA activity in Canada.

At the Irish Desk team meeting on the situation, most of the key investigators had concluded that the meeting would probably be focused on improving the flow of money from Canada to Ireland. The Security Service was certain of two things: Money was coming in as a result of Byrne's efforts, and they hadn't a clue as to how it was getting back to the IRA in either Ireland proper or Northern Ireland. More work obviously needed to be done on this front.

While the Security Service had eyes on Byrne and Driscoll, they did not have bugs inside the home of Collin Boyle. So, in terms of what went on once the front door closed behind Byrne, they were clueless.

Byrne was singularly focused on his meeting with the IRA man. He exited the foyer, waved across the open-concept living room at Boyle's wife in the kitchen, then turned to his right to see a man sitting on the couch reading the *Toronto Sun*. The man finished what he was reading, put down the paper, and turned to the two men who were looking at him.

Byrne smiled and said, "So we're calling you 'Mr. Driscoll' today."

"Darcy Byrne," Driscoll responded dryly. "My old friend from the playground at St. Pats. Dylan sends his regards from South Armagh. My visit is his way of saying, 'Thank you.'"

Boyle smiled nervously, knowing now that the handle "Thomas Driscoll" was an alias, but not caring to know the man's real name. "Let's take this to my office," he said, motioning them toward the hall of the large ranch-stye bungalow. The office was adjacent to four bedrooms and a bathroom that completed the east wing of the house. The west wing, which contained the living area, was just as massive and conveniently cut off from the office and sleeping area. Boyle closed the office door and poured the men a whiskey.

"So, how've you been, Darcy?" Driscoll asked as he took a generous sip of the liquor. It went down like water. No sign of the whiskey burn with this experienced drinker.

"Oh, a bit better than when last we met," Byrne responded. "Still managing the armoury in Monaghan? Any new Armalites arrived?"

Driscoll glanced at Boyle before responding, "Oh, the armoury is a moving fixture in Monaghan, friend. We have our little system to avoid incursions from the authorities, even if we are in the safety of the South. But we're not here to speak of my skill at running a floating arms-storage facility or my knowledge of Armalite rifles—admittedly purchased with Canadian money on occasion. We've gathered to discuss something bigger and better."

"So, what's the plan?" Byrne asked. Boyle looked on with an almost confused expression.

"The plan? Well, someone's in a hurry. Okay, here's the plan. I have everything you need from a knowledge standpoint to train one of your men in explosives."

Boyle's eyes shifted away from Driscoll as a smile crept onto the IRA man's face.

"I assume you are still interested in applying my unique skill in the appropriate situation," Driscoll said.

"Mr. Driscoll, I have recruited the ideal student for your mentorship," Byrne replied in an upbeat tone. "Tomorrow we'll take a road trip up north and make a proper introduction."

The arrival of Jimmy O'Connor—who everyone else would call Thomas Driscoll—introduced new possibilities for Bryne and his associates. It suggested that the South Armagh Brigade had established some renewed confidence in him, and he was eager to prove himself.

Darcy Byrne downed his whiskey in one shot. No sign of the whiskey burn for him either.

A trip to Montreal - *November 26, 2003*

It wasn't easy, but Karuna and I took the evasive measures that Redmund had recommended and were on our way to Montreal. Those measures included sneaking out our back door, hopping a fence onto a neighbour's property, and catching a taxi on an adjacent street. We took the taxi to Karuna's parents' house and borrowed their car for the five-hour drive across Highway 401 to Canada's second largest city. If we were being followed, we couldn't tell. We were amateurs both at detecting surveillance and shaking tailing vehicles.

The ride to Montreal was a largely silent one. Both of us were digesting Redmund's instructions and parting remarks. Plus, Karuna was finishing her reading of *A Nation's Shame*. I wondered about the importance of Maloney in relation to the mysterious tapes he had mentioned in his brief phone call with the reporter.

Karuna broke the silence just outside of Cornwall, some four hours into the drive. "So, we're going to see Terry Maloney in Montreal, and a phone call wouldn't garner the information we need. Why is he such a big deal?"

I shifted into my memory and gave her what I knew. "According to Redmund, Maloney's the RCMP man—known as Sully—who tried to infiltrate the Irish community at Foley's Pub. Redmund makes a big deal about Sully in the book, because he claimed that the Service Mountie should have been able to provide information to nail the bombing on those responsible. However, the RCMP maintains that there was no inside man."

Karuna let that sink in before asking, "Did your dad ever mention Maloney?"

"My dad didn't mention anybody. The only other Service Mountie I knew was Warren Belwood, because Dad had a friendship with him."

"And Belwood basically snubbed you when you mentioned the bombing of the plane."

"He actually startled me. His whole face transformed. Maybe it started as fear, but it converted to ice-cold anger."

"Sounds like self-defence. He knows a lot," Karuna concluded. And the silence set in again, this time taking us most of the way to Montreal.

We pulled into a rest stop on the outskirts of the city a little after noon. I retrieved our *McNally Map Book of Canada,* and Karuna deciphered the best route to where Maloney lived.

Back in the car, we began competing with Montreal's drivers for our share of the road. These folks were aggressive, and their abrupt lane changes and high speed, combined with the pothole-ridden road, made navigating to the Shaughnessy Village apartment of Terry Maloney a white-knuckle experience.

Shaughnessy was a rundown part of town and littered with tall apartment buildings and some low-rise, rough-looking townhomes. Let's just say the place was not terribly welcoming. We found the address that Redmund had provided for us, parked the car, and made our way to the entrance. When my attempts at buzzing in through the apartment intercom failed, Karuna pulled on the entrance door, and the lock simply gave way. Anyone could get in.

We took the elevator up to the twelfth floor and knocked on Maloney's door. We heard some shuffling, and a gentleman, a little younger than my dad had been, answered the door.

"Yes," he said with a suspicious look in his eyes.

"Hello, Mr. Maloney. My name is De—"

"How did you get in here? No soliciting. Period. Take your sales pitch someplace else." He started to close the door.

"No, sir. We are not selling anything," Karuna cut in. "My husband and I were sent here by Jack Redmund in Toronto."

"The reporter? Well, why the hell isn't he here himself?" After a brief pause, he added. "I'm not talking to a couple of strangers. This could be a setup. Now, find your way out of here and leave me alone." He started to close the door again.

"Mr. Maloney. My name is Declan Keenan." Now it was my turn to give it a shot. "Did you happen to know my father, Patrick Keenan? A fellow Security Service agent?"

Terry Maloney stared at me. He needed a shave—and most certainly could use a shower. It was hard to read what was going through his mind. Finally, he said, "You kind of look like your old man. Heard he passed recently. Tell you what, show me your licence. If it says 'Keenan' on it, I'll talk to you."

While I found this strange, I showed him my driver's licence.

"You drove all the way from Toronto?" he asked, looking at us like we were crazy. "Well, come on in. Don't mind the mess."

His apartment was a one-bedroom unit, and Maloney lived on his own. He was clearly a drinker—empty bottles of Jack Daniels were placed on the floor just inside the kitchen door. There was an open bottle on the counter. The dishes weren't done, and to put it plainly, the place was a mess—not a terrible mess, but enough of one to be just this side of disgusting.

Before offering us a seat, he pointed a finger at Karuna, and looking at me, said, "The wife?"

"Yes, I am Declan's wife. My name is Karuna Patel," she answered, offering her hand by way of introduction.

"Well, nice to meet you," Maloney said, shaking her hand. It almost sounded like he was apologizing to her. Then he took control of the conversation. "So, what did I say to the reporter that got him to send Patrick Keenan's son to see me? I might have been into my drinks when I was speaking to him, so I can't guarantee any kind of *accuracy* to what I was saying. Have a seat."

Karuna and I sat down on the living-room couch. She spoke first. "We might as well get right to it then. As you know, in Redmund's book he implied that you were the Security Service insider who could have broken the Flight 281 case wide open." Karuna paused. Maloney's expression revealed nothing. He wasn't irritated or surprised; he looked at us as if we had just read him a grocery list.

Karuna continued. "When Jack Redmund contacted you recently, you said to him, 'You probably want to know about the tapes'."

Maloney walked to the kitchen counter and poured himself a tumbler of Jack Daniels before sitting in a nearby chair.

"Well, kids, Mr. Maloney's got a big fuckin' mouth when he's been drinkin'." He grinned. "The tapes. How acquainted are you with the Redmund book?"

"We've both read it," I said, "cover to cover. We've done some additional research too. And Karuna reviewed some of the court transcripts."

"Well, that's pretty acquainted," Maloney said. "In any of your research, did you ever come across a reference to any *tapes?*"

"No, sir. No reference to tapes," Karuna replied.

"So, a retired Mountie on a pension in Montreal gets loose-lipped with a reporter—a reporter who made his life miserable for a little while with that goddamn book, I might add—and now, there's a new mystery surrounding some tapes." Maloney took a generous swig of his Jack Daniels.

I waited a few seconds before answering. "There is one tape. My father sent Redmund a cassette just before he died. It involves two men arguing about the bombing, with one man saying the bomb was supposed to detonate after the plane had landed in London."

"A cassette? In 1972, the Security Service would have been working with reel-to-reel. Better quality." Maloney was stalling. He knew cassettes were used in some surveillance devices in the 1970s. I started to make a small interrupting gesture, because I wanted to say something, but Karuna gently put her hand on my arm. She wanted the silence to do its work.

Maloney finished his drink. His face transformed from a kind of indifference to bitterness to sadness over the course of a few seconds. "Fuck it. This has been on my head for too long. I'm almost seventy-years-old, for Christ's sake. Your reporter was right with the name of that book. That bombing and the lame investigation into it are this nation's shame."

He stood up. "Here's the deal. I am going to tell you something that you won't be able to prove. Sure, there were tapes—loads of them. Your dad and Warren Belwood were the surveillance leads on the investigation. They had wiretaps on the phones of the conspirators and bugs at Foley's Pub. While the bulk of the discussions happened away from the mics, we had more than enough to nail these guys. And now, the problem: The service senior brass knew it and blew it. They could have stopped the bombing, but they took their eyes off the ball. Then they orchestrated a cover-up that made it look like the boys at Foley's were just so damn clever that they found a way to get away with mass murder.

"The tapes—over a hundred hours of them—were erased by a Security Service agent when it became clear that the bombing could have been prevented if we had been paying attention. His superior ordered the agent to erase the tapes and to remove all vital documents from the detachment. He probably sent them to some service vault in Newfoundland. Once the erasing of the tapes and the disappearance of the documents became common knowledge within the detachment, they ordered everyone to maintain secrecy.

"Remember, we're talking about the Security Service. We worked in the *secrets business*. Keeping secrets was our job. The regular Mounties were compelled to follow the criminal code. The service was in charge of protecting Canada's national security. The higher-ups determined that admitting that Canada could have prevented the terrorist attack was not in the nation's interests. All that to say, there are no tapes and there are no documents, at least not anymore," Maloney concluded.

"Well, there's the cassette," Karuna added.

"Yes, the cassette," Maloney returned to the counter and refilled his tumbler. Then he turned to me and said, "Your dad was really torn up about the bombing and the suppression of evidence. He blamed himself, I guess. He was never much of a talker, but after Flight 281 went down, he was practically mute on the job—very good at what he did but never said anything beyond the scope of whatever operation he was working on. Anyway, I don't know anything about any cassettes. My guess is that your dad dubbed one or two of the tapes before the higher-ups got the technicians to erase everything. Maybe Patrick saw it coming. Maybe Belwood talked him into it. Maybe Belwood and your dad did it together."

"So, there may be more tapes." Karuna said.

"Sure, there may be more tapes," Maloney answered. "But cassette tapes were hard to make at the detachment without getting noticed, and time wasn't on our side. We had maybe a week after the bombing to follow the orders set down by the bosses. It would have been easier to copy documents. Anyway, if I knew your dad, and your father-in-law," he said, pointing and looking toward Karuna, "he wouldn't have just made a little cassette and sent up a prayer. There's other material that he had access to."

"A paper trail," I said.

"Yes, a paper trail," Maloney answered emphatically. "We'd been getting warning memos for over six months that the IRA wanted to blow up British planes flying out of North America." Maloney stopped for another not-so-subtle sip of his drink. He started to stare at a spot in front of him. It was like he was ruminating on something, trying to work things out in his mind.

"I'll be right back," he said, as he got up to go into his bedroom. He came back with a sealed manilla envelope. "Your dad sent me this—probably at the same time he sent the tape to the reporter."

He handed me the envelope. "Why didn't you open it?"

Maloney stood there for a minute, his mind slowly reconciling with what he was about to say. In a soft voice, he answered, "Because I'm a drunk and a coward. I protected my career as a Service Mountie and retired with a full pension. Look what I spend my money on." He gestured to the Jack Daniels on the kitchen counter with one hand and his sparsely furnished living room with the other. "When I saw the envelope was from Patrick Keenan, and I knew he was on his deathbed, I had a pretty good idea that I would regret opening it. It's been sitting in there for weeks."

I took my eyes off Maloney and stared at the envelope. "Open it," he said.

I opened the envelope and tipped its contents onto the table. We collectively saw a cassette (labelled *FEB. 12*), three photographs, and a collection of pages stapled together. I positioned the photos in a row so that we could take a look at them.

"Do you recognize any of these men?" I asked.

Maloney grabbed a pair of glasses off a nearby table and answered. "Sure. The first picture is of Darcy Byrne and Owen Ryan in front of Foley's. They were the most zealous members of the group, and this picture was taken early in the investigation. The second picture is from a Watcher Service report. It's a photo of Byrne going into Boyle's house, probably around the time that a suspected IRA man came to Toronto for a visit. The last one is back at Foley's again. Your dad took this picture. This time we have Darcy Byrne, Owen Ryan, and Cathal O'Dwyer, the bombmaker."

We flipped the pictures. On the back of the first two pictures, the word "READY" was written in all caps. On the third, the one of Byrne, Ryan, and O'Dwyer, someone had written the word "BOOM." We didn't say anything to each other. We just shared expressions that indicated simultaneous contemplation was taking place.

My Father's Secret

Karuna moved onto the papers and started reading while Maloney and I looked over her shoulder. The first one was a BOAC telex dated February 11, 1973, and the second looked like some kind of memo.

"The telex is a warning from BOAC. It was pretty risky of your dad to copy it. It's from a few days before the bombing. It was ignored for two reasons: First, BOAC had provided a pile of warnings—over seventy if I recall—for most of 1972 and early 1973. A case of the boy who cried wolf, I guess. However, this telex seemed a little more specific. Second, we were not paying enough attention to the conspirators in the days after the anniversary of Bloody Sunday."

We took a closer look at the telex:

TELEX-Feb. 11, 1973
British Overseas Airway Corporation (BOAC)
IMMEDIATE ATTENTION REQUIRED!
Attention: Canadian Foreign Affairs, RCMP Security Service, Toronto International Airport Security

Assessment of threat received from MI6 reveals the strong likelihood of sabotage attempts being undertaken by IRA sympathizers in Toronto by placing time/delay devices, etc. in BOAC aircraft or registered baggage. IRA sympathizers are also threatening bombings aboard BOAC flights via carry-on baggage.

Directive: Utilize x-ray and anti-explosive measures (including canine units) to assess and counter sabotage threats.

"Very specific. And a couple of days before the bombing," Karuna said.

"And the second document?" I asked.

"It looks like a memo from the CSE," Maloney said, adjusting his glasses. "They're the ones who intercept electronic communication from our enemies at home and abroad. There are eight threat assessments addressed to John Bakersmith, Director of Intelligence for Foreign Affairs, dated two days before the bombing. It looks like your father has highlighted the one we care about."

Irish diaspora threatening British flights
- MI6 has informed the British Overseas Airway Corporation (BOAC) of potential threat to aircrafts departing from Canada—specifically Toronto with peripheral concerns in Ottawa and Montreal.
- Signals shared by MI6 include intercepts relating to bombing plots in luggage (checked and/or carry-on).
- Threat level: 4 – SERIOUS/PROBABLE – CSE recommends follow up with RCMP Security Service and British consulate. CSE also recommends enhanced security at Canadian airports, particularly Toronto.

"Do you know if Foreign Affairs followed up with the Security Service?" Karuna asked.

"That wouldn't have been something I would have known about. I imagine they did follow up."

Maloney slowly made his way back to his chair and removed his glasses. He looked defeated. "Do you know how many times I wanted to say something? ... Do something? ... Instead, I followed the chain of command, ignored my conscience, then got lost in the bottom of a bottle ... a thirty-year whiskey serenade. Such a waste."

"Maybe we can do something now," Karuna said, leaning toward the distraught man.

"Maybe," Maloney said with a profoundly sad expression on his face. "Maybe."

A dense quiet enveloped the room. This time it assumed the air of defeat that Maloney had introduced.

Maloney broke the silence, "Here's what you're up against. The Security Service buried almost all the evidence. While they erased the tapes, they didn't shred the documents. I heard they just stowed them away in a variety of RCMP archive facilities across the country. They did this to create a kind of disjointed jigsaw puzzle that no one would be able to put together. While some incriminating things might be dug up in Edmonton, they'd never be able to connect it to a confirming piece of evidence in Halifax. They were just lucky to find that one report in Moose Jaw in 1985. Archiving the documents is a way of hiding evidence instead of destroying evidence, which would be illegal and very un-Canadian."

'This all seems very un-Canadian,' I thought, but I resisted the temptation to interrupt.

He went on, "It looks like Patrick Keenan kept a few bits of paper and audio tape for himself. God knows how or why. It must have been some kind of compulsion to do the right thing. Or insurance. For what, I don't know. I suppose, as a retired Security Service man at the end of his life, he felt their emergence into the world could do some good."

"Do you have a cassette player?" I asked.

Maloney looked up, making eye contact with me for the first time since he'd slipped into defeat. "Does it look like I even have a DVD player?"

"Fair enough," I answered. "We'll take these? The cassette, the photos, and the paper?"

"You will. Get them out of here. Do what you need to do with them," he said, waving a hand at us as if to symbolically sweep the contents of the envelope away.

We got up and prepared to leave. Karuna stood frozen, looking intently at Maloney. "Are you going to be okay?"

"No, I am not," Maloney replied with a note of surrender. "But I haven't been okay since 1973. I hope I was able to help, but I'm not sure what good it's going to do. The Security Service were experts at burying secrets, and burying those who *betray* those secrets … which explains why none of us went public after the bombing. I am not sure what those who took over at CSIS are like, but if they're half as good as the Service, you'll be chasing the wind." Then he added, "Be careful with what you've learned."

He downed the rest of his latest tumbler of Jack Daniels, got up, and led us to the door. As we stepped out, he looked at me and said, "I liked your dad."

Then he slowly shut the door behind us.

In the woods behind the farm - *August 1972*

The Watcher Service had been following Byrne with various surveillance cars since he'd left Boyle's the previous evening. When he'd come back the next morning, the new "Byrne unit" waved off the surveillance team sitting at Boyle's house and waited to see what their target would do next. At around nine, Byrne and the man from Ireland (who for operational purposes the Watcher Service Mounties had begun to refer to as Mr. X, because they had determined that Thomas Driscoll wasn't his real name) got into Byrne's Nova and headed out on the road. Eventually, they made their way to Highway 401, then the 400, and proceeded north to Barrie, about an hour north of the city. They exited on Essa Road, pulled into an industrial park, and went to a unit owned by Simcoe County Demolition. Byrne honked the horn twice, and then they waited in the car.

The Watcher Service Mounties were RCMP veterans Bill Short and Heather Jansen. Both could boast that, since their rookie year, they had never blown their cover while tailing a suspect. Short didn't live up to his name—he was actually quite tall and slim, with blond hair and a moustache. Short was a very confident agent who always put his assessment ahead of everyone else's. Ninety percent of the time, he was right.

Jansen had a less dynamic presence than Short. She was of average height with short, brown hair, a bit lean, and had mannerisms—particularly the way she walked and talked—that some might say were more on the masculine side.

While they waited in front of Simcoe County Demolition, Jansen asked, "Anything in particular we're supposed to be looking for beyond what's in the brief?"

"No. Just maintain the tail on Byrne and document what he's up to," replied Short, five years Jansen's senior. No sooner had he finished saying this than a man emerged from the building.

"Look, someone's coming. Get the camera. We should get pictures of all these guys," Jansen said, pointing at the main office door to the industrial unit.

"Get the camera? First of all, I'm the senior agent here, and second, you were supposed to bring the camera," Short shot back.

Jansen said nothing. She knew they'd had the conversation before leaving the Watcher Service detachment. Short had been fussing about the gear in the vehicle's trunk and she'd asked, "Do we have everything we need?" He'd given her a look that said both "*yes*" and "*mind your business.*" Now, they were without a camera, and he was blaming her.

They shifted their attention back to what was happening in front of them. The man exiting the building made his way to Byrne's car window. After a brief discussion, he got into a nearby station wagon and drove ahead of Byrne's car out of the parking lot. "Must be a family man. The '68 Country Squire was the family car of the year a few years ago," Short quipped. Jansen wondered how the agent could move so quickly from irritation and blame to inane commentary on cars.

The agents followed, keeping their distance. Short was behind the wheel, and Jansen used a map book to determine potential routes that the vehicles they were pursuing might take. This was a precaution in case they lost sight of the cars.

They ended up at a home a short drive from the demolition-company office. The three men got out of their cars and went inside. Jansen opened the glovebox and accessed the portable radio that was concealed in the compartment. She reached under the seat and grabbed a magnetic antenna, then opened her window, put the antenna on top of the vehicle, and radioed into dispatch, running the plate of the station wagon. The car owner's name was Cathal O'Dwyer, aged thirty-one. There were toys and bikes littering the front lawn of the man's small, rundown bungalow. 'A family man indeed,' Jansen thought.

It was two hours before the three men emerged again and got into O'Dwyer's car. They headed across Essa Road before picking up the 400 mega-highway to Highway 11 just north of Barrie. They navigated through Orillia and made a turn on a county road toward Severn. When they reached the hamlet, they headed east and then turned into a farm lane toward an old house with a derelict barn. While O'Dwyer proceeded up the driveway toward the farmhouse, Short stopped his car a ways back.

Once again, Jansen accessed the Watcher Service radio and contacted dispatch to get information about the address. The farm belonged to Ken O'Dwyer, probably some relative of Cathal's. The property consisted of a farmhouse, desperately in need of paint, and the weathered barn at the rear of the property. Just beyond the barn were a slew of abandoned vehicles: tractors, pickups, cars, and rusted-out farm implements. If this had once been a working farm, those days were long gone. Now, it looked like a wrecking yard.

Short found a place to tuck the Watcher Service vehicle, backing it up a little path that had probably once been used by the farmer who owned the property. It was fairly packed down and well-hidden from the main road, but the agents could still see the farmhouse.

"I'll head up the path to get a closer look. Keep an eye on their car," he said to Jansen.

Short got out of the car, stepping through the tall grass of the old laneway before ducking into the forest and heading toward the farmhouse. He was grateful that the Watcher Service was a clandestine operation. He was dressed comfortably—shorts, a T-shirt, and running shoes, ideal for the hot August weather. He earned a few superficial scratches on his arms and legs from some stray branches as he got himself into position, just in time to see O'Dwyer, Byrne, and Mr. X exit the house and head up a path a short distance from where he was situated. O'Dwyer led the way, followed by Byrne and Mr. X, who was carrying a small duffle bag.

Short did his best to keep up with them in the intervening five or so minutes. He could hear their voices, but he couldn't discern what they were saying. However, he dared not get any closer for fear of blowing his cover.

At one point, the voices went mute, and Short wondered if they'd gone further into the bush. He got up from his prone position and took a few steps toward where he had last heard their voices when a sudden loud boom rocked the area. Short dove to the ground.

"For fuck's sake!" he muttered through clenched teeth as he propped his head up to see what was going on. 'Was that an explosion?' he thought. 'No, probably a shotgun. Christ, I hope it was a shotgun.'

He retreated to his original position, concealing himself as O'Dwyer, Byrne, and Mr. X walked back down the path toward the farmhouse. Short headed to where the men had come from, looking for the place where they'd fired the shotgun. When he heard a car start back at the farmhouse, he knew that he had to double back to his vehicle or risk losing them as they drove away.

Meanwhile, Heather Jansen lived through the same experience as she waited patiently in the Watcher Service vehicle, confident that Short had parked it in a place that was hard to detect. As the minutes passed, she kept her eyes open for any passers-by, but she knew that they were in a remote location that the prospect was highly unlikely. Her vigilance was interrupted by the sound and vibration of an explosion that shook the car.

"Jesus!" she said aloud.

She stepped out of the car and looked toward the location where she had last seen Short. She made her way up the path, fearing her partner might be in trouble. She didn't get far before she heard voices and surmised that Byrne and company were heading back toward the farmhouse. A minute later, the station wagon started. She doubled back to her vehicle, got in on the driver's side, and quietly closed the car door.

She gripped the steering wheel hard. "Fuck, fuck, fuck!"

A minute later, O'Dwyer's car sped down the road, dust flying up in its wake.

A minute after that, a breathless Short opened the passenger door and dropped in the seat.

"Let's go, Jansen." While his direction was abrupt, he wasn't yelling. He'd been in similar situations before, so he brought as much calm to the moment as he could.

Jansen drove as fast as she could to make up the ground that they had lost to O'Dwyer. Fortunately, there weren't too many route options around Severn, so they had a reasonable idea of where the suspect vehicle was going. As long as they were in position before they turned off the county road north of Orillia, they'd be fine.

"Okay, partner, here's what I saw," Short said, and described the scene.

Finally, Jansen asked, "Any idea what caused the explosion? Dynamite? Something like that?"

"Dynamite would have made a much louder sound, and we would have seen smoke and other evidence of a larger blast," Short responded. "My guess is a high-powered hunting rifle."

"Maybe blasting caps?" Jansen asked.

"I doubt it. I didn't find anything when I went toward the location of the sound. Like I said, if it was dynamite, I would have at least seen smoke. I probably never got to where the three men had gathered because I had to double back to the car once I heard O'Dwyer start his engine."

Short paused, allowing some space for him to think. "We'll call it in to the local police. The OPP will send someone out to look for shotgun shells or any other evidence."

They drove for another five minutes before they were within surveillance range of O'Dwyer's vehicle.

Five minutes after that, Jansen said, "I felt the blast in the car—easily two hundred metres from where those men were located. Does a shotgun have that much vibrational range?"

"I'm going to answer yes to that," Short responded, indicating that the conversation was over.

The two agents were silent for the rest of ride back to Barrie. Once the station wagon arrived at O'Dwyer's house, the three men got out of the car and headed inside. It was about five in the afternoon.

A few hours later, Darcy Byrne emerged from the house. By now, it was just before nine o'clock, and the sun was descending in the August sky. He climbed into the Nova, lit a cigarette, and started to pull out of the driveway.

"Where's Mr. X?" Jansen asked.

Short didn't answer; he was trying to determine what to do next.

As the Nova started heading up the street away from them, Short said, "Byrne is our primary target. We need to stay on him. Let's go."

At that, they followed Byrne through the Barrie suburb and onto Highway 400, heading back to Toronto.

Meanwhile, inside the house, Thomas Driscoll (known as Mr. X to the RCMP and Jimmy O'Connor to Darcy Byrne), with a cigarette hanging from his mouth, had dynamite, blasting caps, a detonator and a stereo tuner splayed out on a table, and started a tutorial that would provide Cathal O'Dwyer with the expertise to bring terror to the nation.

The second tape - *November 26, 2003*

Karuna guided me onto the highway and helped me navigate through Montreal's nightmarish road-warrior motorways (and another obstacle course of potholes). Soon enough, we were headed out of town. Fortunately, the 1999 Honda Accord that Karuna's parents had bought a few years back had a cassette player in it. She put the cassette in the player as we crossed the Trans-Canada Highway bridge between Girwood Island and Ile aux Tourtes.

The tape, labelled *FEB. 12*, was quiet with light static for about twenty seconds. Karuna and I shared a glance and wondered if we were about to listen to a blank tape before a click sound gave way to two men talking.

Voice 1: Hello.
Voice 2: It's me.
Voice 1: I've been waiting for your call. And you know I don't like to wait.
[five seconds of silence]
Voice 1 (continues): Is everything in place for my niece to attend the concerts?
Voice 2: As you already know, the first concert ticket is all set. The second concert ticket is not confirmed. I am going to have to see what I can do at the ticket window at the venue.
Voice 1: What are you talking about?
Voice 2: It relates to the complication. Do you want me to go on?
[brief silence]
Voice 1: Yes, go on.
Voice 2: The concert ticket at the first venue is purchased, and she will be able to attend that show. The second concert

ticket is a different story. They are asking that she pick up the ticket at the venue before proceeding to the concert.
[another brief silence]
Voice 1: I see. This is the problem we were discussing prior to your departure.
Voice 2: Yes.
Voice 1: Well, if we're going to make this work, we should review the plan. I don't want her to miss the concert. I'm not sure when she'll get another chance to see this band.
Voice 2: That makes sense. Do you want me to call you at the alternate number?
Voice 1: Yes. How does thirty minutes from now suit you?
Voice 2: That works fine for me. I'll be calling collect.
Voice 1: I'll be sure to accept the charges. How's the weather there?
Voice 2: Goddam freezing.
Voice 1: Hope you packed for it.
Voice 2: I sure did. Talk to you soon.
[click]

Karuna spoke first, "I have a feeling they're not talking about a niece going to a concert."

"There's no question about that," I responded. "Who do you think's talking?"

"No idea. One guy's got an Irish accent. Darcy Byrne? Collin Boyle? Paddy Kerrigan? Redmund might be able to help us with identifying who's talking. The one without the accent is probably Owen Ryan, and since he and Byrne were essentially partners, my guess he's the other speaker."

"They're speaking in some kind of code. What do you think they mean when they mention concert tickets?" I asked.

Karuna gave it some thought. "Could be the plane tickets. Could be the bomb."

"Yeah, it could be either of those things. And the two concerts could be a reference to the fact that the bomb was first loaded on a CP Air flight from Ottawa to Toronto before being transferred onto BOAC Flight 281."

"Two concerts. Two cities," she said.

"I imagine that—since the conspirators were based in Toronto, the Security Service was onto them, and BOAC had been warning about potential attacks—everybody had an eye on flights out of Toronto headed for the UK."

Karuna turned to me and said something that we'd both realized at the same time: "This is a tape that confirms the planting of the bomb on the plane in Ottawa. This is the conspirators talking about some kind of glitch in the plan."

"Why the hell didn't this come out in the original investigation?" I asked, knowing Karuna couldn't answer the question.

"Well, they thought they'd destroyed all of the tapes," she answered. "It looks like your dad was able to acquire and dub this one onto cassette." She paused to think. "Maybe we're back to what Maloney said. The Security Service were experts at keeping secrets. This one's a huge secret. Imagine if the authenticity of the tape could be verified." Karuna was thinking out loud at this point.

"I guess we'd have to assume that CSIS is maintaining those secrets now," I added. "It makes sense, since the Security Service was disbanded in favour of a civilian spy agency with the formation of CSIS in 1984. I imagine that quite a few Security Service personnel simply migrated to CSIS. If some of those agents were close to the Flight 281 bombing probe, they might have made sure that evidence remained buried." I paused before adding, "This is what I don't get: How were they able to simply bury things like this?"

Karuna was quick to respond. "Because the Security Service and CSIS are not law enforcement; they're intelligence-gathering agencies. They are not legally obligated to share the things they know unless it's directly related to national security matters. In fact, spy agencies are not supposed to focus on gathering evidence for criminal matters."

"Well, that doesn't make any sense. You wouldn't think that the two are mutually exclusive. You need cooperation, don't you?"

"You'd think so. However, they separated the RCMP Security Service and the RCMP Criminal Branch back in '84. There was a perception that the two units were bleeding into one another. While the Security Service tried to maintain autonomy, the head of the RCMP was still *technically* the head of their branch. CSIS was created to provide a clear delineation between the spies and the cops."

"Well, aren't you a bundle of knowledge, Karuna," I quipped.

"Grade-eleven 'Intro to Law.' You should know this Mr. Teacher-man."

"Thanks to your tutoring, I promise to do a better job teaching my students about the framework you just described so clearly," I responded with a smile.

We made our way across the Trans-Canada, bound for home, with over five hours of thinking and deciphering to pass the time and kilometres ahead of us.

Committed to *the rifle theory - August 1972*

Bill Short put the finishing touches on his report. Heather Jansen was reviewing the pages Short had just typed as he returned the carriage, scrolled up, and removed the final page from the typewriter.

Short looked at his colleague. She had a confused look on her face. Not trying very hard to hide his irritation, he asked, "Thoughts?"

Jansen made eye contact. The previous day had been pretty exhausting. They had picked up the tail on Byrne at eight in the morning and not gotten relief from another unit until they'd left him at his house at around ten that night. Short and Jansen had arranged to meet the next morning to prepare the report. The main storytelling component of what went on fell to Short, the senior agent on the case. Jansen simply typed up a logistical analysis of the day's events. But when she read Short's report, she struggled with one point in particular.

She let out a sigh. "You're pretty committed to the idea that it was a rifle."

Short was pissed. 'Here she goes again,' he thought before responding, "Agent Jansen, I have been at this a long time. I also hunt every November with my buddies. Believe it or not, there are weapons that can make quite a lot of noise—explosive noise as a matter of fact. Now, let's put this one to bed and move on. The report's done. Make a few copies on the Xerox machine, get in your car, and drive the report bundle out to the Security Service detachment by the airport."

Jansen stared at Short.

"Agent Jansen, this needs to be done. Understood?" he said assertively.

Jansen picked up the report, tapped it on the desk, and headed for the Xerox machine. She dared not bring up the fact that they hadn't sent another unit to O'Dwyer's house to see what had become of Mr. X.

"And don't forget to contact the OPP about visiting the scene at the farm," Short barked as she walked away.

Jansen was visibly frustrated as she stood over the Xerox machine. She made the appropriate number of copies and set her mind to delivering them to the Toronto Airport Detachment after she completed her next chore.

It took her a few minutes to find the contact number for the OPP's Orillia headquarters. She was put through to Inspector Robert Miller, who made it clear from the beginning of the conversation that he was very busy.

"You want what, young lady?" Miller asked after hearing the service agent's request.

Jansen put the derogatory tone aside, as she so often had to in a male-dominated profession, and explained herself for the second time. "Inspector, my partner and I, members of the RCMP Watcher Service, need you to send someone to investigate a potential crime scene on a farm property in Severn. We need this done without tipping off the property owner, because we do not want to compromise our investigation. We need you to look for shell casings or evidence of a small explosion just off a path on the northwest portion of the property."

"All right, Jansen, is it? You're asking me to investigate whether or not someone shot a rifle on a farm near Severn? First of all, the actual hamlet of Severn is a population of about twenty-five people, and second, if I investigated every gun fired on a farm around Orillia, I'd be dead from exhaustion—mostly because I'd be investigating rabbit and coyote killings," Miller responded.

"I can assure you, Inspector, that this is a matter of national security."

"National security?! A farmer shoots a rifle on his own farm?! Come on, little lady," Miller said, once again taking on a condescending tone.

She sighed before reiterating her point. "Inspector, I appreciate your experience and your resistance. However, this needs to be investigated. Can I expect the cooperation of the Orillia OPP in this matter?"

Miller started laughing, "Yes, princess. I'll look into your *'national security issue.'* Goodbye." As he was hanging up, she could hear him say, "What a fuckin' joke."

She made a note to follow up in a few days.

CHAPTER 6:
IRISH GAMESMANSHIP

Target: Prince Charles (?) - *August 1972*

The Irish Desk team convened in the late afternoon at the Toronto Airport Detachment. A copy of Short and Jansen's Watcher Service report rested at each place of the conference table. A bit of social banter was followed by a review of the document. Staff Sergeant Millington was at the head of the table with Dawson to his immediate right. Around the rest of the conference table sat Keenan, Belwood, Maloney, Nugent, and Stratford.

Belwood was the first to break the silence. "A loud gunshot ... probably a high-powered rifle?"

Keenan nodded. "I'm seeing the same thing. Why go all that way to test a rifle? The report says the drive from Barrie to Severn is forty-five minutes. They could have gone to the gun club on Pinegrove Road if they wanted to test a rifle. That's five minutes from O'Dwyer's place."

"Maybe they were trying to be extra secretive and not reveal the type of weapon they were testing. Gun clubs check you in and make note of the weapon you're using. This way you prevent a paper trail?" Dawson added.

Millington turned to Dawson. "You know this Bill Short fellow? Good operative?"

"Yeah, Bill Short's a good man. Very experienced. Rushes to write his reports sometimes, but he covers all the bases."

Millington moved on. "So, we've got a high-powered rifle being tested on a farm in Severn—essentially the middle of nowhere. Three guys go to test the rifle." He paused. "Do you think they are planning to use the rifle as part of an assassination attempt? Maybe the British Consulate-General in Toronto."

"Shit, we're not expecting a visit from the British PM to Canada anytime soon, are we?" Dawson asked. "Or the Queen?"

Millington was quick to respond, referring to his notes, but clearly knowing the details, his answer already committed to memory. "The Queen and Duke of Edinburgh were here in June for the Queen's Plate over at Woodbine Racetrack. A two-week tour of Ontario was highlighted by the horse race, so that one's already in the books. There's nothing on the docket for a visit from Prime Minister Heath. The next royal slated for a trip to Canada is Prince Charles in December. He's representing his father at the Duke of Edinburgh Award ceremony at the Royal York Hotel. He's only scheduled to be in the city for a few days. I guess they're trying to get the twenty-five-year-old heir to the throne a little overseas experience as a dignitary."

Silence settled in for a moment.

Keenan was the first to say what they were all thinking. "An attempted assassination of the Prince of Wales?" He sounded unconvinced. "That's pretty bold for a bunch of ex-pat Irishmen hanging out at a pub in Toronto—even if they are IRA sympathizers."

"So, how do you explain a clandestine trip to a forest behind a farm to test a rifle?" Dawson asked.

No one answered.

"Well, gentlemen. Our working theory is a potential assassination attempt, maybe against a person working at the British consulate, or perhaps, the Prince of Wales. This is obviously very significant. Let's flesh this out a bit more before I alert the higher-ups. Suffice to say that, with the proper level of diligence, these people will never get close to anyone at the consulate or to the prince when he's in Toronto."

They spent the next few minutes reviewing logistics and assigning tasks to make sure no stone was left unturned. Keenan and Belwood would continue their surveillance and could requisition more resources if necessary. Nugent and Stratford were directed to see how much more information they could squeeze out of Kerrigan without tipping him off that they were onto potential threats against consular officials or Prince Charles. Maloney would strengthen his efforts to try to get beyond Foley and earn the trust of Boyle. And Millington and Dawson, the senior administrative officers, would alert the top brass as needed. They wrapped up the meeting, confident that they could protect those working at the consulate and the heir to the throne.

As they were beginning to get ready to leave the conference room, Keenan asked, "What happened to Mr. X? Does anyone know where he is at this point in time?"

Millington responded, "That's on the Watcher Service. We need to trust that they have taken the appropriate steps to keep an eye on him."

I'm not Redmund - *November 26, 2003*

By the time we got back to Toronto it was almost nine o'clock at night. Our commute to and from Montreal had been just over twelve hours including pit stops. Throw in an hour or so at

Maloney's, and you can see it was a very long day. We were both exhausted and elected to take the Accord back to our place and drop it off at Karuna's parents' the next day. To be on the safe side, we parked the car on the adjacent street and hopped our neighbour's fence again.

As soon as we got settled, I retrieved the Nokia cellphone that Redmund had given me and called his number—not his home number but the number of his corresponding Nokia cellphone, which had been purchased for the sole purpose of our secret conversations.

I filled him in on everything from Maloney's insights to the photos, documents, and new cassette. He listened intently before saying, "I think we are going to have to move fast on this information. My guess is that we are going to start to draw more attention, which probably means they will start to follow you and Karuna more closely."

I took a deep breath and raised a palm to my forehead. "Understood. What do you recommend we do next?"

I could picture Redmund sitting in his cluttered office and coming up with his response. "Our current disadvantage is also our current advantage. It's been thirty years since the bombing. That means that time will have eroded a lot of people's memories, but it also means that a lot of people have had to live with the bombing on their minds for that long too. They're older now. Most people who were directly involved in this would be in their late sixties and early seventies. This is why people like Maloney are a little more willing to talk. They're tired of holding onto the demons that have haunted them all this time."

"Next steps?" I reiterated, palm still held against my forehead.

"Bring the tape, the photos, and the documents over to me in the morning. I'll work my sources to see if I can identify the people on the recording. Then I want you to talk to John Bakersmith,

My Father's Secret

the Foreign Affairs Intelligence Chief who is cited in the memo you were given. He's long since retired but lives in Toronto. He's in his mid-eighties, so he's sticking pretty close to home. I know him from when he worked for Foreign Affairs. I'll give you his address when you drop off the material tomorrow. Does that work for you?"

"What choice do I have, Jack?" I responded in a despondent tone. "We're in this thing now. We have to see how it plays out."

If Redmund detected my insecurity, he blew right past it. "Good. See you tomorrow." He hung up before I could say anything else.

I tossed the phone onto a nearby couch. Now both hands came to my face. I have never been very courageous, and I certainly have never found myself in a situation like this. I have lived a life of low-risk strategy and calculation, always striving to avoid uncomfortable situations. When my parents had told me that they wanted me to be a good boy, I was a good boy. When teachers had told me to pay attention in class, I paid attention. I file my taxes on time, and I constantly defer to authority—my principal, the police, the government.

And here I was, chasing seemingly legitimate leads to a largely unsolved mass murder, perpetrated just minutes from my home. I wasn't like Redmund. From the little I knew about his career, he could be chasing and reporting on four stories at the same time with at least three of them involving people I'd never want to be my enemies. His most recent series was on the tow-truck industry in Toronto. The one before that was on bike gangs and how they were laundering money through fitness centres. All the stories were accompanied by threats on the life of the reporter.

My point? I'm not Redmund. I'm not the kind of guy to put myself (or my family!) in harm's way. Yet, here I was: *in harm's way*. And my wife was here with me. But like I'd said to Redmund on the phone, what choice did I have? Sometimes, a situation presents itself, and you have to either make the courageous decision or wonder how things could have been different. Circumstances dictated that I was going to see Bakersmith; there was no doubt about it.

They can enjoy their hockey moment - *October 1972*

Darcy Byrne took a long drag on his cigarette as he looked into the night sky. The weather was changing. The warmth of September was diminishing, and the cool of October was setting in, particularly in the evenings. He sat on his back patio, thinking about his life, where he'd come from, and where he was going.

It had been an eventful month. Plans were coming together. While he wasn't really sure if he was being watched by the authorities, he couldn't take any chances. A few days after Byrne's Irish comrade Jimmy O'Connor (aka *Thomas Driscoll*) demonstrated the power of the blasting caps with a bit of gunpowder on the O'Dwyer farm in Severn, Cathal's father, Ken, had reported the presence of an OPP cruiser along the road leading to his house. The elder O'Dwyer told his son that he had never seen a cop out by his farm before. He wasn't sure, but he thought the cop may have left his vehicle to walk up the long-abandoned combine trail on the west side of the property.

This was enough for Byrne. He knew that it was just a matter of time before he drew the attention of the authorities. His fundraising efforts had been spectacular from an IRA standpoint, with most of the money going back to Belfast. A handsome amount was available to fund the Canadian effort to strike back at the British—an effort that was slowly taking shape. There was also enough money for him to buy a house that more than met his needs in Mississauga.

The month of September had become a critical month of planning for him and his associates. The explosives expert was long gone by the time September came, but Jimmy O'Connor had assured Byrne that O'Dwyer had learned enough and knew what he was doing. Meanwhile, Byrne began floating ideas about what to do with O'Dwyer's new talent. Of course, the primary purpose of having an explosives man in Canada meant mimicking what was going on in the Provos battle with the British in the North of Ireland. A car bomb outside the British Consulate in Toronto could do the trick. A time-release bomb in an English pub was another option, so long as there were ex-pat Brits frequenting the establishment. But Byrne's ideal target emerged after many discussions with his associates at Foley's and many nights pondering ways to strike at his enemies.

Bombing a passenger jet that was bound for the UK had become his favoured strategy. BOAC had regular flights leaving Toronto for London, and destroying one of those planes would certainly deliver the kind of message he wanted to send. One message would be for the British, letting them know that IRA operatives were everywhere—not just in Ireland. The other message would be for the Provos, forcing them to recognize Darcy Byrne as a legitimate leader of the IRA in the diaspora.

While Byrne enjoyed his cigarette on the patio that October evening, he really had no idea of the level of scrutiny he was actually under. The RCMP Security Service were certainly keeping a close eye on him. They had him tailed regularly by the Watcher Service, and despite some warrant delays, they had managed to start surveillance on his home-phone conversations.

However, September 1972 proved to be a time of major distraction for the RCMP. Early in the month, three drunken idiots had gotten kicked out of the Blue Bird Café in Montreal. In their deep state of intoxication, they'd thought it would be a good idea to head out, acquire some accelerants, return to the venue, and set fire to the entrance of the club. Little did they know that the Blue Bird had not honoured the fire code, and the emergency exits were blocked. As the fire had made its way up the stairs into the club, the patrons had no place to go. In all, thirty-seven people were killed. The local police were running the investigation, but the RCMP—both the Criminal Branch and the Security Service— were offering as much support as they could. In the early hours after the fire had run its course, it was an all-hands situation for the Security Service, because initial fears surfaced that this could be a deranged FLQ attack—fears that had been dismissed within a day or so.

A few days later, thieves had broken into the Montreal Museum of Fine Art and stole eighteen paintings, a Rembrandt among them. The thieves also made off with a collection of jewelry. Once again, local police were on the case, but the RCMP Security Service had been recruited to see if this was the work of some untoward foreign outfit. Large-scale thefts were often linked to criminal syndicates that were looking to bankroll terrorist operations. Once again, no evidence of any such links were found, but manpower had needed to be redirected to confirm this. Then, the day after the Montreal heist, the Palestinian terrorist group Black September had stormed the Olympic Village in Munich, killed two Israeli athletes and taken nine others hostage. They'd demanded the release of Arab prisoners taken by Israel and their allies over the years. The entire episode had ended in a bloodbath that saw the hostages and the terrorists killed in a foiled rescue attempt. Intelligence services around the world, including the RCMP Security Service, were on high alert, running down leads and making sure that something similar wasn't going to happen in their own countries. For a time,

My Father's Secret

Nugent and Stratford were called off their duties on the Irish Desk to check on Palestinian Canadians and anti-Semitic threats aimed at Toronto Jews.

Meanwhile, it seemed like the entire nation was distracted not only by the global events of early September but also by the epic hockey series between Canada and the USSR. After a poor performance on the Canadian leg of the contest, Canada was behind the Soviets. Things got worse when the series shifted to Moscow and Canada lost the first game there. The Canadians were trailing in the series, three games to one with one tie. But then Canada ran the table on the Russians, winning the final three games of the series. The last game delivered the most dramatic of endings with a goal by Paul Henderson with under a minute to play. It was a moment frozen in time for Canadians from coast-to-coast-to-coast.

Byrne was a keen reader of the newspaper, so he knew about all these events. He felt no sympathy for the assholes who'd started the fire in Montreal. He admired the planning and cunning of the museum robbers. He empathized with Black September, feeling a loose solidarity with his comrades who were fighting to win back their country; the loss of life was simply part of their efforts.

In terms of the hockey, Byrne really didn't understand the fuss, but he sure saw the impact. People were obsessed with watching the games. He knew that, after the fourth game, the Canadians (who were supposed to dominate the series) had been booed off the ice. Then he saw all the drama in Moscow and the iconic goal scored by Paul Henderson. Byrne made a point of watching that final game on a small TV with a few patrons at Foley's. They downed a few pints as the game progressed that morning, not really understanding the rules, seeing a loose similarity to rugby, but having difficulty keeping up with the speed of the match. They drew their cues from the broadcast as they tried to keep track of the *good* things that were happening in the game by the excitement of the announcer and the reaction of the crowd.

When Henderson took the pass from Esposito and scored the winner with just thirty-four seconds left, they'd stared at the screen, listening to Foster Hewitt excitedly announce the goal and watching the three thousand Canadians who'd made the trip to Moscow go wild. As the seconds ticked down, and the Canadians worked desperately to protect their lead, the Irishmen at the pub regarded the spectacle with only a few of them demonstrating any kind of excitement. When it was all over, and Canada was declared the victor, Byrne downed his pint, placed his empty glass on the bar, and said, "I don't get it." He then proceeded to the washroom to make room for his next pint.

Back on his porch in Toronto, Byrne lit another cigarette. He stared down at the pile of newspapers scattered beside his chair. One of them, from September 29th, displayed a huge picture of two Canadian hockey players embracing and the Soviet goalie splayed out on his back while a defender impassively skated away. 'Canadians,' he thought. 'No real clue of what it means to struggle. No real sense of what it means to fight for something. They'd rather focus on a game than on the injustices of the world.'

For Byrne, the struggle and the fight had been a passion through his entire life. His father and uncle had shared story after story of Irish persecution. He'd learned the lore of the IRA in his formative years in Armagh, and when the Provos were founded shortly after the Troubles began, he'd become an eager foot soldier.

And now, he had something to prove. He'd helped the South Armagh Brigade stockpile weapons with some of the money he'd raised in Canada. And as a thank you, the Provos had sent an IRA bombmaker to Canada to teach a local his craft. Now, he was in position to plan an operation of his own—one that would draw the praise and admiration of his comrades in the North of Ireland.

Byrne looked down at the hockey picture again. 'They can enjoy their hockey moment. My moment is coming.'

Choosing family - *October 1972*

Eamon Kerrigan waited at the Howard Johnson's for Nugent and Stratford to show up. At this point, he had been under their control for a few months. He was reluctantly sharing information with them—enough information to keep them from revealing his secrets. However, the process had been humiliating, and Kerrigan figured, when the time was right, he needed to choose his family and start working against the RCMP. While he waited for Nugent and Stratford, he was working out what he would share today to satisfy the agents. He was also trying to figure out how he would break the news to his godfather and father that he was being used by the RCMP. It would be a tricky situation, but he was reasonably certain he could make it work—keeping the RCMP at bay and keeping his Irish kin satisfied with whatever information he was able to glean from Nugent and Stratford. He needed to balance all this while maintaining his own secrets.

Finally, the agents arrived. They exchanged a reserved greeting with Kerrigan, ordered coffee, and got to work.

"Okay, Eamon. What have you got?" Stratford asked.

"Well, it's been pretty quiet, but I do know that my godfather has had a number of meetings with Darcy Byrne at his house and at Foley's. From what I gather, based on what my dad has said in calls with my godfather, it's been mostly about money," Kerrigan said.

Nugent shot Kerrigan an impatient glance, "Money for what, jackass."

"I'm not really sure."

"What are they up to, Eamon?" Stratford asked, taking on a more reserved tone. "You've been light on the intel, and we're losing our patience. We're about ready to let them know about your financial indiscretions at Nova Star and your personal life."

"So, if you want them to know you've been robbing them and that you're a faggot, just keep dicking us around," Nugent added.

Kerrigan looked down at the table. He knew he was in a spot. "Is there anything in particular I should be looking for? I mean, all I know is that you guys want me to spy on my family. I have no idea what you're after."

Nugent noticed the waitress approaching and waived her off. He leaned toward Kerrigan and said, "How about their direct ties to the IRA, dipshit? How about how they're getting the money to Belfast? It's time to get real, Kerrigan. Get in there and get something, or by this time next month, we'll sell you out to your dad and Uncle Collin."

Kerrigan continued to look down at the table.

"Eamon, you know what to do," Stratford added.

Nugent, undeterred, irritated, and a bit unhinged, went on. "How about the assassinations they're planning? The consular staff they're targeting for death? Their plan to go after Prince Charles?"

Now, Kerrigan raised his head. He looked at the two agents in a state of utter disbelief. "I don't know anything about that. I swear. I haven't heard a thing."

"Well then, get closer. Find out. We need to know if we are dealing with a bunch of Irish drunks or an IRA terrorist cell," Nugent concluded. He stood up, threw a few one-dollar bills on the table, and walked out of the restaurant.

Stratford hung back for a minute. "Eamon, we need something. Just get us something." His was a tone of appeal. Then he got up and left.

When Stratford got to the parking lot, he immediately confronted his partner. "What the fuck was that, Mike?"

"What are you talking about?"

"You essentially just told our informant that we are looking at his family in an active IRA terrorist investigation that includes an attack on Prince Charles! If Millington gets wind of this, you're in deep shit."

Nugent pulled out a cigarette and lit it while Stratford was delivering his reprimand. "And who would tell him I said any of that, Dave?"

Stratford stared at his partner anxiously. "Jesus, Mike. I'm not going to report you, but for Christ's sake, stop saying shit that could compromise our investigation."

"Okay, partner. Got the message," Nugent responded, gesturing a salute, and making no effort to hide the arrogance in his voice. "Let's go."

While the two RCMP Security Service agents drove away from the Howard Johnsons, Eamon Kerrigan remained in the restaurant, slowly eating his breakfast. His plan to double-cross the RCMP had just taken a turn for the better. He would speak with his father and godfather as soon as he could. He needed to let them know that the RCMP was keeping an eye on them. He hoped that they would value the information he was able to share more than their disgust at the idea that he had been working with the authorities.

In Irish culture, there's nothing worse than a *snitch*, a *rat*, or a *tout*. He had become that, indeed, but perhaps he could keep his family out of trouble with the law. That said, his first volley of information would be of great interest to his father and godfather: The RCMP believed the Toronto Irish were fundraising for the IRA with the hope of murdering British consular staff or assassinating the Prince of Wales. Would this be enough to spare him ostracism and disgrace? If he were in Ireland, he'd be killed just for talking to the cops.

A trip to Rosedale and an unsettling dream
- *November 27, 2003*

I dropped everything off at Redmund's as planned the next morning. I didn't notice any questionable vehicles on the street by his house. Maybe the monitoring operation was over. After he made me a copy of the CSE threat-assessment memo, I climbed back in my car and drove to the home of John Bakersmith, the former Foreign Affairs Intelligence Chief for Canada when BOAC Flight 281 had gone down. Redmund had already spoken to Bakersmith that morning to arrange the meeting.

Bakersmith lived in Rosedale, probably the most exclusive and wealthy neighbourhood in Toronto. He owned a handsome brick house, located beside a church on Roxbourough Avenue. Signs of wealth abounded as I drove through the neighbourhood. Every home was immaculately cared for. 'Professional landscaping must be mandatory,' I thought. There wasn't a junky house in sight. Almost idyllic. Mercedes, BMW, Audi, Porsche ... all standard fair in the driveways on this crisp and cool fall day in Toronto. I tried to clear my mind of envy as I parked my aging Honda Civic and approached Bakersmith's front door.

Before I could knock, the door opened. "Right this way," an elderly gentleman said as he guided me down a narrow corridor toward a small office. I caught a glimpse of his wife, sitting in a high-back chair in the living room and reading a book, a cat on the arm acting as her companion. I waved, and she reluctantly waved back. No smile or exchange of words accompanied the encounter.

"Mr. Keenan," he said. "Jack told me why you're here, and I have to say, I'm a bit surprised. A journalist, a schoolteacher, and his wife teaming up to investigate a thirty-year-old terrorist action. A pity this all wasn't dealt with properly within thirty *days* of the actual event, but I digress. Please take a seat." While I knew Bakersmith was Canadian, his tone took on a cadence that almost made him sound English.

I sat down in a beautiful leather office chair, probably a World War Two vintage piece of high-end furniture. Bakersmith sat down behind an ornate wooden desk, most likely from the same era. Behind him was a large window that revealed a backyard lined with mature trees and shrubbery. I imagined the garden would be fantastic in full bloom, but November in Canada had snuffed the life out of it.

"Thanks for agreeing to see me, Mr. Bakersmith," I said, assuming the old man was more comfortable with being referred to formally than by his first name. "I'll get right to it. My wife and I came upon a few items that might be pertinent to gaining an understanding of the circumstances that brought down Flight 281. Maybe they were missed back in 1973. Maybe they were ignored or stuffed away."

Bakersmith gave no hint of reaction to anything I was saying. He was still an intelligence officer, even in retirement, and even in his eighties. His white hair was parted to the side, and his cardigan, dress shirt, and slacks suggested a casual formality, if such a thing exists.

"One thing we uncovered is this memo…" I said, reaching into my pocket and unfolding the photocopy that Redmund had given me "…from the CSE, which appears to have come across your desk a few days before the bombing."

I handed Bakersmith the memo. He put on his glasses and started reading it carefully, but I got the sense that he knew exactly what he was going to see before the paper touched his hands.

"Yes, I saw this. It was part of my daily briefing. I usually reviewed about five to ten threat assessments per day. Obviously, ninety percent of them were either exaggerated or thwarted by our intelligence community. This one was concerning." Bakersmith looked up from the paper, making eye contact with me. "I'm an old man, Mr. Keenan. The bombing of BOAC 281 haunts many of us who lived through that period. I recall this memo vividly for obvious reasons."

"So how did you handle it back in 1973?" I asked out of curiosity, not provocatively. Unfortunately, Bakersmith thought I was accusing him of something.

"Mr. Keenan, I can assure you this matter was *handled* effectively and efficiently. As the Intelligence Chief of Foreign Affairs, it was my job to follow protocol to the letter. That is exactly what I did—"

"Sir, I didn't mean to imply—"

"Then you should mind your tone, Mr. Keenan," he said sternly. For the record, my tone was fine. I'd obviously struck a nerve with Bakersmith.

"A threat of this nature needed to be vetted and verified. I didn't run to the Minister of Foreign Affairs with every CSE threat assessment. I ran the chain of command, and as a professional, I determined it was not necessary to jump the queue and go to my boss in this particular case."

I cleared my throat before asking, "May I ask why, sir?"

"Because I took the threat assessment straight to the RCMP Security Service. I was informed that they knew about the threat and were acting accordingly," Bakersmith said, removing his glasses and looking directly at me. "My job was to examine threat assessments and act on them. I acted. I went to the people who were working to deal with this specific threat." He held up the piece of paper as he finished his sentence.

"And they waved you off?"

"They certainly did. In fact, they weren't terribly diplomatic about it either. It was as if I were getting in their way simply by bringing it to their attention."

"Mr. Bakersmith, do you remember who you talked to at the Security Service?"

"I do. I started with the head of the Security Service, who handed me off to a subordinate. He got me the name of the lead agent in charge of the Toronto Airport Detachment. His name was Millington. Staff Sergeant Gordon Millington."

The name didn't really mean much to me; I think I remember his name being mentioned in *A Nation's Shame*. I made a mental note to run it by Redmund.

Bakersmith turned and began looking out the window. A deep, pained look took over his face. "When the investigation into the bombing started in February 1973, I made a point of following up with Staff Sergeant Millington. He assured me that the CSE memo and my intervention had been noted, and that they would move with haste to apprehend those responsible. Well, we all know how that went. They got the bomber, but the rest of the Irish mob went free."

I didn't know what to say. I just sat there, and when he turned toward me, I looked down at my hands. I felt like he and his soul were having a conversation, and I was just an unwitting witness.

"I should have made more of scene back in 1973. I assumed that I would be interviewed for the criminal case against the man who built the bomb, but they never summoned me. Years later, when they went after the other conspirators, still no summons. I just assumed they knew what they were doing. I opted to defer rather than challenge," he said in a low, sad voice. "How very Canadian of me."

I was still at a loss when it came to comforting the old man. I finally said, "Maybe some good can come out of what we are doing now." I realized I was trying to reassure him in the same way Karuna had tried to reassure Terry Maloney. I stood up to prepare to leave.

Bakersmith turned to me with a half smile. "Maybe."

I could see from his expression that he didn't believe it was true. Not for a minute.

• • •

As I was driving home after leaving Bakersmith's, a sudden wave of exhaustion overtook me. Maybe the days of having adrenalin steadily coursing through my veins had run their course. Maybe the overwhelming nature of my father's secret had sent me into a funk. Whatever it was, I had nothing left in the tank and needed a rest.

I got home and made my way to the couch. Karuna was out, and I didn't have the energy to phone her on her cell to see where she was. I laid down and sleep came almost immediately.

And so did the dream—or at least that's how it seemed.

I was walking on water.

It was a large open expanse of water like a great lake or ocean. The water was choppy but not too unsettling. The sky was tumultuous and dark, and a great storm was approaching from the direction I was facing.

I walked toward the tempest for what seemed like a very long time. The storm began to get closer, dark clouds tumbling in mystical circles, and as I narrowed my focus to the distance, I

My Father's Secret

saw people walking toward me. Hundreds of them. Men, women, and children were scattered across the vast expanse of sea with the storm progressing behind them. Once the first people were close enough for me to see clearly into their eyes, I raised a hand to wave. They smiled and waved back. Suddenly, their expressions changed to surprise and fear as the sea sucked them underneath the water.

I came to share their fear as I approached new clusters of people. The same pattern repeated itself, except the initial smiles were gone, replaced by a strange recognition from each person. They knew who I was. At the exact moment when this realization crossed their minds, the sea took them and under the water they went. My fear gave way to sadness as the grim procession continued: recognition ... disappearance ... recognition...

As I approached the last person, I was in a complete state of despair. It was a little girl, no more than six years old. We got very close. The water did not take her. She smiled at me as I knelt down to greet her, tears trickling slowly down my cheeks. Waves splashed against me, but they didn't affect my balance or concentration. She held out her hands, and I took them with both of mine. The storm had caught up and swirled around us, the water getting choppier as we looked into each other's eyes. We were in a state of calm as the storm grew more and more intense. She was not afraid. Suddenly, a wind emerged and pulled our hands apart. Up she went, into the sky, into the clouds, into the ether. She held her gaze on me, her smile replaced by a look of stoic inevitability, her ascension so vivid that it burned into my consciousness. I reached up and tried to say something—anything—to bring her back. But she disappeared into the grey clouds.

I woke to find Karuna sitting on the couch, looking at me gravely, "Are you all right?"

I didn't respond.

"Declan," she said. "You were dreaming. When I came in, you were moving around, and then you suddenly raised your arms upward, and your eyes opened up as if you were trying to pull something back from the air."

Still in a daze, I raised myself up and pushed my back up against the armrest.

Karuna continued to look at me, because I still hadn't spoken. "Are you all right, love?"

"It was quite a dream," I said. I breathed deeply as my body began to awaken.

That look of concern didn't leave Karuna's face.

"What's wrong?" I asked.

"You were calling for your mother when you were reaching up," she said.

It appeared my dream had been delivering multiple messages.

The bigger target - *October 1972*

The day after their latest meeting with Eamon Kerrigan at the Howard Johnson's, Nugent and Stratford found themselves around the conference table with the other members of the Irish Desk. Nugent was bored beyond belief as he listened to Keenan and Belwood drone on and on about the tapes, which had essentially revealed nothing.

Eventually, Dawson turned to the two field agents. "What's your informant got for us?" he asked, looking at Stratford.

"Mr. Kerrigan has been given until the end of the month to give us something concrete. If he fails to do so, we'll let his family know what we know."

"This is dragging on," Dawson said.

Nugent spoke up. "We're confident that he'll start to deliver, Sergeant."

"We better be confident, Nugent. If we have to cut this contact loose, and reveal his secrets, the people we're investigating will know we're onto them."

Stratford shot Nugent a glance. His mind was in fits with the knowledge of all Nugent had given away the last time they had met with Kerrigan.

"We know what's at stake, Sergeant Dawson," Nugent responded calmly.

The meeting then shifted gears into logistics dealing with the visit of Prince Charles in December.

•••

Meanwhile, at Foley's Irish Pub, Terry Maloney tried but couldn't get close enough to hear what was being said at the table where Darcy Byrne, Collin Boyle, and Paddy Kerrigan were sitting. If only he could have gotten closer.

"So, your son says the RCMP are trying to get information on us for leniency on a drunk-driving charge?" Boyle asked.

"Not leniency. Forgiveness," Paddy Kerrigan responded. "He says they want information on money, guns, and bombs. They think we're planning to go after the British consulate, and get this, Prince Charles when he comes to Toronto before Christmas."

Kerrigan and Boyle burst into laughter while Darcy Byrne simply smiled. He spoke up when the laughter died down. "Gentlemen, perhaps we can use this information to our advantage. I think going after the Prince of Wales is a splendid idea. I also know that such an effort would take planning and equipment beyond our means and be tantamount to suicide. That said, we could certainly act as though we were going to do something.

This would give Eamon something to take back to the Mounties and give us a chance to plan what we really want to do while the authorities look the other way."

The conversation had turned serious in a hurry. Paddy Kerrigan and Collin Boyle realized that their relationship with Darcy Byrne was about to shift. Apparently, the "trust" that Byrne had spoken about at their first meeting had been earned. Plans were about to be revealed that would set them on a course that would change the struggle for Irish independence with a decisive blow delivered from the diaspora.

"We're going to go along with their suspicions," Byrne said. "In the meantime, I want to set our sights on a bigger target. Do you remain interested in this type of action, gentlemen?"

Kerrigan and Boyle exchanged a glance and nodded.

"Good. It will involve explosives, the results will be devastating, and I'll need the two of you to make the plan work. Paddy, you'll be the lead on logistics. Collin, you'll be my money man, and don't give me that look," Byrne said, pointing at Boyle. "You think I'm flush with cash, when you know I've used your network to send most of the money back to Ireland. Now, it's time to direct a bit of that money into action, and you're in charge of that. See that friend of ours up at the bar, close to Foley?" Kerrigan and Boyle turned to the bar, and their friend waved at them. "You know Owen Ryan. He'll do anything for the cause. The four of us—with a few other helpers—are going to go after some of Her Majesty's assets." Then Byrne waved Ryan over to the table, and the real conversation began.

Terry Maloney watched Ryan walk away from the bar toward the booth. As the man joined the group, he knew something significant was taking place.

Misdirection - *November 1972*

Now that Darcy Byrne knew that he was being watched, he started to take even more precautions. Telephone conversations were kept short, with no hint of his plans allowed to surface. He laid claim to a new booth at Foley's and instructed Boyle to avoid any talk of Irish scheming at his booth. He and Ryan, his main co-conspirator, established a code of sorts for telephone calls, and if something needed to be really fleshed out, they arranged for clandestine meetings around west Toronto. In the meantime, Byrne began to formulate a plan to see just how closely the authorities were watching him.

Since the Prince of Wales was due to make his visit in mid-December and Eamon Kerrigan's handlers had tipped him off that they were worried something was going to happen, Byrne initiated the process of making it look *as if* he were going to attempt to bring an end to the life of the heir to the throne.

His first step was to have Owen Ryan play up his Irish anger and IRA sympathies at Foley's to try to see if there was a leak that was leading straight back to the Mounties. Byrne instructed Ryan to make a generic claim of his intention that, if given the opportunity, he'd love to do something to disrupt the prince's visit. He'd visit various individuals and groups gathered around the pub and work the topic into a conversation. There was one conversation in particular that achieved Byrne's desired purpose.

It was a busy Friday night at Foley's. Ryan came to the bar and grabbed a stool next to Terry Maloney, who was having a hard look at the double whiskey on the rocks that was sitting in front of him. Foley asked Ryan what he could get him.

"Just a pint," he said, and the bartender set about pouring him a dark stout.

"Well, Sully," Ryan started. "You're awfully quiet tonight."

The RCMP man was ready to play his part and looked up with a smile. "Just contemplating the nature of existence, Owen. This whiskey is my companion on the journey."

The two men shared a glance and a short laugh.

"Did you hear the news, Sully? Her Majesty's puppet, the Right Awful Edward Heath, Prime Minister of the Dis-United Kingdom, warned the good folks of Ireland to avoid a Unilateral Declaration of Independence yesterday. Fucking asshole." Ryan took the first sip of his beer.

"A kind of *'don't do it, or else'* dare, as I see it," Sully responded. "You figure the boys back home will heed Mr. Heath's warning?"

"Sully, they'll heed it with a hundred car bombs and a *'fuck you'* to the royal family."

Their conversation gave way to the many other loud conversations occurring around the crowded bar.

Ryan leaned in toward Maloney. "You know that fucker Prince Charles will be in town next month?"

Terry Maloney's heart began to race, but he focused on maintaining the Sully persona, trying not to tip his hand. This could be fruitful indeed. "Is he now?"

"Yes, sir, Sully. Heading to the fancy Royal York hotel to give out some monarchist award."

"You don't say."

"Yep, a member of the Dis-Loyal Family right here in our own backyard."

Ryan let that sink in. Again, the noise of the bar filled the air.

"This could be an opportunity," Ryan said.

Maloney looked at him. "An opportunity for what?"

"Action, I suppose." Then he gave Maloney a friendly slap on the back. "But tonight's a night to get pissed, eh, Sully. Let's not get caught up in the struggles of the homeland on this jovial Friday night."

At that, Ryan got up, pint in hand, and walked away, smiling at Sully as he left.

Maloney picked up his whiskey and turned on his stool to see Ryan make his way to a group of men at the far end of the bar. He tipped his drink to the man's back, thinking, 'Sounds like you're about to bring the struggles of the homeland here to Toronto.'

When he got back to his apartment later that night, he phoned Dawson to tell him what he'd learned. An Irish Desk team meeting was scheduled for the next morning.

The plot to kill the prince - *November 1972*

Byrne gave Ryan three days to work the pub and make his veiled threats against the Prince of Wales known to the regulars at Foley's. He was suspicious of just about everybody, so he couldn't quite figure out who to point the finger at when it came to leaks to the RCMP. He was fairly confident that Paddy Kerrigan had brought his son back to the fold, making him a loyal servant for the diaspora Provos, not a double agent working both sides. If he were, it would be deadly for the young man; he'd see to that himself.

Now, it was time to move forward with the game of deceit. About a week after the seeds were sown, Byrne instructed Ryan to contact Cathal O'Dwyer and create a list of what would be needed to build a bomb. While they weren't going to build one, they wanted to acquire the items that would create the impression that they were on a deadly mission. List in hand, Byrne and Ryan concluded that a car bomb would be the most interesting option.

Then Ryan went shopping. He started at a used car lot on Dundas in the Junction, where he purchased a vehicle. The make and model were irrelevant; he just needed to pick up a car that was mechanically sound. He paid cash for a '65 Ford Fairlane. Next, he went to the local Radio Shack to buy miscellaneous wires, transmitters, batteries, and gadgets, along with a stereo receiver and an alarm clock. O'Dwyer insisted that a good bombmaker always concealed their explosive—and a stereo receiver was an ideal cabinet for hiding a bomb.

Ryan also ramped up the chatter about the coming visit of the Prince of Wales. His tone became more and more angry, and his threats more and more *real*. By this point, it was late November, and the prince's visit was just weeks away. Maloney was taking notes throughout this entire period. While he wasn't totally convinced that Ryan was on the verge of assassinating the prince, he was concerned that something dangerous was about to happen.

These developments were the central theme at the Irish Desk meeting at the Toronto Airport Detachment on the last day of November. Once again, the team was assembled around the familiar conference table.

"So, nothing concrete," Staff Sergeant Millington said.

"No, sir. But there's something going on," Maloney responded.

Millington turned to Nugent. "And does your informant have anything to share?"

"He says that Ryan is a bit of a zealot for the Irish cause. Serious IRA leanings and a propensity to speak almost like a preacher when it comes to the plight of the Irish and the need to strike back at the British and Ulster authorities."

"Enough zealousness to do something?"

"Our informant says yes," Nugent responded. "He says Ryan is a bit crazy, and that given the right set of circumstances, he'd do something dangerous."

"Keenan and Belwood, the tapes?"

Belwood decided to take the lead and provide an answer. "The tapes remain vague and innocuous. Some conversations are downright confusing, but maybe that's just my perception. However, a few conversations confirm what our agents on the ground have told us: Orders were given to purchase a car and pick up miscellaneous electronics. There's no indication of anyone accessing explosives or firearms."

Dawson cut in. "The Watcher Service report says that they purchased a 1965, two-door, blue Ford Fairlane. One of the Watcher Service agents went into the Radio Shack while Ryan was purchasing items. From what he could see, it looked like he picked up a Pioneer stereo receiver, an alarm clock, some wiring, and batteries."

"This doesn't feel right," Keenan said. "It looks like they might be building a car bomb, but they're being pretty obvious about it. You'd think Maloney would be noticing all kinds of hushed conversations and whispers at Foley's. Instead, this Ryan character is practically screaming about it all over the pub. And the tapes would have indicated much more conversation that would at least support the idea of a car bomb."

"But we can't assume this isn't the real deal," Millington said. "This is the Prince of Wales, so let's keep on the trail and see where it leads. About a week ago, I briefed our superiors, and they shared some of our intel with the Metro Police and the security detail for Prince Charles. They now know to look for a blue Ford Fairlane anywhere near the places that the prince is scheduled to visit. In the meantime, Maloney, keep your eyes open for anything at Foley's, and Belwood and Keenan, keep your ears open for anything on those tapes. Nugent and Stratford will arrange a meeting next week with their informant to see if they can get us some more information prior to the royal visit." He began gathering the papers in front of him. "Gentlemen, we cannot make a mistake here. If the life of the Prince of Wales is in jeopardy, we must neutralize the threat. No one relaxes until the prince is safely back in England."

Time for the fireworks - *December 1972*

Byrne sipped his morning coffee and took a long drag of his cigarette. He was sitting at his kitchen table and thinking, 'It's a fine day to fuck with the cops.' He was confident that his efforts with Ryan at Foley's would reveal how closely the authorities were actually watching him.

He picked up his phone and called Ryan. "Good morning, young man. Are you ready to deliver the package?"

"I've got the package ready, and the address is committed to memory," Ryan replied.

"Looks like quite a day out there."

"A day brimming with possibility, sir. I'll talk to you after I've delivered the package."

Ryan knew that the call was the signal that the operation was a go. He would spend his day working on the assumption that Byrne's phone was tapped and that he was being monitored by the authorities. Owen Ryan would try to be as conspicuous as possible.

However, there was plenty of time until he needed to make his move. The prince wasn't due at the Royal York hotel until six in the evening.

Just before lunch, he left his apartment, took the elevator down to ground level, and went out to the parking lot. He was dressed in a winter bomber jacket and wore leather gloves. He went straight to the Ford Fairlane, took off his gloves, and opened the trunk with his key. Looking inside, he rummaged around aimlessly, using his peripheral vision to see if anyone was watching him. So far, he didn't see anything.

Meanwhile, in a Watcher Service car hidden close by, Bill Short and Heather Jansen had a keen eye on the movements of Owen Ryan. They knew that the ideal time to attack the prince would be that night at the Royal York hotel. They had no intention of letting him get close.

The agents just watched. There was nothing to say. Their car was equipped with a radio, so if they needed to do anything dramatic, they'd be able to call for help.

Ryan went back into the apartment building. While they waited, the team at the Irish Desk relayed a message that Byrne had called Ryan that morning. Something about "delivering a package." They needed to be hyper-vigilant to make sure that package was never delivered.

Hours passed. Then at about three, Ryan emerged from the apartment building, carrying a box and headed toward the Fairlane. He was walking slowly, in an overly cautious manner. Jansen pulled the binoculars, which had been lying on her lap, up to her eyes.

"PIONEER. That's the stereo receiver from the report," she said.

An anxious minute passed.

Ryan got to his car, carefully removed his gloves, and opened the trunk. He gently placed the box inside and closed the trunk in a slow, deliberate manner before going around to the driver's side of the car, getting in, and starting the engine. When he began driving, the Watcher Service agents knew something needed to be done.

Short grabbed the radio. "We need to call it," he said to Jansen before relaying the message. "Dispatch, have the Metro Police unit that's standing by follow and stop the blue Ford Fairlane that is leaving the target's apartment building. We also need the bomb squad at the ready to inspect a suspicious package."

Ryan was about two kilometres from his apartment when the yellow police cruiser pulled him over. Short and Jansen were well back, but they could see what was going on.

Ryan got out to meet the police. The officers stepped out of the squad car, hands on their holsters.

"Sir, we're going to ask you to raise your hands," the officer on the driver's side said, gesturing for Ryan to stop progressing toward them.

"Of course," he replied, as his hands went up and a wry smile swept across his face.

Jansen, watching through her binoculars from down the road, whispered, "The son of a bitch is smiling."

"My partner is going to approach you, and you are going to provide your driver's licence and ownership." The officer on the passenger's side approached. Ryan slowly lowered his hands, reached for the wallet in his back pocket, and gave the officer what was asked of him.

"Mr. Ryan," the officer said. "We need you to come with us."

Normally, Owen Ryan would tell these cops to go fuck themselves, but he knew he needed to play along to see where this was going. Under normal circumstances, he'd ask why they needed to take him anywhere.

However, he did ask, "Am I under arrest?"

"No," said the officer who held his identification. "We just need to speak with you down at the station."

Ryan was escorted to the back of the cruiser. Before the policeman opened the door, he patted Ryan down to make sure he wasn't carrying anything that would surprise them. He took his car keys and kept his wallet. While one officer put Ryan in the cruiser, the other officer put the car keys on top of the Fairlane's left front wheel.

And down to the station they went.

As soon as the cruiser was out of sight, Short and Jansen drove to the Fairlane. They were followed by a second cruiser and a large van from the bomb squad. They grabbed the keys, opened the trunk of the car, and saw a Pioneer stereo receiver in a sealed box. Beside it, rested a Radio Shack bag that was filled with wires and gadgets. They also saw a blanket, and when they moved it, caught sight of a small rifle.

By this time, the head of the bomb squad had parked his truck and ordered his men to unload some equipment. He approached the back of the Fairlane.

"What the hell are you two doing?!" his tone was incredulous. He was at least fifteen metres from the Ford when he spoke.

Short calmly turned to him, making his posture a little more erect. "Just seeing what we are dealing with."

"You called in a bomb threat. Get away from there before it blows up in your face."

Short raised his arms in surrender as he and Jansen backed away from the vehicle and headed back to their own. On their way, Short said, "That's no bomb. The box is still intact, with no sign of tampering, and the wiring, transmitter, batteries, and alarm clock are still in the bag that Ryan was given at Radio Shack. Plus, I know that rifle. It's the same pellet gun I bought my son for Christmas. This is some kind of stunt. They're fucking with us."

They were almost back to their car at this point. Jansen turned and saw a bomb squad officer in heavy armour removing the receiver and putting it into a large steel box on a trailer that was attached to the bomb squad van.

The officers got into the van and drove to an abandoned lot down the street with Short and Jansen a short distance behind. Once in a clearly open area, the bomb squad officers guided the box slowly off the trailer and pulled their vehicle away.

'Time for the fireworks,' Jansen thought. "They're going to blow it up here. If it's a real bomb, that box will come apart and the steel housing will probably fly a good distance. If it's not a bomb, the box will stay together."

Jansen and Short rested against the hood of their Watcher Service vehicle. It took a few minutes, but the detonation told the story: *no bomb*. They had just destroyed a perfectly good Pioneer receiver.

Short motioned for Jansen to come around and meet him at the back of the RCMP vehicle. He opened the trunk and pointed to a Pioneer receiver, the exact same type as the one from the back of the car belonging to Owen Ryan. "Hopefully our cover isn't blown with all the fuss. We'll throw this in the back of the Fairlane and then drop the car and the keys off at the police station where they are questioning Ryan."

By the time the original Pioneer receiver was obliterated and the replacement receiver placed in the trunk of the Fairlane, Owen Ryan was in the midst of his interrogation. He was comforted by what he deemed to be the idiocy of the men standing in front of him.

The Metro cops gave way to two members of the RCMP, a couple of fellows named Nugent and Stratford. Nugent did all the talking.

From Ryan's perspective, there was a lot of bullshit "getting to know you" back and forth before he heard a rap on the door. Stratford answered and then waved Nugent over. They shared a few words, then the truth of his detention came out.

"Mr. Ryan," Nugent said, standing on the other side of the interrogation table. "We have gained information that has led us to believe that you have uttered threats against the life of the Prince of Wales. While we are not in a position to detain you, we are in a position to deliver you a warning. We are on to you and your compatriots, and we'll do everything we can to defuse any threats—and arrest you if we even get a whiff of you planning something."

Ryan couldn't help himself. "You must have already had a whiff. Why else would I be here? How much more of a whiff would you need before I'm in serious trouble, Officer?"

Nugent put both hands on the table, leaned across, and looked Ryan squarely in the eyes. "I am going to ask you not to fuck with me, you piece of shit. You think this is a game? Then let's play, and watch me bury you."

Stratford looked on. He was almost rolling his eyes. He was growing tired of his partner's propensity for tough-guy drama.

Nugent stood up. "Now get out of here and hope that you never see me again."

It was actually Nugent and Stratford that left first. Ryan waited in the interrogation room for about two hours before a Metro cop came and got him. They took him to a custody-release area where he was given his keys and his wallet. He was then escorted to the parking lot adjacent to the station and directed to his car.

By this time, it was close to eight at night. The sun had long since descended in the western sky, and a cold, clear night had settled over Toronto. Ryan briefly surveyed the skyline before he pulled his coat collar up toward his ears and headed to the Fairlane. He'd started to unlock his door to get into the car when a subtle thought swept into his mind. He reversed his course, looked around—he was completely alone—and opened the trunk of the car. And there it was: his receiver, the bag of gadgets, and the pellet gun, still hidden under the blanket. 'How much do these cops really know?' he wondered.

Trimming the fat - *December 1972*

The day after Nugent issued his stern warning to Ryan, the Irish Desk team was back at the Toronto Airport Detachment to discuss the most recent events. It was like déjà vu all over again as they collectively and silently read a Watcher Service report from Short and Jansen.

"So, they put a replacement receiver back in the suspect's car?" Keenan asked.

"Looks like it. That might fool him into thinking that we were only concerned about the threats about harming the prince, and it might keep him in the dark about our suspicions of a car bomb," Dawson responded.

"But they'll know that we were aware of the specific target, the Prince of Wales." Keenan shrugged. "Agent Nugent told Ryan that much during the interrogation."

"That's true," Millington cut in. "But, gentlemen, let's be clear. This is a win. We heard about a threat, and it amounted to nothing. This is very good news."

Belwood was the next to speak up. "It just feels like they're toying with us. It's like they lured us to Ryan—or Ryan lured us to him—and then they staged the situation to see how we would react."

"And we did react. That's the point," Millington said sternly.

"We're not letting up on these guys, are we?" Belwood asked. "The anniversary of Blood Sunday is six weeks away. That was the event that led to the establishment of the Irish Desk."

Millington smiled, "Rest assured, gentlemen, our efforts will continue. We might need to trim a little fat, but we are committed to making sure the anniversary of Bloody Sunday comes and goes with the same degree of operative success that we had with the visit of Prince Charles."

Silence enveloped the room. Pretty much everyone present knew what "trim a little fat" meant.

1973

CHAPTER 7:
RIGHT UNDER OUR NOSES

A new year of promise and revenge - *January 1973*

Not long after the successful game of misdirection with the RCMP Security Service, Byrne and Ryan were able to share all of the details of their gambit with Collin Boyle and Paddy Kerrigan. They did this at a Christmas celebration at Foley's, taking care to avoid the ears of the mystery rat that lurked somewhere in the pub. While they knew someone must have provided inside information to the authorities, they weren't sure who the snitch was, though Darcy Byrne wondered if Eamon Kerrigan was playing the role of double agent with the Mounties. It would be pretty risky of him to play this game, given the fact that Byrne and company had cut him so much slack when he'd revealed his involvement with the RCMP. However, there was something a little off about Eamon that Byrne wanted to keep in mind going forward.

Byrne let everyone enjoy their holidays with their families before moving onto the next phase of his plan. Only Ryan knew the topic of conversation prior to the meeting held at Nova Star Pharma when everyone went back to work early in the new year.

Darcy Byrne was the last to arrive. Owen Ryan, Paddy Kerrigan, and Collin Boyle were waiting in a small meeting room adjacent to Boyle's office—no phones, no windows, just a table and four chairs.

"Well, isn't this cozy," Byrne said, as he entered the room.

"We wanted to make you feel comfortable, Darcy," Boyle responded with a smile. "You want a coffee? I'll get my girl to fetch you one."

"No, Collin, thank you."

"Right, then. Let's discuss what you're thinking—something you didn't want to bring up at Foley's, so I assume it's something sensitive."

"Yes, it is ... sensitive, I suppose," Byrne said. "Gentlemen, the whole purpose of our alliance has been to strike back at the British and to open a front for the IRA in the diaspora. Now's the time to make that happen. The anniversary of Bloody Sunday is at the end of the month. It goes without saying that striking on that day would provide the maximum effect both logistically and symbolically."

Two of the three men around the table didn't know what to say. Owen Ryan already knew the plan.

"Owen, fill Collin and Paddy in," Byrne said.

Ryan moved forward in his seat and put his forearms on the table, "The British Overseas Airways Corporation—"

"No one calls it that," Kerrigan interrupted.

Ryan looked at him, running a hand through his red beard, and smiled. "Right. BOAC flies four days a week from Toronto to London. The flights leave on Mondays, Tuesdays, Thursdays, and Fridays at eight p.m. and land in London at around eight a.m., Greenwich Mean Time. Three of the flights are smaller Boeing 737s, but the Tuesday plane is the big one, a 747. Our plan is to target the January 29th flight, with the bomb exploding on the anniversary of Bloody Sunday in London."

"Target?" Boyle asked, frowning.

"Yes, target. With explosives."

"You're going to blow up a fucking BOAC plane," Kerrigan said incredulously.

Byrne stepped in, "No, Paddy. *We're* going to blow up a BOAC plane. We've trained a man to assemble a time-activated explosive device that will be placed in the aircraft's cargo hold. It will blow up about an hour after the plane lands. The hope is to destroy BOAC property; the plane, if they're late getting the baggage off; maybe the gate; maybe the luggage carousel at Heathrow. While the goal would be a limited loss of life, we would probably wind up killing someone—a baggage handler, a member of the ground crew, or a customer service rep in the luggage area. In fact, for the operation to be a success, we would want to have at least a few people die to show the British how serious we are."

Kerrigan looked at Boyle with an angry expression. Boyle simply nodded and said, "So death is part of the objective of this mission?"

Byrne replied, "It certainly is."

"And the IRA is onboard?" Boyle asked.

"Well, they sent their bombmaker to train our man, didn't they?" Byrne responded. Neither Boyle nor Kerrigan took note of the fact that Byrne had answered the question with a question.

The room was quiet. Boyle and Kerrigan needed to wrap their heads around the plan.

"Okay, what do you need, Darcy?" Boyle asked.

"We'll need some cash. I think $5,000 would allow us to prepare the explosives and buy the plane tickets," Byrne responded.

Kerrigan shuffled in his chair.

"Does this make you uncomfortable, Paddy?" Byrne asked.

Kerrigan was red in the face at this point. "Of course, it does, Darcy. So many things could go wrong. How we manage to keep the authorities from knowing it's us doing this is the main concern, seeing that, according to Eamon, they are already keeping an eye on everyone in this room."

"There are no guarantees, Paddy. This is war, and we're trying to make it easier for our comrades on the frontlines back in Ireland," Byrne said. "Where are your people from, Paddy?"

Kerrigan hesitated. "Cavan," he replied. "And a few relatives in Derry."

Byrne looked him the eye. "Cavan's in the thick of it, Paddy. Sure, they're in the republic, but they're a hub for smuggling arms shipments to the North."

"I know, Darcy. I have been supporting them for years. This is an entirely different enterprise," Paddy said, holding Byrne's gaze.

"An entirely different enterprise is what we need to change the course of the war with the British and their Ulster pawns," Darcy said. "We need to do something bold and unprecedented. And we need you to agree with the plan, Paddy Kerrigan."

Kerrigan looked down at the table. He was conflicted, not because he didn't support the cause but more out of a fear of getting caught and jeopardizing the life he had built in Canada.

Finally, Boyle reached over and put a hand on his shoulder. "Paddy, what about your relatives living in squalor in Derry? How many times have you told me about the shit they're dealing with? The Orangemen parades coming right past their house. Your cousin, arrested and killed by the RUC. It's time to strike back."

Kerrigan knew he was worrying about himself and not about the plight of the Irish back home. While his reservations were understandable, he knew he needed to shift his support behind something more impactful. He looked at Byrne and said, "All right, I'll make arrangements to access $5,000. We have cash put away for unexpected situations. I'll work with Eamon to make sure you get the money in a timely fashion. Will that work for you, Darcy?"

"It would, Paddy," Darcy said with a smile. He turned to Boyle. "Communication from here on in will have to be very concise ... and clandestine. Owen is going to explain what I mean by that."

As Darcy Byrne sat back in his chair, Owen Ryan described the coded message system that the men would use when speaking on the phone. If they needed to talk in person, he had a list of locations where they could meet. They spent the next half hour going over logistics. In addition to securing the funds, Paddy Kerrigan would purchase the airplane tickets for a decoy surveillance flight on January 22nd and the actual one on January 29th. Owen Ryan would check in with the ticket and the explosives on the target date. Boyle and Byrne would lead the operation and troubleshoot should any complications arise. They had less than a month to pull everything together. If all went according to plan, the bomb would explode on the anniversary of Bloody Sunday at Heathrow Airport in London.

They're up to something - *Mid January 1973*

Keenan went to the detachment before his shift across the street from Foley's. He knocked on Dawson's office door. "Do you have a minute, Sergeant?"

Dawson took off his glasses and offered Keenan a seat. "This is a surprise. I thought you'd be heading to the surveillance apartment. What's on your mind?"

"Well, the tapes have shifted from boring and mundane to bizarre. It appears that the Irish are starting to speak in some kind of weird gibberish. This suggests two things: First, they know we're monitoring their calls; and second, they don't want us to know what they're talking about." Keenan had a file folder in his hand.

"Is that the transcript?" Dawson said, reaching out to indicate he wanted to read it. He reviewed the document and said, "What do you make of it, Patrick?"

"I'm not sure yet, Sergeant," Keenan replied. "Belwood and I will work to break the code. At the very least, they're up to something."

Dawson was trying to make sense of this new development. "It might be time to get the Watcher Service to keep an eye on Boyle and Byrne for a few nights. Are they the main people talking on the tapes?"

"It seems so. Maloney says that Byrne's main associate is Owen Ryan and Boyle's main man is Paddy Kerrigan, the father of the informant Nugent and Stratford have been working with. Do you think we should be keeping an eye on them as well?" Keenan asked.

"Patrick, it's going to be hard enough for me to get approval to put another tail on Byrne and a new one on Boyle. With the boss wanting to 'trim the fat,' I doubt I'll be able to stretch the surveillance beyond those two," Dawson said, a tone of frustration clearly coming through. He was growing tired of begging for Watcher Service efforts to complement what they were trying to achieve with the wiretaps and bugs.

If Dawson had been able to secure unlimited resources, here's what he might have picked up on: Eamon Kerrigan making regular visits to the Toronto airport.

Byrne knew it was important to confirm that the young man was really on his side, so he gave him an important mission. Eamon Kerrigan was tasked with making trips to the airport to monitor the security at the BOAC counter. He didn't need to get too close—just grab a coffee and watch the check-in process for the London-bound flights. Byrne asked him to make note of personnel, police, and people he figured could be plainclothes cops. His visits would allow him to confirm who the key players were at the ticket counter and surrounding area.

After three such recognizance missions, Eamon Kerrigan reported to Byrne. They met at Nova Star Pharma during the workday in the same room where the original plan had been revealed a week earlier.

"Well, Darcy, they've got two cops who are stationed a short distance from the BOAC counter," Kerrigan started. "They really don't pay much attention. Half the time, they go walking around and then reconnect and talk for long stretches."

"How about the ticket agents?"

"A couple of women the first night. A woman and a man the last two times I was there," Kerrigan said. "I sit on a bench well away from the counter, so no one notices I'm looking at them."

"Plainclothes cops?"

"Not that I've seen."

"Okay, Eamon. Keep doing what you're doing," Byrne said. He noticed Kerrigan looking down at his hands. "Something on your mind, Eamon?"

He looked up and said, "Well, yeah, actually. I have a meeting with the RCMP this week. I have no idea what to say to them. Normally, I can make something up to keep them off my back, but I've run out of things to share."

"I see," Byrne said. "Here's something. Tell them Quinn Foley is working with a Belfast contact to ship weapons overseas. You're not sure how he's doing it, but he's the ringleader."

"I don't want to sell out Quinn."

"Eamon, you're not selling anyone out. It's a bullshit story that they'll chase for the next few weeks. I'll lend the story some credibility by having a few conversations with Quinn at the pub. Don't worry about Quinn; I'll take care of him. All right?"

"Okay, thanks, Darcy," Eamon Kerrigan responded. Things were starting to get complicated, and he hoped he was up to the challenge.

The tickets - *Mid January 1973*

While Darcy Byrne and Eamon Kerrigan were meeting in one part of Nova Star Pharma, Collin Boyle and Paddy Kerrigan were off in a corner of the shipping and receiving area, discussing what they needed to take care of. Byrne had put Paddy in charge of purchasing the plane tickets—both the decoy on the 22nd and the target flight leaving on the 29th, landing in London on the anniversary of Bloody Sunday. He wanted Boyle's input on his plan.

"I've used a travel agent in Scarborough and ordered the two plane tickets," Paddy Kerrigan began. "My plan is to have Eamon check in on the flight on the 22nd. He can scope out security around the gate, but he won't be boarding the flight."

"Sounds reasonable. Can we trust the travel agent?" Boyle asked as he took a drag of his cigarette. He had a coffee in his other hand.

"There won't be a problem there, Collin. He's a cousin of mine. Family first and all that," Kerrigan responded. "I just need to make arrangements to pick up the tickets at BOAC's office downtown."

"When are you picking the tickets up?"

"I'm not," Kerrigan said. "I was hoping we could find someone to do that for us—create a little separation between ourselves and what is about to happen, if you know what I mean."

Boyle nodded while Kerrigan shared his idea.

"The BOAC office is at Yonge and King. My cousin made the reservation. Can you think of anyone who might be willing to pick up the tickets? Someone we can trust."

"Does the person need to know anything other than the fact that they are picking up a couple of plane tickets?" Boyle asked. "I mean, they don't need to know the plan."

"No, it's better that they don't know. How about Foley or Sully? One of them could pick them up," Kerrigan suggested.

My Father's Secret

"Not, Sully," Boyle shot back. "I don't trust that guy. Let's get Foley to do it."

And so, Paddy Kerrigan arranged for Quinn Foley to pick up the two plane tickets at the downtown BOAC office. He said it was Nova Star business, and he needed to get two business associates to London. He claimed he was too tied up at work to do it himself. Foley didn't really challenge Kerrigan, he just agreed and said it was not a problem. He could pick up the tickets before coming into the pub one morning, not to worry.

The two had the discussion on a Friday. When the BOAC office opened on the following Monday morning, Quinn Foley, with a wad of cash in his pocket, approached the agent at the ticket desk. It was a particularly cold January morning, so Quinn was wrapped up in his parka, scarf, hat, and gloves when he walked inside. 'Jesus,' he thought. 'I'll never get used to these Canadian winters.'

He approached the agent with a smile on his face and said, "Hello, I am picking up two tickets. The reservations are under the names Michael Flannery and Brian Fitzpatrick. One's for the 22nd and the other for the 29th. Toronto to London." Foley said as he checked the piece of paper Paddy Kerrigan had given to him with the details.

"I see the reservations were made by a travel agent," the clerk said.

"I am not sure about that. I'm just picking up the tickets for a friend. He's busy at work."

The clerk kept the conversation going while he checked the reservation system, "Aren't you a good friend… Let's see… Here they are, both booked through Cormac O'Malley Travel. The contact phone number for the travellers is 973-4200."

That's when Quinn Foley realized that he was not simply helping a friend with a chore he was too busy to do himself. He had never heard of Cormac O'Malley Travel, and the contact number for both passengers belonged to the pub. In the interests of getting this handled as quickly as possible, Foley said, "Yes, Cormac O'Malley Travel. How much for the tickets?"

"Before I take your payment, I noticed these are one-way tickets. Did the travel agent make a mistake booking them? Should we call him to see if these gentlemen should be booked on a return flight?" the clerk said, punching keys on his computer. Foley was grateful that the man wasn't looking at him. He was too busy fiddling with the keyboard and looking at the reservation information. Foley was also happy he hadn't removed his hat and scarf.

"No, sir," Foley said, thinking on the spot. "They've finished work here and are returning to London, where they live."

"All right then … one way to London. Let me just prepare these for you," the clerk said as he continued to punch the keys.

Quinn Foley turned away from the clerk and looked out the storefront window. People bundled up, combating the freezing temperatures, shuffled past on the street, making their way to work.

After a few minutes, his attention was drawn back to the clerk when he said, "That'll be $1,085."

Foley reached into his pocket and counted out eleven one-hundred-dollar bills. The clerk gave him the tickets and the change, and Foley headed back out into the cold. The chill felt deeper as he made his way down Yonge Street toward his car—and he knew exactly why.

Little did Foley know, but the Watcher Service had been following him ever since Nugent and Stratford's informant claimed he was smuggling weapons to the IRA. He was now in the crosshairs of the RCMP.

The best laid plans - *Late January 1973*

Eamon Kerrigan met with Nugent and Stratford as planned at the Howard Johnson's. If the agents were upset about the Prince Charles wild goose chase, they didn't indicate anything. They also seemed satisfied with the idea that Quinn Foley was working on smuggling weapons to the IRA. The agents had been briefed by Keenan about the coded chatter, and they assumed the arms smuggling was likely what they were talking about. They also learned from Terry Maloney that Foley, Paddy Kerrigan, and Darcy Byrne had engaged in a rather heated exchange about a recent purchase and the pub being used as part of the process. Maybe it was a dispute over the way the weapons were being handled. Maybe the guns were going to run right through Foley's business, and the service could be there to cut them off, hopefully putting this whole Irish crisis behind them.

Kerrigan was pleased that the two service agents were backing off a bit. He needed the space, because he was becoming a more important player in the activities of Darcy Byrne, Owen Ryan, Collin Boyle, and his father. He wasn't sure what this whole "go to the airport" assignment was about, but he was happy to do whatever they asked to earn their trust. With the focus on cops, security, and airport staff, he knew it must have something to do with the people working the London-bound BOAC flight. Perhaps they were targeting BOAC employees, or maybe they wanted to disrupt a flight. He wasn't sure, and he wasn't about to ask. He was lucky to be in their good graces after revealing that he was being blackmailed by the RCMP. To be on the safe side, he shut down his admin-fee revenue-skimming scheme at Nova Star Pharma and kept his dating limited to a few small bars on Church Street. Eamon Kerrigan was trying his best to keep a low profile.

What he wasn't managing as well was his drinking. Eamon had developed a habit of self-medicating. He was good at masking his alcohol consumption at work (he never missed a day) and when he had to perform some important task (like the assignments given to him by Byrne or his father). He kept numerous small flasks of Jameson Irish Whiskey at the ready, accompanied by corresponding packs of Wrigley's spearmint gum. Kerrigan was so well trained as a drinker that, most of the time, the average person would never know he had been drinking, and his breath always smelt minty fresh.

However, the average police officer is not the average person, and when, on January 22nd, Eamon Kerrigan checked in as Michael Flannery for the Toronto to London flight on BOAC, he learned that the hard way.

Eamon arrived at the airport at the appropriate time. He was a little bit deeper into the whiskey than he should have been, but he checked in to the flight without a problem. He told the BOAC ticket agent that he didn't have a bag and would just need his carry-on for the trip. This drew a disinterested look as the man confirmed his reservation and directed him to his gate. There was no security check of any kind. He walked straight to his gate. He might as well have been flying to Winnipeg.

He sat in the waiting area and started to focus on the personnel around the boarding area. He took mental notes: the position of the cops and security guards, the location of the flight staff and airport employees.

He reached into his inside coat pocket, cast a quick glance around him, and took a sip out of his flask. He watched, and he listened, and he waited. The cops at the gate and the extra security guards indicated that they were being a little more vigilant when it came to the BOAC flight.

My Father's Secret

And then he heard a small commotion behind him.

"Of course, we inspected the luggage. We started doing that earlier in the week when you guys raised a stink," a man said loudly.

"Keep your voice down, please." Eamon recognized that voice. He looked back and saw RCMP Agent Dave Stratford. The man he was talking to was wearing a shirt and a tie with a BOAC name tag affixed to his shirt pocket.

Kerrigan turned away from the two men and looked straight ahead. That's when he noticed Mike Nugent at the ticket counter, smiling and chatting with the twenty-something, blonde flight attendant. 'Holy shit,' he thought.

He got up and walked quickly away from the waiting area, straight past Nugent who was too focused on flirting to notice him. However, he was within earshot to hear him say, "Okay, sweetie, let me take a look at that passenger list."

Once he was clear of the gate, he started to run, and as he took a corner, he crashed right into a cop. The collision sent both men to the ground.

The police officer got up first. "What the fuck, man?"

Kerrigan stood up, pleading, "I am so sorry."

"What's the hurry?" the officer said, looking into Kerrigan's panic-stricken eyes. "Have you been drinking, sir?" At first, Eamon thought his breath or his glassy eyes had given him away, until the cop pointed to the floor where the flask, jarred loose by the collision, was lying.

Kerrigan knew he was caught. "Just a little, officer. I like to take the edge off before I fly."

"Let's see your ticket," he said impatiently

Kerrigan complied, and while the constable was reviewing the plane ticket, another officer came around the corner. "Johnston, we need you at Gate 6. Two idiots in a fight."

"Wait here," he said sternly, reading the name on the ticket. "I'll be right back, Mr. Flannery."

And when the cop ran off to Gate 6 with "Michael Flannery's" ticket in his hand, Eamon Kerrigan headed right out of the airport exit to his car and drove straight to Foley's.

He rushed into the pub and went to his father, who was sitting at Collin Boyle's booth. He breathlessly started explaining what had happened in disjointed sentences. Boyle and his father calmed him down and pulled him away from where they were sitting to a quieter part of the bar.

"Son, what's the problem?" Paddy asked.

"The Mounties who have been handling me were at the London-bound gate at the airport. One of them was talking to a BOAC man about checking the luggage, while the other was at the boarding desk reviewing the passenger list," Eamon said.

"What did you do?" his father asked.

"I just took off."

Boyle stepped in, "Did anyone see you take off, Eamon?"

Eamon hesitated. "No. I mean, no one close to the gate saw me leave. The RCMP have no idea I was there." It was lying by omission, but he felt like this was his best option, given the situation.

"Okay ... okay," said Boyle. He turned to Paddy Kerrigan. "We need to bring this to Darcy. Go get yourself a drink, Eamon. This is all the information we need. We'll take it from here."

Meanwhile, back at the airport, Constable Johnston of the Mississauga Police Department, fresh from helping break up a fight and working with his colleagues to take two men into custody, made his way to the boarding area for the BOAC flight corresponding to the ticket he held in his hand. He approached the BOAC agent who was collecting the final few tickets from passengers boarding the plane bound for London and asked about Michael Flannery. She said he hadn't checked in. He surveyed the waiting area, and seeing no sign of Flannery, tossed the ticket into a nearby garbage can. 'Stupid drunk,' he thought, before turning to the young woman and saying, "There's no way he gets on that flight. Contact me if he tries to board the plane, though I'm pretty sure he's gone home to sober up."

Crisis averted - *Mid to Late January 1973*

What Eamon Kerrigan and the gang at Foley's didn't know was that the RCMP Security Service had recognized the potential Bloody Sunday threat and had taken steps to shut it down.

Keenan and Belwood monitored the coded conversations and then spent hours trying to crack the code. The references all surrounded one word: "book." They listened to messages that talked about purchasing a book. Then there were conversations about the book having been purchased. Then there were conversations about what should be done with the book now that they owned it.

At first, they thought the "book" referred to the shipment of weapons that Nugent and Stratford had said Quinn Foley was trying to move from Toronto to Ireland. However, the Watcher Service was keeping an eye on Foley, and there was no sign of any kind of activity that might indicate arms smuggling. The only thing he did that was out of the ordinary was go into the BOAC flight office in downtown Toronto. Other than that, it was to and from the pub every day.

After chasing the weapons angle for days, Belwood finally made the connection. He and Keenan were at the surveillance apartment across the street from Foley's, reviewing the transcripts of the eight taped conversations dealing with the book as well as the Watcher Service reports.

"Why did Foley go to the BOAC office in Toronto? The Irish are boycotting the airline," Belwood said. "I mean, that's the only thing that doesn't really fit at this point. The only reason he'd go there is to purchase a plane ticket."

It dawned on both of them at the same time.

"And BOAC has been warning us for months that the IRA in North America could be targeting their planes for hijackings and bombings," Belwood said.

"So has MI6," Keenan added.

Keenan picked up the phone and called Sergeant Dawson, who happened to be in a meeting with Staff Sergeant Millington. Dawson put them on speakerphone, and they filled the bosses in.

Millington took charge. "Sergeant, arrange for Nugent and Stratford to run active surveillance on all BOAC flights out of Toronto bound for the UK—specifically London. Review passenger lists and confirm that bags are being inspected and x-rayed by BOAC staff. They also need to keep an eye on the waiting areas around targeted gates to see if they observe anything or anyone suspicious."

Dawson spoke next. "Gentlemen, keep reviewing the tapes. If you've broken the code, you'll probably be able to gather even more information now that we have an idea of what these people might be doing."

Millington spoke up again. "Another thing, Sergeant Dawson. Contact the police detachment that serves the airport. Have them put some extra uniforms around the ticket counter and boarding gates for BOAC. This might be enough of a deterrent to scare these guys off, if they're really up to something. Let's keep this state of vigilance active for the next few weeks. That'll take care of the anniversary of Bloody Sunday."

Keenan and Belwood were about to hang up when Dawson said, "And, gentlemen. Good work." An unnecessary affirmation, but appreciated nonetheless.

By the time Eamon Kerrigan had shown up at Toronto International Airport and made his way to the BOAC gate, the service agents were on day two of their surveillance and inspection of the situation surrounding the London-bound flight. No anomalies according to Nugent and Stratford—just the odd person not showing up for their flight. The situation stayed safe right through to February 1st. "Crisis averted," Millington announced at the team meeting the next day. He ordered that the active surveillance of BOAC flights should continue until the beginning of March.

It looked like they had forced the Irish to shelve the "book."

Plan B - *February 7, 1973*

Byrne was angry and frustrated after learning about the heightened security at Toronto International Airport. In the days after Eamon Kerrigan had reported that the RCMP, local police, and private security personnel were monitoring outgoing BOAC flights bound for the UK, debates raged among the conspirators about whether or not to proceed on the target date, the anniversary of Bloody Sunday. The arguments continued right up until the day before the flight they wanted to hit. That's when Byrne, bowing to intense pressure from Boyle and Kerrigan, called it. The operation was off.

Byrne went home and slipped into a depressive state. He avoided Foley's for almost a week. Finally, Owen Ryan came to visit him at his home; he'd had an idea.

They met in the kitchen. It was ten in the morning, and Byrne was still in his pyjamas and robe. He was looking ragged, needing a shave and a shower. He was spending a prolonged time on each drag of his cigarette with only the odd sip of his coffee interrupting his smoking. Ryan looked at him with concern before sharing his idea.

"Darcy, this isn't done," he started. "Sure, we missed the Bloody Sunday anniversary. But I think I've come up with an alternative."

Byrne just looked at him like he was an idiot.

"While the authorities are keeping an eye on the BOAC flights out of Toronto, it's probably safe to assume that they are not looking at connecting flights coming in from other Canadian cities."

Byrne continued to stare impatiently at Ryan. "What the fuck are you talking about, Owen?"

"Okay, just hear me out. If you live in Ottawa or Winnipeg, and you want to go to London, you have to connect to that flight through Toronto. A national carrier—Air Canada or Canadian Pacific—flies you into Toronto and then you transfer onto the BOAC flight. Your luggage just gets shifted from one plane to the next."

Now Byrne was sitting up a little. His vacant expression was slowly diminishing.

"So, what are you suggesting?" Byrne asked, gesturing for Ryan to continue.

"Let's get back on track," he said. "Let's put the package on a plane from Ottawa that connects to the BOAC flight to London out of Toronto."

"So, the bomb essentially flies from Ottawa to Toronto and then gets transferred onto the BOAC flight. How'd you come up with this idea?" Byrne asked.

"I've got relatives in Moncton. They're always complaining about how they have to go to Montreal or Toronto whenever they want to travel across the pond. They're often heading to Dublin, but I did a little digging, and it turns out that it's the same deal for

London," Ryan said, who'd had a smile on his face the whole time he was talking.

Byrne hesitated. He had lost interest in his cigarette. He was thinking.

"If we find a flight out of Ottawa that connects to the BOAC flight in Toronto, we're in business," Byrne said excitedly.

"That's right, Darcy."

"I better get a shower. Go to the doughnut shop down the street, you know the one. Use the pay phone and call Boyle; tell him we're coming to Nova Star to discuss our new plan. We'll call it Plan B," Byrne said.

As Byrne headed down the hall toward the bathroom, he could feel himself coming to life again. They could still open that second front. This plan just might work.

Redeployed - *February 10–13, 1973*

Staff Sergeant Millington called the Irish Desk team to a meeting in the conference room early that afternoon. Everyone except Nugent was there. He had left a few days prior for a holiday in Mexico.

Everyone assembled was fairly pleased with the current situation. Stratford reported that the heightened security at the airport was doing its job. The RCMP, local police, and private security were present for the check-in and boarding of every flight. BOAC said they were x-raying each customer bag that was checked in at their counter before putting it onto their airplanes. Once again, nothing unusual. Maloney reported a rift between Foley and Byrne, and by extension Boyle, Ryan, and Kerrigan. From his perspective, this might be a sign that the passion for plotting was diminishing, and the Irish-Canadian plot was fading away. Only Keenan and Belwood reported anything out of the ordinary. While the Irish had gone silent after the Bloody Sunday anniversary, they had started a new round of sporadic discussions that could be construed as code.

Millington brushed past the potential code theory and moved onto the next priority. Earlier that day, Service HQ in Ottawa had reported that a high-value Soviet target was making the rounds in Toronto. The resources at the Toronto Airport Detachment were stretched thin, so Millington made the decision to redeploy the Irish Desk agents to the new target and announced it after everyone on the team had finished reporting.

This was all news to Sergeant Paul Dawson, who spoke up after the announcement. "I understand the need to redeploy, sir. But the entire team? I think the news is good from an operational standpoint on the Irish front, but we were in a similar situation around Christmas. Shouldn't someone stay on the case? Maybe Keenan or Belwood on surveillance or Maloney at the pub?"

"No, Sergeant, the entire team will be used to deal with the Soviet target for the next five days," Millington responded with irritation. "The last thing we need is for a Soviet agent to procure national secrets while we chase phony leads from an exhausted case. Besides, it's only for five days. At that point, the downtown detachment will have secured the resources for their Soviet Desk to take over."

The men sat in silence, processing what they had been told.

"Anything else, Sergeant Dawson?" Millington said, challenging his second-in-command.

Dawson looked at Millington. "No, sir. Nothing at the present time."

"Fine. Here's the intelligence brief and the assignments. The Irish Desk is on hold until further notice. Our current priority is the Soviet target. Review the brief and the roles I have assigned to each of you. If you have any questions, come see me

My Father's Secret

in my office." Millington abruptly left the room after making the terse announcement.

Keenan picked up the brief and took it to his desk. He knew that Ottawa had been hyper-sensitive about the Soviets for years. That had reached a new crescendo in 1972 when the Cuban Trade Commission in Montreal had been firebombed. When firefighters and police had arrived to put out the blaze, Cuban security personnel had held them off with submachine guns while the commission staff destroyed documents. It was a typical spy-play situation. Someone on our side must have firebombed the Commission. Hidden within the ranks of first responders would have been a team of Security Service agents who were charged with the responsibility of heading inside and stealing documents or anything else of value. At the time, everyone knew the Cuban Trade Commission was a clearing house for Soviet intelligence.

This was on Keenan's mind as he read the brief. The Soviet target was named Igor Fedesov. He was in Toronto to allegedly connect with a service agent who was believed to be willing to provide the spy agency's counter-intelligence playbook to the Soviet operative. This would give Canada's Cold War enemies the opportunity to train their agents to work around the service's operational strategies. The Toronto Airport Detachment had been assigned the case because the agent in question worked on the Soviet Desk out of the downtown office—the one that was being reorganized, and in five days, would take over the case (presumably with the agent at the centre of the controversy arrested and charged with treason).

Essentially, Keenan and Belwood were partnered up to play the role of Watcher Service agents—since the real Watcher Service couldn't be used lest they tip off the agent from downtown. The other pairing, Stratford and Maloney, would perform the same duty with the sets of partners providing twenty-four-hour surveillance on Fedesov.

This would not go down in the annuls of espionage history as one of the great episodes in spy lore. For three days, the men followed Fedesov. He went to a movie, a play, and a hockey game. He wined and dined with a few friends. Meanwhile, the Security Service agent in question was never seen near Fedesov and reports from the downtown office indicated that he performed his duties without a hint of suspicion.

On his final night in Toronto, Fedesov enjoyed a rendezvous with a high-end escort in his hotel room before catching a flight to Montreal around noon on February 13th. As the plane ascended into the sky, he became Montreal's problem.

Keenan and Belwood were back at their desks, typing up their reports after Fedesov left.

"That was a waste of time," Belwood said over the clatter of the typewriter keys hitting the page, interrupted only by the odd carriage return.

Keenan stopped typing and looked up. "Half the time, this job's a waste of time."

The two shared a smile and kept typing. They looked forward to submitting their reports and heading home. Three days of twelve-hour surveillance shifts had proven exhausting. They both needed a good night's rest.

Late that afternoon, they packed up to leave the office. Belwood walked straight out, got into his car, and started driving home. Keenan was not in as much of a rush. As he made his way out, he caught sight of a stack of reel-to-reel tapes and some files in the Irish Desk mail bin. While the work of the team was on hold, neither he nor Belwood had bothered to shut down the surveillance. The tech team must have retrieved and delivered more tapes. As the surveillance leads, he and his partner were the only ones who emptied the mail bins, because most of the items were there for them to catalogue. They'd make sure any other items—mostly files and documents—got into the right hands. 'We'll get to those tomorrow,' he thought, then shook his head and left the detachment.

• • •

The Security Service wasn't the only organization redeploying their personnel. Byrne and Ryan took their connecting-flight idea to Boyle and Kerrigan. Everyone agreed that the plan was feasible, but with less than a week to get organized, they needed to work fast.

Kerrigan contacted his cousin the travel agent, who with no questions asked, determined that a connecting CP Air flight from Ottawa on Tuesday the 13th would work best. The flight left around five in the evening and connected to the eight o'clock overnight flight to London. 'Valentine's Day by the time the plane reaches London,' Kerrigan thought as he sat and waited for his cousin to reserve the tickets. There turned out to be one wrinkle: Because they were dealing with two airlines, the travel agent was having problems transferring the bag from one carrier to the other. The BOAC reservation system was insisting the passenger, "Mr. K. Doherty," retrieve his bag from the CP Air Ottawa to Toronto flight and check in again for the BOAC Toronto to London flight. This wrinkle could undo the whole plan. Kerrigan's cousin worked hard to convince BOAC to take care of the luggage for his client, but the airline wouldn't budge. Not even a move to first class would make a difference.

Nonetheless, Kerrigan made the reservations and sent his son to pick up the BOAC ticket downtown. The CP Air ticket would be picked up by Owen Ryan in Ottawa the day before he checked the bomb in on the originating flight. Byrne and Ryan schemed about ways to handle the luggage-transfer issue and came up with a few strategies. Ryan (Mr. K. Doherty) would call BOAC every day and insist that they rectify the problem. Failing that, he'd try to plead his case at the check-in counter. If he couldn't get them to transfer the bag, he'd abort the mission. All this was confirmed between Ryan and Byrne in a phone conversation using code words "niece," "concert tickets," and "venues," just in case the authorities were still listening in on their calls. To be on the safe side, the two men met on a Mimico park bench to confirm that they were on the same page.

In terms of the explosive device, Cathal O'Dwyer had assembled the bomb in a stereo receiver in January in preparation for the Bloody Sunday anniversary target date. He had disassembled the device when that plan fell apart, only to reassemble it again for the February 13th flight. When Darcy Byrne told him that the plan was back on, O'Dwyer was instructed to drive the package to Ottawa, something that didn't please him very much. It was one thing to bring an explosive down the highway from Barrie to Toronto; it was another thing to drive it five hours to the nation's capital. But O'Dwyer was a loyal disciple, and he kept his displeasure to himself.

The conspirators were extra vigilant in the lead up to February 13th. They suspected that they were being monitored and that their conversations were being recorded. However, they needn't have worried. The RCMP Security Service was chasing a Soviet to gather valuable intelligence of the utmost importance in terms of national security. They had learned that the suspect liked to eat, go to shows, and partake in the company of escorts. No eyes or ears were on the Irish in the days before February 13th.

My Father's Secret

Planting the devastating cargo - *February 13, 1973*

Cathal O'Dwyer made the five-hour drive from Barrie to Ottawa in his '68 Ford Country Squire station wagon. It was a long and boring commute to the nation's capital, just a series of flat roads with few turns and quite a bit of snow making the landscape even more nondescript.

He got to thinking about his role in the operation. He had meticulously followed the directions of Thomas Driscoll (at least, that's what he said his name was), given to him months earlier, and assembled the device. He'd taken the dynamite and blasting caps from work. No one at the demolition company would notice they were missing—at least that was what he was banking on. Next, he purchased the items that would set the bomb off and concealed the simple arrangement of parts—a Quartz alarm clock, a 12-volt battery, a detonator, and a bit of wiring from Radio Shack, all housed around the dynamite and blasting caps in a Sherwood S-7100A stereo receiver—in a regular-sized Samsonite travel suitcase. The stereo receiver was key. Driscoll had insisted that an assembled explosive should always be concealed, providing the perfect disguise for a bomb in the unlucky event that the wrong eyes—a spouse at home or an eager cop inspecting a suspicious vehicle—spotted the device.

While he was told *not* to do this by Driscoll, eventually he wrote down as much as he could remember of what he had learned from the explosives expert. He didn't want to screw up the assembly of the device because his memory had failed. Once the bomb was built, packed back into the receiver, and stored in the suitcase, O'Dwyer had gone out to his backyard and burned the page on which he had written the deadly details. Hopefully, there wouldn't be any more false alarms.

The drive to Ottawa gave him plenty of time to think about other matters as well. He was thinking about the mechanics of the device—so simple, yet so powerful. He was thinking about the plan, finally set in motion, a day away from coming to fruition, and officially opening the second front for the IRA against those Ulster demons and their British overlords. And he was thinking about his father, Ken O'Dwyer, a man who had left Ireland a generation earlier, and who had told him many stories of the Irish struggle for independence.

He had always felt like his father was disappointed in him. Now, he hoped his role in the plot would give his dad some pride in him and give his pathetic life some kind of meaning or purpose. In a perfect world, this would be the first step in the British withdrawal from the island and the unification of Ireland. Cathal O'Dwyer would be the one who delivered the decisive blow.

He met his contact—a man in a new Lincoln Continental Town Car—in a Canadian Tire parking lot in Nepean, just minutes from the Ottawa airport. 'Beautiful car,' O'Dwyer thought. 'And not too hard to spot in a lot full of pickup trucks and family cars.' He arrived in the early afternoon. It was bitterly cold with mounds of plowed snow bordering the half empty parking lot. He pulled the suitcase from the back of the station wagon and climbed with it into the back seat of the contact's vehicle.

"Good drive?" his contact asked. The man stared forward. All O'Dwyer could see in the rearview mirror were the man's eyes and the neatly cut, red hair on the back of his head.

"Pretty smooth," O'Dwyer responded. "A bit of blowing snow, but nothing I couldn't handle." He hesitated before asking, "What's next?"

"Activate the device and head home. I'll take it from here."

O'Dwyer was a little disappointed. He was expecting some recognition of the work he was doing for the cause. He thought the man would at least introduce himself and shake his hand. Instead, he was welcomed with a *"turn the thing on and get out of here."*

"Is there a problem, Cathal?" the man asked. He turned in his seat. Now, O'Dwyer could see that it was Owen Ryan, well-dressed with a shirt and tie beneath a suit, and a handsome overcoat. His long hair was cut short, and his face clean-shaven, looking very much like a businessman of some sort.

"No problem, Owen," O'Dwyer responded.

He opened the Samsonite suitcase and performed a series of tasks to activate the device. There was plenty of room to manoeuvre in the back of the Town Car.

While he was working, Ryan said, "You went with a Sherwood."

O'Dwyer, who was setting the time on the clock, looked up. "Excuse me?"

"A Sherwood receiver. Top quality. Top price too."

O'Dwyer looked back, puzzled. "Yeah, I guess so. Lots of room inside the housing box. Nothing to do with the sound quality of the amp."

Ryan held his gaze on O'Dwyer. "I'm just saying. You could have saved a little money with a Pioneer or a Sanyo. You didn't need to spend the extra and go with the Sherwood."

It was a surreal moment. Here O'Dwyer was, activating a powerful explosive, and he was being quizzed on his choice of electronic housing for an instrument that would change the course of history.

"I thought the Sherwood was the best choice," O'Dwyer responded as he finished activating the device. He put the cover back on and screwed the housing back in place. He carefully put the receiver back in the cardboard box and returned it to the Samsonite suitcase, surrounding it with clothes in as logical a fashion as possible.

"The device is set to detonate—"

"That's fine," Ryan interrupted. "You can go now."

O'Dwyer hesitated, surprised at being interrupted, before slowly shuffling out of the vehicle. He was barely out of the car when the Lincoln pulled away. He stopped and watched it disappear from the parking lot before getting back into his station wagon.

By the time O'Dwyer started the trek back to Barrie, the Town Car was heading for the airport. Owen Ryan was the perfect man for this particular task, because he knew what needed to be done. The CP Air flight left at five for Toronto. It would connect with BOAC 281 and head for London at eight. If O'Dwyer had done what he was supposed to do, the bomb would explode the next morning, about an hour after the plane had landed.

Ryan was a cool customer. Byrne's chief disciple, and anxious to play an active role in the operation, Ryan insisted on making the trip to Ottawa to place the bomb aboard the plane. It was a bonus that he got to use Collin Boyle's Town Car to make the journey. Getting a haircut and shave was a bit of a disappointment, but his hair would grow back.

He knew the deal: Pick up and pay for the ticket the day before the flight that would leave Ottawa, then on travel day (today!), get the bomb onto the CP Air flight, making sure it was transferred onto BOAC Flight 281. This was going to be the biggest challenge, because from the perspective of the airlines, there was no clear link between the CP passenger and the BOAC passenger.

He arrived at the airport, parked his car, and proceeded to the CP Air ticket counter. Arranging for the transfer of the suitcase onto the target flight via a connection was a bit of a stroke of genius. The RCMP were monitoring the BOAC ticket and luggage areas at Toronto's airport, looking for anything suspicious. In Ottawa, CP Air was subject to nothing of the sort. Nonetheless,

Ryan was conscious of every police officer and security guard as he nonchalantly made his way into the ticket line.

Finally, it was his turn. Ryan stepped to the counter, presented his ticket, and lifted the suitcase onto the conveyor belt. A young lady named Tammy was working the counter.

"Hello, Tammy," Ryan said. "I just want to double-check my connection to London. BOAC 281."

Tammy started searching through her system. After a minute, she said, "Unfortunately, there are no notes on our reservation platform, and I don't have access to BOAC's. You'll have to retrieve your bag in Toronto and check in for the BOAC flight with their people."

Ryan had been expecting this, so he started the act he rehearsed on the drive from Toronto, "Oh, for God's sake. I am just trying to get from Ottawa to London with as little hassle as possible. Here is my BOAC ticket, confirming that I am on the flight," he said, holding up the ticket Kerrigan had given to him before he left. "Please don't make me deplane and then go hunting for my bag, just to line up again in Toronto."

Tammy looked at the BOAC ticket before handing it back to him. "I'm sorry, Mr. Doherty, my hands are tied. There is a very specific process for interlining a bag from one aircraft to another, and it needs to be done well in advance. It will mean a bit of bother in Toronto, but—"

"Tammy," Ryan paused and put a stress-filled smile on his face, as if he was desperately trying to keep a lid on his temper. "I paid cash for my ticket at the CP office here in Ottawa. I have also paid cash for, and made the appropriate arrangements with, BOAC. They assured me that I had given them enough time to make the necessary arrangements."

"Sir, if those arrangements were made, there is no indication of that in our system," Tammy replied emphatically.

Ryan's pleading was getting him nowhere, so he tried one last tactic to see if he could avoid aborting the mission.

"Well, Tammy, you leave me no choice. I am going to have to contact BOAC in Toronto and get them to call CP to fix this unacceptable situation." He started to walk away from the counter, leaving the Samsonite suitcase behind.

"Mr. Doherty, please. You need to take your bag."

"Tammy, that bag is going to London. I will call BOAC to ensure that it does."

By this time, the line behind Ryan had grown substantially, and Tammy was getting stressed. She was not comfortable arguing with a customer with a crowd watching. She could also see that the people waiting in line were getting increasingly agitated.

'Why should this guy be inconvenienced just because BOAC couldn't get their act together?' she thought. She also concluded that, if she didn't transfer this bag, an already busy lineup of passengers was going to be even more delayed, leading to a series of stressful interactions with disgruntled customers.

She waved him back. While she switched the tags on the suitcase to guarantee that it made its way onto the BOAC flight, she said, "Mr. Doherty, I am taking you at your word. Your bag will be transferred to the connecting flight, but you need to confirm your reservation with the BOAC flight as soon as you land." Ryan assumed this was bullshit. Once that bag was tagged to transfer onto the London plane, there was no way they'd take the time to fish it out just because Mr. Doherty hadn't talked to the right people in Toronto.

"That's great. A real relief," Ryan said. "Thank you very much, Tammy."

As the bag rolled away on the conveyor belt, she added, "CP Air thanks you. Have a good flight."

Owen Ryan did not have a good flight, but he did have a good drive back to Toronto in Boyle's Town Car. His bag—with its devastating cargo—would arrive in Toronto hours before he did. As he made the turn onto Highway 401 heading back to Toronto, he pulled over onto the paved shoulder. He ripped his BOAC ticket into pieces and threw it out the car window, watching the winter wind throw it into the air like confetti. A few cars honked at the disgraceful act of littering. "You'll be talking about more than the guy who threw garbage on the highway this time tomorrow, so honk all you want," he said out loud with a smile lighting up his face.

The story of a Samsonite suitcase - February 13–14, 1973

The suitcase belonging to 'K. Doherty' was tossed unceremoniously into the cargo hold of the CP Air flight bound for Toronto. Mr. Doherty was not in his seat aboard the plane.

If the suitcase could tell a story, this would be it:

So, I get to Toronto, and they pull me off the CP plane. They don't care what's inside me; if they knew, I think they would have been more careful. I hear the baggage handlers say, "We better get these interlined bags for the BOAC flight over to the x-ray machines with all the other ones checked in from upstairs." They take me and a few other bags over to the x-ray area, where there are hundreds of bags already waiting. They had processed about half of the Toronto to London bags when I hear this guy say, "Oh, for fuck's sake! The damn thing's busted again." A supervisor comes down, hears the x-ray machine is down, and says, "We can't have another delay. This flight is always late taking off. Just get these bags on the plane." A security guard who is standing by says, "I called the K-9 unit when I saw the x-ray wasn't working. Those dogs are great at sniffing out drugs, and they can find guns and bombs too—though I've only seen them find drugs. Shouldn't we wait?" The supervisor stares at this guy like he's an idiot and then turns to the baggage handlers and says, "Just get these bags on the plane. It's already an hour late because of all this bullshit. It'll be nearly two hours late by the time the plane takes off."

These guys were a little gentler putting me on the new plane. Shortly after they stuffed me in the front cargo hold, I heard one of the handlers say, "Shit, the cop with the dog is here." They all looked back at the cop and the dog. "Oh, well, too late now." One of them was laughing as the door closed, and shortly after that, I began my trip to London.

My life ended—along with everyone above me—about an hour from London. I was obliterated and felt nothing.

It's time to commit - *February 14, 1973*

Darcy Byrne started to listen to CBC radio at just before four in the morning, knowing that it would take time for news of the bombing to reach the airwaves. He created a cloud of cigarette smoke and drank multiple coffees until, just before seven, the CBC interrupted programming with breaking news about a plane that had crashed off the coast of Ireland. Initially, Byrne was confused. 'The bomb was supposed to explode at Heathrow,' he thought. This meant that everyone on board the plane had perished—not the intended outcome, but one that just might serve the cause better than the explosion of a bomb-laden suitcase as it circled the baggage-area conveyor belt in London. The original plan was to kill a few employees and seriously damage the BOAC and Heathrow infrastructure. Now Byrne and his conspirators had sent a much bolder message.

Soon after the news broke, his phone started to ring. Each time he picked up and said, "If you have something to say, come to the house." Everyone complied except Owen Ryan, who Byrne had to shut down, assuming the line was still being monitored by the authorities.

By eight, he was sitting in his living room with Ryan, Collin Boyle, and Paddy and Eamon Kerrigan. Things were quiet for the most part. They watched the news on a small television set. CBC was providing news bulletins—coverage that consisted of news anchors reading updates from the AP and Reuters wires, since it was too soon to broadcast actual visuals of the crash scene. When the news anchor bailed out for regular programming, Byrne got up and turned off the TV.

"All right, it's done. We've opened the second front," Byrne said in an even, dispassionate tone.

Ryan had a fanatical smile on his face, while Boyle and the Kerrigans looked like they had seen a ghost. Boyle was the first to speak up.

"Darcy," he took in a breath and let out a stressful sigh, "the plan was to plant a bomb on a plane that would detonate in England. My understanding was that the goal here was property damage with limited loss of life."

Byrne got up from his chair and spoke to everyone, ensuring he looked into the face of each man. "There is the plan, and then there is the operational result. I don't need to explain the result to any of you, because it is clear what happened over the Celtic Sea." He paused before continuing. "The results are bold, aggressive, and clear. The Provisional IRA, both on the island and in the diaspora, are to be taken seriously. This will inspire others to plot similar attacks. God willing, this is the start of a campaign that will lead to Irish unification, the removal of the occupying British forces, and the subjugation of the Ulster loyalists. If you can't see the significance of this moment in history, then I don't think you're paying attention."

"Limited loss of life," Boyle repeated.

Byrne lost his temper. "Oh, for fuck's sake, Collin! We put a bomb on a fucking plane! What did you think was going to happen? Everything would work out, and some lacky would get incinerated tossing the bag onto a conveyor belt? Or some customer service agent would be looking for the idiot who forgot to pick up his suitcase, and the bomb would blow up in his Saxon face? You…" Byrne pointed first at Boyle, then at everyone in the room. "You all had to know that this was a potential outcome. And here we are, the group of gentlemen who made it happen. Bloody Sunday is avenged one-hundredfold, and now the British are going to be scared shitless everywhere they go."

The mood in the room was heavy. Paddy Kerrigan was staring blankly at a spot on the wall while his son sat with his head buried in his hands. Collin Boyle cast an angry look at Darcy Byrne, who refused to make eye contact with him. Only Owen Ryan seemed pleased—even more pleased than Byrne.

"This is it, gentlemen. The die is cast. Don't mourn the dead on the plane, because we haven't been given the time to mourn *our* dead since this deplorable occupation started with Cromwell in 1649. Over three hundred years! A few people dying on an aircraft hardly makes up for the ongoing atrocities our people have faced."

More silence.

"It's time to commit to the preservation of this group and the plan we've enacted. None of us is any more innocent than the other. We must all commit to protecting each other from here on in. Everything has worked out for us so far. We were able to detect and work around the surveillance of the authorities. We were able to test, construct, deliver, and detonate a bomb onboard a British aircraft. And now, we will protect each other at all costs. Agreed?" Byrne looked around the room.

Ryan was the first to answer, as if there was only one obvious response: "Agreed."

Boyle was next. He knew that the money trail would eventually lead back to him. He needed to accept the situation and live with it. "Agreed."

Paddy Kerrigan, still staring at the wall was next, speaking numbly, "Agreed."

A despondent Eamon Kerrigan remained silent. Byrne got his attention by snapping his fingers. "Eamon?"

He looked up and, through bloodshot eyes, mumbled, "Agreed."

CHAPTER 8:
IT GETS WORSE

What's our exposure? - *February 14, 1973*

Patrick Keenan thought he was going to have a heart attack. The phone rang a little before seven in the morning while he was at the kitchen table, reading the newspaper and sipping his coffee. It wasn't the phone ringing that shocked him; it was the dire message delivered by the caller. The voice on the other end of the phone was Sergeant Dawson.

"Get to the office ASAP. A passenger plane that left Toronto yesterday evening has crashed."

"Which airline?" Keenan asked, fearing the worst.

"BOAC. Bound for London. We expect the entire team to be here within the hour. Understood?"

"Yes, sir," Keenan replied, shock reverberating through his response.

He hung up the phone and stood silently.

"Who was that?" his wife called out from the upstairs bedroom.

"I have to get to work," he answered as he rushed through the hallway and into the bedroom to get dressed.

He was at the office well within the hour given to him. Millington and Dawson were already in the conference room, pinning sheets of paper up on the bulletin board and writing messages on the chalkboard. They looked at Keenan as if in a daze as he came into the room. "Morning," they said to each other, sharing a ritual that defied the gravity of the situation.

When Keenan retreated to his desk to get some of his files, Belwood and Maloney showed up, glancing at the conference room. They shared a shocked look that said *"disaster"* before they all headed into the room around the same time.

While the others were getting organized, Stratford came in, coat still on but a notepad and pen in his hand. "Any word from Nugent?" Dawson asked.

"Nugent's on vacation, sir. Two weeks in Mexico," Stratford responded, eyes down, clearly uncomfortable.

"Okay, let's start," Staff Sergeant Millington said, remembering that he had authorized the trip.

Millington was shuffling papers when he started speaking.

"How exposed are we, gentlemen?"

No one answered. If they understood the question correctly, a passenger plane had just been blown to bits, and their emergency meeting was going to deal with the RCMP Security Service's ... *exposure*?

Dawson, as second-in-command, decided he should be the one to respond. "Staff Sergeant Millington, I am not sure about the idea of exposure. Shouldn't we put our efforts into seeing what information we need to share with the Criminal Branch?"

"No, Sergeant. Today, we will begin our discussion by examining our exposure as a special-investigation team that was looking into the activities of potential terrorists at a time when they managed to blow up a fucking plane on our watch!" Millington said firmly. His tone indicated a bottled-up anger that, if prodded further, would completely explode. "And don't any of you dare say *'they're calling it a crash at this point,'* because we all know that's bullshit, and the fucking plane was bombed."

Dawson looked at Millington almost in disbelief. He shifted his attention to some papers in front of him, reluctant to make eye contact, and started to give his staff sergeant the information he thought he needed to hear. "Well, sir, we are the RCMP Security Service, working independently of the law enforcement side of the RCMP. As an intelligence service, we are charged with examining and protecting national security interests. We have no exposure if we choose *not* to share information pertinent to the criminal investigation, provided that *not* sharing the information is in the nation's interests. Are we positioning ourselves to not share information in the interests of national security?" Dawson said this with a passive-aggressive level of disdain in his voice.

"Sergeant, I don't need a lecture on how the Security Service operates in relation to the RCMP Criminal Branch. I also don't need a civics lesson on our moral responsibility to share information with criminal investigators. As your superior, I can assure you, and the rest of the men in this room, that I will make the decisions that I deem fit moving forward, and any challenges will be deemed insubordination."

He let the message sink in. The service agents were in shock.

"Exposure, gentlemen. What do we have? How does it make us look? Maloney, let's start with you."

Maloney cleared his throat and started speaking. "Staff Sergeant, I was unable to get close enough to the group likely responsible for the downing of this aircraft to say definitively that they are the ones who did it. However, judging by the activities of the group and my observations from the week prior to being reassigned to the Soviet target, I believed that something was imminent. I communicated this to you and Sergeant Dawson prior to being reassigned—"

"Where's the report, inspector?" Millington cut in.

Maloney looked at him with a surprised expression. "I reported this to you verbally, sir."

"Not much for paperwork are you, Maloney?"

The silence in the room was deafening. The two men glared at each other. Maloney's anger and humiliation gave him the strength to hold his gaze. Millington was driven by an unrelenting desire to maintain his dominance of the room and the men in it. He was succeeding.

"Stratford, how exposed are we when it comes to Eamon Kerrigan?"

Stratford was finishing a smoke when Millington asked the question. His hand was shaking as he butted out the cigarette in the ashtray in front of him. "Well, sir, my partner has been the main handler when it comes to Kerrigan. However, my observation is that he was providing enough information to keep us engaged, but not enough information to reveal a conspiracy to blow up a plane."

Dawson stepped in. "Do you think he was working both sides? Tipping off the conspirators while distracting us?"

Millington didn't let Stratford answer. "The agent's message was clear—nothing that indicates a conspiracy to blow up a plane."

Dawson was in a daze. What the hell was happening? The Staff Sergeant was shaping the message to suit his needs. Was he trying to preserve the 'integrity' of the Security Service, and save his own skin in the process?

"Surveillance. Our exposure?" Millington went on.

Keenan spoke up. "Staff Sergeant, we are greatly exposed when it comes to surveillance, because we have a wealth of material that could be used as evidence against the perpetrators—"

"Exposure is our focus, agent," Millington interrupted again,

Keenan looked down, nervously shuffling the papers in front of him. "Sir, we have hours of audiotape from the phone

My Father's Secret

conversations emanating from Foley's, Nova Star, and the homes of Boyle and Byrne. We have Watcher Service reports that identify the movements of the key figures in this attack. As far as something definitive—"

"Good, no smoking gun."

Keenan spoke up, not out of defiance but out of a mistaken belief that Millington was missing the point. "Sir, we know with a near one hundred percent certainty that Byrne, Ryan, Boyle, and a few others are the one's responsible for the downing of this aircraft. We knew they were up to something. We chased the Prince Charles theory, and that proved false, thank God. We noticed a ramping up of action prior to the anniversary of Bloody Sunday, and when that passed, we were relieved that nothing had happened. However, as we reported to you recently, the activity of the group, after stalling for about a week after the Bloody Sunday anniversary, began to intensify. When you pulled us off the Irish file to pursue the Soviet target, we postulated that something imminent might be on the horizon."

Millington responded, "And the written report outlining all this, Agent Keenan?"

Keenan was back to fumbling with the papers in front of him. "No formal operational report, sir…" Then he appeared to find something as he leafed through a file and pulled out a sheet of paper. "… but I did submit this threat assessment to you the day before we were reassigned to the Soviet target."

"Let me see that," Millington said roughly. As he was reading the report, a slight look of panic settled on his face. Finally, he asked, "How many copies of this threat assessment do you have?"

Keenan looked up at him suspiciously. "There were three copies made, sir. One for you, one for Sergeant Dawson, and one for my files. You are holding my copy."

"Fine, thank you, Agent," Millington said, putting the threat assessment in a file folder in front of him.

The collective disorientation of the men in the room was palpable. The silence gave way to rapid, confused thinking on the part of the agents. *Were they about to bury the evidence?*

Millington brought their attention back, "Next steps, gentlemen." He stopped to clear his throat. "This is our operational headquarters for the foreseeable future. I want every file, every tape, every bit of information we have on Byrne and his associates brought into this room. We are going to review everything scrupulously to see what information should be shared with the Criminal Branch. Stratford, you'll be heading downtown to get any Watcher Service reports relevant to our inquiry. This is the team; no one else will be joining us. We need to keep our circle tight, and leaks of any kind will not be tolerated."

Millington was a powerful Security Service officer. If he asked for cooperation and obedience, he'd get it, because a transfer to Whitehorse, Prince George, or Labrador City awaited anyone who got out of line. They had all known this when they started working for him. His reputation for assertive revenge was legendary among Service Mounties.

He wrapped up the meeting. "A terrible tragedy has occurred. Obviously, we bear some responsibility because our intelligence skills eluded us, and a group of Irish extremists were able to bring down a plane right under our noses. We need to get to the bottom of this. Now go and start gathering your files. And get them back in here, so I can review them expeditiously. Dismissed."

The agents slowly stood and exited the room.

The meeting seemed to take on two lives: the *exposure* life and the *information-gathering* life. What were they going to do? Save their own asses or share the evidence that would help in the prosecution of the men who'd brought down BOAC Flight 281?

The legend of Darcy Byrne: *Rejection - February 1973*

Darcy Byrne went to Foley's that Valentine's Day to gauge the mood of the Irish-Canadian community—at least the more extreme members who hung out at that particular pub. He arrived around five and sat at his usual booth. By this time, the media was already reporting that the plane must have been bombed. There was no way a plane in descent and heading for Heathrow, after seven hours in the air, was going to suddenly explode without any mayday signals or alerts being shared with air-traffic control. The pub was full of the usual suspects. The plan was to have dinner and share a few conversations with the regulars to see what the patrons thought of the events of the day.

Byrne was joined by Owen Ryan, who was still invigorated, overjoyed that they had been able to pull it off. But as he and Byrne made their way around the pub, the feelings among the patrons were mixed. Some were speaking openly about how good this was for republicanism in Ireland while others were mute. No one was really coming out against the downing of the aircraft, but the silence of roughly half of the people Byrne and Ryan spoke to was very telling indeed.

As the evening wore on, people shifted from the news of the bombing and just settled in for a typical night of drinking. At one point, Byrne and Ryan waved Paddy Kerrigan and Collin Boyle over to their booth. Eamon Kerrigan sat at the bar, sulking into his drink.

The four sat across from each other and shared a bottle of Irish whiskey along with some discussion.

"What are you hearing?" Byrne asked.

"Mixed reviews to be honest, Darcy," Paddy Kerrigan responded. "A lot of the people here could give a shit about what happened. Others are stirred up, but not as many as I would have thought."

"Agreed," said Boyle. "I thought this crowd would rally around the bombing of the plane. I guess, because so many people died, they're a little reticent."

Darcy Byrne took a drag of cigarette before saying, "Reticent, eh? That's a shame, Collin."

The men spent the remainder of the evening together, finishing the first bottle of whiskey and following it with another. Combine that intake with a few pints and they were so inebriated that Foley had to drive them home at closing time.

Byrne was the last one to be dropped off. As he was getting out of the car, he slurred a goodbye to Quinn Foley before adding, "We did a good thing for the united republic today, Quinn. Maybe those fuckers will get the fuck out now." Darcy Byrne would have no recollection of ever saying these words. Quinn Foley would never forget them.

The next morning, Byrne drove to the Country Style Donuts down the street from his house. It was another freezing February day in Toronto, but the sunshine helped take the edge off a bit. Byrne's hangover warmed him up a little as well. He bought a coffee and doughnut before heading to the pay phone outside. He dialed the number of a friend in Armagh who could get a message to Dylan Costello, his old commander in the South Armagh Brigade. The message was simple: "Beyond giving you money, I made myself useful yesterday morning."

Byrne was certain Costello would grasp the reference. Confirmation of this thought came the next morning when his phone rang at home.

"Darcy? It's Dylan. Do you have time for a chat?" Costello asked.

"I'll have to call you. Can you head to our mutual friend's place? The one who gave you the message."

"I can be there in fifteen minutes," Costello said.

"Good," Byrne replied. "I'll be talking to you shortly."

My Father's Secret

And so back to the Country Style Donuts pay phone Darcy Byrne went. He was ready to receive the accolades owing to a conquering hero. He had shown the bravery of an IRA soldier and sent a message that was arguably the loudest and most forceful of the Troubles to date.

The operator connected the call. Dylan Costello was the first to talk.

"Well, Darcy, it appears you'd like to tell me something," Costello said, sounding a little tense.

"I think the news speaks for itself, Dylan," Byrne replied.

Costello sighed. "Spell it out for me, please."

Byrne was confused. Why wasn't Costello congratulating him on the success of his renegade mission?

"Well, Dylan ... a plane was bombed by an IRA cell out of Toronto—"

"I'm going to stop you right there," Costello interrupted. "The IRA exists in Ireland, is headquartered in Ireland, and gives orders from Ireland. What you've done is considered an *'off the books attack'* on civilians living abroad. The IRA can, in no way, be associated with what you've done, Darcy. Am I making myself clear?"

Confusion gave way to anger, "You know what, Dylan? I don't get it. First of all, I was your best friend when I was funnelling money to you to buy guns and explosives, so much so that you sent Jimmy O'Connor over here to help me with explosives training. Second, the IRA set off more than a thousand bombs last year, killing many—including Catholic republicans who happened to be in the wrong place at the wrong time—and these collective bombings are declared operational successes. I take down a *plane*—an asset of the British colonial regime—and you tell me it can't be associated with the IRA!" Byrne's breathing was laboured, his anger taking over his entire body. "Why aren't you telling the boys in Belfast to jump for joy? The second front is opened. I did it. You asked me to do something useful, and I did just that."

Costello listened patiently, though his anger was on the rise as well. Byrne needed to be handled. There was a direct link between the man he had ostracized—basically banished—to Toronto and his own command in South Armagh.

"Darcy, it's been over a day since this plane went down. Have you been reading the press? The aircraft was loaded with *Canadians* going to London, some on business, many for pleasure. Thirty of the passengers were part of a school group going on a pilgrimage to the Globe Theatre to honour William Shakespeare. They were no more than seventeen-years-old, Darcy! The press is also reporting that you killed three babies and their mothers and fathers on that plane. A total of twenty-two passengers were British citizens. Twenty-two … of three hundred and twenty-nine! This is not coming together as a legitimate IRA attack; it's coming off as mass murder, plain and simple."

Byrne started to slump in the phone booth, his head pressed against the cold glass, the chill of the Canadian winter starting to get into his bones. Only the heat of his anger was keeping the cold at bay.

"I suppose it's all how you tell the story, Dylan," he finally said.

Another pause.

"You cannot say this was IRA, Darcy."

More silence.

"Are you still there?" Costello asked. "I need you to tell me that you understand what I'm saying, so I can tell Joe Cahill and Seamus Twomey that you have received the message."

Now Costello was issuing a direct threat. He was invoking the names of the IRA leadership in Belfast to let Byrne know that, if he didn't comply, he was as good as dead.

"I got your fucking message, Dylan. So just fuck off!" Byrne responded, slamming the phone onto the receiver repeatedly until the earpiece broke.

There would be no credit for Darcy Byrne in the eyes of the IRA. He'd officially been cut loose.

Maybe you should do it - *February 1973*

The repeated knocking on his door jarred Byrne awake. He checked the watch on his bedside table. 'It's three-thirty in the morning, for Christ's sake! Who the hell could that be?' The woman he had invited to his bed began to stir, and he told her to stay put. She continued to stir as he got up. "Seriously, don't leave this bed." He headed downstairs.

When he opened the front door, he encountered a distraught and intoxicated Eamon Kerrigan. Byrne gestured for him to remain quiet and led him into his living room.

Kerrigan was breathing heavily—the strained, exaggerated breathing of someone who was very drunk. Clearly the liquor had settled into his system.

Byrne motioned for him to sit in a chair, the same chair he had sat in the day of the bombing, and pulled up a chair for himself from the adjacent dining room, sitting down and leaning forward, almost knee to knee with the young man.

"What's troubling you, Eamon?" Byrne asked.

Tears welled up in Kerrigan's eyes. "I can't take it, Darcy. The pressure. The act I have to put on for those RCMP fucks. The secrets. The guilt."

Byrne sat up. "A troubled young man, indeed."

After a moment, he stood up and made his way to a small bar table where he poured himself a drink.

"I imagine you've had enough of this," Byrne said, holding the glass up to Kerrigan, who dropped his head into his hands.

"That's an all-too-common pose for you these days, Eamon," he said, slumping his shoulders to mimic Kerrigan's posture. "It is the gesture of a man defeated, resting your weary head in your hands."

Kerrigan said nothing.

"Pressure. Secrets. Guilt," Byrne said, leaning against a wall. "I understand the pressure. It's the secrets and the guilt that I'm curious about." He tipped his whiskey glass in Kerrigan's direction before taking a drink. "Tell me a little about that."

Kerrigan's thoughts moved like a slow-motion, stupefied movie about the misery of his own life. "Secrets," he whispered.

"Sure, Eamon. Let's start there."

More silence as the movie continued to play in Kerrigan's head. Drunkenness, theft, deception, violence, promiscuity.

"I think I need your help," Kerrigan said quietly. "I've been taking money from my godfather's company. It's been a little over a year now. I did it out of resentment. I thought I deserved it."

"This poses a significant family problem for you," Byrne said. "Is this why you have taken so earnestly to the drink, Eamon?"

Kerrigan looked up, "Partly."

"And what's the other part?"

Kerrigan was silent.

"Does it have anything to do with your preference for the fellas?" Byrne asked.

Kerrigan looked up, revealing a painful, shocked expression.

"Eamon, your lack of feminine attachment has been noted by some. I, for one, know more than you think."

"Does my father know?" Kerrigan asked, panicking.

"Not for now."

Kerrigan was too afraid to pursue exactly what Byrne meant by this response.

Byrne swallowed the rest of his whiskey and laid the glass down loudly on a nearby table.

"Eamon, is your guilt related exclusively to the theft of the money from your godfather and your ... social life?"

Now, the tears started streaming down the young man's face. His body heaved as if a deep remorse was rising up from the depths of his soul. "We killed all those people," he said through the quiet weeping. "We killed all those people."

"Indeed, we did," Byrne responded calmly, lighting a cigarette. "Eamon, you have served a greater good. This is about the liberation of an oppressed people. You did your part."

"I feel terrible about the part I played."

"How terrible?"

More hesitation as the rat's wheel spun relentlessly in Kerrigan's head. Then he responded: "Like I don't deserve to live." The loud whisper cut through the tears, as though Eamon Kerrigan was struggling to say words that were trapped in his body by some breathless shame.

"I see. Are you saying you want to kill yourself?"

Byrne took a slow, deliberate drag on his cigarette. Kerrigan didn't answer.

Byrne put his cigarette in a nearby ashtray and moved back to the seat across from Kerrigan. He leaned toward him, kissed his tear-soaked cheek, and whispered, "Maybe you should do it."

Byrne got up and went to the foyer, picking up his cigarette along the way. He motioned to Kerrigan. It was time for him to leave. Kerrigan, the very embodiment of defeat, got up slowly, made his way toward the foyer, and straight out the front door.

As Byrne watched him leave from the living-room window, he hoped the young man would do it soon. Eamon Kerrigan was the weak link. If the conspiracy was to fall apart, it would be because of his inability to hold it together. The fact that he was gay was the least of Byrne's concerns. The fact that he might—in a fit of misplaced conscience— reveal the inner workings of the plan to open a second front for the Provos was the real concern.

If Eamon Kerrigan didn't kill himself soon, Byrne would have to make other arrangements to permanently silence the young man. He butted out his cigarette in the ashtray and went back to bed.

They're burying it - *February 1973*

The Security Service men gathered the files, tapes, and other evidence that had become the mainstay of the Irish Desk for over a year and placed them in the Toronto Airport Detachment conference room. Millington vowed to pass along anything that the criminal investigators would need. Mike Nugent, who had rushed back from his Mexican vacation, was his go-to man through the entire process. Anything that came into the room went directly into the hands of one of the two men. Evidence was dropped off, separated into files and tapes and photographs, logged on the staff sergeant's clipboard, and left with either Nugent or Millington (mostly Nugent, because Millington had so many other responsibilities within the detachment). The items were then placed into Security Service storage boxes.

A few days into this process, Belwood shared an observation with Keenan. He was sitting at his desk and looking over at the conference room. Nugent was shuffling some of the files into one of the boxes.

"Does it strike you as odd, Patrick?" Belwood asked.

Keenan, buried in papers at his desk, replied, "What are you talking about, Warren?"

"Well, we gather evidence. We bring it into that room," Belwood said, pointing at the conference room. "It gets catalogued and sorted, but none of it has been shared with the Criminal Branch."

"You don't know what Millington has shared," Keenan said. "Do you think we should ask what we can do to help with the sharing of information?"

Belwood hesitated before responding. "Why would we have to ask? This is pretty straightforward. Share the evidence and charge the bastards who brought down the plane. In fact, the relevant information should have already been shared with the Criminal Branch."

Keenan was confused. "That's got to be what Millington is doing. He's just getting a proper file together to seal the deal on the people who did this."

That idea, though he'd shared it with such certainty, didn't sit quite right with Patrick Keenan. Maybe Belwood had planted a seed. Doubt was sprouting in his mind. A nagging feeling enveloped him, and so he worked late that evening. When everyone on the Irish Desk team was gone, he accessed the conference room. What he discovered shocked him.

Keenan and Belwood had recorded hours and hours of tapes that could bring the conspirators to justice. He decided to go straight to the boxes that held the tapes, but when he opened the first box, it was empty. The second, third, and fourth boxes, the same story. Empty. Where the hell were the tapes?

Next, he shifted to the files. While not as barren as the tape boxes, they held scant information, mostly related to the man who they believed had built the bomb: Cathal O'Dwyer. Where were the other files? He had to believe that they had already been passed along to the Criminal Branch. There were three or four files that hadn't been handled by Millington or Nugent yet. Keenan opened one of them and saw some photos, a few Watcher Service reports and the threat assessment Millington had taken from him on the day of the bombing. He looked around. The detachment was practically empty; only a few agents were reviewing things at the Satellite and Soviet Desks, and the night custodian was emptying the trash bins. He pulled a few items out of the files, walked across the office to the mail room, and put what he had taken into the Irish Desk mail bin, amidst the other material that hadn't been processed while the team was pursuing the Soviet target. Then he went back to his desk, gathered his things, and left the detachment in a daze. His suspicious mind kept him from sleeping soundly that night.

The next morning, he knocked on the conference room door as Millington and Nugent filtered through the evidence, clipboard in hand.

"Excuse me," Keenan asked. "Just wondering how it's going, Staff Sergeant."

Millington looked at Keenan incredulously. "What do you mean, Agent?"

"In terms of the information sharing, sir. The tapes, the files, the other evidence. I am wondering how soon we can expect to hear that they are charging Byrne and the other conspirators."

Millington responded, clearly annoyed. "Patrick, this is not something you need to be concerned about. Let us catalogue the information and share it at the appropriate time."

"Apologies, sir," Keenan said sheepishly. "I was just trying to gauge the status of…" His voice trailed off for a moment. "So, nothing has been shared yet?"

Nugent, always impulsive, responded, "We haven't shared a goddamn thing yet, Keenan. Can't you see all these fuckin' boxes? Now get the hell out of here, and let us sort this shit out."

That's when he knew that they were definitively up to no good.

My Father's Secret

He went back to his desk and said to Belwood, "They're burying it."

Belwood shot a glance at the conference room before turning to Keenan. "What?"

"They're sorting through the evidence and burying most of it. Our tapes are gone," Keenan said in a whisper. "Let's talk about it at lunch. We can't discuss anything here."

They arranged to meet well away from the Toronto Airport Detachment, at The Canadiana Restaurant in Six Points Plaza. Keenan knew the place and trusted that they could speak openly there. They sat in an isolated booth a good distance away from the bar and with no one at the adjacent tables. After they ordered their drinks, and the waiter took their food order, Patrick Keenan told Warren Belwood about his adventure the previous night.

"So, the tapes are gone?" Belwood asked.

"I am not sure if all of them are gone, but the boxes I checked were empty."

"Jesus Christ." It was Belwood's turn to be shocked. "And the files?"

"I could only find the ones dealing with Cathal O'Dwyer. I was in there for about ten minutes and then thought it best to get out before the night owls working one of the other Desks noticed me and asked me what I was doing."

The two men sat in silence. This seemed way too surreal.

"What can we do?" asked Belwood.

"Chain of command dictates that we defer to Millington," Keenan responded.

Belwood nodded, hesitantly. "Defying the staff sergeant is a career killer."

More silence. More murky surrealism.

"I'm not sure I can live with this," Keenan said.

∙ ∙ ∙

Earlier that morning, Millington had found a note on his desk from the night custodian.

Saw a man in the big room last evening.
Sits at the desk by the window (third desk from the entrance).

That was enough for Millington to know that Keenan was sticking his nose where it didn't belong.

So, when Keenan popped his head into the conference room and started asking questions, the staff sergeant knew he needed to accelerate the plan. Millington's superiors, while not explicitly ordering him to make sure the reputation of the Security Service wasn't tarnished by the Flight 281 bombing, did direct him to be very selective with what he shared with the Criminal Branch. If a piece of information even hinted at being a national security issue, it was not to be shared. The takeaway for Millington was that the Canadian people could not be exposed to the idea that the Security Service might have let a terrorist attack happen while the suspects were under surveillance. The staff sergeant, always a good soldier and a fanatical defender of the chain of command, read between the lines, understood the directive, and started to sort the evidence in a manner that would bring as little embarrassment to the Security Service as possible. He'd need help, and Mike Nugent, though crass and vulgar, was the best man for the job. Nugent was cunning and ambitious enough to understand what was being asked of him. He would also understand the transactional nature of his participation, knowing that there would be benefits for him in the future.

Millington and Nugent had already sorted most of the files, removing them from the investigation file boxes and putting them into the archive boxes that he planned to ship to remote locations across the country. The tapes were another matter; there were so many of them, and they were bulky. He had Nugent take them to the basement to be erased by the tech department. After Keenan's not-so-subtle visit, Millington went to the head of the tech department to make sure the erasing of the Irish Desk tapes would be given priority. Once they were wiped, the tapes needed to be relabelled and put back into circulation, as if they'd never existed.

Of course, Keenan had figured out what they were up to the previous evening, and he knew he also needed to move fast. They were burying the evidence too quickly. What they didn't factor in was the file Keenan had moved and the new batch of tapes and documents that were still sitting in the Irish Desk mail bin, waiting for Keenan and Belwood to process.

That's when Patrick Keenan did something that could not only cost him his job but also land him in prison. He careful scoped the area around the mail room before making his move. He had emptied his briefcase prior to coming into the office that morning, and with it, he went to the Irish Desk mail bin and packed ten reel-to-reel tapes, a few photos, and a small collection of documents into the attaché. That night, he would listen to the tapes on the reel-to-reel player he had in his study, sort through the photos, and read the documents. He'd dub the most important tapes onto cassette and put the most important photos and documents to the side. If Keenan had his way, they weren't going to bury everything.

He did it - *February 1973*

Eamon Kerrigan drove to Danforth and Broadview at around nine o'clock at night. The last week or so had been a period of relentless torment. He'd been played for a fool, by both the RCMP and Darcy

Byrne. And as time passed, he'd come to the following conclusion: 'They played you for a fool because you are a fool.'

He had been drinking steadily since the bombing of the plane. He did whatever he needed to do to maintain the buzz, to suppress the pain, and to avoid waking up to the misery. With each passing day, it took more booze, which he complemented with quaaludes and weed. He hadn't been back to work. His father was concerned but couldn't get through to him. Eamon Kerrigan descended further and further into the darkness, creating a hell for himself that he felt he deserved to inhabit.

As he sat in his car, he watched people moving about. Some had just finished dinner and were heading to their cars. Others were just arriving. The Danforth had its usual vibrance—restaurants, bars, coffee shops—a place of pleasant escape.

The twenty-sixer of Jim Beam was almost gone. A functioning alcoholic like Eamon Kerrigan would need to get deep into a second twenty-sixer to really feel inebriated. His eyes were glossy from the booze and the tears. He had helped kill three hundred and twenty-nine people. It didn't matter that he hadn't known he was helping until the deed was done. He was also a liar and a thief—hiding his sexuality in the closet and stealing from his kin. Even before the bombing, he had hated himself; the bombing just confirmed and highlighted that hate.

He surveyed the area. It was time. He took a final swig from the bottle, downing four quaaludes in the process, and got out of the car. The drugs wouldn't have enough time to take effect.

He walked west from the intersection, looking back at the Charger, and thinking, 'I left the car running,' before continuing on the path to his fate.

The Bloor Viaduct was busy for a Sunday. That really didn't concern Eamon; he was just observing both the east and west flow of cars moving along the five-lane bridge. It was a cold night with a few flurries starting to fall as he approached the mid-point of the bridge. He stopped and rested his back against the concrete. 'This is it,' he thought. 'This is my release. A permanent solution.' A car honked its horn as another sped past. 'Road rage. My last encounter with humanity,' Eamon Kerrigan thought. He even allowed for a half smile.

"All right," he said aloud before quickly climbing the barrier and launching himself into the air. Gravity did its work, and a few seconds later, Eamon Kerrigan had accomplished what he had come to the Bloor Viaduct to do.

Owen Ryan was not far behind Kerrigan when he'd gone over. He looked down to see the man's body splayed out on the highway below. Cars began screeching to a stop. Ryan just turned around and headed to the nearest pay phone. Darcy Byrne picked up on the fourth ring.

"He did it," Ryan said.

After a few seconds, Byrne said, "Okay."

"A bridge."

"No need for details," Byrne said, hanging up the phone.

A perfectionist and a narcissist - *November 27, 2003*

Karuna and I headed to Redmund's that evening to discuss my meeting with John Bakersmith. Of course, Karuna and I had already reviewed everything, and we had our own ideas, but in many ways, Redmund seemed to be the conductor of this particular orchestra, and we wanted to make sure we were all in sync.

We arrived, and in typical Jack Redmund style, he gave us a distracted greeting and led us to his gizmo-laden, anti-surveillance vault of an office. We sat down, and I told him how it had gone with Bakersmith. Karuna and I had decided to keep my afternoon dream out of the conversation.

He leaned back in his wheelchair. "So he went to Millington with the CSE threat assessment." It was like a minor revelation.

"What can you tell us about Gord Millington?" Karuna asked. "You might have mentioned him in your book but—"

"He was the head of the RCMP Security Service's Irish Desk back in 1973. Actually, he was in charge of all of the Desks, since he was the staff sergeant for the detachment. He held the position until he retired in 1976." Redmund began rummaging through a filing cabinet beside his desk.

"He was a pretty tenacious leader. He got results, but the people who worked for him didn't have a lot of positive things to say about him. His military background fit well when he transitioned into the RCMP command structure. The higher-ups liked his no-nonsense, win-at-all-costs approach to handling his subordinates."

"Military background?" I asked.

"Yeah. World War Two and Korea," Redmund answered, opening a file. "He was part of the D-Day invasion in 1944 and stayed in the military as an officer after the war. He served for the entire Korean conflict—from the amphibious landing on the Korean peninsula in 1950 to the withdrawal of troops in 1953. He was a commander of one of the regiments of the Princess Patricia Light Infantry, the Princess Pats. These guys were part of a contingent that slowed down the North Korean advance in Kapyong Valley in April 1951. He left the military to take a leadership post in the RCMP Security Service in 1955."

Redmund continued leafing through the file. "Spotless record really. Like I said, not very well liked by the people I talked to back in the seventies, but very well respected in the Security Service."

"An unblemished record." Karuna had something on her mind. "Then BOAC goes down a few years before he retires."

Redmund and I let that sink in before she added, "A bit of a perfectionist? With a hint of narcissism, maybe? I'm just trying to reconcile the fact that we are coming across evidence that he should have shared with the criminal investigators back in 1973."

"So," I said, "Millington might be the link to the tapes and the documents. I know they came from my dad, but he somehow acquired them without Millington's knowledge."

It was Jack Redmund's turn to speculate. "The funny thing is that the criminal investigators were vilified for bringing only Cathal O'Dwyer to justice. They were accused of incompetence, but they'd long maintained that there was more out there—information that wasn't being shared with them. Certainly, there were suspicions when it came to Byrne and Boyle and the others. If there weren't, I wouldn't have had a book to write. Then that CSIS clerk opened the file boxes in Moose Jaw in 1985. That's when people took a harder look at the conspiracy to bring down Flight 281."

A discovery in Moose Jaw - *April 1985*

How the files had come to be in Moose Jaw was a bit of a mystery. Adam Schultz, a new agent helping to set up the Saskatchewan CSIS field office for the Ontario North/Prairies Division, was sifting through boxes that had been transported from the now defunct RCMP Security Service a few months earlier. It was a shitty job. Most of the stuff was old junk that the Security Service just kept in storage vaults at various detachments. But there was an outside chance, Schultz figured, that some national-security nugget might be in one of the boxes. As an ambitious and meticulous CSIS operative, new to the organization, he wondered if the contents of the boxes could help him make an impression with his bosses. However, when it came right down to it, he didn't have a choice; his supervisors told him he had a week to work through the more than four hundred storage containers and destroy the items that were no longer relevant.

It was day three when he came across the two archive boxes marked *Toronto Airport Detachment*. He wondered what files from Toronto were doing in Saskatchewan, but he'd been encountering surprises (mostly deadly boring surprises) for a few days. He popped open box number one. It contained Watcher Service reports, complete with narrative accounts and logistical information. Box number two was filled with random documents, mostly invoices and work orders—nothing of consequence at a glance. However, something about the first box seemed intriguing, and Schultz was drawn back to it. He started reading through the Watcher Service reports. He was about fifteen minutes into his review when he came across a report written by agents William Short and Heather Jansen from August 1972. The report talked about a high-powered rifle being fired near a farm in Severn, Ontario. This is not what caught Schultz's attention. He sat right up when he read the name Cathal O'Dwyer, the BOAC Flight 281 bomber. Then he saw the name Darcy Byrne, the alleged mastermind behind the bombing. While O'Dwyer had gone to jail for the bombing, authorities were never able to charge Byrne with anything. Here was a document that linked O'Dwyer and Byrne. This was huge.

Here's what Schultz didn't know: No one was ever supposed to discover the two boxes from Toronto that had wound up in Moose Jaw. In an effort to hide the fact that the RCMP Security Service had completely missed a national security threat, Staff Sergeant Gordon Millington and his lacky, Agent Mike Nugent, had put the most incriminating evidence into file boxes and shipped them across the country. Some wound up in Halifax, others in Lethbridge, one even made it to Yellowknife—and, of course, two had made their way to Moose Jaw. All the file boxes were labelled INACTIVE/ARCHIVE, and as per procedure, were shipped for storage in detachment vaults. What was unusual was that they were being stored thousands of kilometres away from where they'd originated.

Staff Sergeant Millington had signed off on every shipment, which lent the move some credibility. He'd also personally called each detachment and asked if he could send some archive material their way due to a flood at his Toronto precinct. When they'd arrived at their destinations, they'd been put in the appropriate archive storage room, with all the security you'd expect, in a vault that could only be accessed by the leadership at the RCMP detachment. These were the nation's secrets after all.

What Millington didn't expect was that the RCMP Security Service would be disbanded in 1984 and replaced by the Canadian Security and Intelligence Service. The new leadership wanted to vet the files, pare them down, and computerize the ones that remained relevant. CSIS personnel across Canada were charged with this tedious, though important, task. While most of the files that wound up in Moose Jaw were simply discounted and destroyed, those two boxes had stood out for the curious clerk in Saskatchewan.

When Schultz came along that fateful spring day, he exposed fresh evidence that implicated O'Dwyer (who was already in prison for building the bomb), Darcy Byrne, and Collin Boyle. Byrne was a subject of the Watcher Service reports, and Boyle was tied to many of the receipts and financial documents found in the other box. Once the material reached CSIS command, they were promptly shared with the RCMP. After a two-month review, the Crown prepared to lay charges against Byrne, Boyle, Patrick 'Paddy' Kerrigan, and Owen Ryan. On June 23, 1985, they executed the arrest warrants in a controversial show of force that had shocked Canada.

The legend of Darcy Byrne: *Reckoning - June 1985*

There were rumblings in the press that new evidence had been unearthed and charges were about to be laid in the Flight 281 case. Darcy Byrne wasn't worried—in the aftermath of Jack Redmund's reporting, the authorities had done their level best to pin the attack on him, failing to achieve their goal every time. Plus, the media and prosecutors seemed happy that they, at the very least, were able to convict the bomber, Cathal O'Dwyer.

This latest gambit was sure to follow the same path. He continued to feel no remorse. He was proud of his attempt to open a second front for the IRA in the diaspora, even if his fellow Provos had not appreciated his efforts and weren't willing to accept the help of groups like the Toronto Irish. He believed himself to be a republican hero and made sure that, in the years following the attack, he surrounded himself with people who felt the same way.

He was having problems sleeping that June night. It was about five in the morning when he got up and went down to the kitchen. His wife barely stirred when he got out of bed. His son and daughter, just seven and eight respectively, were very sound sleepers, so they didn't hear him either. He headed outside to the back porch and took a seat on the chaise. As he looked into the sky, with the sun starting to present itself in the east, he reflected on his life.

In the aftermath of the bombing, he had faced a dilemma. What was he going to do for money? How would he make ends meet? An IRA fundraising tour, similar to the one that preceded the bombing, was out of the question. His name was linked—even if only by rumour and inuendo—to the downing of Flight 281, and by many people's standards, the bombing constituted a gross overreach by a rogue IRA wannabe. The solution to the problem had come to him one day not long after the bombing, as he was staring at a pile of bills on his kitchen table. He'd gotten on the phone and scheduled a meeting with Collin Boyle and Paddy Kerrigan at Nova Star Pharma. That's when the arrangement was made. He was officially put on the company payroll as a consultant. For the record, that was the last time he entered the premises of Nova Star, and his consultancy had a negligible (non-existent?) effect on the company's bottom line. He also used the opportunity to tell Boyle and Kerrigan that the authorities were closing in on the bomber, Cathal O'Dwyer, and that if they wanted the man's cooperation, they had better take care of him. Within a week, a generous stipend was placed in O'Dwyer's family bank account to take care of his financial obligations. The stipend came in biweekly instalments with no end date indicated. To be on the safe side, the money had been assigned to O'Dwyer's wife, who was about to become the lone parent to four children under the age of ten when her husband went to prison.

Darcy wondered about the decade or so since the bombing: how almost immediately he had been condemned by his IRA comrades in South Armagh, Belfast, and Derry; how he'd been forced into a different kind of alliance with Boyle and Kerrigan (one he'd been reluctant to accept at first, but one that had grown to be mutually beneficial); and how he and Ryan had arranged for the execution of *The Toronto Star* reporter who'd implicated them in the bombing a few years after it happened. Too bad Redmund had survived, though he'd been left crippled. Fortunately, they'd never caught the shooter that Byrne and Ryan had recruited for the job. After the reporter's book on the bombing, Byrne had endured months of police surveillance and a half dozen interrogations by the RCMP. In the true spirit of Irish republicanism, he'd given them nothing—not even his name.

On this particular June morning, he wondered how his life had become so meaningless, slothful, and boring. Sure, he had met a woman he was comfortable with and gotten married. They even had a couple of kids. But Darcy Byrne had grown fat and lazy. His hair had morphed from a black and white mixture to a solid white mane—a fairly typical hair colour for an Irishman, but he was only in his early forties. He spent most of his days watching television and reading the newspaper. Evenings were spent at Foley's with a few republican friends who weren't afraid to sit with an "outcast." He'd found a home on the opposite side of the pub away from Boyle and Kerrigan. They seldom talked, not because of any animosity but more out of an understanding that there was really nothing to talk about.

Meanwhile, Owen Ryan, who had been Byrne's primary ally back in the early seventies, was the unofficial spokesperson of disgruntled Irish republicans in Toronto and the surrounding area. The tours that Byrne used to take part in had been taken up by Ryan, who would make appearances, stir up crowds, raise money, and funnel the cash back to Belfast. He was no different from zealots working in Montreal, Ottawa, New York, Boston, and Chicago. Byrne would hear all about Ryan's efforts at Foley's. He remained a good friend, and Byrne didn't begrudge Owen his success.

All this was running through Byrne's mind when he heard some cars coming down his street. He got out of the chaise and lumbered through the kitchen and into the living room to peer out the front window. He saw four police cars and two unmarked vehicles. Everyone got out of their cars and gathered as a group. One man, from one of the unmarked cars, was doing most of the talking. He was kind of tall with short, thick brown hair and a goatee, and was dressed in a tailored suit. After a brief discussion, the cops returned to their squad cars. The man from the other unmarked car split from the group and made his way up the front walk on his own. He looked familiar. Maybe one of his interrogators from years ago.

Before the man could ring the bell, Byrne opened the door. "What do you want?"

"We want you, Darcy Byrne. I need to come in for a minute." The man was a bit rotund, wearing an ill-fitting suit and shoes that needed a polish. His slicked-back hair made him look slimy. There was something about his moustache that complemented the sliminess. The man entered the house, as Byrne instinctively moved backward, and closed the door behind him.

What happened next is *not* something one would expect in the execution of a Canadian arrest warrant. The man ('He must be a detective,' thought Byrne) told him to take a few more steps back, toward the threshold by the kitchen. Byrne, smiling the whole time, complied. Then the man pulled out a revolver and shot Byrne, once in the head and twice in the chest. He swiftly moved to the body, pulled out a pistol he had concealed behind him and placed it in Byrne's lifeless hand, making sure to release the safety. By the time the backup troops burst through the front door and Byrne's wife and kids had reached the landing at the top of the stairs, the man was over the body, checking for a pulse—part of the act he had rehearsed in his head prior to arriving.

When the first officer entered the house, the man raised his hand and said, "He pulled a gun on me as soon as I told him we were here to arrest him."

The man with the goatee, wearing the nice suit, pushed past the officers in the doorway and said, "Jesus, Director Nugent, what happened?"

The scene was one of traumatic pandemonium. The man in the suit, Crown Attorney Oliver Hunter, pulled Ontario's CSIS Director Mike Nugent into the living room while two officers climbed the stairs to try to calm Byrne's family. Nugent, in very matter-of-fact, technical, law-enforcement jargon, explained how he'd entered the premises, faced the suspect, who'd pulled a pistol from his robe, and before Byrne could shoot, was forced to fire three times to subdue him. Sounded like a textbook shooting as Nugent told the story.

Crown Attorney Hunter was beside himself. "Why did you enter the house? Why did you close the door?" He was bewildered by the high-ranking CSIS agent's behaviour. "You specifically asked to join us in the execution of this warrant. As a professional courtesy, I invited you because of your involvement in the case years ago." He started pacing, trying to make sense of the situation. "We agreed, just a few minutes ago—*at your insistence*—that you be allowed to apprehend the suspect and bring him to us in handcuffs. This is a highly unusual agreement given the fact that, as a rule, CSIS do not arrest people. I conceded based on your rank within Canada's spy agency."

A different point of contention entered Hunter's mind. "I was also under the impression that CSIS operatives don't carry guns unless they are in a foreign hotspot." He glared at Nugent. "Arrest warrants are pretty straightforward. Law enforcement enter the premises, identify themselves, and seek compliance in the safest manner possible. You entered this house, closed the door—an action I just cannot understand—and now Darcy Byrne is lying there dead." He pointed at Byrne's corpse, which was surrounded by a pool of blood.

"What can I say, Hunter?" Nugent said calmly, looking down at Byrne. "He lived by the sword, and now he's died by the sword."

The other pre-dawn arrests went off without a hitch. No one else insisted on apprehending Boyle or Ryan or Kerrigan on their own. No one else found themselves in a situation where they felt they had to shoot the suspect as they arrested him.

Charges and a trial - *June 1986*

"I know you're frustrated about the verdict, but you don't need to take it out on me!" his wife shouted as he went into his study.

"Just give me some space," he yelled, slamming the door.

Oliver Hunter took off his suit jacket and threw it on the floor. He dropped heavily into his reading chair. He was boiling, finally surrendering to the frustration that had been building over the course of the entire trial. After the verdict—an acquittal for Collin Boyle, Paddy Kerrigan, and Owen Ryan—Hunter had been obligated to face the families. They'd begged him to appeal the verdict, but he knew there was no appeal coming. For the life of him, he couldn't find a legal mistake by the judge that would warrant another trial. The fact of the matter was that they didn't have a case.

The previous six months had seen witnesses provide hearsay testimony that the men were part of a conspiracy to bring down BOAC Flight 281 in 1973. They even had a girlfriend of Collin Boyle testify that, during a heated argument driven by rumours regarding the bombing, he'd shouted, *"We bombed the plane! So what? Are you going to turn me in or are we going to keep seeing each other? Get off your high horse for Christ's sake!"* The defence had torn her to shreds, and in the judge's ruling, he'd challenged her reliability as a witness because she'd made two errors of fact in her testimony. 'She's a human being, telling her story years after the fact. Cut her some slack, Judge,' Hunter had thought.

The defence had also hacked to bits the forensic accounting prepared by the Crown that linked Collin Boyle and Paddy Kerrigan to the bombing. Every bit of money—including a sizable cash advance that was probably used to buy the plane tickets for the bombing—was accounted for in some murky argument that created a Crown attorney's worst nightmare: *reasonable doubt.*

Besides, no one had really gotten past the fact that the ringleader, Darcy Byrne, was dead and buried after a "shootout" with police. Hunter had been there. Mike Nugent had executed Byrne in cold blood. He never should have agreed to allow Nugent to take the lead. But what could he have done? Here was the Director General for CSIS in the province, a man who had been instrumental in sharing the evidence that had brought Cathal O'Dwyer to justice back in the seventies, begging to finish the job and arrest Byrne. He had been so persuasive. But once Darcy Byrne had been pumped full of bullets, the air had come right out of Hunter's case.

He could imagine the headlines in tomorrow's paper. His failure would be the talk of the country. Eventually, he'd have to tell the families that all hope was lost, that there would be no appeal, and that the perpetrators were protected from further prosecution by the principle of double jeopardy. They'd suffered trauma when the plane had gone down. Now they'd suffer trauma again, because a desperate attempt to bring the conspirators to justice had collapsed in a flurry of persuasive defence arguments. It was as if their family members were being killed all over again.

2003

CHAPTER 9:
DECLAN'S LAST STAND

Belwood breaks and a graveside visit
- *November 28, 2003*

The morning after our debrief at Redmund's, I decided that I needed to take another trip over to Warren Belwood's house. The visit would be unannounced. Karuna, on her insistence, decided to join me. Redmund was onboard and gave the visit his blessing.

It was another drab, overcast November day. There was no snow in the forecast, just cold—unseasonably cold for November, with almost January-type temperatures (something the weather lady on the radio called "the polar vortex")—so Karuna and I were bundled up in winter coats, hats, and gloves and had the car heater cranked the whole drive over.

We rang the doorbell, and Belwood answered, glasses on the tip of his nose and a newspaper in his hand. His head dropped in an expression of resignation as he waved us into the house and closed the door.

As we stood in the foyer, he said, "So, you're back."

"Yes, sir. I am," I replied with as much courtesy and respect as I could find. "This is my wife, Karuna."

"Hello," he said, looking at her. "I think we met at Patrick's funeral." Then he turned to me. "I was hoping I had scared you off."

I knew exactly what he meant. "It seems my father has sent us on a bit of a mission, Mr. Belwood."

"On this matter, I have no doubt," he said, with a sudden, serious look on his face, glancing at his wife in the kitchen. "A bit of hot coffee for our guests, dear." We didn't object to the unsolicited offer.

He turned back to us. "Take off your shoes, and put your jackets on the deacon's bench, then have a seat in the living room, and I'll be with you in a moment."

We followed his directions. I hadn't really taken in the décor of Belwood's home the last time I'd visited. This place was certainly vintage 1988: puffy furniture, vertical blinds with floral curtains on either end, a pastel-blue paint on the walls, and a beige carpet (clean but worn). The Belwoods came from the generation that would rearrange their furniture, every once in a while, before they'd even consider buying a new living-room set. Karuna and I sat next to each other on the couch and waited for Belwood to return.

He came into the room just as his wife brought in a tray with mugs of coffee from the kitchen. He turned to her. "You might as well stay for this, Sally."

She looked at him with surprise. "What's going on, Warren?"

He pointed at Karuna and me. "I think they want to talk about Flight 281."

She paused, gave a slight nod, and sat down in a wingback chair across from us. Warren Belwood followed suit, sitting in a matching chair beside his wife.

"Well, Karuna and Declan, where are we at with your *mission?*"

We told Belwood what we'd discovered: the tapes of the conspirators, the meeting with Maloney, the documents, the photos, and what Bakersmith had had to say.

Belwood had a puzzled look on his face. "Why? What prompted you to pursue this investigation of yours, and who is helping you?"

I hesitated. I hadn't updated him on how all this started. "Mr. Belwood, it seems my father felt a burden of guilt regarding the bombing of Flight 281. He left me a videotaped deathbed directive to retrieve that box from you. That's why I really came here that last time. That box you had contained clues that led me to Jack Redmund of *The Toronto Star.*"

"Jack Redmund," Belwood muttered in frustration. He wasn't being rude, just repeating the name of the man who'd always known (or at least suspected) the story of what really happened but had been unable prove it—a man of tenacity that Belwood wished had left well enough alone. He'd always hoped that the disgrace of Flight 281 would just be forgotten and put away.

"Yes, sir, Jack Redmund. It seems my father sent him an audiotape prior to his death. On the tape, two men discuss the bombing in anxious tones, claiming it was only supposed to do minimal damage on the ground in London."

Belwood was looking out his living-room window. "Collin Boyle and Paddy Kerrigan," he said. "I know the tape."

The room went silent. Belwood's wife reached across and put her hand on her husband's arm. "Hasn't this gone on long enough?"

Tears welled up in his eyes as he shifted his gaze to a spot on the carpet in front of him. One lonely tear left his eye and dropped from his cheek onto his lap. While the floodgates didn't exactly open, the tears began to fall in a steady drip.

Belwood broke the silence. "Cowards," he said.

More silence.

"You take an oath to serve and protect the nation. But then you join the service, and it becomes all about the chain of command. You have to trust that the commander above you in the chain will do what's best for the country. You have to trust that they are governed by a moral compass that goes beyond their own damned egos. You have to trust that the decisions that are made will benefit the country in the long term."

He looked directly at Karuna.

"We failed miserably. We should have stood up to the bastards. I am so ashamed," he said, not really speaking to her, just sending his confession out to the universe. He took a breath and abruptly wiped the tears from his eyes. "I'm seventy-six-years-old, for heaven's sake. The only time I've ever cried was at the funerals of my parents."

No one responded. He was entitled to cry.

"Okay," he sighed. "Let's come clean."

Belwood started his story at his transfer to the Security Service Toronto Airport Detachment and outlined the Irish Desk investigation, right from Bloody Sunday to the odd developments after BOAC 281 had gone down. He said that the man in charge, Staff Sergeant Gord Millington, had realized that the service had blown it, and had wanted to find a way to save face. So, he'd come up with a plan.

"Millington told us to get all of the intelligence on the men we knew were responsible for the bombing and bring it directly to him. He said that he and Agent Mike Nugent would catalogue it and share the most important information with the Criminal Branch so that charges could be laid against the main suspects. What we didn't know was that Millington and Nugent were working together to make the evidence disappear."

"Why would they do that?" Karuna asked.

My Father's Secret

"I'm not exactly sure. Your father-in-law and I spoke about this a little after we knew the evidence was gone. At first, we told ourselves that Millington was acting in the nation's interest. While it bothered us deeply, we wondered whether Canada was ready to hear that the Security Service had watched the conspirators hatch a plan, and execute that plan, *while* we had eyes on them. With such tragic results, we wondered if Millington was protecting Canadians from the shame associated with the terrorist act and protecting the reputation of the RCMP Security Service in the process. Later, we thought that Millington was trying to protect his *own* reputation. He had an unblemished career in the military and the RCMP. The work of the Irish Desk had ended in a terrorist group achieving their objective *while* we were watching them. Millington, by burying the evidence, created the impression that we didn't know what was going on, and that these guys were able to pull off the bombing without us being able to predict it was going to happen."

No one said anything. This was a lot to digest. I wished Jack Redmund could have been there with us to hear this confession and weigh in. However, I had to ask myself one question: Would Warren Belwood have been this candid with anyone other than Karuna and me? We were my father's proxy. He was a party to my father's secret. The Flight 281 torch had been passed to us, the family of Patrick Keenan, not a *Toronto Star* reporter, and it was us who would need to see things through.

Karuna broke the silence. "We need to find Gord Millington."

"Dead. Had a stroke a few years ago. Patrick and I chose not to attend the funeral," Belwood responded quickly. "He finished his distinguished career with the Security Service with high honours and a full pension. He, along with his lacky Nugent, were even credited with helping the Criminal Branch gather the evidence to convict Cathal O'Dwyer for building the bomb that blew up the plane."

Karuna was restless at this point. "Well, then, who can we talk to?"

"Paul Dawson was as torn up about Flight 281 as we were," Belwood responded. "He had a heart attack a few years ago, just seventy-three. We did attend that funeral."

"How about Mike Nugent?" Karuna asked.

"You cannot trust that son of a bitch," Belwood responded. His eye's flashed with anger. You could tell cursing was a rarity for the man.

Then Belwood drifted off into his thoughts. Maybe anger at Millington and Nugent. Maybe some fond memories of Paul Dawson and my father. Maybe some other dreamland that took him mercifully away from Flight 281.

I leaned forward and tried to bring Warren Belwood back to us. "Can you think of anyone who can help us? *Anyone?* We need to know where to look next."

He thought about the question. "Go see you parents. Your dad told me it would mean a lot to him if you went to visit Assumption Cemetery every once in a while. I don't know why he made a point of telling me this, but he did—on more than one occasion."

This was entirely unhelpful, but I had to respect the fact that the man had just poured his heart out to us. Our family was never the graveside-visit type. When my grandparents died, we were at the grave for the burial and never went back. It was just not in our tradition. Once a person died, they were gone physically and lived on in our memories, and dare I say it? Our hearts.

"We'll do that, Mr. Bellwood," Karuna said. "We'll go see Kathleen and Patrick at Assumption."

I looked at Karuna with a bit of shock in my expression. We had never spoken about visiting my parents' graves. I'd never had a desire to do so. I hoped she was just being kind to the Belwoods, a final act of gratitude before we left their home.

"If you can think of anything else that would help us, please let us know," Karuna said. "We appreciate your candour, Mr. Belwood. We'll leave you and your wife to get back to your day."

It was an awkward goodbye, partly because it felt incomplete, and partly because (if I was reading Karuna correctly) we were about to go to visit my parents' graves.

• • •

We had an argument in the car. In my irritation, I asked my wife what the hell she was up to. Why would I want to spend my afternoon in the cemetery where my parents were buried? Karuna implored me to stop being so ridiculous (which went over really well!) before the two of us stopped talking. There we were, silently bundled up in our hats, gloves, and parkas. The loudest noise in the car was the heater that blew rather desperately, moving mostly cold air around the cabin of our tiny Honda Civic. We were heading to Assumption Catholic Cemetery in Mississauga.

I parked the car in front of the cemetery office when we arrived and jumped angrily (and noisily) out without saying a word. One thing my wife hadn't considered was the fact that neither of us could remember where the hell Kathleen and Patrick Keenan were buried, even though we had just been there a month earlier. I guess the grief and funeral-home limousine proved to be too much of a distraction. A helpful clerk gave me directions to the plot, and I returned to the car.

I got back into the Civic, with a dramatic door slam, and started driving toward that section of the cemetery. Karuna eventually assumed a calm tone. "Did it occur to you that your father was directing us to come to the grave for a reason?"

"What the hell are you talking about, Karuna?" I asked, still running hot.

"In my family's tradition, honouring the dead through ceremony and ritual is common. In your family's tradition, it's not. So, why would your father—after leaving you a videotape to start this adventure and sending mysterious packages to a reporter and a former colleague—*repeatedly* tell his best friend to ask you to visit his grave?"

I was dumbfounded and speechless.

"Declan, it appears this is part of the journey," Karuna said gently. "Your father needs us to visit the last resting place of his body. We need to see what he wants us to do next."

Still speechless and still angry, I navigated us to the area where my parents were buried. We got out of the car (no door slam this time) and headed to the grave.

And there it was, the headstone that had been ordered shortly after my mother died. It had been updated to include my father's name and the years of his life. Two names, two sets of dates, and a simple cross etched at the top of the stone. The ground over the grave was still just dirt; the groundskeeper would seed it in the spring. There was only one thing that was different; something we hadn't asked for was affixed to either side of the headstone: two vases with wilted flowers in each. I knelt down to look at the flowers and saw a card, protected by a small, clear, plastic bag. Karuna noticed the same thing on the other side of the headstone. We both reached for the bags and removed the cards.

As soon as I read my card, I knew why we were there. Karuna was right.

She must have come to the same conclusion as she looked at her card. Instinctively, we held up the cards we had in our hands to show each other what was written.

Mine read: HEATHER JANSEN

Karuna's read: 281
My father was sending us to find Heather Jansen.

What do we know? - *November 28, 2003*

Heather Jansen was not that hard to find. I called Warren Belwood, and he told me that she was alive and well and living in Leaside, a Toronto neighbourhood, though he didn't have her number. Karuna worked the Toronto phone book while I filled in Redmund on the latest developments. He wasn't too surprised to hear about the blatant suppression of evidence.

After a few calls, Karuna eventually reached Heather Jansen. Each call started with Karuna saying, "Hello, I was hoping to speak to Heather Jansen. I am calling on behalf of Patrick Keenan. Did he tell you I'd be calling?" to which the first three recipients provided various responses—some more diplomatic than others—that indicated that she had the wrong number.

On the fourth call, Heather Jansen answered the phone, and after a moment of hesitation, said, "Patrick Keenan's dead. I was at his funeral about a month ago." Her voice sounded gravelly and weathered. A smoker maybe.

Karuna had hit the mark. She identified herself and asked, "Can Patrick's son and I meet with you, Ms. Jansen?"

Jansen considered the question. "Well, obviously, I'd need to know what this is about?"

Karuna suspected Jansen already knew the answer to this question but complied. "BOAC Flight 281."

Karuna told me later that she could hear Jansen exhale into the phone receiver before she responded. "I suppose so." She shared her address, and we were scheduled to meet with her the next morning.

It was a restless night at our house. Karuna busied herself on the computer, once again going down the Flight 281 rabbit hole, while I sat in the living room with a notepad in hand and tried to map out where we'd been and where we were going.

I made a list of names under two headings:

Suspects	Investigators
Darcy Byrne (leader, killed by police in 1985) Owen Ryan (conspirator, acquitted in 1986)	Gord Millington (leader, buried evidence) Mike Nugent (Millington's main ally, buried evidence)
Collin Boyle (money man, acquitted in 1986) Paddy Kerrigan (Boyle's main ally, acquitted in 1986)	Paul Dawson (second-in-command) Terry Maloney (Service insider, Foley's)
Cathal O'Dwyer (bombmaker, 25 years for manslaughter, 1975. Released in 2000.)	Warren Belwood (surveillance) Patrick Keenan (surveillance)

It struck me that the top two names on both lists were rather despicable characters—a truly unfortunate situation that helped to explain how the conspirators had gotten away with mass murder. A second revelation struck me as I made my way down the two lists; both contained silent partners and blind obedience. No doubt Boyle and Kerrigan had been active participants in the conspiracy, but they'd kept themselves far enough removed from the actual construction and planting of the bomb to evade justice. In many ways, they were silent partners in the scheme. Meanwhile, Cathal O'Dwyer had done whatever the conspirators wanted with an ambivalence (*blindness?*) to the fact that he could go to jail for what he was doing. On the other side of the ledger, Maloney, Belwood, and my father had been blindly obedient and silent partners to the whims of the Security Service. They were silent in the aftermath of the bombing and then blindly followed the chain of command to the detriment of justice. It was disturbing to see the "good guys" from the Security Service looking either just as bad as the *"bad guys"* or at least morally bankrupt enough to allow the bombing of Flight 281 to remain, essentially, an unsolved crime.

The only consolation I could draw from my little analysis was that my father and a few of his colleagues were breaking the silence and revealing their secrets now, my father from the grave and the others out of a sense of moral exhaustion.

Karuna entered the room and a new train of thought emerged. "I wonder what happened to Mike Nugent," she said. "We know that Millington is dead, but what about the other guy who buried the evidence?"

I looked at my watch. It was after eleven. "Do you think it's too late to call Jack?"

Karuna gave it some thought before answering, "I think you'll know when you reach him."

I picked up the Nokia and dialed the only number that phone had ever called.

"Yes, Declan," Redmund answered in an alert voice. 'Good. I didn't wake him up.'

"Good evening, Jack," I started. "What do you know about Mike Nugent?"

"Ah, Nugent," Redmund said with a chuckle. "So, I've met this guy, and he's a slippery son of a bitch." That was the second time someone had referred to Mike Nugent as that in under twelve hours.

"Millington and Nugent were front and centre when it came to handing over the evidence that convicted Cathal O'Dwyer for building the bomb that brought down the plane. That happened almost right away. It was as if they were trying to spin a lone-bomber narrative that pretty much went unchallenged."

"That is until you pointed the finger at the others," I interjected.

"I sure did," Redmund quipped. "And it put me in a wheelchair."

"And Nugent?" I asked, getting us back on track.

"So, Nugent gets all these accolades in the O'Dwyer case, and when a wider conspiracy is suggested, he disappears behind a veil of Security Service secrecy. Within two years of the bombing, he rose to the rank of Corps Sergeant Major. When CSIS was formed in 1984, he became an inspector with the new outfit and has been there ever since. Now he's the Director General for CSIS in Ontario. I think he's in his mid-sixties now. Gotta be close to retirement," Redmund concluded.

"Millington and Nugent," I said, as a thought more than a statement. "Two Service men who tried to make the investigation into the conspiracy go away."

"Their plan has been largely successful for thirty years, Declan."

"That's true," I said. "Listen, I'll call you tomorrow after we talk to Heather Jansen. She agreed to meet with us at ten."

I disconnected the call. I didn't have to fill Karuna in because she'd had her ear to the Nokia receiver the whole time Jack Redmund was speaking. "Big day tomorrow," she said. "We better get some rest."

We made our way upstairs and went through our evening rituals. It seemed odd to be flossing and brushing and washing and rinsing while we were in the midst of uncovering evidence in the unsolved murder of three hundred and twenty-nine people.

We put on our pyjamas and curled into each other. Karuna turned toward me and kissed me gently. There was a moment of hesitation and then a decision to forgo sleep for a few moments. What happened next will remain between the two of us.

A candid conversation with Heather Jansen
- *November 29, 2003*

We arrived at Heather Jansen's Leaside home on time. She lived in a luxury townhouse complex—a few rows of tasteful, three-story units that Karuna and I knew we would struggle to afford. We ascended the stairs from the driveway and rang the doorbell. A woman answered. "Come in. Heather will be down in a minute." She looked like she was in her early sixties. Her hair was brown with white working its way through the shoulder-length cut. She looked reasonably fit, dressed in leggings and a long, floral shirt.

She walked us to a nicely decorated living room—simple furniture, landscape artwork, a Persian rug bringing some warmth to the space. Karuna and I sat on the couch and waited. It seemed like we had been beside each other, waiting on someone's couch, through most of this episode.

Heather Jansen came down the stairs and into the living room. She was a little taller than the other woman and around the same age. Her hair was short and dark brown. She walked with purpose ('The gait of a man,' I thought.) and shook both our hands firmly as she introduced herself.

She sat down in a stylish leather chair across from us. "Well, this is your meeting. Tell me what you want."

We reviewed as much as we could with a little extra emphasis on our visit with Belwood. She nodded her head when we mentioned Belwood's name. Her eyes twitched a bit when we mentioned Millington, and her face tightened when she heard the name Nugent.

"Yesterday, we were visiting my parents' grave," I said. "I guess my father ordered two permanent vases for flowers to be affixed to either end of the headstone. I had no idea that he'd done that. When we arrived, we noticed some flowers in the vases, and when we looked closer, we found these two cards, protected in small, plastic bags that were attached to the flowers in each vase."

Karuna handed her the cards.

A half smile crossed her face. "And you're Patrick Keenan's son."

"I am. Now, we just need to know why my father directed us to you. Were you on the same Service Mountie team as him?"

"No," she replied. "I was part of the Watcher Service. We ran physical surveillance on people the investigators wanted us to keep an eye on."

Karuna spoke next. "Who did you follow that could help us with Flight 281? You must have followed someone important, or my father-in-law never would have sent us your way."

Jansen was mulling things over in her mind. Finally, she said, "I'll be right back." She got up, left the room, and headed back up the stairs.

She came back with a manilla envelope that was strikingly similar to the one Terry Maloney had shared with us a few days earlier. This one had been opened.

"Your dad, may he rest in peace, didn't like to leave things alone. It looks like he put together a reminder for my conscience, and he mailed it to me before he died." She put the envelope on the coffee table.

"What are we dealing with?" Karuna asked.

"See for yourselves."

Karuna took the envelope and emptied it onto the coffee table. There was another cassette (this one was labelled *FEB.14B*), a multi-page report, and three photographs—a combination not dissimilar to what my dad had sent Maloney. A Post-it Note on the report said, *"Please review with Declan Keenan when he contacts you."*

Jansen started explaining. "The cassette speaks for itself. The report is not unfamiliar to me, because I am one of its authors. And the pictures..." She paused to take a breath. "The first picture is of Owen Ryan approaching his car with a stereo receiver in his hands. I took the photo. Do you know about the Prince Charles lead?"

We stared blankly back at her.

"I guess that's a no," she said. "At one point, the Irish Desk had us following Owen Ryan in relation to a potential threat to assassinate Prince Charles when he visited Toronto just before Christmas 1972. The report deals with the Watcher Service tail that my partner and I had on Ryan. Our insider told us that he had uttered threats against the prince and then appeared to be purchasing components to house and conceal a bomb: a stereo receiver, wiring, an alarm clock, and some batteries. I suppose you know that Cathal O'Dwyer concealed his bomb in a stereo receiver in the BOAC Flight 281 incident. We eventually concluded that the threat and activities highlighted in the report were part of a game of misdirection, conducted by the Irish to keep us from seeing what they were actually up to.

"The second picture is of Darcy Byrne and Owen Ryan on a park bench in Mimico around the time of the bombing."

I picked up the photo and took a closer look. It looked like they were talking without really looking at each other, as if they were on the lookout for someone watching them—someone like the Watcher Service.

"I don't know who took the third photo, but it looks like Quinn Foley going into the BOAC ticket office downtown." Jansen put the picture down before moving on. "I listened to the tape. It's a series of calls to Darcy Byrne's home-phone line. They're lined up in a row. It sounds like the conspirators all calling in to Byrne to say they'd heard something on the radio, to which Byrne tells them they better come over to his house. One of them, Owen Ryan, says a bit too much. You'll notice that when you listen to the tape yourself."

Jansen stood up and began to slowly pace across the small living room. "Your father approached me in 1973 when it appeared the RCMP Criminal Branch was going to limit its investigation to O'Dwyer. He appealed to my good nature, arguing that there were more people involved and this fact needed to be revealed. I gave the idea of helping him some serious thought, but I chose safety and job security over nobility. Patrick really wanted to do the right thing. No one was willing to step up and help him, because it looked like an unwinnable battle."

I suddenly felt a knot in my stomach. My father, whom I had resented so much, had contended with a crisis that had started in 1972 and followed him for the rest of his life. He had been isolated, alone, and helpless, a condition from which he'd never recovered.

Jansen brought my attention back to the task at hand. "I told you that the report dealt with the Prince Charles threat. That one's never seen the light of day. Another report that you should pay attention to is the one they used at Boyle, Ryan, and Kerrigan's trial in 1986; it speaks about a rifle being fired outside a farm north of Orillia. I am going to tell you what's not in the report, because it was an observation that I made at the time, which was dismissed by my partner, the senior agent on the surveillance operation. We followed Byrne, O'Dwyer, and someone we referred to as Mr. X, whose name remains a mystery, out to a farm in Severn, around

My Father's Secret

Orillia. This was the summer before the bombing. The three men set off a small explosion, probably using a detonator and blasting caps. My partner insisted it was a rifle, and that's what made it into the report." Jansen looked at Karuna. "The forensics proved that a timer set off the blasting caps that detonated the dynamite that brought down Flight 281."

"Why didn't this come out in the investigation?" Karuna asked emphatically. She shifted herself forward to the edge of the couch.

"I wish I knew the answer to that question," Jansen answered, sadness and emotion took over her tone. "While my partner said the sound and vibration were from a high-powered rifle, I felt the explosion hundreds of metres away, sitting in our surveillance vehicle."

'Fuck me,' I thought. "And the report used at the trial only tells the story of what your partner observed that day? Your observations were shut out?"

She nodded. "It tells *his* story. My perspective was ignored."

"That seems to be a pattern in this case," Karuna added. "Ignoring the most relevant information. How did they get away with it?"

Jansen stopped pacing and sat back down in her chair. "There are two answers to that question. The Security Service can cherry-pick anything they want and declare it to be a national security issue, and no one ever will ever see it. There's also the fact that someone in charge made things disappear and selectively shared information so that the Criminal Branch could pin the bombing exclusively on O'Dwyer."

"Millington," I said.

"And Nugent," added Karuna.

Jansen looked down. "Fucking Nugent. I guess he backed the right horse. Millington promoted him within the service, and when CSIS was founded, he made sure he got a leadership spot there too."

"So, he's protected," Karuna said.

"He protects himself. He's deep into a spy's career. He pretty much runs the CSIS staff working out of Ontario. I think he's the director general. That means there are some national leaders above him, but he is free to do what he wants from an operational perspective," Jansen said, maintaining eye contact throughout this part of the conversation.

"What was he like?" I asked.

"Michael Nugent is, and will always be, a self-serving prick. He will do anything to preserve the things that serve his interests. He is ruthless, relentless, and very skilled at protecting himself. He builds alliances that are virtually impenetrable. He's also crass, a heavy drinker, a womanizer, and extremely homophobic—if that helps you understand the man any better."

"A real son of a bitch," Karuna said.

"Yes, that he is. Only this guy is one of the top spies in the country. He's able to hide behind the same national-security wall that he hid behind when he worked with the Security Service," Jansen said, sounding angry. "If you are counting on cracking Mike Nugent, you've got your work cut out for you."

We all took a pause. Jansen's anger hung heavy in the air.

I broke the silence. "Can we take all of this?" I said, motioning to the things on the coffee table.

"Declan, I think that package was always more for you than for me," Jansen responded. "I sincerely wish you the best of luck. If this investigation puts me in some kind of spotlight, I'm ready for it. I'm tired of hiding."

She walked us to the door, we said our goodbyes, and we climbed into the car. Jansen and the woman she lived with—her

My Father's Secret

partner, I thought—looked on from their living-room window as we drove away.

Her partner looked angry.

Jansen looked lost.

As the Honda pulled onto the main street, Karuna put the cassette in the player. The content was just as Jansen described it, but one part of the conversation sent chills down our spines:

> **Ryan:** I can't believe it, Darcy. This is way more than we could have dreamed!
> **Byrne:** Stop talking. Just come to the house.
> **Ryan:** We did it, Darcy! We've opened the second front!
> **Byrne:** Shut the fuck up, Owen! Get your ass over here now.

That sounded a lot like a confession to me.

Close enough to publish - *November 29, 2003*

Jack Redmund was our first call after leaving Jansen's, and he told us to meet him at his house within the hour. He wrapped up what he was doing at *The Star* and made his way home. Both vehicles arrived at the same time, and we rushed into the house. It was around noon.

We got ourselves organized in Redmund's office, and that's when, in typical Jack Redmund style, he took charge of the situation. "We now have three cassettes, a series of photos, and some documents. A lot of this is new material, seemingly smuggled out of the suppressed files of the RCMP Security Service by Patrick Keenan. We need to sift through everything we have and decide what to do next."

So that's what we did. We started with the Security Service documents. We had two Watcher Service reports that were verified by Heather Jansen. One had been used as evidence in the 1986 trial of the conspirators. It put Byrne and a mystery man (Mr. X) together with Cathal O'Dwyer, testing explosive components (probably blasting caps) months before the bombing, not a "high-powered rifle" as was reported during the trial. The second report, buried by the Security Service, outlined an alleged *(foiled? faked?)* attempt to kill Prince Charles just before Christmas 1972. This report spoke of components that were purchased to make it look like they were going to set off a bomb to kill the heir to the throne when he visited Toronto. It turned out to be a ruse staged by the Irish. We also had the threat assessment that had been shared with Redmund back in 1978. It told the story of a heightened level of action by the conspirators in the days prior to the bombing of BOAC Flight 281. While I had no proof, I was sure it was my father who'd sent the threat assessment to Redmund.

Next, we had the documents that we'd retrieved from Terry Maloney: warnings from BOAC and MI6 that the chatter they were monitoring indicated a likelihood that planes could be the target of a terrorist attack. And then Canada's own Communications Security Establishment, the CSE, had warned Foreign Affairs that an attack was imminent in the days prior to the attack. When John Bakersmith took this information to Millington, he'd been dismissed. When he followed up, he was berated.

Then there were the photographs. The scenes were burned into the memories of all three of us.

- Byrne and Ryan outside of Foley's, shortly after the former resurfaced upon his return from Ireland. ("The birth of the conspiracy," according to Redmund.)
- Byrne being greeted by Boyle at the front door of his home. ("Starting to execute the plan?" Karuna asked.)

My Father's Secret

- Byrne, Ryan, and O'Dwyer greeting each other in front of Foley's. ("Recruiting the bombmaker?" I wondered.)
- Ryan approaching a Ford Fairlane with a large box. ("The Prince Charles distraction," Redmund stated.)
- Foley going into the BOAC office in Toronto. ("Do you think he was in on it?" I asked).
- Byrne and Ryan sitting on a park bench days before the bombing. ("They both look like they are on the lookout for cops," Karuna observed.)

Finally, we listened to the tapes. These were the most damning evidence of all in my mind, because the audio seemed to bring the conspiracy to life. The discussion of the "concert tickets" in the February 12th call provided a link to the plane tickets for the Ottawa and Toronto flights (the two "venues"). The February 14th phone call between Boyle and Kerrigan showed that the two men were distraught by the fact that the plane had exploded in mid-air: *"We thought it would go off in the baggage area, not while the plane was in the air,"* one of the two men said. And then there was the third tape, the second one from February 14th. A string of calls to Darcy Byrne's with different people saying they'd heard the news, and Byrne telling them to *"come to the house."* However, Owen Ryan says, *"We did it, Darcy! We've opened the second front!"* to which Byrne angrily tells him to get his ass over to his house.

We poured over the items for hours, deciphering and analyzing every detail. Eventually, it was Jack Redmund who summed things up.

"We can hypothesize on motive, opportunity, and anything else we deem fit, but when it comes right down to it, we have new evidence here that provides a fresh perspective on a thirty-year-old crime. I don't know how this information would hold up in court, but there is certainly enough here for me to publish an incredibly damning piece on the RCMP Security Service and the men responsible for bringing down the plane."

Karuna was the first to respond. "Publishing is our only option, Jack. The Crown didn't appeal the acquittal back in 1986, so they must have felt that their case was either too weak to try again or that there were no errors made by the judge over the course of the trial. The conspirators are protected by double jeopardy."

Redmund mulled over what she said. "I'll say two things about that: It's probably true, and it's bullshit. We've got new evidence here."

"Any good lawyer will challenge how we came to be in possession of the evidence, and more importantly, will go after the authenticity of what we have. Besides, they'd have to come up with brand-new charges against the conspirators." Karuna was right; the things we had come to possess would be attacked by any good defence lawyer.

"*True. Bullshit*," Redmund replied. "Anyway, the law is not my concern. I am writing this up—in fact, I've already started—and we'll let the Crown attorneys decide what they are going to do when they read it."

It looked like our evaluation of the evidence was done, so I decided to try to bring things to a close. "Jack, it seems like you need us to leave, so you can write your story."

"That sounds good. I've got a lot to do," he said, fiddling with things on his desk in front of him.

"All right. Karuna, let's go," I said. "We'll call you tomorrow morning to see where things stand."

"Hopefully, we'll be on the front page by suppertime," Redmund said, before adding. "Thanks for being my legs on this."

Karuna smiled and went over and hugged him. I smiled at the sight of the two of them embracing.

"You're the ringleader, Jack. We're just the performers. There's no 'mission' without you," I said.

He accompanied us to the door. Karuna and I were completely spent.

When I got to the car, I looked back. Jack Redmund was long gone.

I started the car and took a deep breath. "We've done something good here, Karuna."

"Thanks to your dad."

Nugent's had enough - *November 29, 2003*

We got home around seven and ordered a pizza. We might have been tired, but we were also starving. I hoped Jack had stopped to get something to eat before he started pounding the keys on his computer.

I had been sitting in the living room for a few minutes, after placing the order, when the doorbell rang. 'That's kind of quick for the pizza guy,' I thought.

Karuna beat me to the door and opened it to find a tall man in a suit, with a big belly and slicked-back hair. "Ms. Patel. Mike Nugent, CSIS," the man said, holding up his ID.

Karuna took a long look at him. "'What can I do for you, Agent Nugent?"

"Do you mind if I come inside?"

Karuna didn't answer. She just kept staring at him. Her expression had shifted from surprise to contempt.

"Yes," I said from behind her. "Come in, please."

Nugent stepped inside, and after a few seconds, motioned for us to sit down. I guess the shock of his presence had forced him to give us direction in our own house. I had to guide Karuna to the couch. She was raging inside; I could feel it.

Nugent sat down and started talking. "Mr. Keenan. Ms. Patel. I'm here to discuss a national security issue. We need you to stop whatever it is you are doing with Jack Redmund."

Karuna pounced on the statement. "And what do you think we're doing with Jack Redmund, Nugent?"

The CSIS agent raised his eyebrows, surprised at her tone, and smiled before saying, "I think you are digging into a long-forgotten saga that Canada put to bed years ago."

"Specifically," I said, putting my hand on top of Karuna's, keeping her from pouncing again. "What *specifically* are we doing that is not in the nation's interest, Director General Nugent." Unlike my wife, I chose to invoke his title, to see if a little mock respect could earn us some kind of explanation.

"BOAC Flight 281 has been dealt with, Mr. Keenan, both by Canada's intelligence services and the courts," he said coolly. "Bringing fresh eyes to the situation will only frustrate the families of the victims. Haven't they been through enough?"

Now, I was mad. How dare he leverage the grief of the families to try to silence us. "We're not convinced that what we're doing with Jack will frustrate anyone. In fact, we think it will only enlighten people to an injustice. I think you're here because bringing fresh eyes to Flight 281 will frustrate *you,* and quite frankly, you *haven't* been through enough."

Nugent wasn't pleased. He leaned forward. "I'm here as a fucking courtesy to you and your wife, Declan." I figured he was using my first name as some kind of powerplay. "My only frustration is your inability to see that I am trying to do you a solid here. Now, I've tried the soft touch, and you and your death-stare wife appear to have rejected that. So now, the firm hand: Leave 281 alone. It's done. It's over. It's finished."

If one of Canada's top spies came to your house and delivered this kind of message to you, how would you react? I can tell you what Karuna and I did. We just stared at the prick with *"FUCK YOU"* written all over our faces. We didn't say a word.

Nugent stared back, mirroring our sentiment. Finally, he said, "You've got no clue what you're dealing with." Then he got up and left. The pizza-delivery guy passed him on the way up our driveway.

Do it. Tonight. - *November 29, 2003*

Nugent headed down the street to his waiting vehicle and climbed into the back seat, slamming the door of the Taurus behind him.

"How'd that go, boss?" Agent Tim Nugent, Mike's son, asked. He knew better than to call his father "Dad" on the job.

On the other hand, his partner, Gerry Klosky, knew better than to ask a question as stupid as the one his partner had just asked. The door slam had said everything about how well the meeting had gone.

"It went fuckin' great, Tim."

"Geez," Tim said, in a tone that suggested *"Relax, Pops,"* which did not improve the situation.

"You guys have been on Redmund for a few weeks now," Nugent said.

"On and off, sir," Klosky answered. "We've squeezed in the surveillance between our other duties, seeing that this one is … *unofficial*."

"Is there anything you have discovered that would suggest the reporter will let this go?"

"Nothing, sir," Klosky said. "We tried to spook him by tailing him around town. We've listened to a lot of his communication—home phone and cell. The lone bug we planted in his office is pretty sketchy. I think he's using jammers, but the limited audio we've gathered suggests that he is building the Flight 281 story and will be ready to publish soon."

"How soon?"

"It's imminent, sir."

"Fuck," Mike Nugent said from the back seat. He needed to think. The visit to Patrick Keenan's son had been a long-shot attempt to scare the man and get him to withdraw his support for what Redmund was going to write. He didn't know how much they had, but according to Klosky, they had gathered new evidence dealing with the bombing. Flight 281 was going to haunt him again unless…

"All right, men. We've done what we can. People have been warned, and they've rejected the warnings. The story they are trying to tell cannot see the light of day. Do you understand what I'm saying?"

He looked into his son's eyes in the review mirror for a long moment. Then Klosky turned around and looked at his boss. "Understood, sir. The provisions you asked for are in place. We will act on your order."

Nugent hesitated. What a road it had been. A career of advancement, because he'd supported Millington after Flight 281 had gone down, which coincided with a career of defensive posturing in the years since to make sure Flight 281 didn't bite him in the ass. Maybe this was it. Maybe this final action would put an end to the fucking Irish Desk and the case that wouldn't go away.

"Do it," Nugent said. "Tonight."

My Father's Secret

A mysterious fire - *November 30, 2003 (2:30 a.m.)*

Jack Redmund was feeling invigorated. 'This is a story,' he thought. He had worked all evening, writing what stood to be the defining article on the BOAC Flight 281 tragedy. Keenan's son and his wife had done most of the running around, something that had accelerated the investigation, given his limited physical abilities and advancing age. Though he was only sixty-two, years of being confined to a wheelchair had brought with it a host of health problems. The atrophied legs were the tip of the iceberg. He was also dealing with constant neuropathic pain (some of it phantom, emanating from his feet, which had absolutely no contact with his brain), organ dysfunction (strain on his bladder, liver, and kidneys from a lack of movement within the body), and a hard-working heart that was getting tired.

However, on this night, adrenalin was keeping his aches and pains away. He was writing to hit a deadline. If he could get the draft of his article into the hands of the editorial team before their story meeting at ten that morning, he'd be guaranteed a spot above the fold in the evening edition, and the story would dominate the front page the next morning. He had the three cassettes, the collection of photos, and the documents to back up his account. They were all sitting in a large manilla envelope on the end of his desk.

He had nearly completed the draft when he heard a small popping sound from just outside his office. He wheeled around to the office door, and the first thing he saw was a rapidly growing wall of smoke building in the hallway. Firefighters always say, *"It's not the fire that kills you, it's the smoke."* He wheeled back to his desk and grabbed the envelope that held the tapes, photos, and documents. That's when he heard the second popping sound from right inside his office, along the floor beside his desk. More smoke and lots of heat this time. 'I've gotta get out,' he thought.

Smoke-filled tears emerged, followed by a steady stream of coughing. He felt he had little choice other than to wheel his way out of the office, through the now-flaming doorframe, and into the hallway. 'Not good,' he thought as the smoke started to blind him.

His coughing became more intense as he made his move. He got into the hallway and turned toward the front door. He didn't get far. He was disoriented and blinded, which caused him to crash into the walls. Now, he couldn't breathe.

Lost, alone, trapped.

Finally, he was close to the living room—or at least that's what he thought. The smoke was everywhere, and the coughing had been replaced by breathlessness. He was stuck. He couldn't move. The situation had become overwhelming.

As Redmund lost consciousness, he thought, 'We were so close.'

A few minutes later, Jack Redmund suffocated in a toxic cloud of burning wood, insulation, metal, and whatever else his house was made of—the smoke had killed him, not the fire.

Shortly after he died, the fire crept up behind his wheelchair. The large envelope—the envelope containing all the evidence Declan Keenan and Karuna Patel had shared with him—slipped from his motionless lap. His body burned. And then so did the envelope. Its contents, though oddly unaffected by the smoke, were slowly consumed by the fire, which killed the story they had threatened to tell ... once and for all.

By the time the firefighters arrived, the house was completely engulfed in flames. All they could do was bring it under control to protect the neighbouring properties. The next morning, they found what was left of Redmund—his charred remains hunched over a half-melted wheelchair.

Later that day, the fire marshal would conclude that the fire had started via two overloaded circuits, one in the office and one in the adjacent hallway. Two power bars were plugged into the office outlet. The fire marshal figured that the extraordinary number of gadgets in the room had overloaded that circuit, fried the power bars, and caused the outlet to catch fire. This likely started a chain reaction that had caused the second outlet to catch fire. The breakers at the power panel hadn't flipped until the fire had already begun.

The fire marshal would never know that two days earlier, CSIS agent Gerry Klosky had entered Redmund's house while the journalist was at *The Toronto Star*'s headquarters on Front Street. He'd gone into the office and dismantled both power bars, removing the safety components that would trip the breakers. He'd also put a small receiver that, when activated, would start an electrical fire in the power bars. Redmund had done him a favour by having so many devices requiring power in the room. He'd just needed to shift a few from neighbouring outlets into the power bars to sell the idea of neglect on the homeowner's part.

Next Klosky had moved to the wall outlet in the hallway. He'd put another small receiver into that outlet, comforted by the fact that both receivers would incinerate upon ignition, looking like an overloaded circuit and not an act of sabotage. After removing all the batteries from the home's fire alarms and replacing them with dead ones, he'd left the house without a trace.

When the Director General had given him the order earlier that night, he'd been ready. He'd returned to the neighbourhood with his partner and parked on an adjacent street, hopped two backyard fences, and come up behind the house. The lights were still on. 'Night owl,' he'd thought. Then Klosky had taken the transmitter out of his pocket and pressed the first button. He'd heard the faint sound of the hallway outlet popping, starting the fire.

Less than a minute later, he'd pushed the second button. Now the flames and smoke would create a catastrophic situation.

Klosky had retreated to the back fence then, watching as a red and orange glow started to slowly appear behind the windows. The toxic smell had followed.

Finally, he'd crossed the back lawn and gone down the driveway, quickly peering at the front door. Nobody was trying to get out. The man in the wheelchair was trapped. He'd looked up and down the street. The lights were all out. Everyone was asleep.

Whatever threat had existed within the house would be gone before the fire department showed up. Hopping the fences that needed to be hopped, he'd left the scene with his partner in a shitty CSIS Department Ford Taurus.

Farewell to a king - *December 2003*

Karuna and I found out about the fire on the news when we woke up the next morning. First, the kitchen radio reported a devastating house fire in Etobicoke. When we clicked on the TV to follow up, the reporter on the scene was already saying that the house had belonged to renowned *Toronto Star* journalist Jack Redmund. By day's end, the fire marshal was declaring that the blaze had been caused by an electrical problem within the home. No foul play was suspected.

Of course, we knew otherwise, but who was going to listen to us? Our entire connection to Redmund had gone up in flames with the house. Sure, the editor Redmund reported to had an idea of who we were and what we were doing, but without the tapes, the photos, and the documents—and Jack Redmund to vouch for us—we were in a hopeless situation. Karuna wouldn't let matters lie. She contacted the editor and told him that this was "clearly arson," to which the editor responded, "Jack was my friend. Let me grieve." Out of compassion, she backed off.

But it was arson—*and murder*—and we knew it.

And we couldn't prove it.

In the days immediately following the death of Jack Redmund, we stewed and we brooded, and we felt so sad and so angry.

Then came his funeral. We had secured a place at the church as a consolation of sorts from the editor. Jack had a brother and a sister; that was the extent of his family. Work was his real family. Telling the truth had been everything he'd lived for.

And that was abundantly clear at his funeral. A formal, Catholic service was followed by internment at Assumption Catholic Cemetery—Karuna and I making our return there under circumstances that would certainly have disappointed my father—and a wake at a nearby banquet hall. A light lunch was followed by a round of speeches from the "who's who" of Canadian journalism. To say that Jack Redmund was admired would be a dramatic understatement. He was respected and lauded, though not always liked. He was caustic and rough in his pursuit of the truth, with a dogged determination that set him apart from many of his colleagues. He had taken on prime ministers and presidents, governments and corporations, the unethical who made vacant claims to being ethical and the so-called benevolent leaders of society who didn't know the first thing about benevolence.

Jack Redmund was a giant. He was a king to his admirers. Now, with the king dead, who would assume the throne? Truth telling was becoming a dying art in a world where skeptics got the most play. Only the Jack Redmunds of the world had the ability to sway the skeptical undercurrent with words that punctuated, evidence that convinced, and stories that brought everything out into the open.

I could say all this, having known the man for less than a month. If it wasn't for Jack Redmund, this entire journey—from a video message from my dad, to the mystery packages, to the hope that we could right a wrong—would have stalled and faltered before the investigation could have gotten any traction at all.

All that traction had been turned into ash when his home was burned to the ground with him in it. The saddest part of the whole ordeal was that there would be no phoenix rising from those ashes. The truth—at least the truth we could prove—had died that November morning when Jack Redmund was murdered in an act of arson that would never be known.

Arson. Just another way of burying the evidence.

• • •

Karuna and I got home from the wake around dinnertime. Neither of us was hungry, and I was feeling restless, so I told her I needed to go for a drive. Just some alone time. I'd be back soon.

I actually don't really enjoy driving, which made the idea of me clearing my mind or finding peace behind the wheel a little ridiculous. I usually felt irritated and angry when I drove. There was always some jerk driving too fast or too slow, somebody cutting in front of me too closely or slamming their brakes on too quickly... 'Road rage is real,' I thought as I made my way aimlessly east toward the CN Tower—that magnet that tells you you're heading into the city.

In time, I was on Lake Shore Boulevard and decided to head north on Parkside Drive. As I drove along, I glanced periodically at High Park to my left and the steady stream of old Toronto homes on my right. Eventually, I was at the lights at Keele and Bloor. People hustled to and from the subway station. Cars lined

My Father's Secret

the four corners of the intersection—some proceeding, some sitting still—obeying the traffic signals like good Canadians.

That's when a bottled-up rage, simmering for most of the drive, came to the surface. I abruptly pulled my car into the empty turn lane beside me and ran the red light, narrowly missing the intersecting traffic. Cars honked as I floored it, racing up Keele Street—how fast, I'm not sure.

I knew where I was heading. Of course, I knew where I was heading. Foley's Irish Pub was just a few minutes away. The Foley's where all this started. The Foley's that had remained hospitable to the murderers even after the bombing of the plane. The Foley's that still stood as a shameless reminder of how justice of the highest importance is often unserved.

I turned aggressively onto Dundas Street, swinging around slower vehicles, and then I was there, right in front of Foley's Irish Pub. I parked my car beside a fire hydrant, turned off the engine, threw off my seat belt, and climbed out, walking quickly into the place. I stood in the doorway and looked around the pub. I had never been there before, but the layout of the establishment seemed to well up in some ethereal memory. The bar was to the left, with a bartender (young, bearded, and slim) pulling pints for the patrons who lined the bar. There was a series of tables in the middle, and booths to my right, all filled with mostly men. At the end of the row was a larger, semi-circular booth. Two old men sat there. While the surveillance photos were from decades earlier, it wasn't difficult to recognize Collin Boyle and Paddy Kerrigan.

I stared at them for who knows how long; they had no idea I was even looking in their direction. Finally, I made my move. I marched across the pub, dodging a few people as I made my way there, and when I got to the booth, I looked at one of the old men and asked, "Collin Boyle?"

They both looked at me with stony expressions. "It depends on who's asking," Boyle answered.

I felt like I was going to burst with anger. It wasn't an anger where I wanted to kill the two men in front of me. It was an anger that I wanted to remove from myself and impose on them, so it would seep into their pores and devour them. I wanted the truth to wake them to the damage they had done, the lives they had destroyed, the remorse they'd never expressed. Finally, I said, "I've seen the proof. I've heard your voices. I know you bombed BOAC Flight 281."

"Who the fuck do you think you are?" Kerrigan said. He looked to be in his eighties.

"I know the truth," I said.

Suddenly, another man, this one about ten years older than me, came up and said to Boyle and Kerrigan, "Everything okay here?" He shifted his gaze from me to the men. That's when I realized I was standing beside Owen Ryan.

Then two men in their twenties came from the bar. Ryan must have waved them over. They grabbed me, dragged me down a corridor, and shoved me into an office.

Another older gentleman was sitting at a desk, reviewing some paperwork. He looked at us over his glasses. "Boys?"

"Need your office for a few, Mr. Foley," one of them said. "Mr. Ryan and Mr. Boyle need a minute with this guy."

They forced me to sit down in a nearby chair. Foley left the office and in came Ryan and Boyle. A few seconds later, Paddy Kerrigan hobbled to the door. "I'm waiting outside," he said, shaking his head as he closed the office door. He wanted nothing to do with what was about to happen.

The young guys who dragged me into the office stood back a ways. The other two stood in front of me. Owen Ryan turned to me. "First of all…"

My Father's Secret

He slapped me violently across the face. The sting left a lingering tingle and pain that caused the blood to rush to my head.

Boyle put his hand on Ryan's shoulder. "Owen, I've got this. Head back out with your boys. I'm going to have a little chat with this fella."

Owen Ryan looked at Boyle, reluctantly realizing that this was not a request. "The boys will be waiting right outside that door. If you need them, let them know."

"If that's what you'd like," Boyle said.

Ryan left with his henchmen and closed the door behind him. Boyle took a seat behind the desk.

"Now, I'd like you to repeat what you said to me just a few minutes ago," he said. Boyle had been in Canada for most of his life but sounded like he had just arrived from Ireland.

"You killed three hundred and twenty-nine people when you and your fellow conspirators bombed BOAC Flight 281 on Valentine's Day in 1973," I said through gritted teeth.

"Well, that's much more specific," he responded. "You realize there was a trial, and I was acquitted of the charges brought by the Crown, which should have put to rest accusations like the one you are making now."

"Did you know that the RCMP Security Service was on to you and Byrne and Ryan the whole time? Active surveillance that included audiotapes of you and your buddy Kerrigan agonizing over the fact that the bomb had gone off early and killed all those people unnecessarily. I have seen photographs of you and the other conspirators together." I was defiant, emphatic, assertive.

Now Boyle was angry. "Then why aren't I in jail, you useless fuck?" he shouted. Then he paused and collected himself. "If what you say is true, I should be in jail."

"Yes, you should be," I shot back.

"And yet, here I am, free as a fucking bird." He leaned forward, placing his forearms on the desk, and smiled. "Let me tell you a little secret, and I can say this because it's been thirty years since this entire episode happened." For some reason, he looked at the door to the office. Then in a loud whisper, he said, "Of course, we blew up that plane. Everybody knows it. Your RCMP claims are probably true. We were being watched and taped and monitored, and we still managed to pull it off."

I was shocked. A confession. He confirmed what we knew.

Then he leaned back in the office chair. "Here's the kicker though, whoever the fuck you are: *Nobody cares*. It's ancient history. They can't try me again—that's double jeopardy, if you know anything about the law. Plus, nobody has ever *wanted* to deal with Flight 281. After it happened, they looked for their patsy and found him in Cathal O'Dwyer. Years later, when they found a bunch of documents in some Prairie outpost, they came after Owen, Paddy, and me. Their efforts were half-hearted, done more out of a sense of obligation to the families than to put anyone in jail for helping to bomb the plane. Funny how they killed Byrne—the brains behind this whole fucking thing—the day they arrested him. That fat fuck didn't have a gun. Anyway, you are here to fight a battle that no one gives a shit about. They never have."

I couldn't believe what I was hearing.

Boyle lit a cigarette. "Let me tell you something about being Irish. We're fighters. Tenacious, stubborn, and ruthless. We do the things that need to be done to achieve the goals that we are pursuing. When we need to blow things up, we blow them up. We are not afraid of a fight, and we are always in it for the long haul."

He took a long drag of his cigarette before continuing. "Now, let me tell you something about being Canadian. The people in this country don't have any concept of what real hardship is all about. Canada is fantasy land. If something bad happens, Canadians sweep it under the rug and refuse to talk about it. They're addicted to a myth—the myth they are always the good guys. They relish in pointing at the Americans in Vietnam, the Russians in Afghanistan, or the Irish in the North of Ireland and saying, 'At least we're not like them.' Very self-righteous."

Another long drag of his cigarette, followed by a long smoky exhale.

"And this is why shit can happen in Canada. Because no one wants to believe that profound evil can emerge from the streets of Toronto, Montreal, and Vancouver. Christ, 9/11—not even a Canadian tragedy—has gotten more attention from lawmakers and the press here than Flight 281 has gotten in thirty years. Evil happens right here, in this city, in this country, and no one cares. That's Canada, friend," Boyle concluded, taking one more drag before resting his cigarette in an ashtray.

He exhaled and looked at me. "I don't even need to know who the fuck you are. You're dressed in a nice suit underneath that coat, which if I'm right, you don't wear very often. From where I come from, most people put on suits only for weddings and funerals. I am assuming, because it's a Tuesday, you've come from a funeral. That's why I am going to forgive your emotional outburst."

We stared at each other. Mine an expression of shock and dismay, his ... a look of smugness and untouchability.

He got up from the desk and moved around to stand over me. "We did it, and it's over. I don't ever want to see you again."

Then he opened the door. "Show this gentleman out, boys. And none of the rough stuff, please."

The young men took me by each arm and walked me through the pub and out the front door. I was in a daze. On my way out, I noticed Owen Ryan staring me down. The man beside him looked familiar. I later realized it was Cathal O'Dwyer, free after serving a "life sentence" for manslaughter.

I was fortunate that my car hadn't been towed away, less fortunate about the $100 ticket for parking in front of a fire hydrant.

The shock remained for the entire drive home. I'd confronted a conspirator, and he'd confirmed my allegations. Then he'd methodically explained why nothing would come of it. It finally started to sink in. The kind of justice I was seeking—that my father, Jack Redmund, and Karuna were seeking—would never be served.

My rage gave way to humiliation. I knew Boyle was right. That murdering son of a bitch was right.

Requiem for all that was lost - *December 2003*

Karuna wasn't very pleased when I told her that I had gone to Foley's. She told me I was lucky I hadn't gotten the shit kicked out of me—or been killed.

However, after I told her about my encounter with Collin Boyle, she was as shocked as I was. Was there anything else we could do? My father's efforts to bring the conspirators to some kind of justice had gone up in smoke at Redmund's house. CSIS power-player Mike Nugent had warned us off pursuing things any further. Collin Boyle had confirmed the one thing that everyone feared but didn't want to admit: *No one really cared about the fate of BOAC Flight 281.*

All Karuna and I could think to do at this point was retreat to the cottage in Craigleith and see if Georgian Bay could provide us with some space to think. My uncle was open to the proposition, and so we made our way north.

The week after Redmund's funeral and Boyle's heartbreaking proclamation was emotionally tumultuous for me. I realized that I had never really mourned the death of my mother, and the tears flowed. I realized that efforts to at least *expose* the conspirators had failed, and that no one would ever know of our attempt to right the wrong, and the tears flowed. I imagined the tragic scars left on the families of the victims of Flight 281, scars that would never heal, scars that would always reveal themselves on the wounded souls of those who had lost their loved ones, and man ... did the tears ever flow.

And then I thought of my father. I thought of his quiet demeanour and his moodiness. I thought of his emotional detachment and the fact that I was never able to get close to him. I thought of what could have been but never was in a relationship that, until now, I hadn't realized had been permanently altered by Flight 281. Out of the depths of my being came a recognition that Patrick Keenan had done the best he could, and despite his noble intentions, he'd come up short of the moral mark he had established for himself. More than anything, I realized how hard I had been on him and wished he were still alive, so I could tell him what I had realized and ask for his forgiveness. And, yes, upon all this reflection, the tears flowed.

Karuna had to get back to work a few days after we got to Craigleith. She was probably tired of consoling me, but I knew, and she knew, that I needed to spend some time on my own. Everyone reaches a breaking point, sometime or another. I had reached mine, and while Karuna was there to witness the break, she knew I was strong enough to put myself back together. Besides, it was my journey and my responsibility to endure the highs and lows that my life delivered.

Despite the cold weather, I went for walks on the escarpment and for trips to neighbouring towns. I made simple meals and just let my mind and spirit pursue a course that might bring me some peace. One restless evening, I returned to the Jerusalem Bible, the one my father had directed me to, the one my mother had turned to for fellowship with members of her church community, the one that had started this whole adventure. I found the Redmund newspaper clipping and the dollar bill still in place at the beginning of the Book of Job. So, I read that book.

Now, I'm no biblical scholar, and my interpretation of what I read was no doubt coloured by my recent experiences, but the Book of Job basically tells the story of a man who had it all. One day, God is telling a few of his angels that Job is so devoted and loyal that nothing could ever turn him away from all that is holy. Satan, one of God's angels, challenges this assertion, claiming Job's loyalty rests with the many blessings he has received from God, and given the opportunity, he could get Job to curse the day he was born. God more or less says, *"Have at it."*

So, Satan goes to town on Job, stripping him of all that he holds dear, including his children. He also goes after his body, covering it in festering boils. Eventually, Job curses the day he was born and sinks into despair. Three friends visit Job and tell him he must have done something pretty bad to go from being God's most beloved to the most cursed man in the world. Job swears he's done nothing to deserve his fate and rejects his friends' claims, eventually demanding that God explain what is going on. God appears from the whirlwind and provides a brief lesson on the complexity of all that has been created—and how Job's limited human mind does not have the capacity to understand all that the Divine has made. God implores Job to stop trying to find a rational explanation for his suffering and to recognize that some things are beyond reason. Job needs to accept that God, the omniscient and omnipresent, has a plan that no human will ever be able to comprehend. The Book of Job is really a story of accepting one's lot and bearing life's burdens with humility.

While this little bit of reading brought me some awareness, it did not provide me with any comfort. I yearned for some form

My Father's Secret

of justice. However, I knew that what I sought was a justice that I would never see—a justice that my father had tried to bring to fruition only to have the forces that had brought about the tragedy of his life (and now mine) emerged largely unscathed, as an ambivalent nation turned its back on mass murder, pretending it had never happened. Like Job, I would have to accept the fact that no reasonable explanation for the Flight 281 tragedy was forthcoming, and I would just have to accept it.

That's when that dream of walking on water in the ocean, the people being sucked into the sea, the little girl ascending into the clouds, and Karuna telling me I was calling for my mother as I woke from the episode came back into my mind. The dream had innocence, understanding, comfort, and despair all wrapped into one intense visual collage. But it was the yearning for my mother that Karuna had witnessed that felt the most profound to me. I yearned for the comfort of her love, her maternal embrace, and her shelter from the evils of the world. I wanted to take that sentiment and at least provide some emotional respite for those who'd suffered through the BOAC Flight 281 tragedy. Ultimately, my effort to manifest my mother's love and to reveal my father's secret resulted in a journey that only Karuna and I—and the spirit of Jack Redmund—would ever know.

On my last night before heading back to the city, I started flipping through the Bible again. I had a fire going in the fireplace, and a full moon hung over Georgian Bay. I came across another piece of paper tucked into the New Testament. It was an old typewritten note, wedged near the end of the Bible. I saw my mother's handwriting at the top:

For Patrick,
I wrote this in my diary years ago. I thought it might help you. You seem troubled.

Sean Patrick Dolan

Love, K.
Summer, 1978

This is what the entry said:

Be cautious. It is easy to lose sight of the things that are important to you. One day you may be happy with the decisions you are making and the next you may be engaging in activities that are destructive to you and the people you love. If you acknowledge fundamental truths in your life, never compromise them for the benefit of your own selfish needs. One compromise can lead to a series of further compromises that will one day leave you in a state of spiritual starvation.

If you follow your heart and your own instinctive wisdom, you need never worry about happiness. It is important to remember that you are not alone in this world, for a solitary approach to living will never lead to the betterment of the world as a whole or the betterment of your own personal world. It is very easy to lose sight of what is right in a world that caters to your wildest dreams. This is why the maintenance of an altruistic perspective is so important.

You know what is right.

Never try to fool your mind or your spirit, for one day, the two will unite and show you your own foolishness. The human capacity for harmony and contentment is readily available for those who chose the path of honesty.

I thought of my mother giving this gift of writing to my father. Maybe this diary entry is what ultimately prompted him, years later, to contact Redmund, Maloney, and Jansen, and to send me on the mission to expose the truth about Flight 281. Maybe it was his way of making sure he didn't 'fool his mind and his spirit.' Maybe it was his way of making sure I chose a path of honesty, with the promise of harmony and contentment resting in my future.

I put the page back in the Bible and stood up. I looked out over the bay and saw only peace. No good or evil, no benevolence or hostility, no pardon or revenge—just peace. And while peace would elude me in many of the days to come, I knew that I had tried to do my father's bidding. I knew I had tried to make my mother proud. I knew I had tried to work with Karuna and Redmund to right a wrong. I also knew that I had tried to be true to myself. In the end, all I could do was settle into the quiet recognition that at least I had tried.

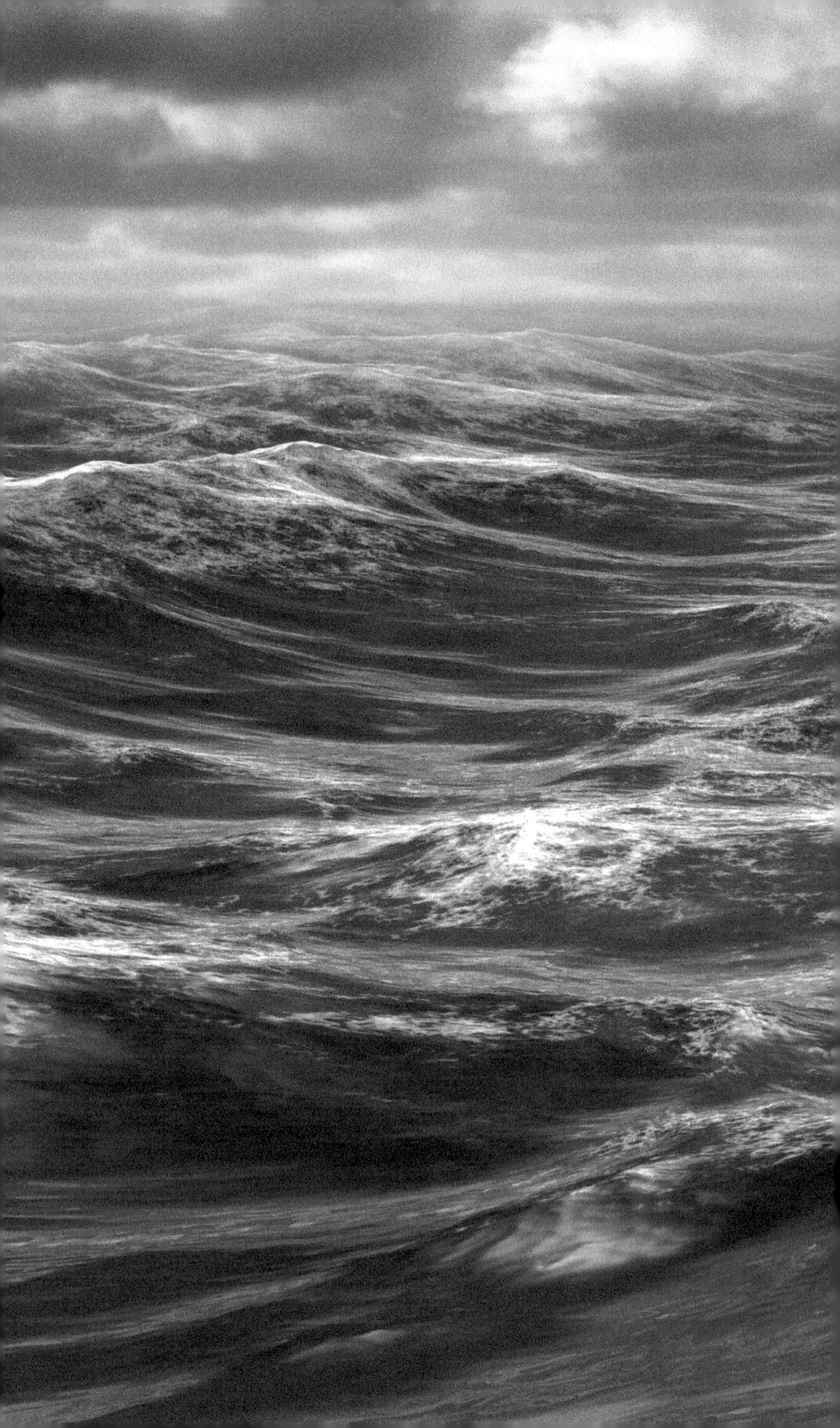

AUTHOR'S NOTE

I was really looking forward to my twenty-first birthday. I rose from my slumber with a bit of a skip in my step because birthdays were a big deal in my family. However, the news that morning was not good. A plane had crashed off the coast of Ireland. There was also an aviation accident on the ground at an airport in Japan. It turned out that neither incident was a crash or an accident; they were both acts of sabotage.

    The instruments of destruction were two bombs, placed onto airplanes that had departed from Canada and exploded within an hour of each other. One went off while baggage handlers were moving suitcases from a CP Air flight onto an Air India plane in Tokyo, killing two and wounding four others. The other exploded off the coast of Ireland, a few hundred kilometres away from Cork, killing all three hundred and twenty-nine people aboard Air India Flight 182. While there was plenty of information that directed the authorities to those who had brought the plane down, only one man has been held accountable. The Air India Flight 182 tragedy—the worst act of global terror prior to 9/11 and the largest mass murder in modern Canadian history—is the inspiration behind *My Father's Secret*. While this novel is by no means a recounting of that awful event, it does draw on some of the principal moments that surrounded this national tragedy.

My hope is that the reader of this novel will have completed their reading and thought, *'Well, that would never happen.'*

But it did ...

Here's a short list of the disappointments that the victims' families had to endure in the aftermath of the bombing of Air India Flight 182:

- The architect behind the bombing, Talwinder Singh Parmar, was under active surveillance by CSIS in the months prior to the bombing. He was considered the most dangerous terrorist in the country. Surveillance was pulled the day before the bombing so that CSIS could purse a *high-value* Soviet target.
- Hours of audio tapes between Parmar and his co-conspirators were erased by CSIS a few months after the bombing. CSIS says it was an error—part of a routine practice of freeing up resources—and that the real mistake lay with the RCMP for not securing the tapes sooner as part of the criminal investigation.
- Three weeks before the tragedy, CSIS followed Parmar and a mystery man (Mr. X) to the home of Inderjit Singh Reyat, a Duncan, BC, mechanic (and the man who was convicted of manslaughter for constructing both the Narita and Flight 182 bombs). They went to a remote location on Vancouver Island, and out of sight of the nearby CSIS operatives, did something that caused a loud boom. CSIS concluded the men had fired a high-powered rifle. Forensic tests conducted in the wooded area after the bombing of the planes found traces of blasting caps. It appears they were testing the bomb materials that would help bring down the planes—all while CSIS was watching.
- In the aftermath of the bombing, Parmar not only eluded Canadian justice but also managed to leave the country. He

was eventually killed in a shootout with Indian police in a town north of Delhi in 1992.
- Days after the bombing, Prime Minister Brian Mulroney reached out to Indian Prime Minister Rajiv Gandhi to share his condolences; this despite the fact that 280 of the 329 killed on Flight 182 were Canadian. Mulroney walked back the condolence call when this fact was brought to his attention.
- It took the Canadian government six months to stop referring to the tragedy as a "crash" and formally acknowledge that the plane had been bombed. It took the RCMP almost twenty years to bring charges against the people alleged to have conspired with Parmar. They were acquitted. A few years after the acquittal—and after two decades of pleading by the victims' families—the federal government finally agreed to a public inquiry into the tragedy. The report of the inquiry is laced with shocking details. Every Canadian should familiarize themselves with *Air India Flight 182: A Canadian Tragedy.*

I've always felt that the victims' families were correct in their main criticism of our nation's handling of the tragedy: that had these been white people instead of brown people, the public mourning, the investigation, and the prosecution of the perpetrators would have been an entirely different enterprise. Instead of being Canada's shame, it would be the story of how this nation brought evil to its knees in the pursuit of justice.

One of my overall concerns in the many years since the tragedy has been the practice—sometimes open and sometimes tacit—of ambivalence and complacency by Canadians in the face of certain episodes in our history. While we are eager to promote how tolerant and accepting we are as a collective, we also either turn a blind eye to shameful things or sweep them under the carpet. I love being Canadian. I love the things that we promote and value and represent on the world stage. We are peace loving. We are compassionate. We are welcoming.

But we are also morally lazy when it comes to certain aspects of our past. I am writing from the perspective of privilege, as a fifty-something white man in small-town Ontario. My privilege has brought with it so many benefits that I am almost afraid to conduct an inventory of all of the free passes I have been given, many based on gender and many based on race. This is why it shocks me to see our nation throw up its hands and more or less deny that bad things ever happen. In terms of Air India Flight 182, we should have done something then and should be regretting what we didn't do to this day. The Air India tragedy should be a lesson on how to move forward, on how to improve our moral actions, and on how to take a stand against atrocities against our brothers and sisters. Instead, it is a footnote in our nation's history that people need to be reminded of by those who have the forthrightness to bring the incident up. It begs the question: Why didn't we respond with passion, anger, and righteousness on June 23, 1985?

My Father's Secret is my treatise on the failure I have felt as a Canadian for all these years. While I do think our national response to the tragedy is disgraceful, I also feel a sense of personal moral failure. Why did it take me nearly forty years to write this novel? Why did it take me so long to confess my complicity as a silent bystander? What should I have done differently?

Maybe it's privilege rearing its ugly head again.

Or maybe it's just the dark side of Canada's national identity—the shadow that no one wants to confront.

Sean Patrick Dolan
June 2021

ACKNOWLEDGEMENTS

I would like to acknowledge the love, support, and encouragement of my wife (and copy editor and business manager), Sharon Goodland. To say I couldn't have done it without you would be a gross understatement. We are the ideal partnership and I love you.

Next, I would like to thank my sons Adam and Liam Coughlin. I am very proud of the men you've become. I snuck your names into the story as a small measure of gratitude for the love you have shown me over the years.

And, to those who have left us, but would have loved to have seen this moment:
- My mother, Fran Seyler/Dolan/Stolte, who I continue to miss each day. I opted to use my full name (the one you used when I was in a bit of trouble) because that's what you would've wanted.
- My second father, Lorne Seyler; you came along after dad died and showed me an evolving path of grace and acceptance up until the day you passed away.
- My father, Paul Dolan. While we lost you many years ago, this novel is, in part, my effort to reconcile with your

paternal legacy, both good and bad. Sometimes I have failed to give your good qualities enough credit.

A special thanks to Lola Murphy, Claude Anderson, and Diane and Greg Miziolek. Thank you for being my consultants and supporters through the writing process.

And, finally, thank you to FriesenPress. Your editorial efforts greatly improved this work, and your professional business model made this adventure as stress-free as possible.

With gratitude,
Sean

Lightning Source UK Ltd.
Milton Keynes UK
UKHW012217181121
394229UK00008B/398/J

9 781039 116351